BOOKS BY D. MICHAEL MARTINDALE

Celeste & the White Dragon
Brother Brigham

Twisted Stories series
Twisted Mind
Twisted Soul

What readers have said about D. Michael's stories

"I found Martindale's writing exciting and compelling. He created a world of nations, customs, and peoples that blends magic with the gods of the lands. It's an exciting read, carefully constructed with sequences and twists to sustain a series. I'm looking forward to the second book of the series."

— Doug Gibson, writer, blogger

"It reminds me of Heinlein in his juvenile years. That's meant as high praise. It's captivating, moves fast, is worth reading a second time immediately after finishing."

— Joe Buchman, adventure traveler

"It's very clean. It gets right into the action, and it keeps up throughout. I think it's a great story."

— Henry Knudsen, screenwriter

"Exciting, clever, and action packed. A great story and a great ending. This is going to be such a hit!"

— Sharon Dodge, database administrator

"The story drew me in right from the beginning. I was so engrossed in the first chapters when I read them that I knew I wouldn't be able to put the book down again."

— Karen Crapo, caretaker

"I absolutely loved it! It was a great read and kept me interested throughout. I can't wait to start the second."

--Valerie Kahler-Cordova, artist

"Jack London once made my heart pound, but Michael Martindale is the first writer to rock me back in my chair in wide-eyed amazement."

— Preston McConkie, journalist

"Like Stephen King, Martindale captures the earthy rhythms of daily life as the characters get caught up in bizarre, harrowing events."

— Christopher Kimball Bigelow, author and editor

"The story still lingers in my mind. It was a real page-turner!"

—Eileen Stringer, reader

"Outrageous, provocative, insightful, courageous and thoughtful. Michael Martindale reminded me of the sensitivities of Orson Scott Card in his novel *Saints*."

— *Eugene Kovalenko, blogger*

"Martindale's frank sensuality...is not salacious; it's simply a matter of fact. A lesser book would have found a way to ignore it completely. It is frustrating when people, in life and in fiction, say what they think should be said instead of what they feel. In that light, Martindale's relative profundity is refreshing."

— *Sam Vicchrilli , In Utah This Week Magazine*

"Reading this fast-paced and quickly changing story is like embarking on a river rafting trip that starts out in placid shallows, never suspecting that around the next corner whitewater rapids wait, anxious to engulf you. The ride never slows down until the last few pages."

— *Jonathan Neville, writer*

"One of the things that a novelist, especially one who writes fantasy fiction, is required to do, is get the reader to suspend disbelief, and then sustain that suspension... This is where Martindale succeeds hands down."

— *David Birley, reader*

"His captivating storytelling keeps the plot moving without being predictable or trite. His descriptions ring true."

— *Wife of reader*

"Skillfully written, creating a realistic, complex, difficult world where everything is not as it initially seems. It's a page-turner, a real heavy weight."

— *Mahonri Stewart, playwright*

"D. Michael has an incredible talent for writing. I was utterly wowed by his characters' inner thoughts."

— *Brian Sheets, digital media specialist*

"I had a hard time putting it down, and as a result I read it surprisingly quickly. I had to know how the whole mess was going to end. It's deep, well thought out, and opens up some interesting and thought-provoking ideas."

— *Lee Penrod, systems programmer*

"Martindale...paints a scenario at once believable and shudderingly delusional."

— *Kim Madsen, readers group coordinator*

TABLE OF CONTENTS

Twisted Soul

4 Slipstream Novellas
by D. Michael Martindale

Worldsmith Stories
Salt Lake City, Utah

ISBN: 978-1-970065-06-0

Published by
Worldsmith Stories
1042 Ft. Union Blvd. #109
Midvale UT 84047

info@worldsmithstories.com
http://worldsmithstories.com

Artwork courtesy of **Pixabay**
pixabay.com

Alexandra

Noah stood at the end of the aisle near the dairy refrigeration units gazing at the girl. She was about his age, eleven years. She had light brown hair that hung straight, almost to her shoulders. Her jeans were faded, and her T-shirt was charcoal grey.

She loitered by the display of doughnuts, watching his father help a customer at the register. He knew what that meant. He'd seen it before.

He walked up to her and said quietly so only she could hear, "You're going to shoplift, aren't you?"

She jumped at his words and whirled around to face him. She looked him up and down and focused for a second on the SpaceX logo on his black T-shirt. She raised an eyebrow. "Who are you?"

"I know that look," he said.

She wrinkled her nose at him. "Go away, Noah." She turned away.

He grabbed her arm and pulled her back. "How do you know my name?"

She studied him with a scowl and a deep concentration, then her face brightened up. "You want a doughnut?"

"I'm not letting you take one."

"I'm not going to steal it. Your dad'll give us one."

Who was this girl? "How do you know he's my dad?"

The customer finished and walked past them out the door, giving them an *Aren't you children adorable?* smile. Noah's father noticed the two of them. "Hello there, young lady."

She gave him an enthusiastic grin.

"You want a doughnut?" He opened the display case.

Noah's jaw practically dropped to the floor. He'd never known his dad to do such a thing since the day he became manager of the convenience store.

"Thank you," the girl said. "The chocolate one with nuts, please."

His father lifted the doughnut with tissue paper and handed it to her. She took it and said, "Thank you very much."

"How about you, Noah?" he said.

"Dad?" Noah said with trepidation. Was this even his father?

"Hurry up. I have work to do."

He tried to think. "Uhhh...bear claw I guess."

His father held it out to him. He took it like it was a tarantula and held it in front of himself, staring at it.

The girl gave him a little smirk and gazed at him as she took a huge bite of her doughnut and chewed. Suddenly she headed for the door.

Noah gaped at her, then gaped at his father, who returned to his duties as if something impossible hadn't just happened. He ran out the door after her.

She walked across the parking lot munching her doughnut. Noah chased after her, his bear claw dangling forgotten in his fingers. "Wait!"

"Go away," she said without looking at him.

He grabbed her arm and stopped her. She glared at him.

"How did you know he's my dad?"

"I got you a doughnut. I didn't invite you to be my friend."

"He never gives me *anything* from the store without paying for it."

She wrested her arm from his grip and took off. He trotted after her and walked alongside her.

"Who are you?"

She whirled on him with a dark expression. "If you don't leave me alone, I'll..." She huffed an exasperated breath and took off at a faster pace. He had to jog to catch up.

"I *won't* leave you alone until you tell me."

She rolled her eyes and stopped. "I'll just make you forget."

"No! Please. I don't want to forget. I want to know—"

"I don't *want* you to know."

"Why not?"

She walked away.

"I won't tell anyone," he called.

"That's what they all say," she said without stopping.

He ran and stood in front of her, forcing her to stop. They glared at each other for a moment.

"I *need* to know," he said.

She sighed with irritation. "My name is Alex. Short for Alexandra."

"I need to know *what* you are."

"What do you think I am? A twelve-year-old girl."

"You know what I mean."

"No...I *don't*." Her expression was full of stubbornness.

He returned the gaze and spoke deliberately. "Yes...you *do*."

She peered at him as she popped the last bite of her doughnut into her mouth and chewed, then licked her fingers. "You gonna eat that?"

He lifted up the bear claw and stared at it, then took a bite out of it.

"You live nearby?" she said. It was almost a statement more than a question. "I could use a drink."

Noah brought Alex to his house and into his kitchen. He headed for the cupboard and pulled a couple glasses down. "Milk okay?"

"Sure."

He grabbed a jug of milk out of the refrigerator and filled the glasses, then took them both and handed one to her. She downed the whole thing.

He studied her. "How'd you know—"

"I just had a feeling. You know, a hunch."

He scowled at her. "You don't even know what I was gonna ask."

"Oh...uh...what were you gonna ask?"

"How did you know my name is Noah?"

"I just guessed."

"You just guessed *Noah*?"

"What's wrong with that?" She went to the counter and poured herself another glass.

"It's such a common name," he said sarcastically.

"I guess I overheard your dad say it."

"No, you didn't. He said it *after* you said it."

She turned her back to him, walked to the sliding glass door, and peered out as she sipped.

He came to her side. "You can't just come into a person's life and—"

"*You* came into *my* life."

"Why won't you tell me?"

She turned to him with a sharp look. "Why should I trust you?"

That gave him pause. "I'd never—"

"That's what they all say." She looked back out the window.

"All who?"

She took a long, slow drink from her cup.

"How'd you get my dad to give us doughnuts?"

"People do that a lot." She smiled mischievously. "Cuz I'm so cute."

He had to admit she was. But to her he said, "I'm not stupid."

She sighed and looked out the window. "Noah, you have to give me time."

"To get to know me?" he said more gently.

She downed the rest of her milk, walked to the counter, and placed the glass on it.

"To see if you can trust me?" he said as he followed her.

She leaned back on the counter with her arms folded and gazed at his hand. "Do you always stand there holding things before you consume them?"

He looked down at his full glass of milk, then chugged the whole thing. He went to the sink and rinsed out both glasses as she watched him intently.

"You want me to show you something?" she said.

He looked at her with anticipation, wondering what strange thing she'd do next. "What?"

"Don't get excited. It's a just a place in the woods."

He had to admit to himself he was a little disappointed. "Okay."

The trees were tall, a mixture of deciduous and pine trees. The ground vegetation was sparse and easy to walk through. A pleasant wind rustled the leaves. Alex led Noah to a lively river maybe thirty feet wide. He gazed around at everything.

"This is beautiful," he said.

"It's where I come to find some peace. One of the places."

They reached the bank of the river and stood watching the water babble past. The splashing sound was soothing.

"Can you believe humans ever left nature to live in cities?" she said.

"Well, it's a nice day. I'm sure it's not always nice, especially in winter."

"Yeah, I suppose." There was a hint of sadness in her voice.

She walked along the bank with Noah following until they came to a place where they could sit. She looked down at the SpaceX logo.

"Nice shirt. You got a lot of friends?" she asked.

"Not really."

She gave him a surprised look—or at least acted surprised. "Why not? You seem like a nice guy. When you're not pestering me."

"Why don't you just read my mind and find out?"

She gave him a dirty look. "What are you talking about?"

"You knew my name. You knew my dad was my dad—"

"The resemblance—"

"I look more like my mom."

"I overheard—"

"No, you didn't! You suck as a liar."

She sighed. "Don't press it, Noah."

"You know there's something special about—"

"*Don't press it!*"

They sat in silence for a moment. Finally Noah asked, "Do *you* have many friends?"

She laughed with a smirk.

"I guess we have that in common," he said. "I'm too weird to have friends. And you—"

"You calling me weird?"

"You're different."

She stared at the river. "Yeah, well, people aren't into different."

She plucked a flat rock off the ground and stood and tried to skip it. It plopped into the water and disappeared.

He stood. "It doesn't work so good when there's a current."

"What makes you so weird, Noah?"

"I don't fit in."

"Yeah, but why?"

He shrugged his shoulders. "I dunno. I'm too smart? I just always seemed to not fit in."

"There has to be a reason."

"I just don't. Don't press *me!*"

She smiled a genuine smile and let a short giggle escape. "I guess that's fair. I should go."

"Can I walk you home?"

She chuckled. "I don't think so." She took off, and he followed.

"Well...can I see you again?"

"Ummmm... Where you gonna be hanging out tomorrow?"

"Nowhere in particular."

They plodded through the trees on their way back to civilization. Noah felt like she was taking her time, almost as if she were reluctant to go. He wasn't in any hurry either.

"We could get another doughnut," she said.

"How about if you just leave my dad alone?"

She smiled again. Her smiles were beautiful when they were genuine. "How about lunch then? I'm buying."

"Like you bought me a dough—"

"Don't press it."

Alexandra stood at the foot of Noah's bed as he lay sleeping. She was stark naked. She watched him as he snored softly. He looked peaceful and kind of cute. It brought a smile to her lips.

She gazed about the room. Posters with science themes hung on the walls, one of the solar system, one of the periodic chart, one of the Hubble image of thousands of distant galaxies.

There was a desk in the corner with a hutch extending above it. The hutch included a bookshelf full of books on physics, astrophysics, cosmology, plus astrology and new age topics. She went over to them and examined them. A strange combination of science and spiritualism. It pleased her.

On the desk she found a magazine with a cover story about the possibility of life on Enceladus, a moon of Saturn. Her smile turned into a grin.

"Quite the geek!" she whispered, and meant it as a compliment.

Noah sighed in his sleep and rolled onto his back. She returned to the foot of the bed and peered at him.

His eyes drifted open. She stood unperturbed. His gaze seemed clouded over, then it focused on her. He jerked to a sitting position and gaped at her.

"Alex?"

She gasped and immediately vanished into thin air.

Noah and Alexandra sat facing each other in the booth of an upscale restaurant—subdued lights, servers in white shirts with long sleeves, more forks than Noah knew what to do with, customers all better dressed than they were. Alex held a menu in her hand and studied it, but he studied her.

"This place is pretty fancy," he said. "You can afford it?"

She never looked up. "Don't worry about it."

He continued to gaze at her as he tried to think how to begin. "So-o-o-o... Whatcha been up to since yesterday?"

"Not much."

"I had a weird dream last night."

She looked up from the menu. "Yeah?"

"I *guess* it was a dream."

Her eyes returned to the menu. "Probably was. Dreams can seem real sometimes."

"Do you wanna hear about it?"

She shrugged one shoulder. "It's your dream."

"I dreamed you were standing in my room, watching me sleep."

She looked at him and smiled. It was not one of her genuine smiles. "Dreaming about me already? How sweet!"

"And you were naked."

She gave him an exaggerated scowl. "What are you, a pervert?"

"*Then*...you vanished."

She looked back at the menu. "Of course I took off, if you were gawking at me naked."

"You *vanished*. Disappeared. Poof!"

"Weird dream, alright. I think I'll have the prime rib. What'll you have?"

He leaned forward and said ominously, "*Was* it a dream?"

She closed the menu, laid it down, and folded her hands on it. "I'm standing in your room naked while you sleep, then vanish. What do *you* think?"

"I'd think it was a dream—if it was anybody but you." He locked on her eyes with his gaze.

"That's ridiculous."

"You're secret's safe with me. Besides, who would believe me?"

"Insanity doesn't help me trust you."

"Is that how it's gonna be?"

She leaned forward and spoke with emphasis. "It was *just...a...dream*."

Noah scowled in exasperation.

The server came and took their orders. Noah was uncomfortable ordering food because he had a pretty good idea how this was going to play out, but when he hesitated, she started ordering for him. He interrupted her and ordered what he wanted—chicken cordon bleu, since the name at least had chicken in it, something he recognized.

The food came and they ate, not exactly in silence, but their conversation was trivial. Alex could shovel the food in with enthusiasm. Noah hardly noticed what he was eating as he gazed at her. He still had half his meal left when she finished.

She looked down at his plate. "You sure don't seem to have much of an appetite around me." She gave him a leering look. "Are you in *lo-o-o-ove*?"

Before he could respond with the irritation he felt, a middle-aged couple passed by them on their way out of the restaurant, carrying a styrofoam container of leftovers. Alex fixated on them.

"What?" Noah said quietly.

She never took her eyes off the couple as they passed. The woman smiled at her. The man's gaze was intense, and he grinned at her.

"Are you done with that?" Alex said after they passed.

"No."

"You're done with that. We gotta go." She stood and tugged at his hand.

"I'm not done!" he cried as he resisted.

"You're getting chubby."

"I am not!"

She yanked and yanked.

"We haven't paid yet!" he said pointedly.

She gave out a frustrated groan and sat back down, then looked around until she found their server. Noah followed her gaze. The server was at another table taking their order. Suddenly his head jerked up, and he looked directly at them. "Excuse me a moment, please," he said to his customers, then walked over to Alex. The customers stared at him dumbfounded.

"Check, please," Alex said.

"Oh, no charge," the server said. "It's on the house."

"Well, let me give you a tip anyway."

"Not necessary. It was a joy to serve you."

"These are not the droids you're looking for," Noah muttered.

Alex scowled at him. The server said, "Pardon?"

"Nothing," said Alex. "Thanks so much for your generosity." She grabbed Noah by the arm and yanked hard. He gave in and stood, and she dragged him out into the parking lot.

"I don't like this, Alex. I'm not a thief."

"*Not now!*" she barked. "Just play along...*please!*"

She dragged him outside to the middle-aged couple just as they reached their car. It was as fancy as the restaurant. She slowed down to a casual pace as they passed the couple.

The woman noticed them first. "Oh, hello." The man turned and looked.

Alex stopped herself and Noah and beamed at them with a huge, friendly smile. "Hi. My name is Alex, and this is my brother Noah." She jerked on Noah's hand.

"H'lo," he muttered.

"Well, aren't you an adorable pair!" the woman said. She exchanged meaningful glances with the man. "Didn't I just see you in the restaurant?"

"Yes, ma'am."

"Where are your parents?" the man said.

"Oh, we ran away from home."

"I see," said the woman with her eyebrows raised.

"But we were kinda thinking maybe that wasn't such a good idea."

Noah whispered, "What are you—" but she jerked on his hand again.

"Do you have a way home?" the woman said.

"Nope, just walking," said Alex.

"Is it far?"

"Pretty far. But we can manage, I guess."

"Nonsense!" She smiled warmly. "Let us give you a ride home."

"Okay!"

Noah gaped at Alex. Was she out of her mind?

The man unlocked the car and opened the back door for them. Noah tried to resist, but Alex pulled hard. They climbed in.

"What are you doing?" Noah hissed in a sharp whisper as the couple got in. "This is nuts!"

Shut up! Alex mouthed.

The man started the car. The woman held up her styrofoam container. "Listen, we need to stop at our house and put this food in the fridge, then we can bring you home. Is that alright?"

"That's just fine, Ellen," Alex said.

A confused look crossed Ellen's face, but her smile quickly returned. The man drove out into the street.

Noah kept giving Alex desperate looks, and she kept gesturing with her hand to calm down. They drove out to a neighborhood Noah had never seen before where the houses were huge and the yards even huger. Each yard seemed to be surrounded by tall fences and thick trees and shrubbery, making them seem like worlds all to themselves.

The car approached one gate, which opened automatically, and drove down a long driveway to the house. The expansive lawn was perfectly manicured, the flower gardens had not a solitary weed sticking out, and the bushes were shaped identically to one another with flat tops. The house was a mansion in Noah's eyes, and the garage attached to it had three doors.

The car pulled into a loop at the end of the driveway and stopped before an ornate door. "We'll be just a moment," Ellen said. "Do you want anything? Some lemonade or something?"

Noah said, "No, tha—"

"Oh, yes, thank you!" Alex blurted. "I'm thirsty."

The couple got out of the car. Alex pushed hard on Noah, but he refused to budge. "Get out!" she hissed.

"This is dangerous! We don't know them."

"It'll be okay. I promise."

"We're gonna die."

"If you want me to trust you, you have to trust me back."

He sucked in a deep breath and loudly sighed it out, then climbed out of the car. She followed quickly.

The man unlocked the door and opened it with Ellen standing next to him. She looked back at the two of them and smiled.

"We should run," Noah whispered.

"Don't you *dare!*" she whispered back.

"Why don't you just stop me with your mind?"

She glared at him and pulled him to the door.

"Make yourself at home," Ellen said.

The couple waited for them to head inside, then followed them in and closed the door. The man locked the deadbolt and pocketed the key. The couple stood in front of the door, almost as if they were guarding it. Noah opened his mouth to speak, but Alex gave him a quick shake of her head.

"Nice place," she said as she gazed about the large, ornately decorated room. "Must have cost a fortune to buy all this stuff."

"We do okay," the man said.

"Would you like to see the game room?" Ellen said. "There's a big screen TV and a pool table—"

"Is that where you keep all the kids?" Alex said.

Noah looked at her in confusion. The couple frowned. The man spoke up. "Uh...yeah...our grandchildren are down there right now."

"Would you like to meet them?" Ellen asked

"I'd love to," Alex said.

The man took them into the kitchen, a huge place with a stainless steel refrigerator bigger than any Noah had ever seen, an island in the middle with a stove and oven and copper pots hanging overhead, and miles of counter space containing blocks of knives and fancy small appliances for toasting, coffee making, and who knew what processing of food. The man went to a door with a padlock on it. He unlocked and removed it and held it up with a sheepish smile. "Can't be too careful when you have a lot of valuable things down there."

"Come on, Noah, let's go meet the grandkids," Alex said with exaggerated enthusiasm. She took his hand and forcefully pulled him to the door. They entered and climbed down the stairs. The couple followed.

At the bottom was an elegant party room with a wet bar, a pool table, an expensive home entertainment center, a ping-pong table, and racks of Blu-ray disks and video games. In one corner was what appeared to be a movie set made up to look like a bedroom with cameras and monitors and lights on stands. There was another door with a padlock on it.

"How do you like it?" the man said.

"Where are the kids, Gregory?" Alex said.

He went to the door and unlocked it. "Right here. Why don't you go in and meet them?" He waited with an inviting smile on his face.

Alex grabbed Noah's hand and brought him to the door. Gregory swung it open. She stood in the doorway and peered in. Noah looked over her shoulder, and his jaw dropped.

There were six bunk beds lined up against the walls. One wall had a small-er wide screen television. On the beds and on bean bags were ten children—five boys and five girls—with ages that looked from about seven to twelve years old. Two older boys played video games as the others watched them or read books. They all turned their heads and looked at Alex and Noah with empty stares.

The oldest boy playing the game smirked and said, "Fresh meat." He went back to his game.

"Alex," Noah said with alarm.

Gregory and Ellen pushed the two of them into the room and slammed the door shut. Noah could hear the sound of the padlock clicking into place.

Alex sighed and turned to face the door. "Gregory, we're not doing this." She waited. "Gregory."

The padlock clicked again and the door slowly opened. Gregory stood there with an uncertain look on his face.

"These kids look pale," Alex said. "They look like they haven't had any sun for months."

Gregory continued to stare with a grim expression.

"They need to get out for some fresh air. Just for a while."

"Fresh air, yeah," Gregory said. "That would be good for them." He stepped aside.

Alex turned to the kids, who gaped at her in amazement. "Move, you idiots!" she barked.

The oldest girl jumped up and ran out. The oldest boy followed, looking suspiciously at Gregory as he passed. The rest of the children dashed out.

Alex and Noah exited. Gregory and Ellen stood in confusion watching the children scurry up the stairs and out of sight.

"Okay, Gregory," Alex said. "You need to call 911 now and turn yourself in. You feel awful for what you've done and you can't take it anymore."

Gregory pulled his phone out and dialed. "Greg?" Ellen said.

"Ellen, you feel just as guilty." Alex looked at Noah, who stared at her in amazement. "Come on."

They climbed the stairs and walked out into the yard. All the kids stood around as if confused. The oldest boy said, "We don't know where we are."

"Just hang tight," Alex said. "The police'll be here soon."

"How did you do that?"

"Do what? They felt guilty for what they did and let us go."

"But—"

"My friend and I were never here," Alex called out to everyone.

The boy looked puzzled, but turned to the children. "Let's just wait here until the police come. They'll bring us home."

Alex took Noah's hand, and they ran out of the yard, pushing the button to open the gate, and across the street. Alex sat on the sidewalk and leaned against the tall fence surrounding another private yard. Noah sat next to her.

"You gonna tell me *that* was a dream?"

"Shut up!"

"Alex, there's no way—"

"I have to concentrate. You think this is easy?"

She closed her eyes and pressed her fingers to her temples. Noah watched with fascination.

Three police cars zoomed up the street, in through the gate, and parked on the driveway. Police officers climbed out, some approaching the children, some heading for the door. One rang the doorbell. Gregory let them in.

"I couldn't take it anymore, officer," Alex said, then paused. "Downstairs. It's all there." Another pause. "Yes, officer, I was part of it too."

She was quiet a moment, then opened her eyes. "I think that's good enough. Let's get the hell out of here."

Alexandra marched angrily through the woods. Noah followed several steps behind her. "I hate people like that," she spat.

"You gonna play games with me now after that?" Noah said.

She headed for the river.

"You gonna pretend that was normal?"

She stopped at the bank and searched for a flat rock, picked it up, and tried to skip it. It plopped and disappeared.

"Tell me what's going on!"

She whirled on him with a fierce gaze. "What the hell do you want from me, Noah? Can't you figure it out for yourself?"

"How—"

"I just do it."

"But how do you make people—"

"I said I just do it."

"You have no idea how?"

"How do you move your arm? You just do it."

Noah took a deep breath to calm down. Alex plopped herself onto the bank and folded her arms across her raised knees. He sat next to her in the same position. "Have you always been able to?"

"Have you always been able to move your arm?"

"That wasn't a dream last night, was it?"

She picked up another rock and examined it. "I wish this was a lake."

"Well...why don't we go to one?"

"There aren't any around. Not within walking distance."

"We could take a taxi. I'm sure you could arrange it."

A laugh escaped her, apparently against her will. "I thought you didn't like it when I cheat."

Carefully he said, "You could wish us there...like you wished yourself into my room."

She glared at him.

He chuckled back. "You know, if that was a dream, it was a nice one."

"You saw me naked. You sure it wasn't a nightmare?"

He could feel the blush burning on his face. "You were...kinda...actually... pretty."

She gave him a heartfelt smile, then gave him a quick peck on the cheek, which warmed him all over. "I better go home." She jumped up and walked into the trees.

"Let me go with you," he said, standing up.

"Thanks for the nice day." She continued walking.

"Alex." He stood there, giving her a pleading look.

She paused and gazed at him.

"Please."

She sighed. "Okay."

They headed back and entered a middle class suburban neighborhood. He gently took her hand. She didn't resist. Out of the corner of his eye, he could see a faint smile on her face.

They walked along the sidewalk in silence, a comfortable silence to Noah's surprise. She stopped at a two-story house and studied it.

"Is this your home?"

"Yes." She turned to him. "I can't let you come in. Not today. Sorry."

"See you tomorrow?"

"If you're lucky."

She peered at him and laughed, and only then did he realize he was pouting. She brushed her fingers against his cheek, then suddenly trotted up to the door and tried the knob. It didn't open, so she rang the doorbell. The door opened.

"Hi, I'm here."

The door opened wider, and she went in. Noah watched as the door closed.

Alexandra's eyes opened, awakened by...something. She stared at the ceiling, trying to get her bearings, and remembered where she was, lying in bed in her "home" for the night.

She looked around and immediately saw Noah standing naked at the foot of the bed. He gazed about as if in a daze, then looked at her. His brow knotted.

Anxious, she sat up and peered at him. "Hi, Noah."

He looked around again, and his mouth moved as if to say something, but nothing came out.

"You're dreaming again," she said. "Why don't you go back to sleep?"

He focused on her, a troubled expression on his face. "Alex?"

"Go back to sleep, Noah."

He looked at her, then down at himself. His face became more confused. "I think I'll go back to sleep."

"Good idea."

He gazed at her for a moment longer, then vanished.

She took a deep breath and sighed it out, then lay back down and stared at the ceiling.

"Holy shit," she whispered.

In the park, Noah and Alexandra sat at a picnic table decorated with sacks and drinks from a very generous McDonald's. He was almost getting used to her unique five-finger discount and wondered if he should feel guilty.

"Did you wish me over?" he said between mouthfuls.

"Dream," she said without looking away from her burger.

"Give it up! How did I do that?"

"You moved your arm."

"That doesn't explain—"

"You want to move your arm, it just moves. You wanted to see me, you just saw me."

"But I don't have your—"

"Obviously you do." She pierced his eyes with her gaze.

He studied her for a long moment. "But how?"

"You love that word."

"Dammit, Alex, I'm sick of—"

"Oh shit!" She stared off into the distance.

"What?" He turned to look. There was nothing but kids playing in the playground, adults tossing balls and frisbees.

"I have to go now." She gave him a forlorn look. "Goodbye, Noah."

She leaped up, leaving her food in place, and marched away in the opposite direction from where she'd stared.

He ran after her and tried to grab her hand, but she jerked it away. "I'm trying to keep you out of this."

"Out of what?"

She let out an exasperated groan. "Then run. But don't *look* like you're running."

She grabbed his hand, but he resisted her tugs. "I don't underst—"

"*Run!*" she cried. He panicked and let her pull him into a jog. "Make it casual. Running for fun, not out of fear."

They trotted to a grove of trees. She pulled him behind a large one and peered around it. "Damn it!" she hissed. "He knows."

A flood of anger swept through Noah. He pushed her against the tree, his face contorting in rage. He wrapped his hands around her neck and squeezed.

She struggled as she choked for air and landed a hard punch against the side of his face. He sprawled back and shook his head, trying to shake away the daze, then glared at her, the wrath returning with a vengeance.

Bracing herself against the tree, she kicked him hard in the chest. He toppled back and landed on the ground with the wind knocked out of him.

"Goddammit, you wimp! Resist him!"

He struggled to a sitting position, trying to catch his breath, then looked up at her glaring down at him. He came to his senses with alarm. "Oh God, Alex! I'm so—"

"Forget it. Just pull yourself together." She offered her hand.

As he looked at it, he felt the anger return, and he snatched at it. She jerked it away, then slapped him forcefully on the cheek. "Get him out of your head!"

He tried to understand what she meant, then it finally dawned on him. He tried to force the anger out. "I *can't!*"

She slapped him again, focusing his attention. "Hello, naked in my bedroom! You have the power." She grabbed both his hands and yanked him to his feet, then pivoted him against the tree. They both peered around it. "Find him."

"What are you talking—"

"Find him! You can do it."

His face went grim, and he peered out into the park, studying each person. A father tossed a baseball to his son. An old man sat on a bench with an old woman, clasping her hand in his lap. A young man sat on the ground leaning against a tree focusing on a book in his hand. A bald man sat at a picnic table with his family, regaling them with a lively story as he waved a fried chicken leg around in his hand.

Noah's eyes darted back to the young man with the book. He could feel something drawing his attention to him. A name popped into his mind.

"Desmond," he murmured.

The man suddenly smiled and turned to look directly into Noah's eyes.

"Now he knows about you too. Damn, Noah, you're a nuisance!"

"What'll he do to us?"

"We need to get out of here."

"Wish us away."

She glared at him. "You numb nuts, I'm not a genie."

"But you and I—"

"We astral projected."

"What?"

"Not here!" She grabbed his hand and forced him to dash away. This time she didn't make any attempt to hide that they were fleeing.

Noah glanced back and found Desmond standing with his book closed in his hand. He grinned knowingly at them as he watched them run away.

They raced out of the park and into a women's clothing shop. She dragged him to the women's restroom. He yanked her to a stop. "I can't go in—"

"Get serious!" She pushed him in.

An elderly woman stood before the mirror touching her hair up. When she saw Noah, she scowled. "What are you two doing in here?"

"He's my mentally challenged brother," Alex said. "He needs my help."

The woman's face suddenly showed pathos. "Oh, the poor dear!"

Alex pulled Noah into a stall and locked the door. She closed the toilet lid and sat on half of it as she patted the other half. Noah shook his head and squeezed down next to her.

The door to the next stall over banged and the lock clacked shut. The elderly woman's shoes were visible through the gap at the bottom of the divider. Clothes rustled, then there was the tinkling sound of flowing urine.

"I'm not comfortable here," he whispered harshly.

"Shut up and let me think." She put her hands on either side of her head while resting her elbows on her knees and closed her eyes.

"Who was that guy?" Noah whispered.

She waved him quiet.

The urine flow stopped and the toilet paper roll rattled. Noah cringed with each sound. The toilet flushed and the stall door opened. Soon water flowed from the sink, then paper towels were yanked out.

The restroom door opened and closed, and he breathed a sigh of relief.

"Alex, you have to tell me, who's Desmond?"

She dropped her hands and stared forward. "He found me when I was ten. That's what he does. Travels around looking for kids with our ability."

"How many kids are there?"

"They all think they're the only ones. They feel confused...alone." She looked at him intensely. "Different."

"Weird," he said, nodding his head.

"Yeah, weird, like you and me. They don't understand why they're so much smarter than the other kids. They don't understand they can sense other people's thoughts and learn about things, many things, long before normal kids do." She patted his knee. "Like you, with your physics and astronomy and chemistry books. You're way older than eleven years..."

He flinched as she rapped the top of his head with her knuckles.

"...up there."

"So he's trying to help them? Why did we run?"

"Oh, Noah, he *grooms* them. He's a pedophile."

"What?"

"He gets them to trust him. He astral projects with them, getting them used to being out-of-body naked with him. Then it's a small step to being physically naked together."

"Why do we astral project naked?"

"You think there's a wardrobe of astral clothing sitting around somewhere?"

"Can't we wish clothing on us?"

She groaned with frustration. "*It's not wishing!* It's a real thing our brains do. With scientific laws behind it. Some mutation, probably."

"Well, it makes me uncomfortable."

"You get used to it. Besides, it doesn't really seem like nakedness when you have no body and no one can see you."

"Except another—"

"Yeah."

The restroom door opened and closed. "Can we get out of here?" Noah whispered.

"Hold on a second." She closed her eyes and pressed her fingers against her temples. "God, he's smug! Didn't even try to follow us."

"Then let's get out of here!"

She opened her eyes. "He knows he'll find us again, sooner or later. He always does."

Alexandra and Noah sat at the edge of the river plopping pebbles into the water. She'd already made her token attempt to skip one before sitting down.

"That's why you helped those kids," he said.

"It's my job."

"Huh?"

"It's what I do. It's how I justify my existence."

"You don't need to—"

"I'm a leech, Noah. I use my abilities to mooch off of people. I don't know how else to survive."

"There must be something else—"

"A twelve-year-old girl constantly on the run from a pedophile?"

"Can't you just...not give in to his grooming?"

"You're so naive for a smart guy. If he can't groom you, he uses his power to destroy your mind. He's more powerful than me."

"Wait a minute! So that wasn't really your house?"

She stood up and walked away.

"Will you cut that out? It's rude!" He went to her when she stopped.

"That family had a son," she said. "He died. I...softened their pain."

"But now they think they have a daughter?"

She turned away. "They'll forget when I leave."

He put his hand on her arm. "What happened to *your* family?"

She turned and grabbed him in an embrace. He heard faint sobs. Uncomfortably he patted her on the back.

"Did you tell the police about him?"

"You think the police can stop anyone like us?"

"Oh...I guess not."

Noah shut his eyes and tried to reach into her mind to comfort her. He had no idea what he was doing.

She giggled affectionately. "Thanks for trying, but I keep a barrier up. I'll be okay."

"But I *did* reach your mind?"

"You did. It would've worked on a normal person. You keep a barrier up too, although you don't realize it. It's a subconscious thing when you can get into people's minds all the time." She gave him her mischievous smile. "Although I can get through yours...if I want to. You'll need to work on that."

He ignored the irritation her taunting caused, because he had something more pressing on his mind. "I want to try it on a normal person."

A smile flickered on the corners of her mouth.

Alexandra and Noah approached the entrance to the convenience store. "On your own dad?" she said.

"I don't feel right messing with a total stranger. Uh...I can't hurt his brain, can I? Accidentally?"

"He'll be fine. Your power isn't developed enough to be dangerous yet."

They found his father inside stocking shelves. "Just in time to help," he said to Noah.

"Um, Dad? Can we maybe have another doughnut?"

"Sure! Help me with this and you've earned one. So who's your friend?"

Noah glanced at her with his brow knotted. She nodded encouragement to him.

He pursed his lips and tried again. "Well...we don't really want to stock shelves. Can't we...uh...just have one anyway?"

His father peered at him for an instant, then smiled. "I suppose I don't want you growing up too fast. Help yourselves."

Noah gazed at Alex with a surprised look. They grabbed their doughnuts and ran out the door as if the police were after them.

"I wish I'd figured out I could do this a long time ago," he said.

"Just be careful. It's easy to become an asshole doing this."

"Like—"

"Yeah, like him."

Alexandra sat in bed with the blankets covering her legs, wearing pajamas with baseball illustrations on them. The lamp on the nightstand glowed. Her clothes were draped over a chair by a desk. She fiddled with a strand of hair that hung past her ear as she gazed about at the boyish trappings of the room that once belonged to the dead son. She wasn't sure, but she had a feeling she'd have a visitor tonight.

Sure enough, Noah materialized naked at the foot of the bed. She smiled at him. "I was hoping you'd come."

He looked down at himself and covered his crotch with his hands.

She smirked. "You didn't cover yourself the first time."

"I didn't know what was going on."

"Did you come to play?"

"I wanted to see if...you're alright."

She sensed that wasn't exactly true. She gazed at him with a half-smile.

He peered at her, then said sheepishly, "I wanted to see if I could do it on purpose."

"I'm fine, thanks for caring," she said theatrically. "And I *do* want to play!"

"Play what?"

She grinned. "Go to our private spot. I'll meet you there."

He looked at her quizzically.

"You know how." She shooed him with her hand. "Go!"

He vanished. She took a deep breath, feeling anxious as she peered about with her mind once more to be sure *he* wasn't around, then dropped back onto the bed with her eyes staring lifelessly at the ceiling.

Noah stood naked at the river, watching the reflection of the full moon rippling in the water. The moonlight fell in streaks through the trees. The chirping of crickets filled the air.

Alexandra appeared naked behind him and walked to his side. His hands reflexively covered his genitals.

She slapped his arm. "Stop that! I've already seen it."

To his surprise, her slap made his arm move a little, although he didn't feel it. Reluctantly he let his hands drop to his side. "So what are we playing?"

"We're skipping rocks."

"They won't skip on the river."

"Try it."

He shrugged, looked around for a flat rock, then reached down to pick it up. His fingers slipped right through it. "You're teasing me. You knew I couldn't do it."

"Why can't you? Look at your feet."

He looked. They were planted firmly on the ground.

"If your fingers slip through the rock, why don't your feet slip through the ground?"

"Um...because gravity doesn't pull on me?"

"Then why don't you float above the ground? Why doesn't the Earth rotate out from under your feet?"

"Well...uh... Why don't *you* pick the rock up?"

She reached down to grab it, and her fingers slipped through. She grinned. "Sorry, I can't either."

"Then why don't *you* float up?"

Her grin became shameless as she floated five feet into the air. Noah raised his eyebrows, not sure if he was surprised or not.

She floated back down. When her feet touched the ground, she kept moving down until she had sunk into the ground to her neck. Now he was sure he was surprised.

"Aren't you gonna join me?" she said.

"How?"

"Move your arm."

He didn't get it.

"You think the ground's holding you up? There's nothing about your astral body to hold up. You're not flesh. You keep your feet on the ground because you don't know anything else to do."

"So if I want to sink into the ground—" He gave out a yelp when his feet began sinking into the earth. He grinned wide and sank to his neck. "This is weird!"

"Fits us perfectly then. You ready to play now?"

"Play what?"

"Superman!"

She raised her arms high above her head and shot straight up into the sky. He gaped with astonishment as she cavorted around in arcs and circles and loop-de-loops. He raised his arms up and suddenly found himself catapulting into the sky. He expected to feel the wind sweeping across his skin and vertigo when he looked down, but he felt nothing. Only his vision told him he was flying.

They swooped around and above and below each other in a graceful impromptu dance, then settled back to where their feet touched the ground again.

"Ready to play some more?" she said.

"What next?"

She pointed to the sky. He looked up and found the moon.

"Take my hand. You don't know any landmarks there."

"You can't be serious! The moon?"

"My hand, or you'll lose me."

Apprehensively he lifted his hand, but stopped. "Won't our...silver cord snap going that far?"

She smirked. "There's no cord."

"Then how does our spirit get back to our body?"

"It's like...quantum entanglement or something. There's a connection. But there's no stupid silver cord."

He placed his hand in hers. He couldn't feel anything in the physical sense, but somehow he still sensed they were joined.

"On three," she said. "One...two..."

"Wait! What am I doing?"

"Instead of wanting to go to the moon, you'll want to follow me. Got it?"

He certainly did want to follow her, or he might end up who-knows-where floating in space. He nodded.

"Alright. One...two...three!"

They vanished.

They arrived together holding hands. He completed a cry he'd already started when they began.

"That wasn't so bad, was it? Distance doesn't matter when..."

She stopped when she noticed him gaping at the view. Before him lay the desolate surface of the moon with the sun in noontime position above them. Below the sun was the Earth, a shadowy globe with just a sliver of sunlight bouncing off its edge and the artificial stars of modern society glittering away on the night side. The real stars blazed steadily throughout the black sky in spite of the brilliant sun. He found he could look directly at the sun without pain or blindness.

But these were things he expected to see, amazing as they were. What mesmerized him even more was on the ground before him.

The American flag stood motionlessly. Behind it was the remnant of a lunar module. Footprints were everywhere. Dozens of paraphernalia were spread about. There was a plaque with two circles representing the western and eastern hemispheres of the Earth. Underneath were the words:

HERE MEN FROM THE PLANET EARTH
FIRST SET FOOT UPON THE MOON
JULY 1969, A. D.
WE CAME IN PEACE FOR ALL MANKIND

Below that were the signatures of three astronauts, and at the bottom the signature of President Richard M. Nixon.

They were at Tranquility Base!

"Beautiful, isn't it?" she said.

"We're here," he whispered solemnly, as if it were a holy shrine. His hand slowly rose to his forehead and stopped at a salute that he held in place.

"On your heart," she said. "You're not in the military." She placed her hand on her heart as if to demonstrate, and his came down to match hers.

"Now repeat after me," she said. "I pledge allegiance..."

He repeated the rest of it with her, almost in a trance. When they finished, they lowered their hands. She said with a grin, "Bet you never dreamed you'd do that here."

He shook his head and headed to the flag. He tried to grab the corner of it with his forefinger and thumb, but they went right through. "I wish I could touch it."

"Sorry. Can't help you with that."

He looked back at her, then up at the sky again. "It's so...so..."

"Breathtaking? Yeah, I was speechless the first time I saw it."

He spun to face her. "How do we breathe? How do we speak without air?"

"You think you're breathing? You think air's coming out of your lungs and vibrating vocal cords? Your mind fills in the details you can't imagine not being there." She pursed her lips closed as she kept talking. "You move your lips because you think you have to when you talk. We're communicating directly, mind to mind, and your mind hallucinates the sound of the words."

He stared at her, so overwhelmed he could think of nothing to say.

"Try holding your breath," she said, moving her lips again.

He clamped his mouth tight and waited for the urge to suck in oxygen. It never came.

"See what I mean?"

"Why do *you* move your lips?"

"Habit. I have to concentrate to not move them."

She came up to him and placed her hand on his arm. He sensed the connection. "You having fun?"

He nodded.

"Are you getting the hang of this?"

"I think so."

"Good." She leaned forward and kissed him on the cheek. He wished it were flesh lips touching a flesh cheek so he could feel it. "I have to go now."

"You're leaving me?"

"I'm sorry, Noah. I've loved our time together, but I have to move on."

"No way! You're not—"

She vanished.

"*Alex!*" he cried.

Alexandra jolted up to a sitting position in the bed, sucking in a huge gasp of air. She quickly scrambled to her feet and rushed to her clothes. She pulled her pajama top off, exposing her barely forming breasts, and grabbed her shirt.

Noah suddenly appeared, naked and agitated. "There's no way I'm letting you face this alone."

She whirled around, clutching her shirt to cover her chest. "Noah, please! Don't make this harder than it is."

"We can deal with it together."

"He's gonna to track me down. I can't let you get involved."

"I'm already involved. You said he knows about me too now."

"You don't understand what you're getting yourself into." She put her shirt on. "He tried to groom me, and I didn't understand what was happening. When I finally realized it, I fought him. I learned to block him." She turned her back to him and pulled the pajama bottoms off.

"So you got away?"

"He got pissed." She slid her panties, then her jeans on. "He started crushing my mind. It was all I could do to hold him back. He was just a little bit stronger. I could hold out for...for...but I knew I'd fail in the end."

"What did you do?"

"I let go, and he eased up, figuring I'd given up. Then I gave him one huge mind blast, all the power I could throw at him. It caught him off guard enough so I could run. I've been running ever since."

She sat and put her socks and shoes on, leaning down so he wouldn't see her eyes moistening. "I ran through the neighborhood. I was naked. Not astral naked, really naked. I ran, and everyone stared at me. I tried to get them all to forget, but there were too many, and I was so tired and so...messed up in the head."

She finished tying her shoelaces and wiped her eyes as she sat up. He crouched before her and reached out to hug her. His arms went through her.

"Dammit!" he said. "Don't go anywhere. I'll be right back."

"Noah, I'm stronger than you. You felt how powerful he is. He'll crush you immediately. Please, just let me go."

"Promise me! Promise you'll wait here for me."

She buried her face in her hands. She should promise him, then run where he'd never find her. What would it matter that she broke her promise if it could save his life?

But she couldn't bring herself to do that. It irritated her that she let him affect her so much. She should know better, but it crept up on her without her noticing. "I promise," she said, and meant it.

He studied her, then nodded. "I'll be right back," he emphasized again, then vanished.

She let her tears flow. She'd keep her promise. She wouldn't leave until he got back. And felt the fool for doing so.

———

Noah quickly dressed and bolted out the door into the night. He raced through the deserted suburban blocks and found her waiting on the steps outside the door. He was a little surprised she was there. He wasn't sure she'd keep her promise.

She stood as he approached, and he swept her into an embrace. She held him tight.

"Let's get out of here," she said.

They walked through the quiet neighborhoods. "It feels strange to have a body again," he said. "Like I'm weighed down."

"You are." She flicked his nose with her finger. "But without one, you can't feel things."

They came to the woods, then made their way through the trees in the dark to their spot. They stood before the river, and she said with determination, "I'm going to skip a rock if it kills me."

"In the river," he said skeptically.

She picked up a flat rock. "I'll use my powers if I have to."

"You can do that?"

She tossed it low along the surface of the river. It hit the water and slipped in with a kerplunk.

"No," she said despondently.

"You know I'm not letting you go."

"You think I *want* to leave you?"

"You can't keep me from finding you."

"Yes, I can."

"No, you can't, or you wouldn't have to keep running from Desmond."

"You're not experienced enough. He knows how to find people like us."

"I'll figure it out."

She sat down and hugged her knees. "Please don't. I'll just have to hide from both of you, and that'll make it twice as hard for me."

He sat next to her. "What if...what if we blocked him together? He's stronger than you, and he's stronger than me. But together?"

"I don't know if our powers add up like that."

"We can test it."

"How? The only way is to let him attack us."

"He already did, but we escaped."

"No, we didn't. He's playing with us, like a cat. He likes the chase."

"Well, what else can we do?"

"You can go home and live your life, and I can run like I always do. He'll probably forget about you. I'm the one he's obsessed with. I'm the only one that ever escaped him."

"Won't he go after me first, because I'll be the easy one?"

She buried her face in her arms folded across her knees.

"If we—"

"Shut up! Let me think."

He peered at her as she kept her face buried. His hand rose, almost of its own accord, and reached out toward her hair. With a fingertip, he brushed a strand into place hanging loose from the rest.

Her head came up. "You're right, Noah. He's not gonna leave you alone, now that he knows you exist. We'll have to try to resist him together."

"It'll work. I know it."

She stood up. "You don't know shit!"

He stood up in a huff.

"Go home," she said. "Get into bed. Then come to me. I'll be waiting for you at...home. At least we can have some fun before..."

He waited for her to finish, but she didn't. "I won't let you be alone."

"Go home," she said softly. "I'll wait for you. I promise."

Noah lay on his bed without taking any clothes off, closed his eyes, and immediately found himself naked at the foot of Alexandra's bed.

She sat on it waiting, still in her clothes. "What took you so long?"

She flopped back, and her eyes stared lifelessly at the ceiling. At the same time her naked projection stood next to him.

"What are we doing this time?" he said.

"I'm giving you a tour."

She took his hand, and all at once they stood in daylight with a long reflection pool stretching out before them. At the other end of the pool was the Taj Mahal. Tourists swarmed about noisily.

"I never thought I'd see this," he said with awe.

"Did you think you'd ever see the American flag on the moon?" she said with a tease.

"It really is the most beautiful building in the world."

"The history behind it is beautiful too. The shah's favorite wife died, and he was grief-stricken. He spent two years building this as her mausoleum. Both their tombs are inside there now."

"That's sad."

"Noah, the code for here is *tomb*."

"What?"

"You'll see," she said with a twinkle in her eye. "Just remember that. The code is *tomb*."

A couple and their two children passed right through them from behind. Noah cried out in shock. "That was creepy!"

"I think it's funny. They have no idea we're here."

"Don't they feel...a chill or something?"

She rolled her eyes. Two women came toward them, and Noah leaped out of their way.

"Alright, you wimp," Alex said. "Let's go."

She took his hand, and suddenly they stood in the middle of a sprawling city. The Eiffel Tower rose before them. He noticed they were standing on a flowing river, and he cried out as he started to sink.

"Move your arm, turkey," she said.

He began flailing his arms around as if trying to fly away. She rolled her eyes and said, "Oh geez!" then took his hand and pulled him up. "Oh ye of little faith!"

They walked across the surface of the river hand in hand. "You're not instilling a lot of confidence in me," she said.

"I'm just not used to this yet."

"You sank because you expect to sink in water."

"Do you have to keep freaking me out with weird places?"

"We're supposed to have fun. You can't say walking on water isn't fun."

"Seems kind of...blasphemous."

She laughed. "You ready for the next one?"

Suddenly Noah found himself standing with nothing around him but sunny sky. He cried out again. Alex shook her head and said, "You're hopeless. Look down."

He found the Eiffel Tower below him. They were standing on its tip. "The code for this is *tower*. Now can you prepare yourself for the next one?"

"Yes," he said testily.

She smiled at him, and they stood in the air with the United States capitol building gleaming at them in the distance in the darkness of night. He looked down and found himself on the apex of the Washington Monument. She looked at him, studying him. "Not freaking out this time?"

He adjusted so his big toe was the only thing touching the apex and floated there, jutting a satisfied chin out.

"Getting cocky, huh? The code here is *cherry*. Get it?"

"Yeah, I get it," he snarled.

"Now let's put you to the test." She slapped him on the shoulder. "Tag. You're it!" She vanished.

He looked around perplexed.

"Hey, cocky!"

He turned and found her twenty feet behind him in the air.

He willed herself behind her, but she vanished before he could touch her and appeared at the apex. "Missed me."

He poofed himself twenty feet above her as she vanished and appeared where he had just left. He immediately jumped behind her and tapped her on the back. "Tag. You're it!"

He vanished and watched from a distance as she scanned around for him. His arm was wrapped around one of the pillars of the capitol rotunda just below the Statue of Freedom on top. Her back was to him as she gazed out ahead, laughed, then vanished.

He sensed something hit the back of his head. "Clever boy, but you're still it!" she said, then appeared twenty feet in front of him. "Hey, Noah. Tower." She vanished.

He looked around, perplexed, then remembered. He jumped to the tip of the Eiffel Tower and searched the blue sky, but didn't see her.

"Hey, Superman!" her voice came from above. He looked up and found her flying in circles above him. He zoomed up to her, but she looped around and avoided him. He tried again, and she veered away again. "Arch!" she said and vanished.

He gazed about and spied the Arc de Triomphe. He popped over there, but she was nowhere to be seen.

She appeared before him. "Not that arch, numb nuts." She vanished.

He scowled as he tried to think of other famous arches, then smiled and vanished.

He stood on the ground with the Delicate Arch in Utah looming over him. The night was as full of stars as it had been on the moon. But he couldn't sense Alex anywhere.

Suddenly her head popped out from the top of the arch. "Not this one either." She disappeared.

He let out a cry of exasperation, then thought and vanished.

He could sense her presence above him, even though all he saw was the underside of the St. Louis arch that he hovered just beneath. Her legs dangled from the top where she sat. He rose up and grabbed her foot. "You're it!" He shot up and away and faced her. "Bridge."

"Not fair! There's a gazillion bridges!"

But he disappeared anyway and reappeared sitting on a cable near the top of a tower on the Golden Gate Bridge. The lights of the bay cities glittered like flashing diamonds below, and the bay itself was a black void in the darkness.

It took a moment, but Alex appeared standing in the middle of the bridge, ignoring the cars zooming through her. "Thought you tricked me, huh?" she called, and it surprised him that he could hear her as if she stood next to him. Suddenly she vanished. Anticipating her move, he immediately began sliding down the cable.

Good thing! She materialized on the tower not far from where he'd been. She projected to the other tower his cable was attached to and waited for him to come. He reached the bottom and began sliding back up the cable on the other side, pleased with himself that he had enough control to go with the cable instead of sliding right through it. She gazed at him with a sly expression and held out her hand to touch him when he reached the top.

Just before he reached her, he disappeared and rematerialized in the air behind and above her. She turned and looked up. "Was that fun?"

He shrugged. "Not as fun as if I could feel it."

But as he spoke, she appeared behind him and slapped his head. "Big clock." She was gone.

He found her in London in daylight sitting on the minute hand of Big Ben as it pointed a little past the 9. He materialized just inside the clock and reached out and tagged her. "Cherry."

He waited within the Washington Monument, feeling weird about being ensconced entirely in rock. A force pushed him from behind, propelling him completely out of the monument. Alex shot out behind him with her hands on his back and said, "Four faces."

Noah reached out from Abraham Lincoln's nostril, grabbed her ankle and pulled. She slid off his gigantic rock nose and hovered before him as he hung by a hand from the nostril. "You booger!" she snapped.

"Tomb."

He flew in circles above the Taj Mahal watching as she appeared at the end of the reflection pool where they'd first gone. The sun blazed its reflection in the water. When she looked up, he waved. She smiled at him and flew up to him. They hovered, gazing at one another, then she sprang at him. He dove away, but she remained hot on his trail.

They veered and looped for a while, then suddenly she appeared right before him. They collided into an embrace and gazed into each other's eyes. Hers seemed filled with emotion.

She gave him a gentle kiss on the lips, said, "Flag," and disappeared.

Noah materialized behind the lunar lander. He jumped out with his hands extended like claws. "Boo!"

No one was there.

He looked around, then flew around, widening his circles more and more. "Alex!" he called in alarm.

He shot straight up so he could gaze upon a wide terrain. He reached out with his senses and detected nothing.

Then he turned to the dark ball of the Earth and stared at it. "No," he whispered in distress.

He immediately projected himself into her bedroom. The bed was rumpled, but the blankets had not been pulled down. No one was in the room. "Alexandra!" he cried out.

He popped into the living room. Nothing. He visited every room in the house. All he found were her substitute parents sleeping away.

Noah stood naked in the middle of the street before her house, looking desperately around.

"*ALEXANDRA!*"

He closed his eyes and concentrated hard to detect her, so hard he didn't flinch when a car drove through him. He felt a presence materialize and opened his eyes. "Why did you leave—"

But it wasn't Alexandra before him. It was Desmond standing naked in the street half a block away.

"There you are, little boy."

He vanished and appeared right in front of Noah, put out his hand and grabbed Noah's shoulder. "Where's your body?"

Noah felt an alien force in his mind. He shut his eyes and moaned. *Block him! Block him!* he shouted to himself over and over. It felt like pain to fight the force.

"*Where's...your...body?*" Desmond said with his teeth clenched and his lips pulled back in a grimace.

Noah started to shake, cried out, and vanished. He stood on the surface of the Seine River in Paris, but Desmond had followed with him, still gripping his shoulder. The man looked down at the flowing water and laughed. "Nice try, Noah, but did you think I'm that easily startled?"

Noah peered wide-eyed at him as his mind fought to resist the force, terror gripping him.

"You know you can't keep this up," Desmond said. "Where's your little friend?"

"I...I...don't know. She...deserted me."

Desmond laughed. "Isn't that like a woman? Uses you and abandons you."

"You...you...use...*children*."

"Oh, Noah. All my kids want it. Maybe not at first. But I grow on them."

Noah jumped again, landing on the top of a tower on the Golden Gate Bridge. Desmond still stood by his side, clinging to his shoulder. "You can't escape me. You'll have to go back to your body sometime, or it'll die."

Noah willed himself to slide down the cable, but Desmond slid with him.

"If I crush your mind," Desmond said, "you'll never get back in your body." They neared the low point of the cable.

Alexandra flew in from the side, barreling into Noah, dislodging him from Desmond's grasp.

"*You fucking bitch!*" Desmond shrieked.

She threw her arms around Noah. "Jump with me."

They vanished.

The terrible force was gone from his mind, but Noah was still in a daze from it. Slowly he became aware that the sky above him was full of stars and black as a void. He sensed the presence of someone enveloping him, and that made him panic, until he realized it was a warm, compassionate presence. His mind cleared enough for him to look up and see Alexandra's troubled face hovering over him.

"I'm so, so sorry, Noah."

He recoiled from her. "You deserted me."

"No, no, I didn't. Well, I did, but—not really."

"You deserted me!"

"I'm here, aren't I?"

"Where did you go?"

"I had to know. I had to find out if he'd only come after me, or..." She fell silent.

"Well, 'or' happened!"

"I'm sorry. I really didn't leave you...not totally. I kept an eye on you."

"You could have told me."

"I was *going* to make you forget, but..." She broke her gaze from him and looked down. "I couldn't." She looked off into the distance. "I should have made you forget me from the beginning."

"Why didn't you?"

She took a moment before answering. "I could tell. I felt it when you accused me of shoplifting."

"You *did* shoplift."

"Your dad gave it to—"

"You forced him."

A smile flickered on her lips. "I sensed you had some power. I didn't realize how much until you stood naked in my bedroom. I didn't want to mess with your mind. It felt too much like Desmond messing with me."

"But you mess with everyone else that way."

"That's different." She glanced at him and looked away, shaking her head. "I know, that's a lame excuse. But I never met anyone else like me—having the same power, but vulnerable. Not like Desmond." She gazed straight at him. "You were special to me. I didn't want to...tamper with you."

"You didn't make me feel so special...in the beginning."

"I didn't want you getting caught up in my life. Isn't it obvious why?"

It made sense. "Okay."

He looked around. They were on a barren, rocky landscape. The horizon was shockingly close. The sun blazed in the sky. There was a bright blue dot in the distance. "Where the hell are we?"

"This is my asteroid. Asteroid Alexandra. It follows the Earth around the sun, about...I don't know...a million miles behind it or something. I come here when I need to escape."

He grinned. "You go to an asteroid to escape from him?"

"I told you I could take care of myself."

"He doesn't know about it?"

"He hasn't figured it out yet. Space is a pretty huge place to search."

"He was trying to find our bodies. You can't bring your body here."

"No, I can't."

"It just lays there helpless for him to do whatever he wants to it."

"He can't track our bodies. Only our minds. Noah, did he break through into yours?"

He tried to think. "I...uh..."

Her face became worried. "Did he get into your mind?"

"I think...I...kept him out."

"God, we need to go back now. If he found out where your body is, you're screwed."

"He was still trying to get me to tell him when you came."

"We need to go anyway, just to be safe. Go home." She disappeared.

Noah gasped for breath as he opened his eyes and sat up on his bed. Alex stood naked beside him.

"You need to get the hell out of here," she said. "Somewhere you've never been before."

"Where's your body now? It's not still at that house, is it?"

"What you don't know, you can't tell him. Just...go somewhere random. I'll follow you, then I'll know where to come after I go back to my body."

He climbed off the bed.

"Wait a sec." She rose up through the ceiling and out of sight. In a moment she came back down. "I don't sense him anywhere. Go."

"But where?"

"Somewhere. Anywhere you've never been before. Anywhere you never thought of going before."

He shrugged, then headed outside. She followed him. He stood in the street looking in either direction.

"Just pick."

He turned toward the direction that would take them out of the suburbs into the country. They walked until they came to the woods.

"Don't go in there. We always go in there."

He nodded and continued along the highway that ran beside the woods and headed toward the mountains. It entered a small canyon with steep, jagged slopes on either side and trees everywhere except where the highway cut through. The sound of rushing water was loud, even though the river was hidden in the trees.

After a half hour, dawn colored the sky. "This far enough?"

"Good enough. You'll be able to see better in the light now."

He plunged into the trees, a wild forest here with the trees closely clumped and the ground vegetation thick. The sun rose as he picked his way through the thick growth. Alexandra slid effortlessly through the trees, always keeping beside him.

They came across a trail. He turned left, ascending higher into the canyon. After another half hour the trail came to a small clearing that stretched to the river. He figured it was the same river Alex kept trying to skip rocks on.

There had once been a bridge over it, but that was long ago washed out, and all that remained was the rock walls on both banks of the river that once supported it.

"Alright, wait here for me," Alex said. "I'll call out to you when I get near. If you hear *anybody* else coming, *run!*"

"Where?"

She looked around and noticed a barely distinguishable deer trail stretching into the trees opposite from the regular trail. "Down there, then hide. Don't use your powers. That'll only help him track you."

He opened his mouth to say more, but she vanished.

He sat on a boulder and waited, keeping his ears sharp for any sound.

He stood and gazed down the path. Nothing but trees rustling in the breeze.

He felt the urge to urinate, and did so against a tree.

He jumped at every natural sound the forest and its inhabitants made.

He leaned against the wall on the nearby bank that jutted up a few feet above the ground and peered down at the rushing water.

After what must have been an hour, he heard footsteps pounding on the trail. "Noah, it's me!" Alex's voice called out.

He sighed with relief and went over to meet her as she appeared, breathing heavily. She rushed into his arms and clung to him. "You're okay."

"What do we do now?"

She brought him to the boulder he was on before. They sat, their hips snuggled tightly together. "We know neither one of us alone is strong enough to fight him," she said.

"So we combine our blocks together."

"We don't know if that'll work."

"All we can do is try."

"And be screwed if it doesn't work. But if we do it out of body, we can get the hell out of there and flee to Asteroid Alexandra before he overwhelms us."

"Leaving our bodies vulnerable."

"Leaving our bodies somewhere it would take him forever to find." She looked around. "We've never been here before. This is a nice random place."

"Until a bear eats us."

"Geez, Noah! Don't be so morbid." She looked around. "We don't want to leave our bodies right here. Too open."

She stood up, walked over to the deer trail, and peered down it. "Let's see what's in here."

They headed carefully down the trail, pushing branches aside from trees and bushes. There was hardly a trail at all. This would be a great place to hide their bodies—if no bears came along. He wondered if a bear could even squeeze through these tight spaces with all the trees and growth.

The trail fizzled out. The ground sloped down to the river. There was a rock outcropping at the end.

"Good as anywhere," she said and sat down leaning against the outcropping. He sat beside her. She put her arm in his and leaned on him. "We need a code word. If either of us says it, that means we can't hold him back any longer, so we get out of there."

"How about *ouch*? The code word."

Alex laughed. "It'll be natural to say. Just make sure we're both touching each other when we do it, so we go to the same place. And for God's sake, don't *ever* let him touch you."

She squeezed his arm. "You ready? Let's just project to right here."

He nodded.

They stood naked on the deer trail gazing at their bodies. For all the world it looked to Noah like they had just implemented a suicide pact. "This is so creepy to see."

"Shall we go where he found you first? Shouldn't take him long to show up there."

"Okay."

She hugged him with her head on his chest. "Now."

They stood in the middle of the street outside Alex's pretend home. She still clung to him. At first she didn't let go, then she relaxed and started looking around.

"How long?" he said.

"Minutes, probably. Maybe seconds if—"

Desmond appeared before them grinning. "Good to see you again, Alex." His face became somber. "You're not stupid enough to come back here. What are you up to?"

She took a step back, pulling Noah. Her face was tight as if in pain.

"You gonna run again, like the coward you are?"

With difficulty she said, "It's not cowardly to run from being raped." Her face contorted with effort.

Desmond's face became more intense. "It's not rape if you consent. And you *will* consent."

"Statutory rape," Noah said.

Desmond looked at him with annoyance. "She can always try pressing charges, little boy."

Alex gave off a pained grunt. Desmond broke into a dash with his hand outstretched. Her eyes bulged, and she vanished without a word before he reached her.

Desmond peered at Noah. He panicked and jumped.

He materialized on Asteroid Alexandra, but she wasn't there. That filled him with dread. He quickly flew around and surveyed the entire asteroid. What happened to her?

He returned to his body and gasped his first breath. Alexandra was already in hers, clinging tightly to him with her head on his shoulder.

He pulled her into an embrace. "Are you okay?"

"God, that hurt," she said.

"Why didn't you say the code word? Why didn't you go to the asteroid?"

"I didn't have time to think. If he touched me..."

He knew what that meant.

"We didn't do so good, did we?" she said.

"We hardly had a chance at all."

"Did *you* do anything?"

Sheepishly he said, "I guess I...I don't know what I thought. I guess I thought we'd have time to give each other a signal or...something."

"Okay, we didn't plan good enough. Now we know he'll attack immediately, so we have to act immediately. We have to...blast him with our minds as hard as we can the second he shows up. And we never let go of each other."

"Are you too weak right now to face him?"

"No, let's get this over with."

They stood before their prone and lifeless bodies. Alex grabbed him in a hug. "Same place."

They projected into the middle of the street, still tight in each other's arms. Within seconds Desmond appeared.

"Now!" Alex shouted.

Noah pushed all his anger at Desmond with as much force as he could. At once his mind was battered with the same power that hit him in the park. He pushed back, but he could feel it slowly overwhelming him. Alex let out a grunt as her face contorted with her attack. Suddenly the force in Noah's head stopped, but Alex cried out. Noah hit back hard with all his strength, now that his mind was clear.

Desmond's face grimaced with effort. Suddenly the force was back with a vengeance in Noah's head. He cried out and almost fell back. Alex gave off a long, angry wail as she began to shake with her effort. Noah felt his mind slipping. Desmond crept toward them as he assaulted their minds, one after the other, with his hand extended.

Noah knew his block was crumbling. "Ouch," he said weakly and jumped back to his body.

They woke up with gasps in unison.

"Did he get through to you?" she asked.

"I don't know. Maybe."

"We have to get out of here *now*."

She jumped up and pulled him to his feet. It took him longer to shake the wooziness from his mind. She led him down the deer trail, then the main trail, jogging as fast as they could. They ran until they came to a side trail that led in the direction of the highway. She headed down it.

The screech of a car coming to a stop came from ahead, then tires crunching on gravel. Alex stopped short. "God, he's here already!"

She pulled him back to the main trail and dashed farther down, away from where their bodies had been. A car door slammed followed by pounding footsteps.

"We gotta hide." She dragged him into the trees where they crouched behind some thick bushes.

"Won't he feel us here?" Noah whispered.

"Shhh!"

Desmond appeared at the intersection and immediately disappeared down the trail toward the washed-out bridge.

"Let's go!" Alex pulled him out onto the trail, heading in the direction Desmond had gone.

"Shouldn't we be going—"

But she turned down the side trail and headed toward the highway. "I'm hoping he's so obsessed with finding us, he was careless."

"Is that why he didn't feel us?"

They found the car on the gravel parking area at the trailhead. She opened the door and peered in. "Ha! Arrogant asshole still thinks I'm a stupid little girl." She climbed into the driver seat. "Get in before he comes back."

Noah ran around the car and climbed in. She turned the keys sitting in the ignition switch and fired up the engine.

"You know what you're doing?" he said.

"Theoretically." She threw the automatic transmission into reverse. "I've never actually done this before."

The car jerked back with a jolt, then jerked to a stop as she slammed on the brakes. "Oooookay," she said sheepishly. "More finesse."

Carefully she eased the car back, turning her head constantly all over the place to make sure she was clear. No vehicles were coming, so she shifted into drive and peeled out onto the pavement.

Noah looked back and saw Desmond appear from the trailhead. "He's—"

"I see," she said, looking in the mirror. "Get ready to grab the wheel."

"Huh?"

She cried out in pain and held her head. He grabbed the wheel and tried to steer. The car swerved all over the road. "You okay, Alex?"

"Shut up and drive. Get ready. You're next."

A pain stabbed him in the head. He cried out. The car headed for the ditch. She grabbed the wheel back from him. "Fight him, Noah."

He grunted in pain, clinging to his head. The pain left as Alex cried out. She tried to keep her hands on the wheel. He grabbed it too. Together they fought to keep the car on the road as the pain bounced from one mind to the other.

"How far can his power reach?" Noah cried out.

Suddenly they both gasped with relief. They waited quietly for something more to happen. "Is he out of range?" Noah said.

"It was too sudden. He's doing something else." She kept glancing in the mirror. "Oh shit!"

He looked back and saw a truck bearing down behind them.

"It's a goddam four-by-four," she said and gunned the engine.

"Don't *you* kill us," he said, gripping the door handle.

"Hit him!" she cried.

"What are you—"

"Hit him with your mind!"

Noah scrunched his face with the effort, watching the four-by-four in the side mirror. It wobbled but still gained on them.

"Hit him again!"

"I'm hitting him!"

Pain swept through his head. He let out a long groan as he endured the pain while trying to keep his attack going. Alex sped up as she reached a long, straight stretch, then hit the brakes as another curve veered to the left. The tires squealed through it and began to slide. They hit gravel and slid more. Noah watched with alarm as the wall of the canyon rushed toward him.

She screeched the car to a stop. The corner fender crumpled into the cliff.

The truck squealed around the corner and screeched to a stop, bumping the back of the car and jostling them.

"God...*damn!*" she said and gunned the engine. The tires spun, then caught the ground. The side of the car scraped against the rock until it broke free. It veered back and forth until Alex regained control.

She grunted in pain again. It grew into a soft wail. "Keep hitting him," she whimpered.

He pushed hard with all his psychic energy and was answered with a stabbing pain. He cried out. The pain stopped, and she began a moan that grew and grew. He hit Desmond again. At once her moan stopped. He braced himself for the next attack, but it didn't come.

They looked at each other with surprise. She stomped on the gas and zoomed the car down the highway, taking the curves precariously.

"Okay...we've learned two things," she said as her hands gripped the steering wheel with white knuckles.

"Don't talk! Concentrate on your driving."

"We've learned together we're almost a match for him."

"What's the other?"

"We'll never beat him."

He gaped at her. "What do we do?"

"Don't talk. I need to concentrate on my driving."

They emerged from the canyon without any sign of the four-by-four or the pain in their heads. Alex relaxed with a sigh and slowed the car down. Noah took a deep breath to calm himself.

"I guess he's regrouping," she said.

They reached the city. She drove what seemed aimlessly to him, until they swerved behind a department store where there were dumpsters and docking bays and no people. She eased to a stop near the building and stared straight ahead, breathing heavily. "We gotta ditch his car."

They climbed out. She marched around the car and stared at the ugly gash along its side. With an angry cry she bashed the sole of her shoe into the door. "Serves you right, asshole!" She grabbed Noah's hand and yanked him into motion.

"He shouldn't know where we are now," she said. "We're harder to track in our bodies."

"That means he is too."

"We'll detect each other when we're in the same area."

"How big an area?"

She shrugged. "You think I ever hung around to test it?"

They headed to the front of the store and through its sliding doors. It was busy, and that made Noah feel better. He was beginning to sense the presence of others automatically, and he could feel their individuality blending together into chaos. He hoped that meant they'd be harder to locate in a crowd.

She dragged him to the back where a family restroom was and pulled him in, ignoring the glances people gave them. There was a sink and a child toilet and a regular toilet and a diaper changing station. With the door shut and locked, she leaned against a wall with her eyes closed, panting heavily. "I gotta pee." She looked at him. "You gonna be too uncomfortable?"

He shook his head, feeling very uncomfortable. She marched to the toilet and pulled her jeans down. He leaned against the wall, fidgeting and looking everywhere except at her. He cringed at the sounds of her business. The toilet flushed and the sink water turned on. He looked at her as she washed her hands.

"What do we do now?" he said.

She dried her hands with paper towels, then leaned against the wall next to him and slid down into a crouch with her arms crossed on her knees. He joined her.

She stared ahead and shook her head. "We can't beat him. Together we're still not strong enough. There's only one thing we can do."

He waited for more. "What?"

She was silent a moment, then said, "Kill him."

He squinted his eyes. "What do you mean?"

"I mean physically kill him. Bash him on the head with a brick. Stick a knife into his chest. Shoot him between the eyes. *Kill* him!"

He stared at her in shock. "I can't do that!"

"Can you help *me* do it?"

"I can't let you do that!"

She glared at him. "It's because of you I have to kill him. Or I'd just run again."

"So run. We can run together."

She looked at him accusingly. "Never see your family ever?"

He paused and thought. Could he do that?

"And what about all the other kids he'll victimize?" she said. "We have to end this now."

Desperately he thought, trying to find some way to keep her from doing this. "Can *you* bring yourself to kill him? Why haven't you done it already if it's so important?"

"Alone? He'd see it coming." She patted his arm. "But I have you now. Together we might have a chance."

"A *chance*? Might have a *chance*?"

She dropped her forehead onto her arms. "Shut up, Noah. I have to think."

He waited. She didn't move. He shifted impatiently. She remained silent. He tried to think of anything he could say to stop her.

"Don't say it," she said, muffled through her arms.

He let out a long sigh and waited.

Finally her head came up. "We can't do it."

That surprised him and flooded him with relief.

"We'd never get close enough without him detecting us."

"It's just as—"

"We need to find someone else to kill him."

"*What?* No way—"

"It's the *only* way."

"You're going to force someone to kill him?"

"Better idea? Let's hear it!"

He didn't have a better idea. He had no ideas. And there was no way he could let her do this.

"You think I like this any better than you?" she said.

He noticed her eyes misting and took a moment to gently reach into her. He could feel her turmoil over this.

Suddenly he was pushed out. "Stay out of my mind," she spat, stood up, and marched out the door. He followed.

Outside a woman looked at them coming out of the restroom with a disapproving scowl. As Alex passed her, she shouted, "Get your mind out of the gutter!"

The woman balked.

Alexandra veered toward the dairy section. "I'm hungry." She picked up a quart of milk and headed down the snack aisle, hooking a bag of chips as she passed. She marched to the deli section. "Ummmm...some potato salad, and that hoagie there."

The woman smiled and packaged it up and slapped a price tag on it.

Alex took it, grabbed a plastic spoon, and headed for the exit. "We already paid for this," she said loudly, "and besides, you never saw us."

The people surrounding them suddenly avoided looking at them. Alex marched outside and plopped down on a bench. He sat next to her. She opened the milk and took a deep swallow, unwrapped the package, opened the potato salad, and took a huge bite.

"You want some of this?" she said through her food.

After contemplating murder, shoplifting seemed trivial. And yes, he was starving. He took a huge bite himself. She offered the milk, and he washed it down.

As they shared the food, she said, "You can look into my mind now."

"I don't need—"

"Please. I want you to see something."

Reluctantly he said, "Okay." For some reason he felt self-conscious doing it so deliberately with her knowing, but he reached out anyway and touched her mind.

In shifting images, he saw her a couple years younger. She seemed fragile compared to herself now. She was with Desmond. Dread shot through him. Desmond acted friendly, affectionate, spoke to her flatteringly. Her feelings as he did so churned, apprehension and guardedness mixed with longing for the attention and tenderness he showed her. A part of her rebelled, but his insistence overwhelmed her.

Noah could feel every emotion as if it were happening to himself.

Desmond began touching her, first in harmless ways, then becoming more and more intimate as his soothing voice washed over her, expressing his love for her. Noah cringed with panic. He couldn't tell how much of the panic was his and how much was hers.

By the time it became unbearable, Alex pushed him out of her mind.

"Enough," she whispered as perspiration glistened on her face.

It took a moment to collect himself. "I'm so sorry that happened."

"Look at that girl," she said, pointing to a woman pushing a cart toward the parking lot with a daughter who must be eight or nine. "Imagine Desmond doing those things to her."

The thought of that made him ill.

Alex studied the people coming and going, then zeroed in on a couple with three children from about their age on down. She peered for a moment, then said, "Look at that man. Look into his mind."

He didn't want to, but he reached out. Flashes of a young girl nude and writhing with pleasure pawed by hands that looked like a man's. Noah pulled back with a jerk, closing his eyes.

"That's his next victim he's already grooming," she said. "He's fantasizing what it'll be like."

"He looks so normal with his family. You'd never guess..."

"They all do. They know how to blend in. Remember Ellen and Gregory?"

"We need to do something—"

"We will. I've already noted where he lives. He won't be with the girl again for three days."

"It's like they're everywhere."

"Imagine that man with Desmond's powers, what he'd do with that girl."

A dark rage welled up inside Noah. He wanted to run to the man and confront him immediately. He wanted to...

"What do you want to happen to that man?" she asked.

Quietly so he could barely hear himself, he whispered, "He doesn't deserve to live."

She nodded.

They sat in silence as Noah let all he'd seen sink in. "But we can't force an innocent person to kill Desmond."

She peered at him for a moment, then gathered the trash from their lunch and stood up. "Meet me at the park."

She walked away. He jumped up and chased after her, reaching her as she threw the trash away. "What are you gonna do?"

"I'll take care of it."

"Are you going to do something danger—"

"Stop!" She sighed in exasperation. "Noah, can't you *just once* trust me?" She glared at him.

He didn't know what to say.

"Meet me at the park."

She marched away.

———

Noah sat at the same picnic table as when they first saw Desmond. His back was to the grove of trees a distance away. He looked around, focusing on every individual before him—man, woman, or child—putting out feelers for any other person who might have their power. Dwelling on it spooked him. What if there were a dozen Desmonds in the crowd?

He felt her sit beside him before he saw her.

"Now we wait," Alex said. "I'm sure he'll show up soon. We made it easy for him, coming here."

"What did you do?" He realized he was shaking.

"Now this is important. We can't let him into our minds and see the plan."

"I don't even know the plan."

"Exactly. He'll expect us to attack him, so we do that immediately."

"Because that worked so good before."

"Listen to me!" She reached over and squeezed his hand. "I'm really counting on you to keep Desmond occupied, so I can concentrate on what I need to do."

He nodded, but her words only made him tremble more. What was she going to do? He tried to focus on what she'd been through, how he felt about her. He was surprised to realize that his feelings for her had grown to something more than just a friend. It was almost like...like...well, he wasn't sure what to call it exactly. But it helped to think of himself as protecting her instead of helping her to...do whatever she needed to do.

That was the goal he'd focus on, to protect her. He couldn't bear the thought of Desmond being victorious.

They sat in silence for a while, then she said softly, "There he is."

Without moving, Noah reached out with his mind and sensed the man coming slowly toward them from behind.

She swiveled around on her seat, then cried out painfully and buckled over. "Hit him!"

Noah whipped around to face Desmond and blasted him with all the force he could muster. The man stopped and reeled from the attack, but regained his balance and marched slowly toward them, a deep scowl on his face.

"Harder!" she cried.

He tried to push harder, but he was at his capacity. He groaned with the effort.

Her breaths came out in noisy spurts. "He...he knows...he knows..."

Noah panicked. He saw the plan?

"He knows I'm...I'm not concentrating on...him. He's wondering why." She gave out a long wail. "Please, Noah, harder!"

He tried, but he could feel himself faltering as Desmond switched back and forth quickly, bombarding his mind, then hers, in close succession.

"Now!" she cried.

Noah didn't understand what she meant because he was already attacking, until he saw a young man with tattoos and a thin Latino mustache creep out from the grove of trees.

She must have been talking to him.

Alex cried loudly with tears streaming down her face. "He's...he's gonna break through. Noah! He's breaking through!" She cried out with anguish and dropped to the grass on her hands and knees. People in the park stared at her.

The Latino man crept up behind Desmond and pulled a gun out. Desmond's eyes popped wide open, and he whirled around. The man stopped with a shocked look. He looked down as the muzzle of his gun crept up and pointed at his own face.

Noah leaped to his feet and charged, giving out a banshee scream. Desmond whirled back and hit Noah with the full force of his mind. Noah stumbled to his knees and ended up planting his face on the ground as he slid across the grass.

Desmond turned back to the man to find the gun aimed at him again. The man cried out and grabbed his head with both hands. The gun pointed skyward.

Alex cried out with rage as she rose up on her knees. Noah lifted his torso up by his arms and blasted Desmond with all his might. Pain stabbed Noah, and he fell back to the ground.

"He's got a gun!" someone shouted, and people screamed.

The pain stopped. Alex howled and crumpled to the ground sobbing. Noah blasted Desmond again. He whirled around and hit Noah with a crippling blast.

A gunshot rang out, then another, and another. Screams echoed everywhere and people ran. Six gunshots in total until the echo died away with the gun trigger still clicking several times more.

Noah lifted his head and saw Desmond standing with a horrified look on his face, eyes and mouth wide open. Blood blossomed from his chest in six places. His head swiveled around to look at the man, but he lost his balance and plummeted like a plank onto the ground, hitting hard on his side. The man stood behind him pointing the gun with a smoking muzzle.

Noah reached out to Desmond with his mind. He could find no mind to sense in the man. He jumped up and ran to Alex. She lay in fetal position on the ground sobbing, her hands clutching her head.

Noah dropped to his knees and gathered her up in his arms. "Are you okay?"

She clung to him desperately, breathing in fitful bursts. "Help me up," she whispered in his ear.

He lifted her to her feet. "We gotta get out of here."

"Wait." She broke free, turned to the shocked people in the park, and shouted, "Call the police! Tell them what you saw!" She threw her arm around Noah and pulled him in. "And we were never here!"

Phones appeared everywhere. The Latino man came to his senses and looked around with horror at everyone staring at him. He turned to flee, but several men charged him and tackled him to the ground. One of them pulled the gun from his hands.

"*Now* let's go," Alex said.

They dashed away. By the time they were a block from the park, they could hear multiple sirens wailing. They ran until they came to the woods and darted through the trees to their place by the river. They stood gaping at each other, panting heavily.

"Did we do it?" she said.

"We did it. He's dead."

She laughed exuberantly and threw herself into his arms. "We did it!" She planted a powerful kiss on his lips. It shocked him, but he quickly regained his composure and kissed her back. Electrifying tingles swept through his body.

She broke away and launched into a victory dance. "We did it! I'm free! I'm free!"

Watching her made his heart leap with delight. Any remaining guilt he felt about what they did evaporated away. To see her so joyful was the happiest thing he'd ever seen in his life. It was then that the word came to him that described how he felt toward her. It was a word he never dreamed of using before on anyone but his parents and never expected to for many more years.

He loved her.

She stopped dancing and gazed at the river, breathing heavily with a beaming, flushed face and a silly grin. "I'm going to skip a rock in that damn river if it's the last thing I do!" She searched around for a good one, wide and flat and rounded at the edges. She positioned herself and looked at him. "Here goes."

Noah wished hard that it would skip for her and felt bad that it wouldn't work. She flung it with a perfect move and watched with anticipation as it hit the surface of the water.

And skipped back into the air one time before it plopped out of sight.

She gaped at it, and he gaped at it, then they gaped at each other and laughed. They embraced again and kissed again.

"This is my lucky day!" she cried.

They sat together naked on Asteroid Alexandra, taking in the breathtaking view as they spoke.

"So his name is Raoul," Noah said.

"He sells drugs to minors. Grade school kids even. He's killed about a dozen people to control his territory. And he slips drugs into the drinks of teenage girls and rapes them."

"Wow. He *is* nasty."

"He deserves every year of prison they give him."

"How'd you get him to do it?"

"I put an image of Desmond in his mind. He thought Desmond was a new drug lord coming into town, wanting to muscle in on his territory." She giggled. "He was very confused, since he never knew Desmond existed until I popped that image into his head."

Noah laughed. He looked around at the asteroid, the close horizon, the fierce stars, and the little blue marble of Earth in the distance. "I guess you'll never have to hide here again."

"But I'll still come. I like the peace and quiet away from people's thoughts." She patted his hand. "You will too over time. Feel free to come here whenever you want."

"Wait a minute. Does that mean you're still leaving?"

Her expression became forlorn. "I have my job to do. There's lots of cities in the world with kids to save."

The joy he felt vanished. "But..."

She gathered him into an embrace. "I know. I love you too."

Those words didn't give him the happy feeling he thought they would. Not if she was leaving. He pulled away. "We make a good team."

"You have a family."

He thought hard about leaving his father and mother. He loved them too.

But it was a distant love. He'd observed other families in action and saw greater warmth among them than he had with his parents. After all, he was weird, and that impacted his family life as well. His parents made great effort, and he made great effort, but somehow the warmth never quite developed.

He struggled for words to explain that to her, and settled on something simple. "I love you more."

She gazed at him with an affectionate look, but mixed with concern. "Do you understand what it means to come with me?"

"After all we've been through? Don't you think I understand more than any other person in the world?"

"You'll either have to break your parents' heart or make them forget you ever existed."

"I'm not sure how much their hearts would be broken. I mean, we love each other, but..."

She nodded. "I think I understand. But still, how fair is it to force that choice on them?"

"How fair is it to force people to give you food, or to replace their dead son so you have somewhere to sleep, or—"

"Okay, I get it."

"Who else can do what we do? How much better is the world with us doing our job?"

"*Our* job now?" she smirked. "You sound like me arguing the guilt out of myself."

"It's a pretty good argument, isn't it?"

She laughed. "I never thought I'd have a true friend until I met you. But I really never thought I'd end up with a disciple."

He chuckled. "It's because you're right. This *is* our job, and we deserve to be paid for it. How many kids will be harmed if we don't do it? How many more Desmonds are out there?"

She shuddered. "People like us are rare. But there's also billions of people in the world. I'm sure a lot of them with our power use it for terrible things. Maybe most of them."

"So we've got our work cut out for us. And you need a partner. All you ever did before me was run away."

She held her hands up. "Hey! You don't have to convince me. I'd love having you tag along."

"Tag along?" he said, feeling offended.

She laughed. "I think you're trying to convince yourself more than me."

A retort almost escaped his lips, but he decided against it. This was who she was, and teasing was her safe way of being affectionate. Not surprising after all she'd been through.

With more seriousness, she said, "I just want to make sure you understand what you're giving up."

"I understand. I can't live a normal life anymore, knowing how much of a difference I could make." He added with a touch of self-consciousness, "Knowing you'd be facing horrible things on your own."

She smiled her genuine smile and gazed up at the stars. "I suppose we could pass as brother and sister so people don't—"

"Brother and sister! I don't want...I mean...when...when we might...you know...when we're...uh...older..."

She grinned at him. "It'll seem too much like incest?"

Noah's jaw dropped. He could almost feel his lifeless face back home turning beet red.

Alexandra laughed and flicked his nose. "You're so adorable!"

The First Mormons in the Moon

Moses Bedford was about to meet the boy who would get Brigham Young killed, but he didn't know it yet. Neither did the boy.

As he strode down High Street in Bromley, Kent, Moses debated with himself whether to attempt one more contact, or to end his missionary efforts for the day and give in to his grumbling stomach. His mood matched the long shadows from the sun as it touched the western horizon. He felt as weary as the half moon looming above was pale. Not one person was willing to speak with him today.

Joseph F. Smith wouldn't let his stomach govern him, he mused. Apostle of the Lord, Second Counselor in the First Presidency, current President of the British Mission—he wouldn't quit until he made at least one contact, no matter how dark the sky became, no matter how tired his body or empty his stomach or demoralized his soul.

But Moses was not Joseph F. Smith.

Few pedestrians and carriages populated the street. Even as he continued debating with himself, he knew in his heart he'd quit for the day.

The young boy suddenly appeared at his side. White shirt underneath a dingy vest, worn knickerbockers, scuffed but sound shoes. The boy looked up and said, "Good evening, gov."

"Good evening, son."

The boy was about to pass by, when Moses realized this might be a sign from God. Quickly he said, "Where are you heading so fast?"

"Home. Just came from school. Morley's Academy."

"That's just down the street. I hear it's a fine school."

"Sure, if you want to learn girl's handwriting and tradesman arithmetic."

Moses smiled, keeping pace with the boy's gait. "I take it you don't."

"I know astronomy and botany and biology and history." He ticked them off with his fingers, starting with his thumb. "I'm no tradesman."

Moses stopped in his tracks, causing the boy to slow to a stop and turn. "How old are you, son?"

"I turn eleven one month from today," he said proudly.

"So the 21st of September. Then...happy birthday."

"Thanks, gov."

"You know a lot for a boy of ten."

"Almost eleven," he boasted. "I knew how to read at three."

Impressive boy! Moses extended his hand. "My name is Brother Moses."

The boy eyed it, then shook it. "I'm Bertie. You a Yank?"

"From Philadelphia."

They resumed walking. "How'd you get a silly name like Brother Moses?" Bertie asked.

"Moses is my Christian name. Brother is my title. I'm a missionary."

That perked his interest. "On your way to Africa? India?"

Moses chuckled. "I'm a missionary right here in Kent."

The boy rolled his eyes. "Don't we got enough Christians here already?"

"I'm a special kind of Christian. A Mormon Christian."

"Never heard of it." He fell silent for a moment, thinking, then stopped before a shop door. "Shouldn't you be off converting heathens? We already got the C of E here."

"I have a message from God for all people, not just heathens."

"Well, me and my pa don't much care for such things." He gestured to the shop door.

Moses looked up and noticed where he was. The block lettering in the window said:

WELLS SHOP
Sporting Equipment
Fine Glass and China Ware

Through the window he could see a man and a woman speaking together toward the back of the shop. The man showed the woman a glass vase.

"It was nice meeting you, gov." Bertie opened the door to go in.

"I think I'll come in and take a look around." He followed the boy into the shop. That seemed to please Bertie.

"Good evening, sir," the man called. "I'll be with you presently. Bertie can take care of you." He went back to the vase and the woman.

Bertie's demeanor instantly became a merchant's. "What're you interested in, gov? Perhaps a cricket bat?" He pulled one off a shelf and held it out with pride. "This is the best bat we carry. Guaranteed to score you at least two runs on average."

"Well, I—"

He leaned in conspiratorially. "This is the type of bat my pa used when he scored his double hat trick. You know what that is, don't you?"

"I'm afraid I don't."

"That's four downed wickets in four consecutive bowls. But he didn't do it in the same over."

"I'm afraid that didn't help."

Bertie's respect for Moses seemed to drop a notch. "The batters missed. My pa knocked down the wicket in the last two bowls of one over, then did it again in the first two bowls of his next over. He was the first bowler to ever do that."

"That's...very impressive."

The boy rolled his eyes.

The man brought the vase and the woman to the register to ring up the purchase.

"You never played cricket, did you?" said Bertie.

"I'm sorry, I haven't."

"You play rounders?" He squinted at Moses' perplexed look. "Baseball!"

"Yes, I do."

"Why do you Yanks play baseball? My pa says you used to play cricket not so long ago."

"Because it's not British." Moses smiled to telegraph it was a joke, but Bertie didn't respond. "Well, why do you Brits play cricket? You invented baseball."

"Because it's not American." A faint smile crossed his lips.

Moses liked the boy. He was smart. And feisty. He'd make a fantastic Mormon.

Her transaction complete, the woman headed for the door. "Thank you, ma'am," the man said. "Good evening to you."

He walked toward Moses and Bertie. "Welcome, sir. I hope Bertie's been of help to you." He held out his hand. "My name is Joseph Wells. I'm the proprietor of this shop."

Moses shook his hand. "He's the best shop clerk I've ever had the fortune of meeting."

Joseph beamed with satisfaction. "And your name, sir?"

"I'm Brother Moses Bedford from Philadelphia."

"Brother? Are you a Quaker?"

Moses smiled. "Brother from Philadelphia. I can see how you might think that. But no, sir, I'm an elder for the Church of Jesus Christ of Latter-day Saints."

"I thought you said you were Mormon," Bertie blurted.

Joseph scowled. "Mormon? You mean Brigham Young?"

"Brigham Young?" Bertie cried. "With his hundred wives? That's what Mormons are?"

"That's an exagger—"

"Have you been preaching to my son?"

"Not at all! He's been teaching *me* about cricket."

Joseph studied him suspiciously, then headed for the register. "Well, you're talking to the wrong chaps. We don't put any stock in that sort of thing. Right, Bertie?"

"Right, pa! We're rational."

"You should talk to Sarah, my wife. She's the religious one." He shook his head with a resigned smile as he opened the register and pulled out the drawer. "You have no idea how religious! Maybe you could steal her away and chain her in that temple of yours."

"Pa!"

"Those are lies!" Moses said.

Joseph peered at Moses with a glint in his eyes. "I beg your pardon, sir. It was said in jest. Bertie, why don't you take Brother Moses to meet your mum and offer him some tea while I close up. It's just across the street, sir."

"Follow me, gov," said Bertie.

The sky was half-dark by now with streaks of red in the clouds. They crossed the street easily with no traffic in sight.

"So you don't steal women and chain them up so you can marry them?"

"No, Bertie. I think you'll find that we're pretty normal."

"But Brigham Young has a hundred wives, right?"

"We do have plural wives, like Abraham in the Bible. But Brigham Young doesn't have *that* many."

"How many then?"

"I...don't really know for sure."

"I heard about free love. I didn't know anybody really practiced it."

Moses sighed in exasperation. "We don't! They're wives, not...not mistresses."

"If you can have as many wives as you want, what's the difference?"

"Marriage!"

They reached the building across the street. Bertie stopped and turned to him. "How many wives do *you* have?"

"I'm not married."

He nodded. "Good."

He took Moses behind the building where some stairs descended into the ground and terminated at a door. In the back was a small garden with a woman on her knees digging. Beyond that was a dilapidated structure that might be a stable.

"Mum, I brought a guest."

The woman looked up. "What?" She eyed Moses up and down.

"Pa said to bring him over for some tea."

Confused, she said, "Um...let me finish here."

"I'll get the kettle going." Bertie started down the stairs, but popped his head up. "He's a Mormon, but all's well. He doesn't have any wives."

Bertie headed for the door below and disappeared inside. The last glimpse Moses had of the woman was her gaping at him, then digging furiously.

Inside Bertie headed for the kitchen area and expertly fired up the stove. "Have a seat, gov."

Moses sat in a frayed chair and peered about the bleak room. Patches of oilcloth and a dingy mat partially covered a darkly stained wooden floor. The fireplace mantel contained a white coral rock and several fossil bones. Above that hung a sketch of a man's head sliced in half to expose the brain within. Bookshelves hung on the wall loaded with books. Next to them hung a tattered and yellowed map of southern England.

Bertie had the kettle heating when his mother entered the room, her hands hanging in front of her darkened with moist soil. "Pardon me, sir, while I wash."

She walked toward a basin in the kitchen area and dipped and rubbed her hands in the water, then grabbed a towel to dry them. "Welcome, sir. My name is Sarah. I guess you've met Bertie."

Moses stood and approached her. "Indeed I have. My name is Brother Moses Bedford." He took her hand, bent over and kissed it.

She giggled and flushed. "I'm not a lady."

"You should be, as beautiful as you are."

Bertie rolled his eyes as the kettle whistled. He grabbed it off the stove and poured three cups.

Sarah indicated the table with chairs around it. "Please." She and Moses sat. She regarded him, then said, "You're a Mormon. Is that like a Quaker?"

He chuckled. "Not at all, although we do call ourselves brother and sister."

"What do Mormons believe?"

"Most importantly, in Jesus Christ. We also believe in modern prophets. Our prophet Joseph Smith restored the pure gospel of Jesus to the world."

Bertie brought a tray with the three cups of tea and a plate of biscuits and sat down, hooking a biscuit immediately. As he chewed he said, "They also believe in lots of wives. But he doesn't have any."

She scrunched her brow at that. "Well, we're C of E. We already have Christ...and..."

"...and we *don't* believe in lots of wives," Bertie said, then sipped his tea.

Joseph burst into the room, and Bertie stood up. "Sit down, boy, I'll get my own." He headed for the kettle and poured himself a cup. "Has he made us Mormons yet, love?"

"You just want to be able to marry that girl at the market," she said.

Joseph grinned at Moses as he came to the table and sat. "Wives. They always know, don't they?"

Moses glanced at Sarah, not sure how to take this. Joseph slapped him on the shoulder. "I jest! You need a better sense of humor."

Sarah never cracked a smile through all of it. "I told him I'm already a Christian."

"I told him he ought to go to Africa where the heathens are," said Bertie.

"Leave the heathens alone," Joseph said. "They're happy with their own religions."

This is the family God wanted him to approach? Moses wasn't sure how to steer the conversation to where he could preach the gospel. He wasn't sure it would do any good if he did.

"Um...as I was telling your wife, we believe that God called our prophet Joseph Smith to restore the pure gospel of Jesus Christ to the—"

"Isn't that what they all say?" Joseph said. "Martin Luther. John Calvin. At least Henry the Eighth was honest about it. He just wanted to shag Anne Boleyn."

Bertie laughed. Sarah hissed, "Joseph!"

Moses was speechless. Where should he go from that?

"Listen, Brother Moses, I'm happy to offer you hospitality, but we're not interested in your little message from your little prophet. Like Sarah said, she's already got religion. And Bertie and I are rationalists."

"Don't be mean, pa," Bertie said. "I like him."

Joseph smiled at him. "You're such a good boy. Thanks for reminding me. Brother Moses, I beg your pardon for being so flippant. I'm sure your religion is as important to you as Sarah's is to her."

"It is," Moses said testily.

"Maybe *you* should be the prophet. You have the name for it."

Moses was about fed up. He must have been mistaken that the Spirit led him here. He should have gone home and eaten. The tea and the conversation were not settling well on his empty stomach.

"Tell you what, governor," Joseph said. "Let me show you something that's part of *my* religion."

Bertie's eyes lit up.

"You can keep a secret, can't you? Your word is your bond as a religious man, innit?"

"Absolutely."

"Come with me." Joseph stood and headed for the door. Bertie scrambled out of his chair and followed.

Moses looked at Sarah.

"He's been dying to show someone," she said. "Please do not betray him."

"I won't, ma'am." He stood and followed the two rational males out the door as Sarah began gathering up the teaware.

The sun was gone, but the sky still glowed enough red streaks to light their way. Joseph led them past the garden to the stable. He paused at the door and pierced Moses with his gaze.

"I need your solemn vow that you'll tell no one about my...endeavor."

"Is it legal?"

Joseph was taken aback. "Of course it's legal! But I don't want anyone knowing about it yet. Do you vow?"

"I promise I won't reveal your endeavor until you've revealed it to the world yourself."

Joseph nodded. "Good."

"You're going to love this!" Bertie said.

Joseph produced a key and unlocked the padlock, then slid the door open. The structure was pitch black inside. "Bertie, let's strike some lamps."

Moses waited at the door as father and son crept into the darkness. He strained to see something in the shadows. He thought he saw a bit of red sparkling on something from the remaining sunlight, almost like fairy dust.

Or maybe a sign from the Spirit? Joseph had called this his "religion." Could this be the starting point for Moses to deliver his message?

Lights flared as Joseph and Bertie ignited the lamps. The blackness flashed into a gloomy illumination. Moses gasped in awe.

Before him were two giant spheres, three times the height of a man, encompassing two-thirds of the space in the stable. The surface of one sphere consisted of many dozens of hexagonal panels that had a bluish-charcoal metallic look. Each panel had embedded in it a square blind. The blinds on the bottom and top were opened, but the rest were all closed.

But the other sphere appeared made of a thick glass with cross work beams of steel reinforcement. A spidery web of wires was embedded in it with the end of each wire poking out as if waiting to attach to something. On the inside of the glass surface the wires attached to small switches mounted at regular intervals spread throughout the entire sphere. Moses noticed the intervals between switches were approximately the size of each hexagon on the first sphere.

The transparent sphere acted as a giant lens, severely distorting the view of the stable wall behind it. Inside there was nothing but the switches. On one side was a manhole tightly sealed with a gasket, with a powerful hinge attaching it to the sphere and a handle like a lever protruding on the inside. On the outside was a socket that appeared to be waiting for an external lever to be attached.

Off in a corner of the stable were stacked other hexagonal panels with blinds, bundled tightly with straps anchoring them to the floor as if to keep them from walking away. Each blind was open.

Overhead, most of the ceiling was covered with a gate—a series of planks with wheels attached on either end of each of them mounted within tracks that ran to and curved down the wall. A rope wove between the planks that connected to a pulley system on the wall that extended to the floor.

Joseph beamed at the spheres with the pride of a creator. "Do you know how many years, how many cricket games, it took me to save up for these beauties? I hired the best glass smiths in London to manufacture the spheres."

"What are they for?"

"Transportation," Bertie said. "They float."

"You mean on the sea?"

"Not on water," Joseph said. "They float on air and...well...anything. Nothing."

"I don't understand."

Joseph walked up to the paneled sphere and lay his hand on it. "I call this material wellsite. It's opaque."

"I can see that."

"To gravity."

"To...what are you talking about?"

"Wellsite blocks out all gravity, as an opaque object blocks out all light. Anything contained within it is completely weightless."

"That's not possible," Moses said, feeling compelled to go up and touch the material himself.

"What's not possible, sir," Joseph said with an edge to his voice, "is your namesake parting the Red Sea, or Jesus walking on water, or your prophet seeing God. *This* is science."

Moses scowled. He suddenly felt a fool. This fellow was no prospect for the gospel. He wasn't the least bit prepared to feel the Spirit. Moses was wasting his time. He could be in his flat right now, reading scriptures with a satisfied stomach.

"Science requires proof," Moses said in his own edgy tone. "I don't see this bubble floating on anything but hard ground."

Scowling at him, Bertie said, "Can't you see? The blinds on the bottom and top are open, letting the gravity through."

"The sphere inside the panels has weight," Joseph said, "keeping it pressed to the Earth. Bertie, show him what happens when it's only the panel."

With a mischievous smile, Bertie marched to the stack and grabbed a top panel with both hands.

"Be careful, son."

Bertie nodded, braced his feet, and yanked hard. The panel slid out from the straps. Bertie fell back onto the floor as he let go. The panel shot straight up like a bullet, plastering itself against the ceiling of the stable with a thud.

As Moses gaped, Joseph said, "That's with the blind open. If it had been closed, the panel would have smashed right through the roof and shot off into the rarified layers of the atmosphere."

"That's...that's...that's..." Moses threw his hands up in the air. "...astounding! Miraculous!"

"Not miraculous," Bertie protested. "Science."

Moses forgot his stomach, forgot his frustration, forgot his calling from God. He grabbed Joseph by both arms and cried, "Do you know what this... this...discovery can do, man? It'll transform the entire transportation industry. It'll transform the world!"

He paced back and forth in excitement. "Massive amounts of freight can be transported across country—across the seas—cheaply. Prices for goods will plummet. This is a godsend to the poverty stricken of the world!"

Joseph watched him with amusement. Bertie grinned wide.

"People will be able to travel to the ends of the Earth, over rugged terrain, bodies of water. It'll promote settling in wilderness areas, scientific exploration." He stopped in his tracks, noticing the two grinning at him. "What?"

"Yes," Joseph said, "wellsite will do all that. But these spheres won't."

Moses studied the paneled one. "It's a transport, isn't it?"

"Yes, but you asked the wrong question."

Moses peered at him, wondering what the right question was supposed to be. It's a transport to...to...

"Transport to where?"

Joseph headed for the rope on pulleys and tugged continuously at it. The gate rolled along the tracks until it exposed star-glittered sky through an opening large enough for both spheres to shoot up out of the stable. Before the gate slid to a stop, it revealed the shining half-moon at the edge of the opening.

Moses peered at the moon, then looked down at Joseph, who peered at him. A moment of silence pulsed.

"Dear God, you don't mean..."

Joseph smiled.

"You...you can't take those things to the moon!"

Joseph pointedly gazed at the panel still plastered on the ceiling. "If the roof weren't there, that panel would be flying to the moon right now."

Moses peered at the panel on the ceiling, then up at the moon. Joseph and

Bertie came up alongside him and gazed with him.

"We're going to the moon," Bertie said with reverence.

"No, you're not, son," Joseph said.

"Pa!"

"It's too dangerous. After a few voyages, maybe then."

"But I—"

"Brother Moses, I'm relying on your honor to keep silent about this."

Breathlessly with his face still aimed at the sky, Moses said, "Who would believe me?"

Joseph chuckled. "Nevertheless..."

"I'm going, pa!"

Joseph tousled Bertie's hair. "Very well...someday."

"Does it work?" Moses said. "I mean, have you tried it?"

"Of course I've tried it," Joseph said.

"I went with him, across the channel and back," said Bertie.

Joseph went to the rope and pulled the gate closed. "Don't you have chores need doing before bedtime, Bertie?"

The boy groaned the international chore-hating groan, the same one Moses had groaned throughout his childhood.

Joseph gestured to the door. "Please." The three of them exited the stable. Joseph secured the padlock behind him. "Has your God ever brought someone to the moon, Brother Moses?"

Moses looked at him and found his eyes twinkling.

Joseph extended his hand. "It was an honor to meet you, sir. Good evening." They shook, and he led the boy to the stairs. They descended into their flat.

Moses stared at the moon. The half-face on it grinned at him. Joseph's words echoed in his mind. *Has your God ever brought someone to the moon?*

Before Bertie's head disappeared, he stopped and peered at Moses. They locked eyes for an instant.

"Bertie?" Joseph's voice called.

The boy cocked his head at Moses, then went in.

Moses walked to the street and headed home, his mind awash in thoughts. He remembered things he'd heard now and then as a converted Mormon, words people said came from the lips of prophets. Joseph Smith said there were men and women living on the moon the same as Earth, who were tall and lived long lives and dressed something like the Quakers. Brigham Young mentioned the inhabitants of "this little planet that shines, called the moon." Hyrum Smith once preached that the moon was inhabited. Several men were promised in their patriarchal blessings that they would preach the gospel to many peoples, including those on the moon.

The thought flashed into his mind, *Yes, Joseph Wells! The answer to your question is yes. My God has brought people to the moon.*

And suddenly he realized the Spirit *had* led him to the boy, to the little sports-and-glassware shop on High Street, and to the extraordinary man of science who had no interest in his message, but had invented a most marvelous machine, a transport that could bring Mormons to the moon.

To preach the restored gospel of Jesus Christ!

His head swam with the implications. He wanted to turn right back and demand he be allowed to accompany Joseph on his voyage into space. God's hand was in everything that transpired this evening. It had to be!

The instant he thought that, he knew it would never happen. Joseph Wells tried to be polite, but his detestation of belief in God was palpable. Moses knew he'd never allow him to accompany him to the moon to preach his religion to any people who dwelled there. *Leave the heathens alone*, he said.

Moses arrived at his flat and immediately dropped to his knees. He prayed for guidance. He thought of Nephi's story in the Book of Mormon, how the Spirit led him on his important mission. After fervent praying, he felt his own assurance from the Spirit. He knew that, like Nephi, he must do something that his conscience would balk at. He must break his vow to Joseph. He must steal that sphere, so an entire nation of moon people would not dwindle in unbelief.

He gathered whatever provisions he could think of, food, bottles of water, a blanket—and several copies of the Book of Mormon, of course. He felt ill-prepared, not beginning to know what he might need on a voyage to the moon. Once again, he felt compelled to trust in the Lord. God knows what he needs, and he will provide. Moses would travel and preach without purse or scrip in a way no messenger of God had done before.

The moon was low in the west as he left to return to the stable, his bag of meager provisions slung over his shoulder. The streets of Bromley were dark and utterly still, without even a breeze to whisper a sound. The moon beckoned...*chase me if you can!*

I will! vowed Moses.

Wells Shop was dark. The windows to the lower dwelling of the Wells family were shuttered. He crept to the stable door, and to his surprise found the padlock hanging open. He looked around in apprehension, but there was no sign of anyone. Joseph must not have pressed hard enough to lock it fully.

Or perhaps...if God can open a prison for the Apostle Peter to escape, he can certainly unlock a stable for him.

He crept inside, confident that he was on a mission from God. He found a single lamp lit, but no one in sight. His head spun, thinking that an angel of the Lord must have prepared the way. He headed for the rope and pulled on it as carefully as he could, minimizing the creaking as the gate slid open.

Requiring the strength of both hands, he tugged on the external lever and swung the hatch open. The gasket made a sucking sound as it let go.

Inside, a single electric glow lamp cast ghostly illumination on a pile of provisions in the middle of the sphere. Shadows behind the pile left the rest of the space in blackness.

Moses climbed in and tossed his bag to the side, pathetic compared to the well-organized stack in the middle. He smiled with gratitude for the angel's preparations. "Thank you, Lord," he murmured as he pulled the hatch closed, tugged the lever back in place to seal it, then smiled. "I don't suppose you included a spacefaring Liahona?"

"What's a Liahona?" said a childlike voice from the blackness.

Moses jumped, expecting to see the shadowy figure of a cherub in robes, until he realized he recognized the voice. "Bertie?"

The boy emerged into the light, grinning. "I knew you'd come back."

"You...you're not supposed to come with. Your father said—"

"And you're not supposed to steal my pa's sphere."

"I can't...honestly, son, I can't bring you with. It's too—"

"Do you know how to navigate this thing?"

"Uh..."

"Have you helped steer it across the English Channel in the middle of the night?"

Moses sighed with exasperation.

"You need me. You'll kill yourself without me. Or get lost in outer space."

"It would be kidnapping."

He grinned. "I think I'm kidnapping you. Brace yourself."

He pressed several switches on the floor in quick succession. The open blinds on the bottom snapped closed.

A sudden force pressed Moses against the bottom. The edges of the opening in the ceiling vanished away. Everything seemed absolutely still except for the force pushing them against the sphere's floor.

"We're heading for the moon, right, gov?"

"What? No!"

A look of alarm hit Bertie's face. He pushed a couple switches that opened lower blinds again. The pressure eased. Moses could see the shadowy buildings and streets of Kent a thousand feet below them with the occasional light glowing. They were still rising far above it.

"Where, then?" Bertie asked.

"I...I can't just *go* to the moon. I'm only called to the British mission. I mean...I have no authority to start up a mission on...I mean—"

"Governor, we're still shooting off into space. *Where do you want to go?*"

"Utah!"

Bertie gave him a strange look. "That's...west?" He opened and closed blinds. Everything and everyone in the sphere jostled this way and that as the direction of acceleration changed with the adjustment of gravitational pull.

By the time Bertie sat back saying, "I think that does it," the half moon could be seen above the edge of the Earth through the open blinds, with nothing but dark Atlantic Ocean below. The sensation of *down* disappeared. They and their supplies rose from the surface of the sphere and drifted casually toward the open blinds pointing west.

"Why are we going to Utah?" Bertie said.

"I have to speak with Brigham Young."

Bertie scowled at him. "You're going to betray my pa. You're giving this to Brigham Young so he can claim he invented it and get rich."

"No! I just need his permission to preach to the moon people."

"Why didn't you just telegraph him?"

"That I want to go to the moon and preach to the people there?"

Bertie nodded as he thought. "You need to show him so he believes you. So you *are* betraying my pa."

"I...I'm sorry. I promise you Brigham will keep it secret too. But this was too import—"

"I was hoping you just wanted to go to the moon, not break your promise."

"The world will never know. Just you, me, and Brigham Young. Your father's secret will be safe."

Bertie turned with a deep scowl to peer out the blinds.

Moses sighed and studied the Earth. The edge glowed with sunlight spilling from beyond the horizon, but the ocean was dark and featureless. "How high are we? How fast are we going?"

"I don't know how high we are. We have to be going fast to orbit."

"Are you sure we're not slowly falling to Earth?"

"Orbiting *is* falling to Earth. We're just going so fast, by the time we reach Earth, it's curved away from us, so we're still orbiting. What's he like, Brigham Young?"

"I've never met him."

"How do you know he's a prophet? Maybe *he's* lying." He squinted his eyes. "Like you."

Moses exhaled with exasperation. "I read the Book of Mormon and prayed, and received a witness that it's true."

"What's the Book of Mormon?"

"It's a new book of scripture."

"So it's the Mormon Bible?"

"No, we still use the Bible. You know how there was the Old Testament first? Then Jesus came, and the New Testament was added?"

"Yeah."

"Then Joseph Smith came, and God gave us the Book of Mormon to add to the others."

"So it's like the Even Newer Testament?"

"Well, yes, you could say that. Except the Bible was written by the Israelites and the Jews, but the Book of Mormon was written by the ancient people of America."

"You mean Red Injuns?"

"Well, their ancestors. They called themselves Nephites and Lamanites."

Bertie scrunched his face up. "I think if there was an American Bible out there, we'd all have heard of it by now."

"That's part of my message as a missionary, to tell the people of England about the...Even Newer Testament."

"You have scholars that studied it? Old manuscripts they translated? What language was it written in?"

Moses smiled at the barrage of questions. "It was written in a special language called Reformed Egyptian—"

"Egyptian? In America?"

"It's a record of the descendants of a man named Lehi who lived in Jerusalem, and they—"

"A record of ancient Americans who lived in Jerusalem?"

"No...yes...I mean, they started out in Jerusalem, but God led them to America. He instructed them to build a boat and—"

"Is this before or after Columbus?"

"It's two thousand years before Columbus, in 600 B.C."

"Where'd they get the Egyptian?"

"Lehi was a merchant in Jerusalem, so he knew Egyptian, and he taught it to his descendants."

"So they wrote their Bible in Egyptian, and after the Rosetta Stone was discovered, Egyptian scholars translated the manuscripts into English."

"No, no! A historian called Mormon—"

"That's why you call yourselves Mormons? After the chap who translated the Book of Mormon? Is that why you call it the Book of Mormon?"

Moses took a deep breath. "If you'd just let me tell the story, you wouldn't have to ask all these questions."

"Very well. Tell the story."

Moses launched into the visit from Moroni, the golden plates, how Joseph Smith used the Urim and Thummim to translate the plates by the power of God, and how he gave the plates back to Moroni.

"So there are no manuscripts and no golden plates," Bertie said with disappointment.

"God wanted us to have faith—"

"That's the stupidest thing I ever heard! That's no Bible. We have manuscripts. We can study them. We can compare them to history. Your Bible has nothing!"

"I have a witness of its truthfulness through the power of the Holy Ghost."

Bertie rolled his eyes and turned to look out the blinds. "I see land."

Moses scrambled to look. They neared the beginning of daylight, and the sun's halo blazed over the horizon. He could make out the coastline of New York and Massachusetts and Maine. The clouds were like a cream pie they hovered above. They must be miles high.

It was a breathtaking sight! Moses realized, except for Bertie and Joseph and the angels and God, he was the only one in history who'd seen this sight.

The Earth seemed to roll below them. In a moment the Great Lakes appeared, glistening in the sun.

"We *are* going fast!" Moses said.

"Now where's Utah?"

"Still a thousand miles west."

"Will you recognize it when you see it?"

"Well...there'll be the Rocky Mountains and the Great Salt Lake."

"We'll get there in daylight. You promised no one but Brigham Young would see us."

"Didn't anyone see you when you crossed the channel?"

"We went in the middle of the night and avoided any lights."

"Well, Utah has a lot of empty country."

"Does Brigham Young live in empty country?"

"Salt Lake City."

"So we need to land far from him, then travel to him, then convince him to travel back with us and see the sphere. How many days will that be?"

"We can land in empty country and wait for dark, then travel to Salt Lake in the middle of the night."

Bertie thought about that, looking somber. "Very well."

"I'm deeply sorry about this, but this is extremely important to me. It's as important to me as building the sphere was to your father. As important as going to the moon is to you."

"By the time we reach Salt Lake City, my pa will figure out the sphere is gone and figure out I'm missing. Maybe he'll suspect you came back and stole it. Or maybe he'll think I did."

The Great Lakes had rotated out of sight below the sphere. Hills and plains loomed ahead.

"Bertie, when we make it to the moon, I'll stay there. You can return and tell your father I kidnapped you and made you take me there."

"You don't understand. He has that other sphere."

"But it's not finished."

"All he has to do is install the panels. It took him four weeks to install these panels, but he was in no hurry. Believe me, he'll be in a hurry this time. He'll close the shop and work on it every hour. I figure, a day or two and he'll chase us down."

"But chase us where? How will he know?"

"That depends on what he thinks happened. I suspect he'll either head for the moon, or to Philadelphia thinking you brought it home. Or maybe he'll guess we're in Utah bringing it to Brigham Young."

"Whatever happens, I promise I'll explain it to your father so he's not angry with you."

"You hand out promises like candy." He tried to face away while floating in the weak gravity.

They traveled in silence until the plains rolled past and the mountains began. The tops had a dusting of early snow. Bertie fell asleep. Moses kept an eye out for the Great Salt Lake.

He almost missed it. It was miles south of them. He gently shook Bertie awake. "We need to go south. We're passing the lake."

Bertie shook the grogginess away and rushed to the open blinds. He worked switches and snapped blinds open and closed until their trajectory headed south to the shimmering lake. "It looks empty on the north," the boy said. "We can set down there."

Bertie worked the blinds like a master, easing the sphere toward the northern edge of the lake, and using various tugs of gravity from the Earth and the moon to slow their descent. By the time the sphere touched ground, it was no more jarring that a jump from four feet up.

"The air's stale," Bertie said. "Let's get out of here."

Moses opened the hatch. A blast of warm, salty, dry, but fresh air hit his face. What a change from England!

The two climbed out and stretched their legs in the sun. Bertie was mesmerized by the sparkling lake and the mountain range off to the east. Moses was just as impressed, never having been there before.

They explored, talked about endless subjects, kept an eye out for anyone coming along. No one ever did.

Bertie was insatiable with curiosity, and knowledgeable beyond any ten-year-old Moses had ever known. Moses learned as much from him as he did from Moses.

Bertie gave Moses an inventory of their provisions. Packages of compressed food, water bottles and a condenser, steel cylinders of oxygen, a contraption that removed stale gasses from the air, a portable heater, basic things like tools and knives and rope, and blankets. Joseph Wells anticipated the moon may have an atmosphere, may even have life, but would probably be colder than what humans were used to.

Moses learned that Bertie developed his curiosity and knowledge when he broke his leg one day. As he lay in bed recuperating, his father and mother brought him book after book to read. The range of topics varied widely. He soaked it all up and demanded more. He was not exaggerating when he said he studied different fields of science.

Neither of them brought up religion again. Moses was certain that his mission was not to the Wells family. They were not spiritually ready for the gospel, and he was only making it look more foolish in their eyes when he talked about it. Bertie appeared to have satisfied his curiosity when he declared the origins of the Book of Mormon "stupid." But it disappointed Moses because he liked Bertie, and it saddened him that he couldn't share the truth with a boy that sought so passionately for knowledge.

In the heat of the afternoon, they stripped down to their skin and dove into the Great Salt Lake. The buoyancy of the lake delighted them. The salt drying on their bodies afterward did not, and they brushed it off feverishly from themselves, helping each other clean their backs, before getting dressed again.

They slept on blankets inside the sphere for the rest of the day into the night, keeping the hatch open for fresh air.

The moon was almost set in the west when they awoke. The stars blazed brighter than they would in smokey London or Philadelphia with their city lamps.

They closed the hatch and quietly began their approach to Salt Lake City. "Do you see the lights?" Moses asked.

Bertie looked at him with offense and eased the sphere toward the city, about a thousand feet below. "Where should we set down?"

"I'm not sure yet," Moses said as he studied the landscape.

Downtown was easy to find. There was the broad roof of the Tabernacle, and next to it the shell of a partially completed building that must be the temple. It had a box shaped exterior of walls, but no roof or spires, and nothing inside but a floor. A block or two away was the telltale beehive spire of Brigham Young's home.

"There, in the temple," Moses said.

"Which one's the temple?"

"The one that's unfinished."

Bertie guided the sphere in and landed it as gently as he'd done in the desert.

They climbed out and walked through the ominous darkness of the building, their steps echoing on the walls. They headed into the street and toward the Beehive House.

The structure was dark and silent. Moses stood before the door and wondered how to handle this while Bertie fidgeted. Should he knock? There was little chance Brigham himself would answer. Whoever did was not likely to let a stranger up to Brigham's bedroom at night.

Should he sneak in and seek out Brigham's room, waking the man up in the middle of the night like an intruder?

"What are we doing?" Bertie asked.

"I'm not sure what to do."

"Knock."

"But a servant or maid will probably answer and not let us in."

"Want me to climb through a window and open the door?"

Moses knocked.

It took several bursts of knocking before a light went on and the door opened. A woman stood there in sleepware and a robe. "Yes, what is it?"

"I'm so sorry to disturb you, ma'am. My name is Moses Bedford. I'm an elder who's been serving in the British Mission under President Joseph F. Smith. I understand this is where President Young lives?"

The woman glanced back into the house. "Well...yes, this is his home."

"I have an urgent message to give him. I've traveled all the way from England and need to talk with him immediately."

"Is this from President Smith?"

"Um...well...yes, it's...it's an urgent mission matter."

"Can it wait until morning?"

"I'm sorry, it cannot. No, it absolutely cannot wait."

"Very well. Please wait here."

She closed the door on them.

"You should have let me climb through a window," Bertie said. Moses glared at him.

They stood before the door for some time, listening to the night breeze and the chirping crickets.

"I don't think she's coming back," said Bertie.

The door swung open, and Brigham Young stood there in all his majesty—plus a nightshirt. He looked all the part like a prophet with his long grey beard. His expression looked as if he were about to smite them with an Egyptian plague. Bertie gaped with his mouth open.

"What is this about?"

"President Young, my name is Moses Bedford. I'm an elder in the British Mission."

"You have a message for me from President Smith?"

Moses looked at Bertie, who shrugged.

"Who's this young fellow?"

"I'm Bertie Wells. I'm rational."

Brigham looked him up and down. "I'm not surprised, since you're not one of my wives."

"How many do you have?"

"More than I need, boy, more than I need." He pierced Moses with his gaze. "Is this the urgent message? To be interrogated by this young Brit?"

"President, I know what I'm about to say sounds..." He looked at Bertie. "...unrational—"

"It's not unrational. It's science."

"But I give you my solemn word that every bit of it is true."

"He wants your permission to preach to the moon people."

Brigham's dark glare turned darker. "I'd enjoy this prank at a less ungodly hour, Brother Moses."

"President..." He exhaled with frustration. "I'll just come out and say it. Last evening I was with this boy's family in Kent, England. His father—"

"Did you say last night?" Brigham said.

"Uh...yes...you see—"

"You sailed all the way here from England and crossed the Great Plains in one night?"

"That's what I'm trying—"

"Where were you when we left Nauvoo?" Brigham said with a taunting smile.

Moses gave a frustrated sigh. "President, this boy's father invented an extraordinary vehicle that can defy gravity. We've flown it here from England, and it's hidden in the temple right now."

Brigham studied him for a long, withering moment, then turned his gaze to Bertie.

"It's true, gov," Bertie said. "Every word."

"What's this about moon people?"

"Bertie's father intends to fly it to the moon. When I heard this, I thought immediately about how...uh...you and Brother Joseph taught that there are people living on the moon. I was...I felt as though the Spirit led me to Bertie's family so I could learn about this invention, and...and possibly travel to the moon and open a mission there."

"This boy's father handed his invention over to you so you could spread the gospel on the moon?"

"Well, um..."

"*I* handed it over to him," Bertie blurted.

Brigham's eyes became amused as he eyed the boy. "I take it you're a good Christian boy?"

"I told you, I'm rational."

"He means," Moses said, "well...that he believes in science."

"A man could do worse than that," Brigham said, "considering some of the preachers I've encountered. This thing your father invented...you say it can really fly to the moon?"

"That's right, gov."

"And you call yourself the rational one?"

"Well, I don't believe in no Angel Mormoni with golden books."

"And I've never believed a man who claimed he could fly to the moon."

"Please, President," Moses said. "The sphere is hidden in the temple. It can't be there by morning when people come around. We can prove it to you."

Brigham studied him for a long moment. "Proof is good. Let me get decent." Brigham put on his most intimidating face. "But if you two are selling me damaged goods, I swear by all that is holy I'll have Porter Rockwell skin you alive."

He slammed the door shut.

"Whose Porter Rockwell?" Bertie hissed in a loud whisper.

"You'd love him."

Brigham stood before the sphere, staring somberly at it. "Show me."

Bertie climbed in and closed the hatch. In seconds, the bottom blinds closed. The sphere shot up into the night sky as a rush of wind swept into the building.

Brigham gasped and trotted forward to look up. "Leap rogue and jump whore, I don't believe it!"

"Bertie's father has it all supplied for a trip to the moon," Moses said. "He seemed confident it could go there."

Brigham looked back down at him. "You're a good Latter-day Saint, Moses, and a good missionary." He slapped Moses on the back a little harder than was comfortable. "You say this needs to be out of here by morning?"

"Joseph—Bertie's father—wants this kept secret until he's ready to reveal it to the world."

Brigham nodded. "Joseph. Fine name. Maybe it's an omen." He looked up at the sphere once more, hanging in the sky the size of a melon. "Bring the boy down."

Moses beckoned Bertie down with his hand, assuming he'd be watching through the open blinds. Indeed, not ten seconds passed before the globe slowly sank back down to the ground. The hatch swung open, and Bertie gazed out with a face full of pride.

"I may believe in angels, young man," Brigham said, "but I'm rational too, and I believe in science. I believe what I see with my own eyes."

Brigham brought Bertie and Moses back to his home. "I need to do a little talking to the Spirit," he said, then ordered his wives to treat his guests to boiled eggs and buttered corn bread with honey.

"Got any tea, gov?" Bertie said.

"We most certainly do not!" Brigham said.

He made a sour face and munched on his corn bread.

Brigham's expression softened. He said to one of his wives, "Bring the boy some tea," then left the room.

Moses barely noticed the food he was eating. He was too overwhelmed that he was traveling to the moon under the direct authority of Brigham Young to establish a mission there. He could think of no honor greater except to have personally witnessed Joseph Smith receiving the gold plates from the angel.

By the time Brigham came back, they were finished and enjoying the comfort of full bellies. Bertie kept sipping tea. Joseph Smith's Word of Wisdom advised against it, but the boy was English. There was no way he'd give up his tea.

Brigham appeared in a traveling coat. "I have pondered and prayed, Brother Moses, and the Spirit agrees with you. It's time to bring the gospel to the moon people."

"Are you...will you be coming with?"

"Indeed I will. We're bringing the Good News to a whole new world. It seems fitting a prophet should be there."

Moses was beyond amazed. He would travel to the moon with Brigham Young himself!

"My adoring wives," Brigham said, turning toward them. "I'm going on another mission, something I thought I'd never do again at my advanced age."

"What shall we tell the people?" one of them asked.

"Tell them nothing! If you try to explain old Brigham went to the moon, they'll think I'm crazier than they already do."

"But—"

"Tell them..." he said more gently. "Tell them I've come down ill. A stomach malady, perhaps, considering some of your cooking."

Most of his wives made a pouting face.

Brigham looked at Moses and Bertie. "I suppose this could be a dangerous mission. We don't know what to expect." He pondered a moment, then said to his wives, "If I don't return in, say, a week or so, tell them I died of the malady." A smile flickered an instant on the corners of his mouth. "Or tell them one of my beloved wives poisoned me. I think you know who I'm talking about."

He kissed each one of them. "Kiss the other wives for me, and the children." He turned to Moses and Bertie. "We should go, before daylight reveals that contraption."

The three of them settled in to the sphere. The light of the single lamp cast shadowy illumination on their faces. Moses felt excitement tinged with misgivings. It was true, they faced unknown dangers and may never survive this journey.

Brigham looked about with nervous eyes and muttered something.

"What was that, gov?" Bertie said as he went about preparing to launch.

"I said I must be out of my mind, going to the moon in this damn thing."

He shook his head and waved his arm in dismissal. "I need to trust in the Spirit of the Lord."

"Trust in science," Bertie said. "My pa knew what he was doing."

He closed the blinds beneath them most of the way, and the sphere shot up into the sky, knocking Brigham over. "Great Lucifer's turds!" he cried.

"Sorry, gov."

Brigham watched with fascination as Bertie played the blinds like a concert pianist, guiding the sphere westward to chase down the glowing half-moon in the night. "How does this work?"

"The blinds are made of wellsite and block gravity," Bertie said. "By opening and closing them, I can make gravity pull us in the direction we want to go. I closed the bottom ones almost the whole way, so that blocked off most of Earth's gravity. The air pressure shot us up into the sky like spitting a melon seed out."

"I see." Brigham peered out the open blinds. "But do you know what you're doing? Do you know how to navigate?"

Bertie gave him a dirty look. "The blinds facing the moon are opened wide. Its gravity is pulling us toward it."

"Will we hit the surface as fast as we left Earth?"

Another dirty look. "I'll set you down as soft as your bottom on a pillow."

Moses cried out as his bottom lifted above the surface. Bertie and Brigham and all their supplies floated up with him.

"What's this?" Brigham cried.

"I think we left the atmosphere," said Bertie. "It's not spitting us out anymore, so we're floating free. No gravity."

"But you said there was moon gravity," Moses said.

He laughed. "Just a tiny bit. The moon's smaller, and we're still far away. Look what direction you're floating."

It was true. Everything slowly floated toward the moon. After some time they had to scramble around to sit on the surface facing the moon to avoid doing a headstand.

"It feels like falling," Brigham said. "Endlessly falling."

Bertie grinned and nodded.

"Maybe it's what the angels feel."

Bertie shook his head with a smirk and fished out something to eat. "You gonna marry some moon wives, gov?"

"I think I have enough," Brigham said.

Bertie laughed.

"How long will this take?" Moses asked.

Bertie shrugged. "Better get comfortable. Have some breakfast."

As they ate, Moses gazed at the moon. It was hard to tell if it looked any bigger with nothing surrounding it but blackness and stars, and the refraction of the sphere didn't help. The moon seemed to have a slight rainbow edge surrounding it, like a prism. He watched it for some time, but it didn't seem to be growing.

"This could take days," he murmured.

"Yep," said Bertie. "We got supplies."

But the sight of the stars was dazzling. They shone brightly and steadily in the absence of atmosphere and the lamps of the city. They filled the sky. Moses felt like he were seeing the lights of the city of God on Kolob.

Time passed slowly. Bertie regaled them with the rules of cricket and the stories of his father's sporting victories. He and Brigham debated religion and science and rationality. Bertie never was convinced there was a way for religion to be rational, no matter how much Brigham insisted there was. Moses felt entirely out of his league during those debates and could only listen with fascination.

The worst part was the necessities of biology. The supplies included chamber pots that could be sealed with a lid, but using them in front of the others was uncomfortable. In the weak gravity the flow or the solids didn't want to cooperate like they did on Earth, tending to spread. They almost made a game of trying to capture them before they spread too far, and in spite of the sealed lids, the whole sphere accrued the aroma of an outhouse. It took some time before Moses became accustomed enough to not notice it.

Whenever a sensation of needing to catch their breath hit them, Bertie took one of the oxygen canisters and sprayed enough of it into their space to make them feel normal again, then ran the contraption that cleansed the waste gases out. They had to pop their ears each time.

They slept a lot, and when they did, they extinguished the lamp. Complete darkness and silence befell them, except for the faint buzz of their electric heater. Moses had never experienced such an intense blackness before. He thought this must be what outer darkness was like. Thank the Lord he'd never be a son of perdition!

Only by checking his pocket watch could Moses tell how much time had past. He did it too often at first, making it feel like the hands crawled. That was too frustrating, so he stopped checking altogether. But after a long time when he checked again, he realized that had been a mistake too. He knew the time, but he didn't know if it was A.M. or P.M., or how many A.M.'s and P.M.'s had already passed. He wasn't sure he wanted to know. The answer was probably, hardly any.

It was the moon that saved him. He studiously avoided looking at it as much as he could stand, but its size grew noticeably as time passed. He found himself living in a new universe where hours and days had no meaning, and time was measured in units of moon-size. He also noticed the moon seemed to grow at a greater rate as they grew closer. They and their supplies seemed to press against the surface of the sphere with growing pressure. The moon's gravity gripped tighter on them.

It also made passing waste easier with time.

When boredom threatened to bring them to insanity, Moses pulled out his Book of Mormon and read it. At first Bertie groaned, but as the story of Lehi and his sons unfolded, with Nephi the good one conflicting with Laman and Lemuel the wicked ones, as they built a ship and sailed across the sea to a new land, he became mesmerized. To him it was an adventure tale of fanciful far-off lands, as if the Lehi family were buccaneers roaming the oceans.

His excitement infected Moses, and he was able to relate to the Book of Mormon story by thinking of themselves as traveling to the promised land like Lehi's family. He thought of their sphere as one of the tight ships of the Jaredites, sealed against the ocean of black space, with oxygen canisters as the stoppers to let in air and the lamp as the glowing stones that the finger of the Lord had touched.

For Bertie's sake, he skipped the long preachy parts and the endless quoting of chapter after chapter of Isaiah and focused on the adventures. The wars between the Nephites and the Lamanites intrigued the boy. When Teancum came into the picture, Bertie declared him his hero as he slunk around like a spy and assassinated the enemy's king. He groaned when Teancum ended up being killed.

The day came—if it could be call a day—when the moon filled their view, a view which was blocked by almost-closed blinds. Bertie had slowly closed them over time to decrease the gravitational pull and gradually opened up the blinds facing the Earth so its distant gravity could act as a braking force. He was determined to set Brigham's bottom down gently as a matter of pride.

As the surface of the moon hurtled toward them, Bernie launched into a symphony of clicks and clacks as he shut and opened blinds in all directions, easing them closer. Their direction veered horizontally as he peered through the narrow openings in the blinds to gauge their speed and to find a satisfactory landing site. Their speed slowed visibly.

Moses peered through the slits too, amazed at the detail he could see that was never available to him on his home world. For the first time, he felt in his bones how much a world the moon was. Tall mountains in craggy rings surrounding plains of craters. Cracks in the earth—an ironic word to use for the soil of the moon. Colors of greater variety than he expected, white and grey and brown and even olive green.

Bertie settled them down just inside the darkness of night, as gently as he could. He succeeded admirably, only jostling them a little, then flung the top and bottom blinds wide open to allow gravity to hold the sphere on the surface.

"We're here!" Moses cooed. Bertie grinned ear to ear.

"Let's give thanks to the Lord for our safe journey," Brigham said and, ignoring Bertie's rolling eyes, boomed out a prayer worthy of a prophet. Moses tried hard to feel blessed that he had this opportunity to hear a prophet of God speaking to the Lord, but he also wanted to get out of the stuffy outhouse air and stretch his legs.

But Brigham's powers of praying were immense, and Moses conjured up all the patience he could to sit still and feel the Spirit. Bertie's patience was barely contained as he fidgeted in place.

With the resounding "Amen!" Bertie scrambled to side of the sphere so he could gawk at their new world. Brigham and Moses gathered around him, excited as children themselves.

It was a wild and desolate scene. They landed in a vast circular plain with cliffs on every side. The inside of a crater. The sun hadn't risen, but was rising behind them with its rays gleaming on the peaks of the cliffs ahead, showing drab grey rock. Moses was surprised to see what looked for the world like piles of snow lying about throughout the valley and in shadowed crevices on the walls. In spite of the sunlight, the stars blazed clearly, filling the black sky.

"Shall we go out?" Brigham said.

"No!" Bertie cried. "The sky's still pitch dark when there's sunlight. That means there ain't no air."

Moses and Brigham were dumbfounded. "Then how do we explore?" Moses asked.

"We don't," said Bertie, then looked at Brigham with an accusing gaze. "I thought you said there were moon people here."

Brigham brooded as he peered out the blinds.

"Thank God I'm rational and don't believe in silly angels talking about moon men," Bertie sneered.

Moses noted the irony of Bertie's reference to God in that statement, but said nothing. He was too shocked and demoralized. He and Brigham had felt the Spirit telling them to come here. What was God thinking? An even more demoralizing thought hit him. Had he been wrong about feeling the Spirit? Had he been deceived by the wrong spirit?

He could imagine that happening to himself, but to Brigham Young? It was unthinkable! He wished he never brought Brigham on this useless voyage, wished he never saw this infernal sphere.

The sunlight on the peaks advanced down the face of the cliffs. As it hit the snow-like piles, some kind of vapor rose from them. More and more vapor swirled up into the empty non-atmosphere of the crater.

By the time the sun peeked over the horizon, which was much closer than any Earth horizon, the valley seemed filled with a faint haze, and the sky eased into a bluish tint. Stars began to fade. The full force of the sunlight turned the flowing vapor into hissing geysers of steam. A thick fog advanced toward them

With his face glowing in delight, Bertie cried, "It's frozen air!" He jumped to the lever and put his hand on it.

"Wait!" Brigham said. "How do you know it's air like ours? Will we breathe it, or will it kill us with noxious vapors?"

Bertie scowled, then let go of the lever and backed off.

The three of them gazed at each other. Moses felt forlorn, still fearful their journey had been in vain.

"Look at all those pebbles lying on the ground," Brigham said.

Moses looked. They were oval-shaped grey things that did look like pebbles, but pebbles that were more evenly shaped and sized and smoothed than he'd ever seen on Earth. And where was the flowing water that had smoothed them? Moses knew at least that much science to know smooth pebbles don't form in a desolate landscape.

"Look at that one!" Bertie said as he pointed down to a spot on the ground where the sunlight hit it. "It's cracking."

A pebble was indeed splitting, and Moses could see the split growing as he watched. In the crack was a very familiar green, and tufts of fibers flicked out, the color of grass, but frail, flimsy stalks. He glanced at other pebbles. They were all splitting.

"They're seeds!" Brigham cried.

Filaments broke from the underside of the seeds and drove themselves into the ground. *Roots!* thought Moses.

A central stalk rose up, thicker than the fibers, and a tiny bud formed on its tip, orange in color. Buds formed everywhere. The fibers grew out into spiky needle-like leaves, olive green.

Amidst the forest of bulbous stalks, other fleshy vegetation rose up, cactus-like, then ballooned as if water was being pumped into them.

"It has to be air," Bernie said. "They're green like Earth plants."

"There's one way to find out," Brigham said, "if you have a way to strike a fire."

Bernie scrambled to the pile of supplies and pulled out a box of lucifers and held one up.

"Good boy!" Brigham said. He tore a blank page from the end of the Book of Mormon and crumpled it up. "Moses, unlatch that lever and be ready to swing the hatch open for a brief second. Bertie, be ready to strike that lucifer."

They huddled by the hatch. Brigham held the crumpled paper up, Bertie held the lucifer near the plate of a switch, and Moses pushed down on the lever. "Now!" Brigham bellowed.

Bertie struck the match on the panel and lit the paper. Moses swung the hatch open enough for Brigham to toss the flaming wad out. Moses slammed the hatch shut, fighting the pressure of the air inside the sphere trying to escape.

They gazed out the blinds as the crumpled paper withered in the flames. A couple buds nearby were singed. The fire fizzled out, leaving a clump of ash.

Brigham grinned. "There's oxygen."

When they opened the hatch again, it flung out of Moses' hand. The air inside the sphere flew out with a pop as a waft of chilled fresh air moved in.

"It's thin like mountain air," Brigham said. "We'll get winded easier."

"Who shall be the first man to set foot on the moon?" Moses said.

"Who do you suggest, Brother Moses?" Brigham said.

"I think a prophet should lead the way."

Brigham harrumphed, then leaned forward to Bertie. "I think the son of the man who made this journey possible should be the first."

The boy's face lit up, and he dashed out of the hatch and flew threw the air with a shocked whoop and arms flailing. Slowly he dropped to the ground and tumbled, crushing plants as he went. He ended up splatted on his butt, facing them with a sheepish grin. "Low gravity."

Brigham climbed out and took a few tentative steps. Each one was a graceful glide through the air for a few feet. He jumped and zoomed up higher than a horse's ears, then settled down like a swan. A silly grin broke out on his face. "I feel twenty years younger!"

Moses scrambled out, and the three of them frolicked and cavorted like school children filled with hot air. "Just be careful," Brigham said. "If you get injured, who knows what moon infections you might get."

They became winded quickly in the rarified air. "That'll do," Brigham said. "We've played children long enough. Time to get down to business."

"The moon men?" Bertie said. He twisted his head around in exaggerated fashion. "I don't see no moon men."

"There are vast stretches of land in Utah, boy, where you'll see not a soul no matter how many times you twist your neck."

"What is that?" Bertie said as he stared off.

Moses looked, but saw nothing they hadn't already seen. "What are you talking about?"

"That sound."

Moses stood still and heard it. A barely noticeable booming in regular intervals.

Brigham twisted his own head back and forth. "Where's it coming from?"

Bertie concentrated with a scowl, then looked down, then dropped to his hands and knees and pressed his ear against the ground. "Down here. Sounds like...ka-chunk...ka-chunk...factories."

Moses and Brigham looked at each other in surprise. "They're underground," Moses said.

"Makes sense, with only frozen air at night," Brigham said.

Bertie stood up. "How do we get down there?'

"What if they're dangerous?" Moses said.

"You're on a mission from God," Brigham said. "You must be like Alma. You must be like Abinadi. You must be ready to give your life for the Lord."

Moses nodded with pursed lips and a growing resolve. With the wonders and the excitement, he'd nearly lost sight of their purpose here. "Let's bring the good news of Christ to them." He turned to Bertie and smiled. "To heathens this time."

Bernie laughed. "Still don't know how to get down there, gov."

As if in answer, an echoing bellow filled the valley, the sound of a great beast. They all turned as one, with the hair on Moses' skin prickling. Another bellow, then another—a whole chorus of them.

One beast appeared, and Moses thought an entire house plodded toward him. Its massive sides heaved slowly, sucking in gallons of thin air, and breathed them out in a piercing bellow. The body was bloated with rolls of fat, hiding whatever legs it stood on. The skin was rough and white with black dapples along its spine. The maw was a red pit that opened wide, leaving little room left in the head to hold a brain of any size. Its eyes were beady.

Another, then another of these moon monsters appeared, until a whole herd of them advanced. Between bellows they filled their mouths with torn masses of green—fibers and stalks and buds and fleshy cactus appendages— and swallowed them quickly to bellow again.

"They look like giant, disgusting hogs," Moses murmured.

Behind them came small figures, ants compared to the beasts, with long, thin tentacles protruding from their sides, six altogether, that whipped about like writhing snakes. The figures could be no more than five feet tall. They wore something that seemed to be leather from head to foot, but from this distance, Moses couldn't tell. They also had two small arms with hands that carried some kind of staff. On their heads were helmets with spikes on them, which they used along with the staffs to prod the beasts forward.

"It appears they *don't* dress like Quakers," Brigham said.

Bertie gawked at the creatures with his mouth open.

The beasts swarmed around their sphere, and Moses became alarmed. They were three times the size of it, and they bumped and jostled it as they passed. Would those behemoths damage it? If one of them fell on it, it could buckle under the weight, and their carriage back to Earth would be gone.

When the moon men reached the sphere, several of them surrounded it and examined it, their tentacles crawling over the surface. One of them found the lever and caressed it with its hand. Moses held his breath, but the creature never tried to work it.

A moon man spotted them and gave out a piercing cry. All the others gazed at them and gave off noises like clicking and whining and even piping. As a unit, they marched toward them in great sailing strides, covering much ground with each step. Their tentacles flailed.

"We better run," Bertie cried and dashed away without waiting for the two men. They raced after him, covering as much ground with each flying step as the moon men.

A crater wall towered ahead of them. Moses realized they were running nowhere with no plan and would eventually be trapped against the cliffs. But he could think of nothing else to do. He didn't want those writhing tentacles near him.

They became winded quickly, and their strides grew weaker. The moon men closed the gap between them. *They* were used to the thin air.

Bertie's foot suddenly plopped down with a reverberating thud. He stopped, gaping at his feet. Moses and Brigham stopped. There was a seam in the ground where the plants ended and a flat surface of dust extended beyond. Moses swept his eyes across the landscape. The dust plain was a perfect circle, and its far end butted up against the foot of the cliffs.

Bertie stomped on the flat surface with one foot a couple times, listening to the thud. "It's hollow. This must be how to get down there."

Before his words died out, the faint ka-chunks gave way to a loud squealing groan with knocks and throbs. The dust in the circle vibrated. At the edge of the circle next to Moses and Brigham, a crack in the ground opened, shaped like a thin black crescent.

Bertie was jostled and fell to the ground. The crescent widened. Dust on the edge fell into the blackness. "Get off of there, Bertie!" Brigham shouted.

Bertie stood and gaped as the opening widened. He looked around, then raced to the side of the plain where the gap didn't exist. As the crescent grew to meet him, he had to keep veering closer to the cliffs to avoid it. Moses could see he'd never make the edge of the plain before the gap opened enough to swallow him.

"Run to the cliff!" Brigham cried.

Bertie turned and sprinted. Traveling in the direction the surface moved helped him cover more distance with each leap, but each landing caused him to wobble and nearly fall. By the time he neared the cliffs, the gap filled most of the plain. The remaining flat space threatened to disappear under the cliff entirely. Bertie leaped with all his might with each footfall, then took a great two-legged jump right before the gap became a full circle. He barely landed on the edge of solid ground, flapping his arms to keep from falling back into the gap.

Brigham and Moses rushed around the opening to him. "Are you well, young man?" Brigham said.

He nodded as he tried to gasp thin oxygen into his lungs.

The moon men caught up with them and surrounded them with the cliff blocking their retreat. Brigham took a step forward with his arms out in a peace gesture. "Greetings, Men of Luna. I am Brigham Young, prophet of our Lord and Savior Jesus Christ."

The moon men squealed with chatter. One jabbed its staff into Brigham's side. The prophet's eyes popped wide, his body stiffened, and he fell forward onto his face.

Moses was shocked. Without even thinking he cried, "By the power of the Melchizedek priesthood and in the name of—"

A staff jabbed him and froze every muscle in his body as some kind of energy crackled through him. As he blacked out, he realized the foolishness of trying to rebuke a flesh-and-blood creature as if it were a devil from hell.

Moses awoke to a darkness as complete as within the sphere. He was so disoriented, he imagined he were floating again in the tiny gravity of space. "Brigham?" he called in distress. "Bertie?"

"I'm here," Bertie cried.

"Brother Moses," Brigham said, "you're awake."

Hearing those familiar voices helped him clear his head. He became conscious of his body lying flat on his back, pressing against a surface with less force than he was used to on his bed back home. A constant thrumming sound permeated the place. "Where are we?"

"The moonies got us!" Bertie said.

Moses tried to sit up and found he was restrained. "We're trapped!" he wailed. "Prisoners!"

"Thrown into the lion's den," Brigham said. "Pray the Lord deliver us as he did Daniel."

"Swallowed up in the belly of the whale," Moses said. In the stuffy darkness, that seemed the better comparison.

Faint sobbing filtered through the thrumming. It was Bertie. "I don't want to die on the moon. My pa, my mum, they'll never know."

"The Lord will not abandon us, son," Brigham said. "He didn't abandon Jonah in the whale. Jonah completed his mission to the Ninevites, and we'll complete ours."

Bertie's weeping grew louder. Moses didn't think Brigham's "unrational" encouragement comforted him.

A long vertical sliver of bluish light appeared off to his left. The sliver widened, spewing brightness in. Moses had to shut his eyes and slowly blink them open.

"You see, Bertie," Brigham said. "The angel of the Lord swings the prison gates wide."

But when the light stopped widening, a silhouette appeared that looked nothing like an angel of the Lord. It was the shape of a moon man, tentacles and all, with its small hands gripping a staff.

The creature strode forward and stood at their feet. Moses could see Brigham and Bertie lying on surfaces that were not quite beds, not quite tables. The moon man's face was half-lit so only its right side showed. There was no nose. A bulbous hemisphere extended from the side where an ear should be, featureless but for a grey sheen. Moses thought it an eye. There was a slit where a mouth should be that curved down deeply, making it look like the creature frowned. The neck was long and had three joints to it, which looked disturbing like it was broken. Every other part of its body was covered in clothing, except for the tentacles which hung unmoving at its sides and the hands gripping the paralyzing staff.

Brigham cleared his throat. "Greetings, sir. We are men from Earth, that giant ball that hangs in your sky. We come here with a message from—"

A piercing squeal filled the space, reverberating and hurting Moses' ears. It died out into clicks and whistles. Moses was so shocked, he blurted out, "How can the Spirit give us the gift of *that* tongue?"

"I wanna go home!" Bertie wailed, sobbing loudly.

More moon men crowded in and unstrapped the restraints. "Shall we try to escape?" Moses said.

"They'll just hit us with those staffs again," Brigham said. "Trust in the Lord, Brother Moses. We're still alive."

The moon man beside Brigham grabbed him with tentacles and pulled him onto his feet. Tentacles grabbed Moses and slid him off the table. He wobbled an instant before he regained his balance. Bertie stood next to him, gaping at the moon men with terror in his eyes. He wiped tears away.

"May we speak with your leader?" Brigham said.

In response his moon man shoved him with a tentacle until he walked toward the opening. Moses and Bertie were pushed too.

They came out into a corridor lit all around with bluish light that came from below. Streams of a phosphorescent fluid flowed along either edge of the floor where it met the walls like gutters in a street. The thrumming was louder out here. The walls looked cavernous, except they were too evenly carved to be natural. Without their spiked helmets on, the moon men displayed a ridge of dingy white spines extending from their scalps in a line from forehead to nape of the three-jointed neck.

The creatures steered them into a room. One gutter of glowing fluid extended in and flowed around the perimeter of the room, joining the corridor gutter on the other side of the entrance. The place looked like a common area for dining with tables throughout and moon men consuming strange globs of substance from metal bowls. Their speech of clicking and whistling and wails blended with the thrumming noise. When the Earth folk appeared, the moon speech stopped as the heads cocked back and forth so the bulbous eyes on either side could stare at them, then the speech resumed with greater enthusiasm.

The moon men sat them at an empty table and plunked bowls down before them. Their small hands appeared like the prehensile flaps at the end of an elephant's trunk.

A thick aroma assaulted Moses, reminding him of roasting mushrooms. The glob of food looked fibrous like meat, a light brown color, and he thought it must be the flesh of the bellowing beasts. His stomach ached with hunger at the smell of food, but also churned with revulsion at the thought of eating flesh from another world. Would it nourish them or poison them?

Brigham stared at his bowl. "If there was ever a time to pray over food, this is it." He folded his hands in front of him and said, "Dear Father in Heaven, bless this food to nourish us and not kill us as we begin our mission to the moon people."

He must have been thinking what Moses thought.

Brigham stared at it again, looked around at the moon men eating. They used no utensils, only their elephant-flap hands to tear pieces off. He did so himself with his five-fingered hands and stuffed a large chunk in his mouth. As he chewed, he said, "Tastes like mutton, but sweeter."

Bertie studied him with a scowl, then broke off a small piece and slid it into his mouth. He chewed uncertainly, then his face lit up, and he tore off a larger piece and stuffed it in.

Moses tried to swallow his stomach's discomfort, took a piece, and with a shudder slipped it into his mouth and chewed. It was surprisingly tender, almost melting in his mouth. At once he grinned and chewed more enthusiastically. "It's quite delicious," he said after swallowing.

"How you going to preach to these moonies if you don't know the language?" Bertie said.

"We've done it before, boy. We'll just have to learn it."

"They don't talk with natural sounds."

Brigham sat still and listened, then attempted to mimic the sounds he heard. His clicks sounded more like dull clacks, his whistles more like shrill woos, and his wails sounded like a frightened woman. Bertie laughed. Moses cringed watching a prophet make such a fool of himself.

"See? We can do it," Brigham said with no sarcasm in his tone.

Bertie laughed again and made his own attempt to mimic the moon speech. His sounded closer to the real thing. Soon the two of them were conversing to each other in moon speech as if they were saying things. Several of the moon men nearby stared at them. Moses hoped it didn't offend them.

One of them stood and shuffled over. With its frowning slit of a mouth, it looked intensely offended. Bertie and Brigham stopped and looked up at him.

The creature said something back to them. They stared at him without comprehension. It said something again, shorter and slower. Brigham tried to duplicate it. Moses had no idea if he succeeded well enough.

The creature cocked its head to the side and gazed at him with one bulging eye, then turned its head to gaze at him with the other. It said one more thing, then sat back down.

Brigham peered at Moses and Bertie with his eyebrows up. "There you have it, gentlemen. Our first communication with moon men. We *can* do it."

"But you don't know what he said," Bertie protested. "You don't know what *you* said."

"It's a start. We'll build from there." He winked. "It's scientific."

Bertie frowned as he thought about that, then smiled.

They finished their food. Moon men surrounded them and prodded them to their feet and out the door. Down the corridor they went and came to another entrance they were pushed into.

The thrumming and pounding was deafening in this space. The bluish fluid flowed along the walls here too, but the space was so large, its lighting didn't fill it. There was movement in the shadows that corresponded with the pulsing noises. Moses realized it was a vast chamber full of machinery.

The brightest spot in the chamber was a flood of the bluish fluid pouring from the machinery like a small waterfall, flowing along a channel to connect with the gutters along the wall. Moses wished he could communicate so he could find out what the fluid was made of and how they manufactured it.

The moon men gave him no time to ponder. They pressed the three of them toward the machinery. Figures emerged from the shadows next to the thrumming contraptions, moon men operating dials and levers. They were even shorter than the helmeted ones standing beside them, and they had no tentacles.

As they approached, Moses saw they had chains attached to their ankles that were anchored into the ground.

Brigham's moon man prodded him toward an unoccupied station with empty chains. When he realized where they steered him, he stopped and whirled around to face them. "Slaves!" he bellowed in rage.

The moon men backed off a step.

"I didn't come all this way to become a slave!"

A moon guard tried to jab him with his staff, but Brigham knocked it away with a swing of his hand. "I'm no son of Cain!" he howled and punched the guard in the face.

His fist buried deep into the face with a squelch. A greyish-yellow fluid oozed out. Brigham balked and tried to pull his hand out. It took some effort before he dislodged it with a suctional pop. The guard dropped to the ground and splattered open.

Brigham stared at the protoplasm dripping from his hand. "Brother Moses, I like your idea of escaping." He shoved the next guard and the next and ran. They all dropped and splattered on the ground.

"Crikey!" Bertie cried and shoved his own guard.

They ran into the corridor and back the way they came. Shrieks and clicking and hooting filled the space. Moon men darted out of their way as they charged by. Moses had to push off the ceiling with each sailing step to keep from bumping his head.

"How do we get out of here?" Bertie shouted.

"Just keep running until we find something," Brigham said. "They can't hurt us with anything but their staffs." His words came out labored. Moses was glad they were in moon gravity, or he feared Brigham wouldn't be able to sustain his effort.

They dashed for some time through the maze of corridors, pushing the occasional moon man aside who challenged them before they could touch them with their staffs. They left a trail of globs of moon flesh splattered against the walls.

By the time Moses became weary, even with his youth and the weak gravity, they came across a side corridor that ascended. It was dark because the glowing fluid couldn't flow up the slope. "Try that," Brigham said.

Bertie dashed in first. The bluish light grew dim and nearly disappeared as they moved away from the level corridor, but enough of it remained to notice the corridor made a sharp turn ahead.

They reached the turn and found it was a switchback that continued to ascend in the other direction. They rushed around it with Bertie in the lead. The boy came to a sudden halt, and Moses and Brigham ran into him, almost knocking him to the ground.

"White light!" he cried, pointing ahead.

In the distance was a dim glow, as dim as the blue light had been before they turned the corner, but it was a glow of white light. Precious sunlight, Moses hoped. They ran with new energy. The light became brighter as they went, until they could see an opening ahead in the ceiling where the light shone brightly.

They rushed to the opening. The corridor floor merged smoothly with a wide surface above. They ran onto it and stopped to gauge where they were.

They stood in a vast bowl, many times broader than deep, that had apparently been hewed out of the rocky surface of the moon. A carpet of moon plants covered it, some the familiar stalks and cactus types they had watched grow before their eyes, some new types they hadn't seen. Throughout the bowl were moon men of the slave variety with hatchets in their hands, hacking away at giant carcasses of dead moon beasts. Piles of the flesh were transported away on slave-drawn carts to other openings like the one they'd emerged from, scattered all along the edges of the bowl. There must have been dozens of them, which explained why the three of them were able to encounter one of those ascending corridors so easily. With so many of them, they were bound to find one before long.

Moses noticed a wide ramp, wide enough to accommodate the bulk of a moon beast, circling along the side of the bowl, spiraling slowly up until it merged with the surface of the moon above. The lips of the bowl were a perfect circle, and at one end the cliffs of a crater wall jutted above.

It was the empty gap underneath the sliding plain Bertie had landed on.

Moses pointed to the ramp and cried, "Our escape!"

Brigham said, "This must be where they herd the cattle down."

Pounding footsteps and clicks and whistles came from the corridor behind them. Bertie's eyed popped open with alarm. "Time to go!"

He dashed up the ramp. Brigham and Moses followed just as moon guards appeared from the opening. One of them howled something to the slaves, who broke into a run toward them with their hatchets raised.

Guards and slaves pursued the three of them as they rounded the wall of the bowl in a wide corkscrew fashion. Moses glanced behind him. The sight of their pursuers leaping in sailing bounds toward them was comical, but it didn't make him feel like laughing.

Spears shot past them. Moses noticed a new weapon in the hands of some of the guards. They were long with a handle on the end, almost like a rifle, but spears shot from them. He thought of them as land harpoons.

And they were the whales.

A spear hit Brigham directly on the back. He stumbled forward and almost fell on his face, but he pushed off the ramp with his hands and floated up, managing to land running again. The harpoons must have been designed to penetrate soft moon flesh, not the more solid human flesh. Those paralyzing staffs and butcher hatchets worried Moses more.

It seemed to take forever to circle the corkscrew ramp to the surface. Moses wasn't sure, but he thought the moon men were gaining on them. If nothing else, they had the advantage of being used to the thin air. The Earth men gasped for oxygen, and Moses had to grab Brigham's arm to keep him moving along the last few hundred yards.

They reached the surface. The plants they'd first seen had grown taller, and it was like wading through a tall field of grass as they ran again. The top of the sphere was barely visible in the distance.

As they ran, Bertie completely disappeared into the sea of plants every time he landed on his foot and bounded back up. Moses' grip on Brigham slipped, and he slowed down to grab him again. But Brigham waved him off and said, "Go!"

"I can't leave you!"

"Don't coddle me! Go!"

Moses dashed ahead, following the leaping boy as he popped in and out of sight. At the top of one of his bounds, Bertie pointed up and shouted, "Pa!"

Moses looked up and saw the second sphere, now covered in panels, shooting past them in the black sky, coming from the direction of the cliffs behind them and heading toward their sphere. He glanced back. The moon men poured onto the surface in hot pursuit. Brigham bounded up and down, but he was farther back than Moses expected.

He stopped and watched. The moon men leaped toward Brigham, closing the distance quickly. A spear sailed past Brigham and disappeared in the stalks. Another one grazed him and tore his jacket. Moses ran for him.

A third spear hit Brigham square in the back. He grunted and fell forward out of sight. The shaft of the spear stuck up above the stalks. "Brigham!" Moses cried as he ran toward him.

The moon men were upon Brigham and lifted him up with their tentacles as he squirmed to get loose. Slaves with hatchets swarmed past them, heading for Moses. He turned and bolted, but the slaves gained on him quickly.

"Duck!" Bertie shouted.

Moses looked up and saw the second sphere barreling down on him, skirting the tops of the stalks. Moses cried out and dropped to the ground. The sphere whooshed past, thrashing the stalks and hitting him with a blast of wind. He leaped up and watched as the sphere plowed through the moon men, splattering their soft flesh everywhere. Those it missed scattered with piercing shrieks.

The sphere crashed into the crater wall, burying itself into rock that broke apart and showered out at a slow pace that looked unreal. A landslide of rocks rolled casually down, submerging more than half the sphere in its rubble. Fortunately the hatch was still exposed.

The moon men fled back to the spiraling ramp. Multiple guards carried Brigham with their tentacles entwined around him. They disappeared down into the bowl.

Blinds on the sphere snapped open and closed as the sphere jostled around in place, but it couldn't break free of the rock. The hatch flew open, and Joseph Wells crawled out. He broke into a run and had the same shock Bertie did when he tumbled to the ground, bounced up, and landed on hands and knees. He stood, brushed himself off, and ran more carefully, wobbling each time he touched ground until he got used to it.

"Pa!" Bertie cried and ran toward him.

"Bertie, you have the devil to pay!" Joseph cried with smoldering eyes.

Bertie stopped and gazed at him with an apologetic look.

"Run, boy!" Joseph called. "The devil can wait."

Bertie turned and ran. Moses ran. Joseph quickly caught up with him. "I know what your word is worth now, Mormon," he said as he passed by.

Bertie reached the other sphere first, opened the hatch, and climbed in. Joseph came up quickly behind him and followed. He paused inside the hatch and placed his hand on the inside lever, then peered at Moses with a dark expression.

Moses panicked. He was going to close the hatch and leave him there!

Bertie shouted something that Moses couldn't make out. Joseph's face flinched and scowled. He gave out a frustrated groan and disappeared inside, leaving the hatch open.

Moses crawled in. Joseph swung the hatch closed. "Out of the way!" he growled as he clambered into the middle and started operating blinds.

The sphere rose up with a jerk. Joseph seemed in no mood to give them a gentle ride. "You had another man?"

"Yeah, pa. Brigham Young."

Joseph threw him a shocked look. "Mother of God! Are you serious?" He shot a withering glare at Moses. "You told Brigham Young?" The sphere kept floating up away from the surface.

"You can't leave him behind," Moses said. "He's still a human being, not the devil."

"Devil or not, those moon demons already dragged him into hell where he belongs."

"You can't leave him behind," Bertie said. "He was right about men on the moon."

His glare never disappeared, but Joseph adjusted the blinds to deflect the sphere horizontally toward the bowl.

"We can land down inside," Bertie said. "They still have to be leaping along the wall."

Moses watched with anticipation as the inside of the bowl came into view. The surviving moon men were visible moving along the ramp. But to Moses' surprise, they headed back up in pursuit of Brigham Young, who leaped with all his might as he fled toward the surface.

"Hurrah, Brigham!" Bertie cried, thrusting his fists into the air. Moses felt the same exhilaration. Brigham was unstoppable!

He reached the surface. Globs of moon man protoplasm dripped from both hands. He'd put up a hell of a fight! Joseph propelled the sphere toward him, but Brigham didn't notice it. He took one look at the trapped sphere and rushed toward it.

"No!" Bertie cried.

"*The fool!*" Joseph said. "He can't escape in that."

Brigham climbed in and slammed the hatch shut. Moon men swarmed out from the bowl and surrounded it. Joseph dove his sphere toward them. They scattered in chaos.

Blinds on the embedded sphere popped open and closed randomly, one after the other.

"The fool!" Joseph cried. "He doesn't know what he's doing."

The sphere jostled violently in place, but the rock held fast to it. All the blinds started closing.

"Not all of them!" Bertie cried in alarm.

Joseph veered their sphere upward toward space.

"You can't leave him!" Moses cried.

"It's too late," Joseph said. "He sealed his own fate."

The last blind closed. Blasts of wind swept across the entire surface of the moon toward the embedded sphere, thrashing the stalks wildly. Plumes of moon dust shot up from the sphere in a column that swept high into the blackness. Moon men rose from the surface, carried up by the wind, whirling around in the vortex. Dust plumes blasted out from every opening in the bowl below like geysers. With no gravity above the embedded sphere, the entire atmosphere of the moon flooded toward it and up into space in a giant column.

The hatch in the sphere opened and Brigham climbed out.

"No, Brigham!" Moses cried. "No, no, no!"

The hurricane force swept him off his feet in the low gravity and flew him into the sky. Brigham flailed with his hands and legs, but nothing could stop him. Joseph kept the sphere even with him as they all rose.

"What are you waiting for?" Moses said. "Rescue him!"

"We can't," Joseph said. "I open the hatch, we all die."

"You can open it quick—"

"*I open the hatch*," Joseph said forcefully, "*we all die.*"

Brigham's struggles quieted. He drifted away as Joseph rearranged the blinds and steered them toward the dark globe of the Earth. Moses watched with horror as Brigham floated into the dark night, his eyes and his mouth open wide, his arms and legs spread-eagle from the flailing. An entourage of moon men floated around him, escorting him into eternity.

Moses wept.

The gloomy illumination in the sphere was nothing compared to the gloomy mood.

"We killed the moon," Bertie said.

"Brigham Young killed the moon," Joseph said.

"We killed Brigham," Moses said.

"He killed himself."

"It wasn't his fault," Moses said. "He didn't understand how it worked."

Joseph shot a piercing gaze at him. "No. It was *your* fault." He looked at Bertie. "And yours."

Bertie was on the verge of tears. He wiped at his nose with his sleeve.

"No!" Moses said. "It was I alone. I would have taken the sphere with or without him."

"Perhaps I'm to blame," said Joseph. "I should have known better than to trust a man who believes in fairy tales, who steals women and chains them in their temple."

Moses didn't have the moral courage to object to that falsehood again.

They spoke little on the journey home, only what was necessary. Moses' conscience gnawed at him the entire time. This really was all his fault. He made a promise and broke it. He stole property that wasn't his. He coaxed Brigham into a ridiculous adventure that only fools would consider.

But he was so sure the Spirit instructed him to go. Brigham, a prophet of the Lord, was sure the Spirit instructed him. What did it all mean? Brigham was right about men being on the moon. How could he be so wrong about this mission?

None of it made sense. He couldn't figure out who was to blame. Himself? Joseph for showing him the spheres? Bertie for making the journey possible with his navigation skills? Brigham Young for proclaiming it was the will of God? All of them? None of them?

God himself?

It was more than he could bear. He sunk into a depression and refused to think at all.

Joseph guided the sphere into the stable and let it land with a bump. They climbed out without a word. Joseph stood gazing at the sphere. Bertie and Moses stood behind him, watching him.

At once Joseph marched over to the stack of wellsite panels strapped to the ground—considerably fewer than when Moses first saw it. He looked up at the panel still pressed against the ceiling, then pulled out a pocket knife and cut into the straps that held the stack in place.

"No, pa!" Bertie cried and ran over to him.

Joseph pushed him back and sawed at the straps until they gave way. The panels shot into the air and crashed into the ceiling. The full force of so many of them at once smashed through. Moses and Bertie gaped as the panels sailed up into the darkness and disappeared.

Joseph marched over to the worktable and grabbed a roll of twine. He climbed into the sphere with it and his knife in hand.

"What're you doing, pa?" Bertie called in distress.

In a moment Joseph came out with multiple strings of twine in his hand that extended back into the sphere.

"No, pa," Bertie whispered with a tear trickling down.

Joseph yanked on the twine. All the blinds on the bottom of the sphere snapped closed. The sphere shot up through the opening in the ceiling, yanking the string out of Joseph's hands. He cried out in pain and held his hand out, showing a streak of friction burn on the palm. He sucked on it.

The sphere shot high into the night, turned into a dot, and was lost among the stars.

"Oh, pa," Bertie said with silent tears. "What did you do?"

"We've done enough damage with those things." Joseph turned to Moses. "Why are you still here?"

Moses peered at him, then peered at Bertie. He liked the boy and would miss him, but he didn't know how they could be friends anymore after everything that happened. There was nothing left for him to do here.

"I'm sorry," he muttered. It felt terribly inadequate.

As he walked out of the stable, he heard Bertie say, "Is there the devil to pay now?"

"Go to bed, son," Joseph said. "There's no payment for the devil big enough to make this better."

Moses slept fitfully and woke bleary-eyed. He spent the next several days moping around his flat. He couldn't bring himself to do any proselyting when he was so sick at soul. He ate very little.

One day he packed up all his things—a small accumulation as a missionary—into a single bag and took a train to London to meet with President Joseph F. Smith.

The man received him graciously. "Brother Bedford, correct?" he said as he shook his hand.

"Yes, Moses Bedford from Philadelphia."

They sat in a parlor. "How are things down in Kent?"

Moses wet his lips as he gazed at the thin face with the impressively long, ragged beard. The eyes looked at him kindly through the small round spectacles. There was a touch of grey at his temples. "Things in Kent are fine. Things in my life are not."

The eyes became even more tender. "I'm sorry to hear that. Tell me what concerns you."

He planned on telling him the whole story, but as he gazed at the eyes of the man sitting before him in flesh and blood, he realized he couldn't bring himself to do it. How could he possibly tell any rational person such a story?

He almost smiled at the word rational. It made him think of Bertie.

A man came into the parlor. "Excuse me, President, but there's a message from Salt Lake City."

President Smith accepted the telegram. "Excuse me a moment, Brother Moses." He adjusted his spectacles and read it. "Oh, dear Lord in heaven." He looked up. "President Brigham Young has passed."

A thrill shot through Moses. How had the world come to know this in the few days since he watched Brigham float away to the stars? Who could possibly have told anyone? Joseph, Bertie, himself—he couldn't imagine any of them saying a word.

"He died of a stomach malady," President Smith said.

At once Moses remembered the glib words Brigham had spoken to his wives. *If I don't return in a week, tell them I died of a stomach malady.*

President Smith seemed in a daze. He fingered the telegram, his eyes darting around. "They've called me back to Salt Lake." He looked at Moses. "President Taylor will be in charge now." He set the telegram down and moved to stand, but sunk back down as if weighed down by a burden. "I should go prepare."

"Let me accompany you, President," Moses said immediately. He didn't want to stay in England. He needed time to think, to sort things out, to figure out what to make of everything.

"Oh, Brother Moses, I'm sorry. I forgot. There was something you wanted to talk to me about."

"It's not important now. It was a personal matter, and I felt I needed to return home and recuperate."

"Yes, yes. Of course. It would be nice to have your company."

They made arrangements to meet at the train station. Moses was already prepared to leave, but President Smith needed time. Moses spent the time exploring London. His heart wasn't in it, but he didn't know what else to do. He kept gazing up into the sky at the crescent moon hanging low in the west.

He imagined tiny specks above the moon, Brigham Young and the moon men floating away. Would they float forever into the cold vastness of space, or slide into an eternal orbit around the moon, or eventually fall back down to the surface? That dead surface where life once flourished for two weeks out of the month during the daylight period, where thinking beings lived their lives in blue-lit caverns feasting on tender moon cattle. All of it was gone as the atmosphere was sucked from the caverns and swept from the surface into the void. No more snow piles of frozen air, no more pebbles growing stalks and cactus pods, no more guards and slaves, no more moon beasts.

If humans ever ventured to the moon again, they'd find nothing there except moon rocks to bring back as curiosities. That thought filled him with sadness.

Bertie scrawled away in the light of a single candle, not wishing to wake his parents—especially his pa. His experience on the moon haunted him in troubling dreams and waking flashes of memory. He felt a driving need to tell somebody about it, anybody, but he couldn't. His pa forbade it, and he understood why. They could never tell anyone how they killed the moon.

But he couldn't hold it in. He had to let the story out somehow. One night an idea came to him, a wonderful, a marvelous idea. He could write it down. He could tell a story of a journey to the moon. Not the real one he and his pa and the two Mormons lived, but a fanciful one with different names and other made-up things happening besides what really happened. He could pass it off as a romance, a scientific romance. No one would be the wiser.

He wrote down the title of his work in large block letters followed by his full name as he fancied a respected author would do:

THE FIRST MEN IN THE MOON

by Herbert George Wells

He scribbled away, the words flowing freely. His hands could barely keep up with his thoughts. He felt as if he were in a trance with a Greek muse pouring ideas into his head. He covered three pages of scrawl and began on the fourth when a gruff voice boomed from above.

"What the blazes are you doing, boy?"

He sat up stiff with alarm and looked up at the scowling face of his pa, ghostly in the flickering candlelight. That face glared down at the pages, swept them up and peered at the title. Bertie saw the rage bloom in his eyes.

"I told you to never speak of this to anyone!" he roared, crumbling up the pages. His mum jerked awake and sat up in bed.

"I'm not! I'm making stuff up."

"What's going on?" his mum said.

His pa took the candle and marched over to the stove. Bertie jumped up and grabbed his nightshirt, tugging hard. "No, pa, no!" His boyish strength couldn't slow the man down. "I changed all the names. It's not called wellsite. You're not called Joseph Wells. No Mormons'll be in it. It's just a romance. No one'll know."

His pa opened a lid on the stove and dropped the crumpled pages in. He lowered the wick of the candle and ignited the paper.

"No, pa," Bertie wailed with his eyes tearing up.

The pages shriveled into ash in short order. It reminded Bertie of Brigham's test for oxygen on the moon.

Joseph clanged the lid back on. "Go to bed. Never talk about it again. Never write about it again." He marched back to the bed and climbed in with his wife, who looked at him with confusion.

Bertie slumped into his bed and huddled under the covers. "I will!" he whispered to himself fiercely. "I *will* write it. One day, when I'm grown, or when you're dead, I'll write it. *I will!*"

A Face in the Window

A bloodcurdling scream ripped from the young woman's mouth. Her face contorted in terror. A knife plunged into her shoulder and pulled out again. The woman turned and ran as a snarling demon of a man chased after her, brandishing the knife dripping with blood.

Amy sat straight up on the sofa, her eyes bulging with fear. She hugged her legs tightly to her body with one arm. The other hand rummaged in a bowl on the sofa next to her and came away with a handful of popcorn. She stuffed it in her mouth without taking her eyes off the television and chewed slowly as the young woman fled through the cemetery, dodging around upright slabs of stone, tall and ancient, as gravestones in horror movies always were.

The snarling man gained on the woman. She stumbled—of course—and he was upon her driving the blade into her back. Over and over he stabbed. Blood oozed from the woman's mouth.

A phone squawked with a garish ring tone.

Amy nearly jumped to the ceiling with a squeal. The bowl of popcorn went flying. She grabbed her phone lying on the arm of the sofa and fumbled to answer so the noise would stop.

"Tyler, you scared the crap out of me!"

Raucous music and lively voices flooded through the phone. "You're not still watching that movie, are you?" Tyler said, shouting over the noise.

"Course not." She twirled a strand of her blonde hair like she always did when she fibbed. The woman in the movie screamed again. "Maybe," she said with a cringe.

"You always get spooked when you watch them alone."

She cuddled the phone affectionately. "I wish you were here."

"Hey, I offered."

"I know. My mom's a prude."

"I could be there in ten minutes."

That sounded like a fantastic idea to her, but he must be having a great time with his friends, considering all the noise. And she felt silly for spooking herself. "She'll be home soon anyway."

"Is that Amy?" a voice cried on the other end. "I love you, Amy!"

"Is that Liam?" she asked.

"When are you gonna dump this guy and go out with a real man?" Liam shouted.

She smiled. "Tell him when I find a real man."

"She says if you didn't look so much like the Elephant Man," Tyler said with his voice away from the phone.

"She did not!" Liam said. "Amy, he's lying on you again."

"Seriously, Amy," Tyler said. "I'll come over."

"You've got all your friends there."

"They can manage without me."

She thought hard about it. She'd love nothing more than to have his comforting arms holding her instead of sitting alone in the house. But her mother would probably be home before he got there, and then she'd really feel silly for making a fuss.

Her phone emitted a double beep. She glanced at it and curled her lip in disgust. "Oh, and now my battery's going dead."

"So charge it."

She cringed. "I can't find the cord."

"Again?" His voice left the phone. "She lost her charger again."

"I still love you, Amy," Liam shouted. "Even if you are a ditzy blonde."

Amy's phone chirped the tone for an incoming call. "My mom's calling. I gotta go."

"I'll be over in ten."

"No, please don't bother. She's probably calling to say she's on her way."

"You sure?"

"And I don't want you walking alone in the dark."

"Told you that movie would spook you. See you tomorrow for the picnic. I love you."

The phone chirped again. "I love you, Tyler." She tapped her phone and said, "Mom, where are you? You're supposed to be home by now."

"Sorry, honey. They need me to stay another half hour."

"Half hour!"

"Maybe less."

"This happens like every night."

"I'm sorry. The flu's going around."

A piercing scream came out of the television. Amy jumped.

"Are you watching another horror movie?"

"I dunno."

"Quit watching those things when you're alone! How many times—"

"Alright already."

"You're not crawling into bed with me tonight."

"Geez, Mom!"

The double beep sounded again. "My battery's dying."

"Did you lose your cord again?"

Amy sighed.

"This is the second time. I'm not buying you another one."

"Battery's dead gotta go," Amy blurted and ended the call. She dropped the phone on the sofa next to her and looked at the popcorn strewn all over. With a groan, she picked up the bowl and scraped the popcorn back into it.

She caught something out of the corner of her eye and turned her head toward the living room window. The curtains were partially opened, but she didn't see anything but darkness. Without taking her eyes off the window, she rose to her feet slowly, apprehensively.

"I gotta find that cord."

Leaving half the popcorn on the floor, she took the bowl to the kitchen, an open space visible from the living room. With her back to the window, she leaned on the counter. "Relax, Amy. There's nothing there. It's just your imagination." She shook her head. "I gotta quit watching those movies."

She turned and headed into the living room. Her eyes landed squarely on the window. She stared at it a moment, mesmerized, then turned away and held up her hand to shield her view of it.

"No one's there. No one's there."

She headed for the hallway entrance that was just to the right of the television. Partway there, she dropped her hand. Her eyes caught movement again, and she jerked her head toward the window. She barely saw something before it disappeared to the side. She swore it was a face.

Immediately she dove back to the sofa, huddling on the floor beside it. She took a moment to catch her breath and her courage, then peeked over the arm. Nothing but blackness. The television made more horror movie noises.

She reached over the arm and grabbed her phone, never taking her eyes off the window, and dropped down on her butt, leaning against the sofa. She dialed.

"911," said the operator. "What's the address of your location?"

The phone emitted another double beep and shut off. She growled in frustration and threw the phone back on the sofa. "Stupid battery!"

She checked the window again over the sofa arm. Still nothing. She rose up to a crouch, took a deep breath, dashed to the window, and yanked the curtains closed.

She ran to the hallway and to her bedroom where she grabbed a baseball bat. She came back and peered around the corner into the living room. The movie made another horrifying scream.

"Shut up!" She reached over and shut the television off, then pressed her back against the wall and gazed about the room. Her eyes ended up on the front door.

"Judy!" she said as she thought of the next-door neighbor. She held up the bat, crept toward the door while scanning every corner of the room, and reached out for the knob.

Before she could touch it, the knob turned.

She jumped back. The door moved a millimeter, but the deadbolt stopped it in place. The knob and the door rattled, then fell silent. She inched toward the door and peaked through the peephole.

An eye stared back at her.

She recoiled and dashed into the hallway, then peaked around at the front door. Dead stillness permeated the house. She watched, eyes wide.

In her bedroom, glass shattered. She jumped and whirled around. Through the open door of her bedroom she saw the curtains on her window flutter with a breeze. They parted, and the face of a man almost as creepy as the one in the movie jutted through. His face had a determined look, and he held a large knife in his teeth like a pirate.

She shrieked and dashed for the front door as the man climbed through the window. She turned the knob and yanked, then remembered the deadbolt. She flipped it open and swung the door wide. The creepy man charged out of the hallway right for her, brandishing the knife.

She swung the bat as hard as she could, whacking him on the side of the head. He stumbled back with a groan, holding his head.

Amy rushed out the door and slammed it behind her. Her home was in an area of new construction. Only two houses had sold so far, hers and Judy's next door. All the rest displayed FOR SALE signs. Beyond Judy's house was a forest. Their street ended there and turned ninety degrees left to follow the line of trees before it veered into the mouth of a canyon a couple miles later.

She ran to Judy's door, grateful there were lights on inside. She rang the doorbell furiously.

The creepy man bolted out the door of her house, saw her, and raced toward her.

"Judy! Judy! Open up!" She banged on the door with her fists, but Judy didn't come. In desperation she turned the knob and pushed. The door opened.

Amy jumped in and slammed the door shut just as the creepy man arrived. She twisted the deadbolt into place. The door rattled but didn't open.

Amy backed up into the living room. Judy's house had the same floor plan as hers, but was a mirror image. She found earbuds and a phone lying on the kitchen floor. From it the thin sound of music played.

"Judy!" she called.

The light in the hallway was on. She ran toward it. Movement caught her eye, but it was just the curtain on the living room window fluttering.

The master bedroom's door was open with the lights on. She ran to it. "Judy, there's a man—"

She stopped in her tracks and screamed. Judy lay on her back on the bed, completely naked, her arms spread out and bound to each bedpost, her mouth gagged. Her legs were spread open. She stared lifelessly at the ceiling.

Blood was everywhere on the bed and her body.

Amy dashed into the living room and headed for the landline phone sitting on an end table by the sofa. She dialed 911, keeping her eyes riveted on the front door.

"911. What's the address where you're located?"

"It's, uh...well, my address next door is 1618 South Canyon Road."

She heard typing on the other end. "What's the nature of your emergency?"

"There's a man trying to kill me. He killed my neigh—"

A hand wrapped around her mouth. Another hand yanked the phone receiver away and dropped it on the floor. The hands whirled her around. The creepy man grinned at her, knife in his teeth. She glanced at the living room window. The fluttering curtains revealed broken glass. It must have already been broken, since she never heard the crash.

"Please repeat that, ma'am," a tinny voice from the receiver said. "Ma'am? Are you still there?"

The man took the knife in his hand and pressed it against her throat. "Drop the bat."

It rattled on the floor.

He put the knife back in his teeth and pushed her toward the front door. He shoved her against it face-first. The weight of his body held her in place as she struggled to escape. From his pocket he whipped out a cloth, wrapped it around her head, covering her mouth, and tied it behind her head with a violent tug.

"Shtop shtruggling," he said through the knife. She froze in terror.

He opened the door and dragged her out, across the two yards, and back into her house, slamming the door behind him and engaging the deadbolt.

He forced her into her bedroom. The curtains rustled with the wind. He shoved her into a tight corner between the wall and her bed and leered at her. He slid the knife under her gag and yanked. It dropped to the floor.

"Take your clothes off."

Trembling and almost in tears, she shook her head. He leaped at her and held her head by the hair, then pressed the tip of the knife against her cheek. "Do it or you lose an eye."

He drew back. With shaking fingers, she unbuttoned her blouse. He watched with smoldering eyes as she slipped the blouse off, then folded her arms across her bra.

He gestured with the point of the knife to her legs. "Keep going."

She kicked off her sandals, undid her jeans, and slid them off, revealing bikini panties. She sat on the bed to pull the jeans from her feet.

He watched grimly, and when her pants were off, he nodded with a predatory satisfaction.

"And now your—"

She rolled back across her bed and crouched on the other side. He growled in rage and dove for her across the bed.

She bolted for the door. He rolled off the end of the bed onto his hands and knees and grabbed for her ankle. His hand connected, but her ankle slipped from his grasp. She stumbled onto her hands and knees. He reached and grabbed the back elastic of her panties, exposing her buttocks.

She scrambled to her feet. His grasp slipped from her panties. She ran for the front door while he jumped up. She twisted the deadbolt and pushed on the door. He grabbed her by the hair and yanked her back.

"Help! Help!" she shrieked out the open door.

He slammed the door shut and threw her onto the floor on her back. She immediately tried to scramble away, but he forced her back down and straddled her, laying the knife on the floor next to her. He leaned over and pinned her wrists to the floor. A grin formed on his face.

"I love the taste of a young woman."

He leaned all the way down and nibbled on her neck. She whimpered and struggled.

The door burst open, and a police officer appeared. He took a split second to assess the situation and drew his baton. "Get off her *now*!"

The creepy man rose to a sitting position, looking straight ahead with his back to the officer. In a flash, he grabbed the knife and rolled to a crouching position on the floor, facing the officer.

The officer dropped his baton, drew his gun, and aimed. Amy scrambled away and huddled on the floor by the wall and the television stand. She hugged her legs tightly to her chest.

"Drop the knife and place your hands on your head."

A sinister grin crossed the creepy man's face as he gazed at the officer.

Slowly he stood, keeping the knife extended.

"Sir, drop that knife or I'll open fire."

The man's grin widened. He cried out and rushed the officer, knife raised up to stab.

Sarah drove up to her street and became alarmed when she saw a police car in front of Judy's house. Her door was wide open. Sarah passed a man, tall and thin with dark hair, walking his dog. She thought he looked familiar, and remembered seeing him doing the same thing a time or two in the next subdivision over.

The door to her own house was open with light streaming out. She pulled into the driveway and climbed out apprehensively.

Two gunshots rang out.

"Amy!" Sarah shrieked. The man with the dog stopped and gaped.

She ran to the front door.

The creepy man's face filled with pain. He dropped the knife and sank to the floor. Amy stared at him in wide-eyed horror.

Sarah ran in as the officer leaned over the creepy man and felt for a pulse. Sarah gaped at the body in shock.

"Mom!" Amy cried and ran to her.

"Amy!" They fell into an embrace. "Oh, honey, are you okay?"

Through sobs she said, "He tried to rape me."

As they hugged, Amy spotted something lying in the corner by the front door. "My charger cord." She broke the embrace and went over to pick it up. She caught a glimpse out the door of a man walking a dog. He stood motionless, gazing back at her. His expression was somber, perhaps a bit grim.

He stared at Amy, and a faint smile crossed his lips. She remembered her clothes were off and hid behind the door. His dog became restless and tugged at the leash. The man looked down at the dog and continued walking.

Sarah ripped a length of duct tape off the roll and pressed it along the edge of a flattened cardboard box over the broken window. Amy, back in her jeans and blouse, sat on her bed clutching the bat, still shaking.

"Can we get a landline now?" she said.

Sarah sighed. "I suppose you're right."

The doorbell rang, and they both jumped. "It's Tyler," Amy said. She stood and crept to the front door, holding the bat up.

"Check the peephole first," Sarah said.

"Duh, Mom!"

Amy crept over and peered into the peephole, then swung the door open. She grabbed Tyler in a fierce hug, then dragged him in, slammed the door, and locked the deadbolt.

They hugged again. "Are you alright?" Tyler said.

"I'm alright. Thanks for coming over." She kissed him deeply.

"Tell me what happened."

She took his hand and led him into the bedroom. Sarah pressed another strip of tape on.

"That's where he broke in?" he said.

"Yeah." Amy pointed. "And he made me take my clothes off right there."

Tyler put his arm around her and drew her close. It helped calm her. "But he's dead now, right?"

"Yeah." She shuddered. "Right in front of me." Tears formed in her eyes. "He raped Judy, then killed her. It must have been before he came over here."

"I wish I could have been here to protect you." He gave Sarah a pointed look.

Sarah looked down. "Well, we're all safe now. That man won't hurt anyone ever again."

"I'm staying over tonight," he said. "I'll sleep on the sofa." He smiled at Amy. "With the bat."

Sarah didn't look happy about that, but she said nothing as she applied the last strip of duct tape on the cardboard. She stepped back to examine her work. "That'll have to do for now." She gazed at Tyler and Amy with their arms around each other. "I'm sorry this happened." She stepped out of the bedroom.

Tyler and Amy sat on the bed arm in arm. He stroked her hair lovingly as she snuggled up to him. "To think I almost lost you tonight," he said.

"I wish you'd been here with me."

"Next time I will be. I don't care what your mom says."

"I feel safe in your arms."

"You are. Always." He kissed her on the cheek. She turned and kissed him on the lips.

In the morning, Amy woke up, then sat up with a jolt. The events of the night before flooded back into her memory. She looked at the cardboard covering the window, then at the corner where she had to strip down to almost nothing. It seemed so unreal now. She shuddered at how it might have played out.

She wanted to lie back down and curl up in a ball under the covers, but she hated to let that monster have such an impact on her. She swung her legs over the side, took a deep breath, and stood to face the window. She stared at it for some time.

"No," she murmured. "You're dead and gone. I'm not going to let you ruin my life."

She walked to the living room. Tyler was sprawled on the sofa, still asleep. The bat lay across the coffee table. His mouth was open, and a little drool slid out from it. She giggled softly as she gazed at him, feeling better to see him there.

She knelt beside him and gently stroked his hair. He stirred, his head turning, and his mouth started smacking. She timed it so her lips touched his when one of his smacks closed. He jerked a little, his eyes opened to slits, and he smiled and kissed her back, pulling her in.

"I want to wake up to that every morning," he said.

"You'll have to make an honest woman of me first."

He sat up, groaning at his stiffness, and yawned. "Oh, we have that picnic today. Listen, we don't have to do that—"

"No!" She pushed the apprehension she felt down. "I'm not letting that creep ruin our plans."

"You sure? Liam will understand."

She shook her head slowly. "I have to. If I don't do this, I'm afraid I'll be afraid for good." She smiled and sat next to him, taking his arm. "Besides, I'll have two strong men to protect me."

"We could go somewhere more public—"

"No! The meadow in the forest."

Liam called to make sure they were still on for the picnic. Amy assured him she was okay. He drove over, and the three of them walked down the street with backpacks of picnic supplies. They entered the forest at the trailhead near the street corner.

The sun shone cheerfully through the trees. Tyler's arm held Amy by the waist. She clung to him for dear life. As they walked, her eyes darted about anxiously. Any other time they took this hike, she felt excited and invigorated, but today she couldn't shake the jitters. She refused to let it affect her. She kept reminding herself the man was dead, and she had two young men by her side.

"Great day for a walk," Liam said.

"Yeah," she said with forced pleasantness.

"The breeze is nice," Tyler said. "Keeps it from getting too hot."

"Yeah."

They fell silent as they hiked. She realized, maybe the boys were uneasy themselves. That was a relief. She was too on edge to enjoy small talk. She knew it was silly to imagine the creepy man leaping from behind a tree and stabbing them, but that didn't stop her from imagining the creepy man leaping from behind a tree and stabbing them.

They reached the meadow and laid out the blanket and supplies. They sat in a three-point circle and began eating.

"A year ago," Tyler said, looking around. "Hard to believe it's been that long."

"I can still remember like it was yesterday," Liam said. "It was sunny like today. A little windier. Me and Tyler were hiking and came across two silly girls coming the other way."

"Silly!" Amy protested. "Do you remember how you guys acted?"

"It worked, didn't it?" Liam said. "You two were swept off your feet."

"And two months later, JoAnn was swept back on her feet," Tyler said.

Liam rolled his eyes. "Wasn't she a nightmare! How'd you get so lucky, ending up with the good one?"

"Hey!" Amy said. "She was my friend!" Then she laughed. "She *was* a pill, wasn't she?" Amy enjoyed the playful conversation. It kept her mind off her jitters.

Tyler said, "Me and Liam came out of the trees, and there you two were, popping into view on the other side of the meadow."

"That was a hell of a walk," said Liam, "the four of us gawking at each other uncomfortably until we came together."

The conversation lulled. Liam and Tyler exchanged glances. She wondered what that meant.

"Amy," Tyler said somberly, "I've been thinking. Maybe we *should* get married before I go off to college."

A thrill shot through her. "You really mean it?"

"I can't bear the thought of being away from you."

"How will we live?'

"I've got my scholarship, and you can get a job."

"Neither of us has a car."

"We can live on campus in married student housing."

She gaped at him, then glanced at Liam. He looked back with his eyes misting and his face filled with some kind of emotion.

She turned her gaze back to Tyler. "What made you change your mind?"

He scooted over to her and stroked her cheek. "I never want you to be alone again."

She wrapped her arms around him and pulled him into a passionate kiss. "I love you, Tyler."

"I love you, Amy."

Liam crawled over and knelt before them. "Congratulations!" He planted a kiss on Amy's lips. "I love you guys!" Then he planted one on Tyler's lips.

"Yecch!" Tyler wiped his mouth with his sleeve. "You still gonna be my best man?"

"You know it!"

Something snapped in the forest. Amy jumped. "What was that?"

"What was what?" Tyler said.

"I heard...something."

Tyler looked at Liam, who said, "I didn't hear anything."

She pouted at them. "I didn't imagine it."

Tyler hugged her and caressed the back of her hair. "Relax, sweetheart. There's all sorts of critters running around these woods. It could have been anything."

She nodded, but still looked around with apprehension.

"Yeah, it could have been anything," Liam said. He looked around with a suspicious expression.

They sat silently. All they could hear was leaves rustling in the wind and the occasional bird chirping.

"Maybe it's time we headed back," Tyler said.

"Sure," said Liam.

Amy nodded.

They packed up the supplies and headed down the trail.

Tyler and Amy walked arm in arm as Liam followed up behind. Now Amy couldn't hold back the jitters. She hated feeling this way. This was supposed to be a happy place for her with the memories it held. The whole world always seemed safe to her all her life. Now it was an alien place where unspeakable things could happen without warning.

Tyler must have felt her shaking. "Everything'll be okay, sweetheart."

She didn't care about hiding her feelings anymore. "That noise *could* have been anything."

"But *not* that guy from last night," Tyler said.

"He's not the only creepy guy in the world."

"It was one man," Tyler said. "Every creepy guy in the world isn't lined up to attack you."

"I know," she murmured, hugging him tight.

"You know..." Tyler said cautiously. "It might not hurt if you got some counseling."

"Counseling?" she said in surprise.

"There might even be some kind of...victim's fund that would pay for it."

"You want me to get counseling?"

"Well, look at you! I've never seen you so jumpy."

"He has a point," Liam said.

She halted and frowned at them. "Is that surprising? After what I went through?"

"Isn't that the point?" Liam said. "Counseling can help you deal with it. You have PT—"

"I don't want any counseling. I just want to forget about it."

Tyler gazed at her with a troubled look.

"Are you mad at me?" she said.

"I just want what's best for you."

"I know, and I love you for it. But please, just let me deal with it on my own, okay? I'll be alright."

Tyler and Liam looked at each other. Liam shrugged. "She'll be alright."

"Do I have a choice?" Tyler said.

She giggled and brushed the tip of his nose. "Not really."

He shook his head with a faint smile. "Sometimes I wonder why I love you so much."

"It's because I'm so cute and adorable."

He put his finger in his mouth and feigned gagging. She laughed.

A definite crack sounded ahead of them. Their heads jerked to look. "I heard that one," Liam said.

Tyler said, "Probably a deer...or a moose...or..."

"But I don't see anything," Amy said.

"It's a thick forest."

Branches rustled, but there was no gust of wind. She cowered behind Tyler. They peered into the trees.

"You're starting to spook me now," Liam said.

"Good!" said Amy. "Let's get out of here."

"It's just some animal," Tyler said. "Maybe a...cougar?"

She slapped his chest. "That doesn't make me feel any better!"

"No, it couldn't be," said Liam. "Cougars don't hunt in the middle of the day...I think..."

"Let's go home!" Amy moaned.

Tyler pointed. "Home is in the direction of the noise."

She peered around desperately, looking for movement. "I don't want to just stand here."

Tyler's shoulders straightened. "Alright, we'll just start walking. Slowly... casually...like nothing's wrong."

"Okay."

"Don't run," Liam said. "That would just make the cougar charge us."

"Geez, Liam!" she said with a scowl.

They walked, slowly but deliberately. Her tension increased with every step. They stared grimly ahead as she listened hard for any more sounds.

"Wait!" Liam said. They came to a stop. He cocked his head back and forth listening.

"What is it?" Tyler asked.

"I thought I heard something. Too many footsteps."

Amy's hair prickled on end. "Where?"

He turned to look back. "From behind, I think."

Amy squeezed Tyler hard. "Oh God, let's get out of here."

"Walk slowly," Tyler said.

They began walking.

"Yeah, I hear them," Liam said almost in a whisper. "Behind us."

They stopped. Amy heard two more footsteps, then silence.

"Just a hiker," Tyler said without conviction.

"That keeps stopping when we do?" said Liam.

"Just keep going," Tyler said.

They walked faster. The other footsteps started up. The three of them increased their pace. The footsteps increased their pace. They broke into a run. So did the other footsteps.

They ran until they broke from the trees and crossed the street. They huddled behind a large lone tree. Tyler and Liam peered around it. Amy listened carefully. She heard nothing.

"It was just an animal," Tyler said.

"Sounded like human steps to me," Liam said.

"Someone playing a trick on us," Tyler ventured.

"Someone out to get us," Amy whimpered.

"He's dead," Tyler said.

They continued to stare into the forest.

Amy said, "Just take me home, Tyler. And don't leave me."

"I won't."

He wrapped his arm around her protectively. She clung to him with all her might. Liam walked beside them, constantly looking back at the forest.

When they reached the house, Liam said, "Damn, that was weird. I'm sorry that ruined our day, Amy."

"No, it's okay," she said. "Probably...probably just an animal or something." She dearly hoped that was true.

"Maybe we can do something tomorrow," Liam said. "Like in town. Where there's lots of people."

Amy nodded. Tyler said, "Sure. Let's do that."

Liam hugged the both of them and kissed Amy on the cheek. "See ya. Wish Tyler had gotten JoAnn." He grinned suggestively, then got in his car and drove off as they went inside the house.

"Amy? Is that you?" Sarah called from her bedroom.

"Yeah, Mom." They sat on the sofa. The curtains on the window were wide open. Sunlight splashed into the room. Amy realized she sat on the side closer to the window. She stood up. "Move over."

"Huh?"

"Move over!"

Tyler shuffled over. Amy sat on the far end away from the window.

Sarah emerged, dressed for work. "I have to work late again tonight."

"Mom!"

"I know, honey. But I don't have a choice."

"After last night? Call in sick!"

"Amy, the man's dead."

"Somebody just chased us in the woods," Tyler said.

Sarah gaped at him. "Who?"

"Well...we don't know. We didn't see anything."

"Then how do you—"

"We heard him running after us," Amy said.

Sarah turned to Tyler. "Did you hear it too?"

"Yes," he said with irritation.

Sarah looked back and forth at them. "It was probably...some...animal..."

"I'm staying with her tonight."

Sarah eyed him for an instant, then nodded. "Just...don't...*do* anything."

"Mom!"

"I'm only staying to protect her," Tyler said.

Sarah nodded grimly.

Amy insisted they watch a romantic comedy that evening—the opposite of a horror movie. Tyler agreed enthusiastically, even though he usually moaned at romantic comedies. They sat on the sofa snuggled up to each other, Tyler closer to the window, which had its curtains tightly closed. A bowl of popcorn sat on Amy's lap. They stuffed their mouths over and over. Amy's baseball bat leaned up against the side of the sofa, and her phone lay on the arm next to her, fully charged this time. She made sure of it.

"Do you have your phone?" she asked.

Without removing his eyes from the television, he slipped his phone out of his shirt pocket and held it up.

"Is it charged?"

"Fully charged."

He laid it on the sofa next to him. As the night went on, and as they laughed at the movie and made wisecracks about it, Amy was able to relax.

During a loud belly laugh, Amy thought she heard something rattle—something in the direction of the door. She stiffened up.

"What?" he said.

She waited to see if it happened again. "I thought I heard the door."

Tyler stuffed some popcorn in his mouth and said while he chewed, "It's your mom coming home."

She watched the door, but nothing happened. "It's not opening."

"Maybe she forgot the key."

"Then she'd ring the doorbell."

He looked at her, swallowed the popcorn, and headed for the door. He peered through the peephole. Amy waited with apprehension.

"No one there." He turned to face her.

She looked toward the window, the hair on her arms prickling. He marched over and grabbed both edges of the curtains, paused and looked at her.

"Tyler..." she whimpered.

He whipped the curtains open.

There was nothing there. He closed them again.

"The bedroom window!" Amy cried and hurried behind the sofa in a crouch.

Tyler started for the hallway, but stopped and turned back for the bat. He stood in the hall where Amy could see him as he gazed toward her bedroom. She stood and took a couple steps toward him, feeling dread. He looked at her and shrugged his shoulders.

Her eyes were drawn to the curtains. Something pulled her to them. Slowly she walked toward the window.

"Amy?" he said.

She paused in front of the curtains, then grabbed them as Tyler watched her. She took a deep breath, then whipped them open.

The man that had walked the dog stared back at her, leering.

She screamed and fell back. Tyler rushed to her and looked out the window, but the face was gone.

"What was it?"

"I saw him! In the window."

"The same guy?"

"No, a different one."

He ran back to the hallway and looked toward her bedroom, then turned to her and shook his head. She grabbed her phone and dialed.

"911. What's the address there?"

"1618 South Canyon Road."

"What's the nature of your emergency?"

"There's a man stalking us outside my house."

Keyboard clacking on the other end. "Officers have been notified. They're on their way."

She put the phone down. "The police are coming."

He nodded and kept his eye on the bedroom window. Her eyes darted back and forth between the living room window and the front door. It seemed an eternity before the doorbell rang, causing her to jump. She rushed to the door.

"Be careful, Amy!"

She peered through the peephole, then threw the door open. The same officer from the previous night stood there. "Ma'am, we received a report—"

"Hurry! Come in!" She waved desperately. As he walked in she peered behind him. As soon as he was in, she shut the door and turned the deadbolt. The officer looked at her funny.

"I've seen horror movies," she said. "I'm not letting him sneak up behind you and stab you."

The officer sighed as he looked at her, then at Tyler with the bat raised. "What's going on tonight?"

"There was another face—another man—in the window." She pointed.

He looked at the partially opened curtains and the blackness beyond.

"Before that, he rattled the door trying to get in."

The officer studied her, then looked at Tyler. "Did you see anything?"

"I believe her. She wouldn't lie."

"Did you *see* anything?"

Sheepishly he said, "No. But she's not lying."

"I didn't say she was." To Amy he said, "Did you recognize him?"

"I've seen him around sometimes, walking a dog."

"Do you know where he lives?"

"It's got to be the next neighborhood over. Only two houses have sold in this one."

"Can you describe him?"

"Tall and thin, dark hair, about thirty."

A knock came to the door, making her jump. The officer went and opened it. Amy was about to object until she saw a second officer standing there, a woman.

"Did you find anything?" the first officer said to her.

"Nothing."

"But I saw him," Amy said.

"Okay, ma'am," he said. "We'll make a report."

"But I *saw* him."

"You should take her seriously," Tyler said. "Don't you know what happened here last night?"

"I *am* taking her seriously," the officer said. "But no one's out there now."

The other officer said, "We probably scared him away. I doubt he'll come back the rest of the night."

"Can't you stay—at least until my mom gets home?"

"When will that be?" the woman said.

"Soon...I hope."

"Ma'am," said the male officer, "we're the only ones on duty tonight for the whole town. We'll check around your yard one more time. I'll sit outside for as long as I can. But if a call comes in, I'll have to take it."

Amy sighed with resignation. "Thank you, Officer."

The two officers left. Amy closed the door behind them, locked it, then ran into Tyler's arms. "You believe me, don't you?"

"Of course I do."

"What do we do now?"

"I think it's like they said. They chased him away for the night."

"Are you sure?"

"Why would he come back when he saw how quickly the cops came?"

"What about tomorrow night?"

"Um..."

"Tyler, why is another man after me?"

He sighed out a breath. "I don't know."

Amy and Tyler sat somberly on the sofa, still watching the movie. This time there was no popcorn, no lightheartedness. Everything else was in the same place, the bat leaning against the sofa, her phone on the arm next to her, his phone on the cushion next to him. The curtains were tightly closed.

"What's taking my mom so long?" she said.

"You know how her work is."

"Yeah, but I don't think she's ever been this late before."

They fell silent again. Amy couldn't concentrate on the movie. Where was her mother?

She felt a pressure that couldn't wait any longer. "I gotta go to the bathroom." She squeezed his arm and gave him a pleading look. "Will you come with me?"

"To the bathroom?"

"Just stand outside the door." They both stood. "Bring the bat."

He picked up the bat with a flourish and walked with her to the bathroom door in the hallway.

The officer sat alone in his car parked on the far curb from the house. He kept a sharp eye out for any movement in the yard. The radio crackled with chatter now and then, not much this late at night. His fellow officer responded to the calls.

It disturbed him that there was an incident two nights in a row at the same place, especially since the perp from the first one was dead. Normally he'd consider the possibility that the girl was paranoid, but the previous night made that impossible.

While the other officer was out on a call, another urgent one came in. He'd have to take this one. He acknowledged the call and started up the engine, looked around once more, then drove away.

———

Amy flushed the toilet and washed her hands. When she opened the door, Tyler leaned against the frame grinning at her. "It's so romantic listening to you pee."

She stuck her tongue out at him. "Thanks for keeping guard."

His phone rang. Amy jumped and let out a frustrated grunt. She was sick to death of all these scares.

He looked at the screen and put it to his ear. "Hey, Liam."

Amy looked at the cardboard over her bedroom window. Just the sight of it disturbed her.

"We think someone else tried to get in," Tyler said. "Yes, really! Yes, we called the police. They didn't find any—"

The cardboard shuddered as something hit it from behind. The tape on one corner peeled away from the wall. "Tyler!" she cried.

He looked as the cardboard shuddered again, knocking it further off. "Liam, he's trying to get in! Call the police!" He stuffed the phone in his pocket and raised the bat.

Another bang and the cardboard swung to the side, still hanging by a single strip of tape. The neighborhood man leered at them. He put a knife in his teeth and clamped down, then started climbing.

Tyler brandished the bat. "Stay away from her. I'll kill you, I swear!"

The man's feet hit the floor. He pulled the knife out of his mouth and said with a grin, "Please do."

"What?"

The man crept toward them. They ran to the front door. The man emerged from the hallway grinning as Tyler unlocked the door and opened it.

Sarah lay on the porch face down in a pool of blood. Amy screamed and froze in terror.

"Go!" Tyler said and pushed her out the door. She had to step over her mother.

Sarah's car was parked in the driveway. "Your mom's car," Tyler said and dragged Amy to it. He tried the door, but it was locked.

The man charged out the door, leaping over Sarah's body. Tyler grabbed Amy's hand. They fled down the street. She wept as she tried to look back at her mother.

"Help!" she cried. "Somebody help!"

The neighborhood man raced after them with the knife ready. Tyler pulled Amy down the street toward the forest with the bat in his hand. They reached the large tree they'd huddled behind after the picnic. Tyler pushed Amy behind it, then stood with the bat held high. "Leave us alone, or I'll kill you."

The man's grin spread wide. "Okay." He continued to advance toward them with deliberate steps.

Tyler tightened his grip and prepared to swing. "I swear I'll do it."

"So do it." He came within a few feet, just out of reach of the bat, and readied his knife.

Tyler tightened his grip once more, eyed the blade, and swung at it. The man pulled back and stabbed at Tyler's arm. The tip caught skin. Tyler cried out as a line of blood formed.

"Gotcha!" said the man.

Amy watched with terror from behind the tree.

Tyler charged and landed a blow on the man's shoulder. The man groaned, but it turned into a laugh. He jabbed with the knife. Tyler barely twisted out of the way. He continued to spin around and whacked the man on the back.

The man lurched to the side with a cry, then whirled back. "You fucking pussy! Is that all you got? You promised to kill me."

He lunged with the knife, aiming at Tyler's chest. Tyler swung hard and connected on the side of the man's head. The man stumbled back, grabbing his head with one hand. He shook the wooziness away. "God damn you, that hurts! Hit me like you mean it."

"Are you insane?" Tyler said.

Headlights appeared down the street with red and blue lights flashing. A siren gave out a single blast.

The man turned and smiled as the police officer climbed out with gun drawn. "Drop your weapon and lie on the ground."

The neighborhood man looked at Tyler with a disturbing grin. "See you real soon." He charged the officer with his blade raised. The officer pumped two shots into him. The man crumpled to the ground.

Amy gaped in shock. The man had deliberately gotten himself killed—just like the creepy man from last night.

The officer's eyes popped wide open. His body jerked several times. He stopped with a wild look in his eyes. "What the hell?" More spasms hit, then he regained his composure, leered at Tyler, and raised his gun. "Your turn."

Tyler dove to the ground as the bark on the tree behind him exploded. He scrambled on hands and knees behind the tree.

The officer strode toward them with a sneer, firing off three rounds that hit the tree. "Come on out, asshole. I don't want to hurt your girlfriend...yet."

Tyler pressed his back against the tree and lifted the bat. Another gunshot sounded, and the tip of the bat exploded with the impact of the bullet, nearly flinging it out of Tyler's hand. The muzzle of the gun appeared from around the tree. He swung hard and hit the officer squarely in the face.

The officer fell to the ground, dropping the gun. His face was bloody with broken teeth. He groaned with pain, then jerked several more times. "What's happening to me?" he wailed.

His wail broke into a chuckle. "I'm going to taste that girlfriend of yours all over her sweet, sweet body. I love the taste of a young woman."

Shock swept through Amy at the words. They were the same ones the creepy man said.

Tyler cried out in rage and pummeled the officer's head. With each swing, he gave off a cry of fury. He pummeled and pummeled until the officer lay still.

Amy ran to him and stopped his next swing. "Tyler!"

He looked at her with wild eyes, then came to himself and looked down at the officer. The head was a bloody mess. Tyler dropped the dripping bat. His face contorted in horror. "Oh my God, what have I done?"

She pulled him away from the body and forced him to look at her. "You protected us. You protected me! That's what you did."

He stared at her, then at the body.

"He was going to kill us," she said.

He returned his gaze to her and opened his mouth to speak. But suddenly he stiffened up, then contorted. She backed away in shock, her hands covering her mouth.

Tyler twisted and thrashed. He fell back against the tree, struggling as if he were fighting something off. His arms shot forward, palms facing out, as if trying to push something away.

"Tyler," she whispered.

His eyes shut hard, and his face grimaced with some kind of effort. His hands grasped at his body, tearing at something that wasn't there. She watched in helpless horror.

He gave out a long, harrowing cry, pushed forward with his entire body in one mighty effort, then fell forward onto his hands and knees, gasping for air. She rushed to him and threw her arms around him.

"Are you alright? What happened?"

He rose up, still kneeling, and gave out an anguished cry. "*What the hell was that?*"

She pulled back in dread. "Tyler, what happened?"

"I don't know. It was...something...trying to get inside..."

She gasped and stared at the body of the officer, then back at the body of the neighborhood man. "Tyler, the officer said the exact same words the guy last night said."

They stared at each other, speechless.

Rhythmic footsteps came from the forest, the sound of someone running toward them. Tyler grabbed the bat and stood up, waiting.

A man ran out from the trees, emerging into the moonlight. He was dressed like he'd been out camping. He stopped to gaze at Tyler and Amy, then raised a hunting knife and charged them with a war cry.

Tyler swung the bat and connected with his head. The camper stumbled and cried out in pain. Slowly he raised his head. "I'm going to taste her." He struggled to his feet. "I'm going to taste her sweet pussy lips."

He rushed for Amy. Tyler crashed the bat down on his head. The camper dropped to hands and knees and whimpered. Struggling to get the words out, he said, "I'm going to show her what a real man feels like. Then I'm going to make you watch me carve out her insides."

He tried to stand, but Tyler bashed him on the head until he lay still. Amy stared at them both in a shocked daze.

Tyler stiffened and contorted once more. He struggled and pushed. "Not again!" He tightened all his muscles and squeezed, until with a grunt he forced the thing away. "It's trying to get inside me."

"What is?"

"I don't know!"

They heard the sound of a gunning engine. Headlights flashed at them from down the street. The car squealed to a stop. They peered into the headlights, but were blinded by them.

A car door opened and slammed shut. The car still idled. A figure stepped into the light.

"Liam!" Tyler cried. "Thank God!"

"What is going on?" Liam said, staring at the bodies.

Tyler and Amy jogged up to him.

"Are you guys okay?" Liam said, eyes wide.

Tyler spoke as he panted for breath. "These guys...attacked us. Something...it keeps getting into people."

Liam gazed at him somberly. "Hang on a sec." He went back into the shadows behind the headlights. Amy heard the trunk pop open. There was some noise of rummaging, then the trunk slammed shut again. Liam emerged with a tire iron in his hand. "Say again, what's going on?"

"That guy from last night," Tyler said. "It wasn't a guy. It was a...thing... something that jumped into the guy that attacked us tonight, and then to a camper, and—"

Liam swung the iron at Tyler's head. He barely swung the bat up to soften the blow. It caught his ear and deflected off his skull. Blood flowed out from his ear.

"What are you doing?" Amy shrieked.

Liam broke into a dash toward the gun lying on the ground. Tyler rushed at him and whacked him on the back, making him stumble. Tyler ran, grabbed the gun, and pointed it.

Liam stood back up with a troubled expression. "Are you gonna to shoot your old buddy, Tyler?"

"What the hell are you doing?" Tyler said.

"I love you guys. You know that."

Amy picked up the hunting knife and stood beside Tyler. "It's not Liam."

Tyler saw the knife in her hand and pushed her behind him. "Stay back."

"I'm not letting him hurt you."

"I've already killed. You haven't."

"Yeah," said Liam, smirking. "Don't want to spoil her innocent taste." He took a step closer.

"Don't move," Tyler said.

"You can't win." He took a couple more steps.

"Liam..."

"I'll keep coming and coming, until I take you or kill you."

"Take me?"

"You should let me take you. Then it'll be her true love that fucks her blind."

"What do you want?"

Liam laughed enthusiastically. "What do you think I want? She looks so delicious."

"Oh, Liam," Amy said, disheartened. She stood ready to swing the knife.

"Liam, stop it," Tyler said.

"It's not Liam!" Amy cried.

"Yes, it is," Liam said. "Don't you know? I've always loved you. I've always wanted you. But shithead Tyler got you instead, and I was stuck with that JoAnn bitch."

"You're not Liam," she growled.

"I've always wanted to fuck you, Amy. Ever since I saw you. And now I'm going to."

"You can't have her," Tyler said.

"I take what I want, *Tyler*."

"Not this time."

"How you gonna stop me, *Tyler*?"

"Liam," Tyler called, "fight it. *Fight it!* You can push it out."

Liam guffawed. "He can't. He's too fucking weak. You'll have to kill him." He charged with the tire iron. Tyler grabbed his forearm to hold it back. He raised the gun, but Liam grabbed his arm and held it.

The two groaned as they grappled against one another, their arms trembling with the effort. Amy rammed the hilt of the knife down on Liam's head. Tyler pushed him away, twisting his arm out of his grasp.

Liam fell back on his butt. The tire iron slipped and clattered on the pavement. Tyler dropped and grabbed him by the throat, pointing the gun at his face.

"Why don't you kill me, Tyler?" He grabbed Tyler's throat with both hands and squeezed. Tyler dropped the gun and squeezed Liam's throat with both of his.

"I'm sorry, Liam," Amy said and plunged the knife into his shoulder. He cried out and let go of Tyler's throat. Amy pulled the knife out and prepared to stab again. Tyler leaped up and yanked her away. Liam bellowed as he held his shoulder.

"Don't kill him," Tyler said as he held her back.

"That's not Liam anymore."

"He's my best friend."

"That thing killed my mom!"

"If we kill it, it'll just possess someone else."

Liam's bellow turned into laughter. "Tyler...*Tyler*!"

"Let's just get out of here," Tyler said. They turned to leave.

"Liam's not gone. He's still here...with me. Still here, still wishing he could fuck Amy."

Tyler stop and gaped at him with a disturbed look.

"Listen, Tyler." Liam stopped laughing, and his face softened. An expression of fear took over. A weak voice spoke. "Tyler, help me."

Tyler stared in horror.

"Get it out of me."

"Liam, fight it! You can do it."

Liam whimpered. The whimper turned into mocking laughter. He struggled to his feet and spoke in the stronger voice. "There's only one way to remove me from his body." His balance was precarious, but he managed to stand. "Kill the body." He picked the iron up.

Tyler grabbed Amy's hand and ran with her back to her house. "Where does your mom keep her keys?"

"In her purse."

They reached Sarah's body. He upended her purse and dumped its contents on the porch.

"Tyler, we can't leave her like this."

"We don't have time," he said as he rummaged through the contents. "Where are her keys?"

Liam was nearly there, jogging with difficulty. Tyler jumped up and guarded Amy as they backed off the porch onto the sidewalk. He held the gun ready.

Liam grinned at him as he moved in with the tire iron raised and stood over the body. He reached into his pocket, pulled out a keychain, and dangled it in front of them. "Looking for these? The dog walker took them right after he killed her."

"After *you* killed her!" Amy growled.

"And now I got them." Liam slid them back in his pocket and advanced on them slowly.

"Don't you have keys?" Tyler asked Amy.

"In my bedroom."

Tyler looked down the street. "Liam's car!"

They bolted for the car, still idling with its headlights on.

———

Tyler drove Liam's car down the street on the way to the mouth of the canyon. Amy wept quietly. "I can't believe my mom's dead."

They approached the mouth of the canyon. "Why are we going there?" Amy said.

"If we go into town, who knows who else that thing'll possess."

Tyler gazed grimly ahead as he navigated the curves on the narrow two-lane road. His phone rang. He pulled it out, looked at it, and set it down with disgust on the panel between them. Amy looked at it and saw Liam's name. It kept ringing and ringing. When it stopped, a moment passed, then it rang again.

Amy jabbed at it, putting it on speaker. "We're calling the police."

Liam laughed. "Because that worked so good before. Where are you going, Tyler? You think you can outrun me?"

"We *are* outrunning you."

"I'll always be with Liam. Till death do us part."

"Shut that off," Tyler said angrily.

"I'll torment him for the rest of his life."

She disconnected the phone with a stab. "What is that thing?"

"Some kind of...spirit or...demon or...something."

"It's a devil."

"Or some dead pervert's ghost."

"How is that possible?"

He looked at her and shrugged.

"How can it take over people's bodies like that?"

"I guess it's...it's...possession."

Headlights in the side mirror caught her attention, some distance back. "Maybe we can get a priest to exorcise it."

"It said only death can remove him."

"We're believing evil spirits now?"

"What if we did exorcise it? Wouldn't it just possess someone else?"

"At least we'd have Liam back."

"Maybe it's worth a try."

She gazed at him, remembering his contortions fighting it off. She placed her hand on his arm. "It couldn't take you."

"It sure tried. Twice."

"You were strong enough to fight it."

He nodded. "And Liam wasn't."

"So it *can* be stopped."

"For some people, I guess."

"There has to be a way to stop it."

"I'm thinking."

She noticed the headlights were closer. "Tyler..." she said.

"I see it."

She picked up the phone. "I'm calling the police."

"And tell them what? I killed three innocent people. One of them was a cop. I'm a cop killer."

Her finger hovered over the phone. "You know that was the demon."

"But they won't."

"We have to do something!"

"More cops with guns for that thing to possess?"

She dropped the phone in frustration. "It's better than nothing. Maybe with a bunch of cops, they can...I don't know...overwhelm him?"

Tyler stared into the mirror. "Is that your mother's car?"

The headlights swerved into the on-coming lane and zoomed up parallel to them. Amy couldn't see who the driver was in the dark, but it was definitely her mother's car. The driver's head turned to look at them, then surged ahead and veered directly into their path.

Amy cried out. Tyler turned the steering wheel hard and slammed on the brakes. The back tires skidded into the ditch. He gunned the engine, but the tires spun.

Liam climbed out of Sarah's car, brandishing the tire iron and a determined face. Tyler grabbed the knife. Amy grabbed the gun, but Tyler placed his hand on hers. "We can't kill him." He held the knife up. "Come on."

He got out and helped her slide out through his door. The sound of rushing water from the canyon river filled the night. Liam stood between the two cars.

Tyler and Liam stared at each other over the top of Liam's car. Tyler made a sudden move toward the front, and Liam mirrored it.

Immediately Tyler rushed to the back of the car, but Liam followed him there. They both return to the middle with the car between them.

"We gonna dance all night?" Liam said.

"I know what you are."

"Do you now?"

"You're some kind of evil spirit. Maybe a sexual predator that died. Or maybe a demon that got a taste for sex while possessing someone."

"Maybe. Maybe not." He looked like he was enjoying this.

"Now you jump from body to body trying to satisfy your lust."

"Sounds fun."

"But you never will." Tyler tried to sound ominous. "You'll spend eternity lusting and never feel satisfied."

"Step aside, Tyler. Let me have her, and I won't have to kill you."

"Never."

Liam shrugged. "Then I'll just kill you and have her anyway."

"If you can."

Liam scowled at him. "Do you doubt it? No matter how many times you kill me, I'll just come back. You can't stay lucky forever."

"Why don't you leave us alone and go after someone else?"

Liam's scowl deepened. A burning lust filled his eyes. Amy thought she could see the demon inside him, and it chilled her to the bone.

"She's mine," Liam said. The voice was dark and gravelly. "I've claimed her. Such delicious innocence."

"Claim someone else."

"No one escapes me."

"You can't take her."

A look of disgust crossed Liam's face. "*Take* her?" He shuddered. "Women are for having, not taking. Do you know how goddamn disgusting it is to possess a female body?"

Tyler laughed with derision. "Don't like being a lesbian?"

"This conversation is over."

Liam opened the passenger door of their car, leaned far into it, and shut the engine off. He stood back up and dangled the key in front of him. "You're not going anywhere now."

Tyler made a dash around the front, aiming for Sarah's car. Liam rushed after him. Tyler couldn't quite make it and hurried back to Amy.

With a deep scowl, Liam climbed into Sarah's car, keeping an eye on Tyler and Amy. The car headed up the canyon road and drove until it disappeared behind a curve.

"What's he doing now?" Amy said.

"No idea, but I don't like it." They stared up the road for a moment longer. Nothing happened. "Let's just get the hell out of here."

Tyler took the phone from the car, and they walked down the road toward the mouth of the canyon. The headlights of Liam's car stuck in the ditch blazed a streak of light across the road and onto the wall of the canyon. They walked as far off the road as they could without going into the forest. Amy was on the side closer to the forest. Darkness surrounded them.

They constantly looked back, making sure Liam didn't return, but never saw anything except that streak of white light and red taillights. The rush of the river a short distance away was all the noise they could hear.

"Be ready to run into the forest if we have to," he said.

"How far before we get back?"

"About five miles, I think, to your house."

Amy looked back. Her mother's car entered the streak of light, silently rolling toward them with the engine off. "Tyler!" she cried.

He whirled around as the headlights burst on, blinding them. She pulled him out of the car's path, but it veered toward him and caught his hip, throwing both of them to the side. She fell immediately onto the gravel of the shoulder. He spun with the knife flying from his hand, hit the pavement, and rolled a couple times.

The car's brakes slammed on. Liam leaped out. Amy scrambled to her feet, but Liam reached her before she could run and wrapped his arms around her. She struggled and screamed.

Tyler shook his head, jumped up and cried out in pain, grabbing his hip.

Hanging tightly to Amy with one arm, Liam reached into the car and popped open the trunk. Tyler limped to the knife and picked it up. Liam dragged Amy to the trunk as she fought him, but his arms squeezed tightly around her.

Tyler ran to them with a limp, cringing and grunting with each footstep. Liam pushed Amy into the trunk. She pushed back hard with cries of anger. He pressed the lid of the trunk down on her. An arm and leg hung out, keeping it from closing.

Tyler grabbed Liam by the shoulder and whirled him around, stabbing him in the chest near his collarbone. Liam howled and grabbed Tyler's arm by the wrist. Tyler couldn't pull the knife back out.

Amy tried to push open the trunk and climb out, but Liam leaned against it as he and Tyler grappled. She pounded on Liam's hip, but it had no effect. Liam gripped Tyler's arm and held him in place as he strained his head forward. The move caused the knife to twist in his chest, and he groaned in pain. His mouth reached Tyler's arm and bit down.

Tyler cried out and released the knife. He bashed his fist into Liam's head. Liam fell to the side as Tyler stumbled back. The trunk lid flew open, and Amy crawled out. Liam roared with a grimace as he pulled the knife from his chest. Tyler and Amy ran for the car door.

"I am so fucking sick of you, Tyler!" Liam cried and charged them with the knife.

Tyler opened the door for Amy, but Liam was upon them before she could get in. Tyler grabbed Amy's arm, and they rushed across the street toward the forest.

"You can't escape me!" Liam bellowed, taking a few steps in their direction. "I'll find you and I'll hurt you. I'll make you watch while I fuck her over and over."

They plunged into the trees.

"Then I'll kill her right before your eyes. A slow, painful death."

The forest growth was thick, slowing them down. Tyler grunted each time he put weight on his hip.

"Do you hear me, Tyler?" Liam's voice called. "I'll never stop!"

They struggled through brush and branches until they had to stop from exhaustion.

"Your hip," she said. "Are you alright?"

He signaled her to be silent and looked behind them, cocking his head to listen. The river sounded distant now. "I don't think he's following us. Go slowly and make as little noise as you can."

"Go where?"

"Just...away. It should be dawn soon."

They picked their way through the forest as the ground sloped up the mountains. It was hard not to make sounds. Amy felt like she'd collapse from all the exertion and emotional turmoil. She wept silent tears for her mother, for the innocent people they had to kill, for Liam. She didn't want Tyler to hear her crying, like he tried not to let her see how much his hip hurt.

They encountered a small creek gurgling down the slope. and followed it along the edge to avoid the thicker growth. The sky to the east developed a bluish tint by the time they heard more splashing water. It was a tall, narrow ribbon of a waterfall plummeting down from a cliff along the canyon wall. There was an enormous boulder, larger than a car, sitting nearby. He brought her to a spot where they could sit and lean against a flat surface on its side.

"You need to sleep," he told her.

"So do you."

"I'll keep watch. He'll have a hell of a time finding us here anyway."

They sat. Tyler winced with pain while doing it. He put his arm around her. Amy caressed his hip. "Is it bad?"

"I think it's just bruised. I'll be alright."

She closed her eyes and rested her head on his shoulder. "I feel so safe in your arms."

The sun rose as Liam drove along the canyon road. His breathing was heavy with a wheeze, and his shoulder and chest were drenched in blood. He was in no condition to chase them into the forest, so he kept driving up and down, knowing they'd have to come out sooner or later.

He passed an SUV parked at a trailhead on the river's side. There were six college-age kids, four boys and two girls. He eyed the girls. One was a little pudgy, but they were both attractive enough. He took note of them and continued driving.

Further up the road he spotted a young man and woman getting out of their car at a trailhead on the other side. They had backpacks with them. The woman was amazingly beautiful with a baby-face.

This one he had to have!

He drove past and pulled over just out of their sight. He turned the car off, left the keys in the ignition, and stepped out, grunting with the pain.

———

Beth and Nathan hiked along the trail. It paralleled the highway just far enough back for the trees to block their view of it. Beth could hear the occasional car passing by. They held hands affectionately. The weight of her backpack tugged on her shoulders.

"My mother says I could do better than you," she said as she nudged him with her shoulder.

Nathan rolled his eyes. "We're not even married and she's already an evil mother-in-law."

"Maybe she's right. Maybe I should trade up."

"Maybe you should go to Hollywood and find a man worthy of you."

"Or maybe I'll tell my mother to go to hell." Beth grinned at him.

He grinned back. "That works too."

"Maybe I already did."

He laughed enthusiastically. "Now, the matter about kids..."

"Three...maybe four."

Nathan balked. "That's a lot of kids."

Beth shrugged. "There's seven in my family."

"There's only two in mine."

"That's right, so I averaged them out. That comes to four and a half kids."

"That poor half-a-kid! He'll have to go to a special school."

"See? I even rounded down for you. I could have said five." She tossed her head to flip her hair. "I'm being completely reasonable."

"I don't know. That extra half-a-kid sounds intriguing. We could rent him out to circuses."

They came to an enormous boulder, twelve feet high and at least thirty feet long. Its top was flat, gently sloping up as it extended deeper into the forest. Beth stopped and gazed at it, mesmerized by it .

"Look at the size of that thing!" Nathan said. "I'd hate to have been around when it rolled down the mountain."

"Oh, we have to climb on top!" Beth said in delight. She grabbed a protrusion, found a foothold, and pulled herself up.

They climbed. She clambered on top of the boulder, walked along it, and looked around. He came up behind her. She extended her arms out on either side and twirled. "Isn't this great!"

She gazed off in the distance. On the other side of the canyon was a long, narrow waterfall tumbling down a crevice until it disappeared into the trees. "Look at that view!"

He put his arm around her and looked where she looked. She noticed a satisfied smile on his face. She gave him a kiss on the cheek. "You knew this was here all along."

"What do you mean?" he said, doing a poor job of feigning ignorance.

She gave him a longer kiss on his lips. "You're an awful liar."

———

Amy snored softly as she slept. Tyler sat with his arm around her, keeping his eyes and ears open. Morning birds chirped with a frenzy. The waterfall splashed away. Its soothing sound relaxed him, seduced him. His eyelids drooped. He tried to fight it.

Max opened the back of his SUV. A car drove by. The driver stared at him intensely as he passed. No, at Jenny and Nicole. "Asshole!" he muttered.

Everyone milled about, looking at the scenery. Jenny fidgeted. "Let's get moving," she said. "I'm starving!"

Ryan grinned at her. He and Eddie headed for the back of the SUV and pulled supplies out.

"You're the one made us late in the first place," Nicole said to Jenny.

"I was busy." Jenny paused dramatically. "Breaking up with Greg."

All five of them stopped and gaped at her. Ryan perked up with interest.

"You're kidding!" said Zach.

"That's why he didn't come?" Max said.

Eddie muttered to Ryan out of the corner of his mouth, but not very quietly, "Now's your chance."

Nicole sniggered. Ryan threw a glare at Eddie that could kill. Jenny blushed and glanced at Ryan with a poorly suppressed smiled.

With the picnic supplies out, Max locked the SUV and turned to look at his five friends gathering everything up to carry down the trail. Jenny grabbed one handle of the large cooler. "Who wants to help me with this?"

Ryan jumped into action, grabbing the other handle. "I'll help you."

Jenny grinned warmly at him. "Thanks, Ryan."

Max smiled. Eddie came up to him. They watched Jenny and Ryan head down the trail and Nicole and Zach carry bags of food side by side, brushing affectionately against each other.

"I need to get me a girlfriend fast," Max said, then looked at Eddie.

"Don't look at me!" Eddie said with his hands up in the air.

 The six of them carried the supplies into a clearing in the forest near the river. They laid everything out next to a campfire ring of large stones in the middle of the clearing.

"Max, this place is beautiful!" Nicole said.

He grinned with satisfaction. "Told you."

Nicole wandered over to the river and gazed upstream and downstream. Jenny and Ryan placed the cooler on the ground next to the supplies. Max studied them. He didn't know whether to feel envious of Ryan or sorry for him that he was so love-stricken.

Jenny headed over to Nicole and admired the scenery with her. Max decided to wander over.

"Gorgeous, isn't it?" Nicole said.

"Sure is," said Jenny.

Nicole leaned in a little. "I think Ryan has a crush on you."

Max smiled. *Think* he has a crush?

"Maybe I shouldn't have said I broke up," Jenny said.

"Ryan's a sweetheart. Don't you like him?"

"Sure I like him, but I could use a break. At least a few days...weeks... months..." They both giggled.

"What's up, ladies?" Max said as he came up, making them jump.

"Are you eavesdropping again?" Nicole growled.

"Didn't hear a thing." He strolled between them and looked at Nicole, then Jenny, with a big grin. "Poor Ryan, huh?"

They shot him disgusted looks. Nicole slapped him on the shoulder.

"Max, shall we get the fire going?" Eddie called out.

"Get the fire going," Max called back.

"You're not out of the doghouse yet," Nicole told him.

Beth and Nathan sat beside each other on the far end of the boulder, opposite from where they climbed up. They had their arms around each other and their heads touching as they looked out at the forest.

"Beth?"

"Yes?"

"Have I ever told you how beautiful you are?"

She smiled warmly. "Yes, you have."

"Have I ever told you how wonderful life's been since I met you?"

She had to hold back a chuckle. He'd done this often, but always acted like it was the first time. "You have."

He turned and faced her. "Have I ever told you how I couldn't stand to live a single day without you?"

She leaned over and kissed him.

"Have I ever told you I'm dying to ask you to marry me?"

Her eyes went wide, and a tingle swept through her. He hadn't said that one before.

He pulled a little box out and opened it. Inside was a diamond ring. She gaped at it, then looked into his eyes in anticipation, breathlessly waiting for his next words.

She caught movement out of the corner of her eye. A head appeared above the far edge of the boulder. A young man struggled up. She gasped when she saw the blood all over his shirt. "Oh my God! He's hurt!"

Nathan jumped to his feet and ran to him. The man wobbled to his feet with a murderous glare. A dread shot through Beth.

"Enough with you boyfriends!" the man shouted and charged. He rammed into Nathan and pushed him over the edge of the boulder.

"Nathan!" Beth shrieked as she jumped up. She ran to the edge and peered over. Nathan lay unconscious or dead, his head resting on a blood-spattered rock.

"Now it's just you and me, darling," the man said as he stumbled to her with a terrifying leer.

She tried to dodge him and run to the lower end. He blocked her way. "Where do you think you're going?"

"I have to help Nathan."

"Not in this lifetime, darling. You're mine now."

A mixture of horror and rage seethed within her. She looked around at the precipices surrounding them on every side of the boulder.

"Nowhere to run, my delicious morsel. I'm going to taste you all over—"

The rage won out. With a ferocious snarl, she plowed into him with her arms extended. His eyes popped wide open. He toppled back, hit the surface hard with his head, and slid across the boulder. She fell upon him and banged his head against the rock, once, twice, three times.

Between bangs he said with difficulty, "How...dare you...you fucking... bitch!". He tried to push her away and break free, but he was too weak. He swung his fist into the side of her face, knocking her off-balance enough so he could roll over and crawl away. He reached the edge of the boulder, but she leaped on him again and banged his head against the rock until he grew still.

She sat back, breathing hard, fighting the tears that wanted to force their way out. She headed for the low end of the boulder and climbed down carefully, her head still ringing from his punch. She rushed over to Nathan, knelt beside him, and stroked his hair. "Dear God, please be okay."

His head moved, just a little, and a soft moan escaped his lips. She dared to hope. "Nathan, can you hear me?"

His eyes slowly focused on her, and a faint smile crossed his lips. "Help me up," he rasped.

"Are you sure?"

"I'm okay."

She carefully lifted him to a sitting position. Blood smeared the back of his head. He was woozy for a moment, but slowly regained his wits.

"Help me..." He winced with pain and pressed his hand against the back of his head. "Help me to my feet."

She helped him up, then held him in place until he found his balance. He leaned over, bracing himself with his hands on his knees. "That's better."

"We need to get you to a hospital."

Slowly he lifted his head to gaze at her. A snarl broke out on his face. He grabbed her and whirled her around and pressed her against the boulder. With each word he spoke, he pounded her head against the rock.

"No...woman...does that...to me!...Do you...hear me?...No...woman... beats...*me!*"

His rage slowly died with each pounding. Beth slid down, barely able to think. He released her and let her drop as he leaned against the boulder with one hand, panting and grimacing while holding the back of his head.

She tried to focus on him, tried to understand what was happening. Why would he do this to her?

He looked up and saw the face of the other man hanging over the edge, staring down lifelessly at them. He raised his fist and shook it.

"You fucking wimp, Liam! What kind of a pussy lets a woman beat him?"

Her mind spun. She couldn't process what his words meant. He turned his attention to her. She had a hard time focusing on him, and her head slowly lolled back and forth. Her breathing came in faint whimpers and moans.

He leaned in close. "And *you!* Now you see what you get when you fuck with me."

He knelt down and straddled her. She cried out weakly. Her eyes managed to focus on him. "Na...than," she could barely squeeze out. "Wh...why...why did you..."

He grinned and grabbed the lapels of her blouse. "Nathan can't answer."

"Wha...what are you?"

"I'm the only real man you'll ever have." He ripped her blouse apart with the sound of tearing fabric and popping buttons.

Max helped Jenny and Nicole rummage in the supplies, pulling things out and spreading them around. Eddie and Ryan carefully constructed a pile of sticks in the middle of the campfire ring.

Max noticed Ryan casting furtive glances at Jenny. When Eddie caught him doing it, he tried to cover it up by saying, "Where are the matches?"

"Max," Eddie called, "where are the matches?"

"I guess they're still in the van," Max called back.

"I'll go get them," Zach said.

"You'll need these." Max tossed him the set of keys.

Zach caught them and nodded, then headed back to the SUV. "Hurry back, love," Nicole said. He smiled at her.

Nathan stumbled out onto the highway and crossed over. His injuries were severe and too much to handle, now that the rush of adrenalin and sex hormones had been spent on Beth. He entered the trees on the other side and walked as the sound of the river grew louder.

It was all he could do to reach the bank and follow it until he came to a place where the river narrowed and splashed over wicked boulders. He stood on a rock outcropping ten feet above and gazed down at it.

He'd been through this a million times. He lost count how many years. He was used to the pain. Pain was temporary when death was involved.

He extended his arms out on both sides and closed his eyes. He leaned forward until he toppled and hit the boulders in the raging water.

The minute the supplies were spread out, Jenny called, "We're ready to eat." By now she was starving like crazy.

Everyone approached. Max looked around. "Where's Zach?"

Nicole turned and looked. "He must still be at the van."

"How long does it take to get matches?" Max said.

"With Zach you never know," Eddie said.

"Hey, guys!" Zach's voice called. Everyone turned to see him run into the clearing. He held his phone up. "There was a bunch of murders in town."

Everyone rushed over and crowded around him. "Where?" Ryan said.

Zach scrolled with his finger. "That new neighborhood near the mouth of the canyon. There's also a girl and two guys missing. They think they might be victims too." He scrolled further. "They also found two abandoned cars. One of them belongs to one of the victims. She's the mother of the missing girl. The other car belongs to one of the missing guys." Suddenly he looked up with dismay. "They found the cars right here in this canyon. Just a little further up from us."

The group threw each other glances. Max said, "Maybe we should search, see if we can find them."

"That's what I was thinking," said Zach. Nicole walked up to him and put her arm around him. The move startled Zach. He looked at her with his brow knotted, then smiled.

"Alright," Max said, "let's head out in different directions. We'll search for, say, thirty minutes, then come straight back."

"What about the food?" Ryan said.

"Yeah, a bear might get into it," Eddie said.

Eagerly, Jenny raised her hand. "I'll stay with the food."

"You gonna fight the bear off alone?" Eddie smirked.

"I fought you off."

Eddie scowled as everyone laughed.

"We should start searching," Zach said. "Those kids have been out there all night."

"Okay," said Max. "Nicole, head off north along the river."

"I'll head northwest," Zach said.

"Good," Max said. "I'll head west across the road. Eddie, you head southwest, and Ryan, you go south with the river."

Everyone mumbled their agreement.

"Be back in an hour so we don't have to search for *you*. Jenny, keep your hands off the food."

She pouted at Max.

"Does the news mention their names?" Nicole said as she craned to look on Zach's phone.

"Oh...um..." Zach checked. "Tyler and Amy and Liam."

"Good," Nicole said. "Now we can call for them." She gave Zach a quick kiss. It startled him again, then he smiled at her.

Jenny sat on a rock in the campfire ring and waited impatiently for them all to leave. They headed off in their assigned directions. Soon voices started calling out, "Tyler...Amy...Liam."

Jenny checked all around to make sure she was alone, then opened the cooler, pulled out an apple, and crunched down on it.

Max headed to the road. When he saw his SUV, he remembered he forgot to get the keys back from Zach. He continued into the forest on the other side and picked his way through the trees.

"Tyler! Amy! Liam!"

He came to a creek tumbling down the mountainside and followed it. "Tyler! Amy! Liam!"

Eddie called out, "Tyler! Liam! Amy!"

He came across a deer trail that made clambering through the forest easier. He followed it, calling their names.

Ryan followed the bank on his left, gazing into the forest on his side and on the other side of the river.

"Amy! Tyler! Liam!"

Jenny laid the apple core down at her feet. She rummaged in a bag of food, pulled out a banana, and peeled it open.

———

Nicole walked along with the river on her right.

"Amy?"

She peered through the trees, looking for any movement, any out-of-place color that didn't fit nature.

"Tyler?"

She studied the trees on the other side of the river. She was glad she wasn't on that side. The growth there was thick. There was more space where she was.

"Liam?"

She came to an eroded patch of ground where exposed roots spread out from a large tree like snakes. It gave her the creeps, making her feel like she was in some horror movie.

Suddenly someone threw their arms around her from behind. She gave off a squeal and spun around.

"Zach!" She slapped him on the chest. "You scared the shit out of me!"

"I couldn't stay away from you," he said with a suggestive grin.

She squirmed out of his embrace. "We need to look for those poor kids."

"Come on, Nicole. What are the chances they got lost right here where we're having a picnic?"

"You were all for searching when Max suggested it."

"Yeah, and now we're alone in the forest." He grinned suggestively.

She hit his chest again with both fists. "You're such an animal!" She pulled away. "We really should search. If I was lost, I'd want someone out looking for me."

He pulled her into an embrace with her back pressed against him. "I wouldn't let you get lost."

"Stop it! What's gotten into you?" She grabbed his hands and pried them away so she could turn and scowl at him, but his silly grin melted her. "Alright, I'll give you one kiss to hold you till later."

"Make it a good one."

They kissed with passion.

Max heard some splashing ahead. He looked up and saw a rock cliff with a narrow waterfall tumbling down, feeding the creek he followed up.

"Tyler? Liam?"

He climbed toward the waterfall, looking in all directions.

"Amy?"

As he neared, a massive boulder came into view from behind the trees. A young man and young woman sat against it, deep in sleep.

"Tyler?"

The young man stirred. His eyes drooped open.

"Liam?"

His eyes went wide, and he leaped to his feet and stared at Max. The young woman moaned and woke up. She saw Max and jumped up, clinging to the young man.

"Amy?" Max said.

"Who are you?" the man said with deep suspicion.

"Max. We've been searching for you...if you're Tyler...or Liam."

"We who?"

"Me and my friends. We heard about it on the news."

The two of them looked at each other. She said, "We're on the news?"

"With all those bodies, how could we not be?" He turned to Max. "What do they say about us?"

"I didn't read the story. All I know is they think you may be victims too."

"We are, but—"

"Liam's the one killing people," the woman said.

"So you're Tyler and Amy."

They both nodded.

"What happened?" Max asked. Amy's tears welled up in her eyes. "Never mind. None of my business. You must be starving."

"Yes, we are," said Tyler.

"We're having a picnic. Come, you can join us, and we can call the authorities." Max headed for the creek, but turned and found the couple standing in place. "What's wrong?"

"I guess we're jumpy," Tyler said. "Your friends. Are any of them acting... weird?"

"No, just you." Max scrutinized them, studied the surroundings, and noticed a bloody hunting knife lying on the ground where they sat. What the hell was going on? Who were the real victims?

Tyler looked at Amy. "Let's go with him. We need to eat."

"Okay," she said hesitantly. She turned to Max with a pleading look. "Do you think you could...walk a little ways ahead of us?"

"Maybe I do need to make it my business," Max said. "What happened to you guys?"

Tyler sighed. "Her mother was murdered last night by a guy named Liam. He chased after us, and we ran out here to hide from him."

"Why didn't you call the police?"

"We...barely escaped as it was."

"That must have been some night last night."

"It was."

Max nodded toward the spot where they'd been sleeping. "If you're the victims, how come you're the ones with the bloody knife?"

They turned and stared at it, then faced Max with abashed expressions.

"We used to it escape Liam," Amy said.

It was possible. And they certainly didn't look or act like murderers. They looked like the all-American couple straight out of Iowa. He wasn't sure, but that might be what worried him the most. Who looked that pure and innocent? "Step back, please."

They looked at him perplexed

He waved his hand at them. "Please!"

They crept back several steps.

"More.

They moved farther back.

Max pulled out a handkerchief and used it to pick up the bloody knife. He held it before his face studying it. "I'd really feel better if you two walked ahead of *me*."

He headed back to the waterfall and waited. They came and stopped at the creek, several yards from him.

"Follow the creek down."

The couple took hands and made their way down the slope.

Jenny sipped at a can of soda as a young couple suddenly came into view down the trail. She gulped quickly and hid the can behind her, just in time before Max appeared behind them.

"Is this them?" she said.

"Two of them." Max looked at the ground where the apple core and banana peel lay.

Jenny scowled at him and set the can down without trying to hide it. "I didn't eat breakfast, and you weren't due back for another fifteen minutes."

"Well, they haven't eaten since yesterday, so give them some food."

She ruffled through the supplies as they came up to her. "We've got plenty." She pulled out two sandwiches and two cans of soda. They accepted them with thank you's, sat down, and devoured them.

Jenny studied the two. They looked like they'd been through a lot. "You must be Amy, and which one are you? Tyler or Liam?"

"Tyler," he said through a mouthful.

Max looked at his watch. "Everyone should start showing up in a few minutes. Jenny, you have your phone? Mine's locked in the van, and Zach has the keys."

She pulled it our with a flourish. "You want me to call 911?"

"Please don't," Tyler said.

Max eyed him suspiciously. "Why not?"

Tyler seemed agitated as he delayed answering. "We'd rather go in ourselves and explain everything."

"Then we can give you a ride there."

"We don't want to trouble you. We can find our own way back."

Jenny gasped as Max presented a large, bloody knife he held with a handkerchief. "I don't feel comfortable letting you wander off," he said.

"What the hell is that?" Jenny cried.

"They had it."

"Is that blood?"

"Yeah, Tyler, Amy. Whose blood is it?"

"We told you," Tyler said with irritation. "We had to stab Liam to escape."

"Liam's the murderer?" Jenny said.

"Did you kill him?" Max said.

"He was alive the last time we saw him," Tyler said.

Max approached them with a dark glare and hovered over them. "What's really going on?"

"I already told you," Tyler said. "Liam killed Amy's mother and—"

"Oh my God, that's terrible!" Jenny said.

"And he chased us into the canyon. We had to hide."

"After you stabbed him," Max said.

"He's really psychotic, and he's really good. We had to escape from him a couple times."

To Jenny Max said, "Call the police."

"We already tried that. A cop's dead now."

"You're still not telling me something," Max growled.

"Look," Tyler said in frustration. "We really don't want to talk about it. Right now I just need to..." He gazed about the forest. "...think."

Max looked around too, and a worried expression crossed his face. "This fellow Liam. Would he be searching for you right now?"

"Possibly. Probably. Yes."

Max and Jenny looked at each other, then ran to opposites sides of the clearing. They cupped their hands around their mouths.

"Nicole! Zach! Come back!" Jenny cried.

"Ryan! Eddie! Get back here as fast as you can!" Max shouted.

They continued shouting until Ryan charged out of the trees panting, eyes ablaze. "What the hell's wrong?"

"There's a psychotic murderer out there somewhere," Max said, then looked at Tyler and Amy. "We think."

"Are you serious?"

Eddie ran into the clearing. "What's happening?" He noticed Tyler and Amy and grinned. "You found them! That's great!" He swiveled his head around. "Where's the other guy?"

"They say the other guy is a psychotic murderer running around looking for them."

His grin disappeared. "That's not great."

"Where's Nicole and Zach?" Jenny asked.

All faces turned to the north, peering into the forest.

"Oh, no!" Jenny wailed.

Tyler and Amy gave each other alarmed looks.

Max tossed the handkerchief away and gripped the knife. "I'd better go after them."

"We're coming with," Tyler said.

But Max was already gone.

Tyler and Amy raced after Max as he ran alongside the river.

"Nicole! Zach!" Max called. When they caught up with him, he said, "Nicole went searching along the river."

Amy looked around, feeling apprehension. "And Zach?"

Max gestured to the left. "He went off that way." He stopped in his tracks. "Oh my God! What is that?"

He rushed over to a large tree with exposed roots twisting along the ground. A nude body lay at the base of the tree, a young woman. Clothes were strewn about. A gag was in her mouth.

Max dropped the knife and knelt down beside her. "Nicole, Nicole."

He felt for a pulse. Tyler and Amy stood behind him, surveying the trees. Max lifted Nicole up to press his cheek against hers. Softly he began to weep. "Nicole."

Amy noticed bruises around her neck.

"We need to get back to the others," Tyler said, peering anxiously into the forest.

Amy whirled around as she caught movement out of the corner of her eye. Another young man stood a hundred feet away staring at them. "Are you Tyler and Amy?" he said.

The man approached. Amy huddled up against Tyler, who put his arm protectively around her.

"You must be Zach?" Tyler said.

The man looked at Max kneeling on the ground with Nicole in his arms. "Oh God! What happened?" He rushed forward and knelt down beside them. "No, no, no! Nicole! Oh God, what happened?"

"She was murdered," Max said through his sobbing.

"Oh God, no no! Nicole!" He fell back with an anguished cry. "God, Nicole, no!"

Max removed the gag from Nicole's mouth. Tyler and Amy peered around at the forest. "We really should go," Tyler said.

Tears staining his face, Max reached for Nicole's blouse lying a few feet away and slid one of her arms into it. "I'm not bringing her back like this."

Zach turned onto his hands and knees and seemed about to vomit. Max slid the other sleeve onto Nicole and buttoned the blouse into place.

Zach rose to his feet with a thick, dead branch and charged. Before Amy could react, Tyler whirled around, but Zach bashed him on the side of the head. The branch shattered in two. Tyler fell to the ground and didn't move.

Amy screamed and rushed at Zach, knocking him on his butt.

"What the hell are you doing, Zach?" Max cried.

Amy knelt beside Tyler and lifted his head. He was still breathing.

Zach leered at Max and rose to his feet. Alarmed, Max lowered Nicole to the ground and stood. Zach howled and sprinted at him. Max folded his hands together into a double fist and slammed Zach across the side of the head. Zach sprawled to the ground.

"Damn it, Zach! Have you lost your mind?"

"That's not Zach," Amy cried.

Max glanced at her in confusion. Zach shook his head and stood up, glaring at him. Max reached down and picked up the hunting knife. "Don't make me hurt you."

Zach peered at the blade and grinned. Like lightning, he charged. Max kicked him in the stomach, sending him flying backward.

Zach landed with a gasp. "What kind of a pussy kick was *that*, Max?"

"What the hell's gotten into you?"

"*He's not Zach!*" Amy shouted. "That's Liam!"

Max looked at her like she was crazy.

Zach noticed Tyler. A gleam formed in his eye. Amy noticed, and dread gripped her.

"Why don't you kill me, *Max*?" Zach said as he gazed at Tyler.

Amy panicked. He wanted to take Tyler while he was unconscious and couldn't fight back. She slapped Tyler on the cheek. "Wake up!"

Zach stood and marched toward Max, his arms out and his chest vulnerable. "Kill me, Max."

Max gaped at him.

He kept advancing. "You know what I did with Nicole? I beat her head against the tree, ripped her clothes off, fucked her brains out, and choked her to death."

Max shook with emotion. His eyes burned with rage. He reached out and strong-armed Zach to a stop. Zach grabbed Max's throat with both hands and squeezed. Max's eyes bulged. He swung the knife around and stabbed Zach in the side of his shoulder.

Zach stiffened with a cry, but didn't break his stranglehold. "Kill me, Max. You know you want to."

"Don't kill him!" Amy shrieked, still trying to revive Tyler.

"You have to kill me, or I'll kill you."

Max plunged the knife into his back. Zach's breathing became shallow and gargling. His grip loosened.

"You killed Nicole," Max said hoarsely.

"That's right. I raped her and strangled her."

"But you loved her."

"She was so innocent and delicious. Her eyes popped out so sweetly when I squeezed the life out of her."

Max plunged the knife again with a howl of rage.

Amy desperately slapped Tyler. "Don't kill him! Tyler can't fight back."

Tyler moved his head and moaned.

"Yes, wake up! Wake up!"

Max stabbed again, and Zach slumped to the ground. Max fell on his knees, gasping and coughing, holding his neck.

Tyler's eyes flew open as his body jerked. He rolled off Amy's lap and thrashed around on the ground, tearing at his body. Amy watched in horror. With a mighty shove into the air, Tyler pushed the demon away. Amy gathered him up in an embrace. "Are you alright?"

Max stiffened with his eyes bulging. He shuddered, then writhed. Amy and Tyler watched in dread. Max jerked back and forth, tearing at his body with his hands. All his muscles tensed up. He let out a loud, prolonged cry, then fell back against the tree and panted hard. "Holy shit! What just happened?"

"That was Liam," Amy said. "He tried to take your body."

"You were too strong for him," Tyler said.

"What are you talking about?"

"An evil spirit tried to possess you," Tyler said.

"That's insane!"

"You felt it!" Amy said.

"How long have you known Zach?" Tyler asked.

"Since kindergarten."

"Would he ever act like he did today? Would he have murdered Nicole?"

"Never!"

"That demon possessed my friend Liam and tried to kill me and rape Amy. It possessed Zach and killed Nicole."

Max stared at him with wild eyes.

"Just now it tried to possess me *and* you."

Max looked around. "Where is it now?"

Tyler and Jenny gazed at each other, then looked back in the direction of the picnic.

Max's eyes widened in alarm. "Ryan! Eddie! *Jenny!*" He dashed away. Amy and Tyler chased after him.

———

Max barreled out of the forest with Amy and Tyler behind him, surprising Jenny, Eddie, and Ryan.

"Did you find them?" Jenny asked.

Max, Tyler, and Amy examined the other three. Tyler couldn't see anything about any of them to make him suspicious. They all stared back with confusion.

"Is it here?" Max cried.

"I don't know!" said Tyler.

"Did it go away?"

"Not a chance." Tyler peered about the trees. "Maybe someone else is in the area."

"What are you guys talking about?" Jenny said.

Max, Tyler, and Amy kept looking about and staring at the other three. Jenny jumped up and marched to Max. "Did you find Nicole and Zach?"

"They're dead," Max said with anguish.

"What?" cried Eddie. He and Ryan ran up to the others.

"The murderer got them?" Ryan said.

Max's face contorted with grief. "Zach killed Nicole."

"*What?*" Jenny, Ryan, and Eddie cried in unison.

"Then Zach tried to kill me, so I had to kill him."

Jenny gaped at him, then glared. "Max, this is the cruelest joke you—"

"It's no joke!" Tyler cried.

Jenny's eyes shot daggers at him.

"It's no joke," Amy said.

Jenny looked her up and down, then returned her gaze to Max. "Why in God's name would Zach kill Nicole? He loves her."

Max looked at Tyler with a pleading expression.

"Don't look at him," Jenny spat. "Answer me!"

"Zach was possessed," Tyler said.

Jenny glared at him.

"Who are you guys?" Eddie growled. "You show up and two of our friends are dead?" He and Ryan advanced menacingly.

"Then you bullshit us with these ridiculous stories?" Ryan said.

Max stopped them both. "It's true. Zach tried to strangle me, and I had to stab him to stop him."

"This is nuts!" Jenny cried.

"Then the demon tried to possess me and Tyler, but we fought it off."

"Max, so help me God, if you're—"

"Come on, Jennie! You think I'd joke about a thing like this?"

She scowled at him.

"I felt it. It was like a...a...icy wind inside my soul, trying to blow me out. It was all I could do to fight it off."

"Jenny, I swear it's true," Amy said. "That thing murdered my mother, Tyler's friend, and tried to rape me."

Jenny looked back and forth at the three of them. "So where is it now?"

"It's near," said Tyler. "It wants Amy."

"Why her?"

"I don't know. It lusts for her."

Jenny studied the forest. "It's near?"

"I'm sure of it," Tyler said. He gestured toward Eddie and Ryan. "it could be in one of them right now."

Ryan and Eddie looked at each other.

"No way!" said Eddie. "You're not pinning this on me!"

"This is insane!" Ryan said.

"How can we tell which one?" Max asked.

"I don't know," said Tyler. "I'm new at this too."

Jenny walked over and faced Amy. "Well, if it's lusting after her..." She grabbed Amy and thrust her toward Ryan and Eddie. "Here, demon, demon. Come and get it!"

Tyler yanked Amy away and shoved Jenny back. "Are you out of your mind?"

"Are you? Now where are Nicole and Zach really?"

Max pursed his lips and shook his head. Sadly he said, "They're down there, along the river. Go see for yourself."

"No!" said Amy. "It might have possessed someone else...out there."

Jenny smirked and walked into the forest.

"You need to go with her," Tyler said to Max.

Max gestured at Ryan and Eddie. "What about them?"

"What about us?" Eddie snarled.

Tyler studied them. "If it's here, we'll be three against one."

Max nodded and trotted off to catch up with Jenny. Tyler and Amy stared at Eddie and Ryan, and the two stared back.

"So now what?" Ryan said.

"It must be you, Ryan," Eddie said, "cuz it ain't me." He shoved Ryan playfully on the shoulder.

He shoved him back. "No way. You've always been the asshole."

Amy murmured to Tyler, "How do we tell?"

He shook his head. The demon was doing a good job holding back his true nature—if it was inside one of them at all.

Amy stared at the two of them, then leaned over to Tyler and whispered, "Maybe Jenny had the right idea."

"What?"

"Be ready."

"What are you doing?"

She pulled away from Tyler's arm and walked toward the two boys.

"Amy," Tyler called.

Eddie and Ryan watch her warily as she circled around them. "You guys creep me out," Ryan said.

Tyler moved in closer, gazing at them intensely for a sign. Amy stopped behind them. She put an arm around each of their shoulders and leaned in. She blew into Eddie's ear, then Ryan's. They both stiffened up. Tyler's hair stood on end. Amy kissed Eddie on the back of the neck, then Ryan, and switched back and forth kissing them. Tyler watched on his toes, ready to pounce.

Eddie relaxed and seemed to get into it. Ryan's eyes began to burn with a familiar lust.

"It's Ryan!" Tyler shouted and charged.

Amy jumped back, but Ryan leaped to his feet and grabbed her. Eddie fell back, gaping with shock.

Ryan dragged Amy back, but Tyler was on top of him in an instant. Ryan shoved Amy into Tyler's arms and bolted into the forest along the downstream river.

Eddie leaped up and stared dumbfounded at Ryan until he disappeared, then turned to Tyler. "You were serious?"

"Yes, I was serious!" He held Amy in his arms as she panted.

In the distance, Jenny screamed. Eddie turned in that direction. "Oh my God! Oh my God!" He backed up to the campfire ring and picked up a large rock, about a foot in size. He held it up, ready to use. "That thing could have possessed *me*."

Tyler nodded.

"What do we do?" Amy said. "We can't live like this forever."

He pulled her in with his arm around her. "I've been thinking. Killing it does no good. Exorcism probably wouldn't do any good. We could run, but we'd have to run our whole lives."

"We could bash its head and put it in a coma for life." She said it angrily.

"Too risky. We might not bash hard enough, or we might kill it."

"Drugs. We could keep it sedated."

"How do we get the drugs? What dosage do we use? How do we feed the body and keep it alive? We can't just go to a hospital with this story."

"We convinced these guys."

"After two of them died. Do we let more people die to convince the authorities?"

"We can't save the whole world," she whimpered. "Saving ourselves will be hard enough."

Tyler caressed her hair. "Maybe...maybe we *can* save the world. At least for a good long time."

She looked at him. "How?"

"I've been thinking—"

Eddie grunted and stiffened up, eyes wide and staring straight ahead. A dread shot through Tyler. Eddie shuddered, then relaxed and looked at Tyler, grinning as he lifted the rock high above his head.

Tyler and Amy back away. Eddie flung the rock at Tyler's head. He ducked barely in time. Amy grabbed his hand and pulled him into a run. They dashed to the trail that led to the road.

Max and Jenny ran into the clearing just as Tyler and Amy disappeared down the trail to the highway. Eddie chased after them with a large rock in his hands.

"It was Eddie!" Max said. He started for them, then stopped and turned. "Where's Ryan?"

"I don't know!" Jenny said, freaking out. After seeing Nicole and Zach, this was too much.

Max waved his hand in no particular direction. "Go find him!" He raced off down the trail.

Jenny looked around, biting her fingernails. "Ryan?" she called weakly.

She dropped her hand and shouted at the top of her lungs, "Ryan! Get back here! I don't wanna have to look for you!"

Max almost passed the SUV, then skidded to a stop. He should have... something...he could use as a weapon. He went to the SUV, then stopped again. Damn! He forgot Zach still had his keys. He turned to continue running, but a glint caught his eye. He looked down and found his keys lying on the ground near the door. Dropped when Zach got possessed?

He grabbed them, opened the back of the SUV, and rummaged around. All he found was a coil of yellow nylon rope. That would have to do.

He shut the SUV and ran across the road into the forest, rope clutched in his hand.

Tyler and Amy fled through the trees. They encountered the creek they followed down with Max and ran alongside it. Amy glanced back and saw Eddie crashing through the trees with the rock in hand. The steep slope and the rocky terrain made it difficult for any of them to run fast.

Jenny crept through the forest, shaking, gazing all around her. "Ryan?" She was terrified to be alone in the woods, but waiting alone at the clearing was no better. Anyway, the demon was in Eddie, not Ryan, right?

That was the only thought that kept her going.

Max charged through the thick brush, keeping an eye out for broken twigs and bent stalks that indicated where they'd gone. He came to the creek and followed it up.

Tyler and Amy reached the narrow waterfall. They veered to the boulder and ran around behind it.

Amy heard Eddie charge out from the trees and stop. They waited as Eddie's crunching footsteps moved past the boulder on the other side.

Tyler nodded. They crept back toward the waterfall and peered around the boulder. She saw Eddie facing away from them, looking around.

They ran past the waterfall into the forest in the other direction.

Max reached the waterfall and stopped to gaze right, then left. He turned to the boulder and searched all around it. The growth was thick past the boulder, and he saw no indication anyone had gone that way.

He returned to the waterfall and gazed in the other direction. It has less growth and would have been easier to run through.

Jenny noticed something ahead through the thick trees. Fear swept through her. She crept forward, wishing the whole time she could flee the other direction, but she had to know.

The something became clearer. It was a person leaning over a fallen tree trunk. Jenny didn't know if she felt relieved she wasn't alone, or creeped out that the person just lay there without moving.

She crept closer until she could see the face. It was Ryan. His eyes bulged open and blood dripped from his mouth. A broken branch of the trunk stuck out from his back. Blood dripped all around it.

Jenny screamed.

Exhaustion plagued Amy. She and Tyler came to another creek. It flowed into a great crevice on their left that it must have carved out over thousands of years. They could hear the waterfall it became splashing below. Tyler peered over the edge. "It looks like we could climb down there."

"Tyler, I'm so tired."

He nodded. They passed the crevice. "Let's head down to the road."

They turned and crept down the slope, moving as fast as they could picking their way through the growth. The crevice followed them on the left.

She knew they neared the highway when she heard a car drive by. The severe cliff that was the crevice smoothed out into a slope, still steep, but they could climb down it with the help of branches to grasp and exposed roots as footholds. Tyler went first and helped her down. At the bottom they found the creek, wider here. A bend in the crevice hid the waterfall, but Amy could hear it splashing.

In the other direction, she could just see bits of pavement through the leaves. "The road!" Amy cried, ready to run to it.

But Tyler paused, looking up the crevice.

"Let's go," she said. "We can flag a car down."

"How soon will one come?"

"What, then?"

He looked at the crevice. "We could hide in there, and maybe he'd pass us by, looking for us on the road."

"Or maybe he'll trap us there."

"That's why he'll pass us by. We'd be crazy to go up there."

"It *is* crazy!"

He looked at her with a pained expression, then looked into the crevice. "I really think this is the better way, or he'll just keep chasing us."

She was too frightened and tired to think straight. "If that's how you feel." She followed him as he made his way along the bank of the creek. The waterfall came into view. Any other time she'd enjoy how beautiful it was, but now it only represented a trap to her.

Before they reached the waterfall, the bank died out as the crevice wall encroached in on them. She gazed up and saw where they'd stood above to peer down into the crevice. She could see how they might have climbed down, but it looked difficult, and she was glad they didn't try.

Even more roots were exposed here than where they climbed down. They were twisted and gnarled like a desolate, cursed landscape, appearing as if they'd been there thousands of years. But they made climbing possible.

"Let's hide up here," he said. "You first."

He helped her climb up, following behind as she went. She came to a spot where she could sit with some comfort and lean against a thick root that emerged out of the dirt on one side and disappeared back into the earth on the other side.

Tyler sat before her and surveyed the creek below. "At least I have the advantage if it tries to come up here."

That didn't make her feel better. The demon wasn't supposed to come this way at all.

They waited, the sound of the waterfall filling her ears. She wondered, how would they ever know if that thing passed by and it was safe for them to leave?

A rock rattled down the slope beside her. She turned to look, but an arm wrapped itself around her throat and squeezed. She clutched at it in horror, trying to pull it away.

Tyler spun around and gaped in shock. The arm tightened its squeeze.

"Come near me and she gets hurt," Eddie's voice shouted above the noise of the falls.

Tyler's eyes darted around, searching.

"Maybe I'll kick you down to the rocks," Eddie said. "Or maybe I'll throw Amy onto them. I haven't decided yet."

"I know you won't hurt her. Not yet."

Eddie guffawed. "Oh, I don't mind if they're hurt when I have them. But maybe you're right. I don't want to risk killing her first. I guess that leaves breaking *your* bones on the rocks."

Tyler looked down at the rocks below strewn about the creek bank.

"Then I can keep my promise," Eddie said.

"What promise?"

"To hurt you and make you watch while I rape her and kill her."

Tyler tried to make a move, but slipped on the gravel. Eddie lurched, then laughed when Tyler failed. Amy tried to think what she could do, but every time she twitched, that arm squeezed tighter.

"I love this place you picked," Eddie said. "Really gives me the advantage, don't you think?" He chuckled with amusement.

She closed her eyes, spilling tears. *We should have flagged a car down*, she thought, but felt bad that she was being critical of Tyler at a time like this.

"You think you can kick me hard enough without losing your grip on her?" Tyler said.

"Fuck, she might fall!" Eddie said with exaggerated concern. "Then you'll both be injured. Just think of the delicious pain she'll feel as I fuck her while she's broken in pieces."

"She could die."

"Hmmmm. I guess it's a risk I'll have to take."

Tyler's eyes went wide. She swore she saw hope cross his face for a fleeting instant. She wondered what he was thinking. A clever idea to get them out of this, she hoped.

"Tell you what," Tyler said. "I'll back down, then you can come down with her, and we can work this out with no one falling to their death."

"Negotiations?" Eddie sneered. "Why should I give up my advantage?"

"We could be here forever with this stand-off."

"Not really. In fact, why don't I get this fuck party going right now?"

Eddie's free hand grabbed her breast and fondled. She stiffened with a gasp. Tyler jerked forward, but stopped with a pained look. He stared at them grimly.

Suddenly Eddie made a gacking noise and let go of her. She tumbled forward. Tyler caught her and steadied her. She looked up.

Eddie's eyes bulged as his hand grasped at a yellow rope looped around his neck. Above him crouched Max pulling tight on the rope.

"What the hell do I do with him?" Max cried.

"Tie the rope around a tree," Tyler said.

Max yanked on the rope, causing Eddie to rise to his feet, and wrapped the end around a tree trunk.

"Keep it snug," Tyler said, "but don't kill him."

Max tied it in place. Eddie grasped the rope above the knot of the loop with both hands to keep himself from strangling.

"He can't take you and me if we kill him, right?" Max said. "Would he take Amy?"

"No killing! I won't let him take any more people. I have an idea."

Eddie let go of the rope and leaned into the loop, choking himself.

"Don't let him kill himself!" Tyler cried.

Max slid down evenly with Eddie and pushed his head back. Eddie fought him, but kept breathing.

"Now what?" said Max. "I have a damn tiger by the tail!"

"Hang on one second."

Tyler held Amy by both arms and gazed into her eyes. Apprehension filled her. What was he planning?

He gave her a kiss. "Amy, please trust me. There's no other way."

"What do you mean?" She was on the verge of tears.

"I love you." He hugged her and kissed her deeply. "There's no other way," he whispered.

He scrambled up to Max and Eddie. "I'll take over. You protect Amy."

"What are you gonna do?"

"Just do it!"

"Tyler!" Amy cried, weeping openly.

Reluctantly Max moved out of his way. Tyler positioned himself and held Eddie's head back. Max climbed down to Amy and stood beside her with his arm around her. She pressed against him as she watched Tyler with a terrible foreboding.

"Doesn't matter what you do, Tyler," Eddie said. "I'll never stop."

Tyler shoved his face into Eddie's. "I know. You're a pathetic soul that can only get a thrill by terrorizing helpless women."

"I terrorized you pretty fucking good too, asshole!"

"Now it's my turn."

Eddie laughed derisively. "You men are so ridiculous! Always thinking you can save your woman from me."

"You're such a simpering, sniveling *pussy*! You can't even possess someone who has a little strength."

Eddie's eyes glared at him.

What is he doing? Amy cried in her mind. *He's infuriating him.*

"Look who you're possessing right now!" Tyler taunted. "Some pussy little boy who can't even wipe his own ass without his mama."

Max stiffened at the insult to his friend, but said nothing. Amy was utterly confused. Tyler never talked like this!

Eddie thrashed about in a rage, "I'll take you, you son of a bitch!"

"*You're* the son of a bitch! Your mother was a diseased whore and your daddy a crater-faced, sweaty pig that could only get laid by paying for it."

Eddie cried out in a rage and pommeled Tyler with his fists. His leverage was too weak to do any harm.

"And you were a weaselly, sickly thing that wet himself in the presence of females. I bet you can't even get it up unless you terrorize a girl."

Eddied raged and fought with all his might, but Tyler pressed against him with his entire body, holding him in place.

"If you were ever with a real woman, your dick would shrivel up like a raisin."

"*Fuck you!*" Eddie shrieked. "I'll take you, I swear to God! I'll take you, then I'll have her, then I'll kill her. You'll watch ringside as your own body destroys her!"

Tyler pressed his nose against Eddie's. "Come get me."

He pulled on Eddie's head, digging the rope into his throat. Eddie squirmed and choked.

Amy screamed.

Max shouted, "What the hell!"

Eddie's struggles grew weaker and weaker, until he finally became still. Tyler slid down with exhaustion to a sitting position, breathing hard.

Max and Amy moved toward Tyler, but stopped when he suddenly jerked. His head popped up and his eyes widened. He trembled, sucked in a deep gasp, and held it. His entire body relaxed, and he let the breath out in an even flow.

"Tyler?" Amy said with a whimper.

Tyler peered down at them. A grin formed across his face, and a creepy chuckle dribbled out soft and slowly, growing into a loud laugh. Max and Amy stepped back in shock.

Tyler threw his arms up triumphantly. "*I took him!*" He leered down at Amy. "And now I'll have you at last."

Amy shook and wept with despair. Max pulled her behind him. "You still have to deal with me."

Shock splashed across Tyler's face. He trembled all over. It turned into thrashing. Suddenly the thrashing stopped. His face broke into a satisfied smile.

"You didn't take me. I took *you*!"

Tyler's eyes widened with dread. "No-o-o-o-o-o-o!" he howled.

"Tyler!" Amy shouted. "What have you done?"

"My God!" said Max.

Tyler's demeanor calmed down. "Max, it's me, Tyler. I've got him, trapped here inside."

Amy shook her head, tears flowing.

"God, Tyler, why?" Max said.

Tyler jerked and tensed, then relaxed. He tensed again, shuddered, and relaxed again. "It's the only way. He won't hurt anyone anymore, at least for one lifetime."

"No, you can't do this," Amy sobbed.

Tyler tensed, jerked, relaxed, shuddered, relaxed, over and over. "Can't do anything about it now. I can fight him. I can stay in control."

"Holy shit," Max murmured.

"He keeps fighting, but I'm keeping him down."

Tyler suddenly trashed and rolled back and forth. He cried and groaned with effort. Amy clung to Max as she watched.

The thrashing subsided. He smiled wearily with his eyes closed. "So far."

"Good God, Tyler, you can't live like this," Max said.

Tyler whipped his head back and forth. He calmed and opened his eyes. "Amy, I love you. I'm sorry I had to do this, but I had to protect you. It's the only way."

"No! Max, bring him to a priest. We can exorcise that thing out of him."

"Would it work?" Max asked.

Amy pushed on his chest. "Don't give me that! We have to try."

"No, Amy!" Tyler said. "This is the only way to stop him for good. You can go live your life in peace.

"Peace?" she said incredulously with her voice quavering. "You call this peace?"

"Max," Tyler said, "call the police. Tell them there's a raging lunatic—a psychotic murderer up here. Bring them to me. I'll act the part."

A burst of thrashing hit him. After a short time he regained control. "Blame all the murders on me."

"Won't they execute you?" Max said.

"I'll plead insanity. With this thing in me, it'll be easy to convince them."

The thrashing hit harder. "You fucking son of a bitch! You're not locking me up!"

Tyler fought hard to regain control. "They'll put me away. They can treat the hell out of me, but I'll never get better. I'll be locked away in a padded room for life." He smiled at Amy. "They'll give me the drugs you wanted to give him to keep me pacified."

He quelled a quick burst of thrashing, then gazed on her lovingly. "And my Amy will be safe. I love you, Amy."

Amy broke away from Max and climbed up to Tyler. "I can't let you do this. I'll fight that thing for a lifetime with you by my side before I let you live in that hell."

She reached Tyler's feet. One leg drew back. Max grabbed her from behind and pulled her away before the leg thrust forward.

Tyler looked at his leg in horror. "Get her out of here, Max! Call the police. I'll be waiting."

Max nodded and pulled a struggling, weeping Amy down toward the road. "No, Max," she pleaded. "Let me go."

Tyler closed his eyes and rested his head on the exposed root. Amy gazed at him through wet eyes as Max pulled her away. Tyler sat calmly, his head occasionally jerking.

Suddenly his eyes popped open. "Max, *wait!*"

Max and Amy stopped, peering at him. Amy hoped against hope he had a better idea.

Tyler's eyes stared into space. "Amy, I was right." He chuckled. "I was right!" He looked down at them. "It's not a devil. It—*he*—was a human being. A serial killer. A sexual predator who murdered his victims."

He suddenly jerked and thrashed. "Don't listen to him, Amy! He's lying."

Tyler pushed the thrashing aside. "They executed him, but somehow he avoided his eternal destiny. He's caught between mortal life and hell."

Tyler's body made a mighty jerk, then calm eyes gazed at Amy. "Don't let him trick you, my love."

Tyler's head jerked sharply. The calm expression vanished.

"It's me, Amy. Tyler. I discovered another way. I can stop him *forever!*"

He stood and took slow steps toward her. Max pulled her close. "Kill me, Max. I can...I can hold him when we die. I can drag him down to hell where he belongs."

A pleading look appeared. Tyler continued to step toward them. Max backed off with Amy. "Don't kill me, Max. It's just trying to escape."

The pleading look disappeared. "Please, Max, you've got to kill me. I can save everyone from him forever. I won't have to fight him for a lifetime."

"Amy, which one is which?" Max cried.

Mouth gaping, she shook her head.

The pleading look again. "That thing is trying to trick you into killing me so it can escape."

A calm look. "Amy, I'll be free of him, and you'll be safe."

Tyler backed them up against the wall of the crevice.

"I don't know what to do!" Max cried.

"Bring him to a priest!" Amy cried.

"No!" Tyler said. "That'll just release him, and I won't be able to drag him down to hell."

"But it'll save *you*," Amy said.

"Stay back," Max said.

"Please, Max," Tyler said.

Max shook his head. "I can't kill you. I don't know which of you..."

Tyler sighed in resignation. "I understand." He lunged for Amy, shoving Max aside. Max barely caught himself from toppling with a hand on the wall of the crevice.

Tyler squeezed Amy in a fierce embrace. "I love you, Amy. Goodbye!"

He pressed his lips hard against hers, then let go of her and ran down toward the highway. Max ran after him, followed by Amy.

Tyler dashed through the trees until he came to the brink of the road. He waited there, watching. Amy heard a vehicle approaching. "No, no, no!"

Tyler leaped out into the street. A delivery truck collided full force with him and screeched to a stop. Amy screamed.

Tyler hit the pavement hard and lay still. Max and Amy rushed out of the forest. The driver hurried out with a shocked expression. "He came out of nowhere!"

Amy dropped to her knees beside Tyler. Blood seeped from his mouth. His eyes focused on her.

"I love you, Amy," he whispered.

His eyes glazed over. He took one last breath. Amy wept profusely. Max pulled her to her feet and held her as he looked around apprehensively.

The driver pulled out his phone and called 911. Max peered all around. Amy watched the driver, tears streaming, a sickly knot in her stomach.

They watched and waited for something to happen.

Amy sat on the end of the sofa, as far away from the window as she could. She hugged her legs and stared at the television. She didn't pay the slightest attention to what was on. It wasn't a horror movie, and that's all that mattered.

The curtains were closed.

Hard as she tried, she couldn't keep the images from flashing in her mind. The faces of the people who died. The snarling faces of the people that thing possessed. The van smashing into Tyler. His last whisper of love.

She looked at the front door for a moment, then at the window. For a long time she stared at the curtains. Then she stood and crept toward them.

She placed her hands on them and stood thinking. On an impulse, she flung them open.

Blackness.

Leaving them open, she returned to her spot on the sofa and sat angled toward the window, hugging her legs. Without moving, she stared at it as the television played.

The blackness seemed to close in on her.

Godblind

Blinders pulled on the reins, urging Phylo to rise up and whinny. As Phylo's forehooves hit the ground, Blinders kicked him in the ribs. The horse shot forward with a vengeance, running toward the forbidden forest. Forbidden— but only to Blinders.

Father ran out of the house toward him, waving his arms wildly and shouting something Blinders couldn't hear with the wind whooshing past his ears and the hooves pounding. It didn't take much imagination for Blinders to guess what Father shouted. "Don't go in there! The Gods will punish you."

It was an idle threat, made often by the parents of Athens. It had no more effect than the threat of the Minotaur eating misbehaving children. Of course, this time Father was serious when he said it, but it made no difference. The

Gods were too softhearted to ever do anything that could be considered real punishment—not to a boy. A rapist or murderer, certainly, but not a boy.

Yesterday, the first time Blinders tried to escape into the forest, he was on foot. He didn't make a desperate dash then because the forest wasn't forbidden to him then. In fact, he wandered in the forest often. If he went too far, the voice of his family's patron goddess, Athena, warned him.

"Where are you going, Blind Boy?" the soothing female voice spoke from the trees.

"I'm taking a walk in the forest," he answered, and it was the truth.

"Don't go too far," Athena said with compassion. "Since you can't hear us, we couldn't direct you back if you got lost."

Which made no sense, since Blinders heard her just fine. But he knew what she meant. He heard the Gods differently than any other person. Everyone else claimed to hear them in their heads, but Blinders heard them like he heard every other sound—through his ears. And when he heard the Gods through his ears and anyone else was standing nearby, they could hear them through their ears too, not in their heads. Sometimes he wondered if they were all making fun of him.

Mother gave him answers to questions that were as confusing as Athena's. One question bothered him for a long time. He finally got up the courage to ask her. "Why am I called Blind Boy? I can see just fine. Better than some."

"Because you can't hear the Gods speak to you," she said, not looking up from her spinning. He knew she was evading his question, because whenever she answered him openly, she always looked at him.

"But I do hear the Gods speaking, all the time."

"Not in your head."

It was a frustrating answer. Even if others really did hear the Gods in their heads, what difference did that make? Did it matter if you heard them in your head or through your ears? Wasn't the important thing that you heard them and obeyed? Why give him such a humiliating name over a pointless thing like that?

Blinders decided to ask another question. "If I can't *hear* the Gods, then why call me Blind Boy? Why not call me Deaf Boy?"

Mother stopped her spinning and looked up—but not at him—and sighed, then held out her arms to embrace him. He obliged, burying his head into her ample breasts. He always loved Mother's embraces.

"The rest of us can hear words *and* see visions from the Gods in our heads." She stroked his hair. "You were born without any of these abilities. So the Gods named you Blind Boy."

Hear voices. See visions in their heads. It sounded crazy.

That was the day Blinders began to question the Gods.

Not their existence. He heard them himself, speaking from the trees, or the posts of the corral fence, or the walls of their home, or from the linnix on his desk. But he questioned the things they said. What was all this about voices and visions in people's heads? Why was he the only person, apparently in the whole world, who couldn't experience this? And why give him a demeaning name that marked him as completely as the brands Father placed on their horses?

The only thing that kept him sane was the nickname Mother gave him that he insisted everyone call him: Blinders. He pretended it was a reference to the blinders of horses, which he loved, and not derived from his hated Gods-given name.

When his voice began to crack and his underarms grew hair and the fuzz of manhood sprouted on his chin, when his penis enlarged like a cancer and grew a mane around its neck that one day became as thick as a lion's, Blinders had a dream. He dreamed of Lethia, the daughter of their neighboring rancher, walking slowly and voluptuously naked toward him. He was naked himself— not surprising, since they were at the lake where the youth in the area gathered to swim.

He'd seen Lethia naked many times at the lake, but only recently had she begun to change into a woman. She had hair growing from her underarms and her crotch as well, but instead of the beginnings of a beard, her body did more fascinating things. It began to fill out and curve, and on her chest the buds of motherhood sprouted.

So when Blinders saw her naked in his dream, it was no imaginary body he saw. He saw her as she really was. And it excited him greatly, even more than the view in real life.

She strode up to him and embraced him. The touch of her skin against his ignited a fire in his loins. He pushed his lips against hers and caressed her buttocks. The loin fire exploded in a series of bursts, waking him up. He panted as his wits returned from the fog of sleep.

Being a hot summer night, he was sleeping nude with no covers. His body was drenched in sweat and a strange feeling of relief. He moved his hand to touch his penis, remembering the fire that had burned within it in his dream, and found a sticky slime all over his genitals and lower belly.

He remembered Father talking about this, the day he told him about becoming a man. How the changes in his body meant that he was growing the power to be a father himself. He explained the process of creating a baby and the laws of the Gods that he must follow to keep from creating bastard children with no family.

Part of his explanation included the Dream of Eros. It was a gift from the Gods, Father said, to help young boys get a release from the craving in their bodies that kept pressuring them to love women. Blinders had his first Dream of Eros! He was so proud, he couldn't wait until morning to tell Father and show him the first spurt of seed his body had generated, so he ran over and woke them. Dreary from sleep as they were, both Father and Mother celebrated his experience.

The next day, Blinders decided to try out other instructions Father gave him. Since boys had no control over the Dream of Eros, there was another thing they could do to control the urge to spurt their seed into a girl. Father called it self-love, but his friends used the more vulgar term, "Pumping the staff of Zeus."

So he wandered into the forest when no one was looking, and when he reached the point where Athena asked, "Where are you going, Blind Boy?" he gave her a different answer.

"I've come to love myself."

He removed his clothes, sat and leaned against a tree, and played with his penis as he had done many times before as a child. But this time should be different. This time his body could generate the seed of a man.

Compared to the Dream, the explosion was exquisite because he was fully awake and could savor every moment of it.

This time there was no sticky mess on his body—it spattered on the ground. After calming his breathing back to normal and letting the wind dry the perspiration on his skin, he stood, put his clothes back on, and walked.

"Did you enjoy your self-love?" Athena asked.

"Yes, I did, Goddess," he answered. He felt as if Athena were a second mother to him.

"Where are you going now?"

"I'm taking a walk through the forest." He said it as he headed in his usual direction that didn't take him any deeper into the trees. But as he said the words, he felt an urge to go somewhere different. The path he always took before was the path of a boy. Today he had generated the seed of a man.

Abruptly he turned and walked deeper into the forest. "Where are you going, Blind Boy?" Athena said. But this time the compassion in her voice was absent. This time she asked it with urgency.

"Just a walk in the forest," he called back as he broke into a trot. *As a man*, he added to himself.

"Turn back, Blind Boy," Athena called from the same tree she'd been speaking through. "You'll get lost."

Blinders stopped. How could he get lost? Wouldn't Athena be able to watch him from anywhere? Couldn't she speak to him from any tree and guide him back?

"Blind Boy," she called from the same tree, some distance behind him.

No, he realized, she couldn't speak to him from any tree!

His mind began to race. The more he thought about it, the more he realized Athena had always spoken from only certain trees. He never paid enough attention to notice before. He always assumed she could do it from any tree.

This was a more exciting exploration than merely heading deeper into the forest. Trees were trees no matter how far he wandered. But the mystery of Athena's voice was a real thing to explore, a real mystery to solve.

Blinders jogged back and prostrated himself before Athena's tree. "I beg your forgiveness, Goddess," he prayed. "I'll be more careful."

"That is well," said Athena.

Blinders stood and walked his usual path. He needed to keep Athena talking, so he asked her the question he still didn't have a satisfactory answer to, the same one he asked Mother.

"Why am I called Blind Boy?"

"It's the name the Gods gave to you."

"Yes, but *why* that name?"

"Because you were born without Godsight." Her voice came from behind, from the same tree, even though he passed a larger tree at this moment. "You cannot hear the voice of the Gods in your mind, so we must speak to you through your ears."

"But if I can't hear the voice of the Gods, then why not call me Deaf Boy?"

"Your mother already answered these questions for you." The voice was fainter.

"I wanted to ask you, to see if there's more you could tell me." He did his best to keep his voice calm, even though the excitement of discovery grew inside him.

Just as quiet, but from ahead of him, Athena said, "When we speak to the minds of people, we give them visions as often as words. From birth you could neither hear the voices nor see the visions of the Gods. Therefore we called you Blind Boy."

Blinders almost missed the implications of what Athena said. From birth? How would they know a newborn baby couldn't see the visions of the Gods? How would a newborn baby let them know?

He asked Athena that question, tensing a little because it might be considered blasphemy. But Athena responded with her usual kindness. And her voice was louder now as he approached a tree ahead of him.

"We are the Gods. We know everything." If she intended any chastisement in the answer, she kept it from the tone in her voice.

"I beg your forgiveness for such a foolish question." He walked up to the tree that had spoken and stood before it, examining it carefully. He asked the final question on his mind.

"But if I'm already cursed with Godblindness, why make things worse by giving me a name that adds to my shame?"

He studied the tree as she spoke. "Your father is looking for you. It's time to feed the horses. You must return home now."

There it was! A small portion of the bark had vibrated as she spoke. He reached up to touch the portion.

"*Now*, Blind Boy!" Athena demanded. It was the sharpest tone she'd ever used with him.

He dropped his hand quickly to his side and bowed his head. "Yes, Goddess." He turned and ran, buoyed by the excitement of his discovery.

Athena could only speak from certain trees!

If Athena could only speak from certain trees, that meant the trees must have been prepared in advance. And *that* meant the Gods must not be as omnipotent as they claimed.

Or was that fair? Had he actually ever heard the Gods claim omnipotence? Or was it always other people who made the claim? He couldn't remember.

But did it make any difference? Even if the Gods never made the claim, they also never corrected those who did. Wasn't it the same thing?

As he lay in bed that night, Blinders thought out his plans for the next day. His excitement kept him awake for some time. This time when he finally slept, he had no Dream of Eros.

The next day after breakfast and cleaning the stables, he headed for the lake where Mother always expected him to go and wash the horse soil from himself. But when he was far from home and stables, he turned quickly and dashed for the forest, stooped over so the tall weeds of the prairie could hide him. Once he made the protection of the trees, he stood up, stretching his back.

He never entered the forest from this place before, so he wasn't quite sure what to expect. Until yesterday, he assumed Athena would stop him about the same distance into the forest as any other time, but today he wondered just how many trees had been prepared for Athena to speak through.

She also spoke to him through trees elsewhere besides the forest. She spoke to him through trees in the grove next to the lake where all the children swam. She spoke to him from the stray trees on the far side of the ranch, where trees were few and surrounded by pasture. Did the trees that Athena spoke through encircle the entire ranch? Did they extend far from the ranch? Did they fill the world?

As Blinders thought about it, he realized he'd never gone far from the ranch. The lake was as far as he ever ventured alone. When he rode Phylo, he only rode in the near reaches of the forest or on the prairie.

In fact, he'd never been in anyone's home but his own. He usually met his friends at the lake or the temple or the community square. Even the homes of his relatives was a place he'd never been. They always came and visited his family. Visits from others were rare in any case, since everyone had plenty of work to do on their ranches and farms.

Always, whenever he ventured too far from the familiar places, the voice of Athena would vibrate from a tree: "Where are you going, Blind Boy?"

Today he would find out what happened when he didn't turn back.

He trudged through the forest, mottled with stable filth. His path was straight into the trees, away from his house. At the usual distance, the familiar question came to him.

"Where are you going, Blind Boy?"

The voice came from his left, perhaps twenty meters away. He headed for the tree he thought it came from, stood in front of it, and said, "I'm going for a walk in the forest."

"You usually don't walk in this part of the forest."

He had the wrong tree. It was the one to the right of this one. He moved over and stood before it. "I was heading for the lake, but then I decided to come here first."

"Wouldn't it be better to go to the lake first and wash, as your parents expect you to?" There was nothing in the tone of her voice that suggested an accusation, but he felt it nonetheless. *Why did you deceive your parents before coming here?*

Or maybe it was just his conscience bothering him.

He feigned self-consciousness. "I wanted to come here and love myself. I didn't want to wait."

"It would be more sanitary to wash yourself off first."

He found the vibrating patch and wanted to touch it.

"You could force disease into your penis. It would be better if you visited the lake first."

He felt a twinge of guilt lying to Athena, especially since it appeared he got away with it. He had no intention of "pumping the staff of Zeus" right now.

But excitement overcame his guilt. He lied to the Goddess and *got away with it!* Shouldn't a Goddess know he was lying?

Or maybe he hadn't gotten away with it. Did she know, but only humored him out of compassion? After all, in spite of the lie, she still insisted he go to the lake and not remain out here.

But if she couldn't tell he was lying, that would mean not only was his mind blind to the Gods, but the Gods were also blind to his mind!

That would explain why they knew at birth he was Godblind. The blindness worked both ways.

It was all he could do to keep his breathing even and his posture casual. This was something he had to verify! Was there more he could do to test this new idea?

He decided the plans he already made would help him verify the blindness of the Gods. He began to walk. "Perhaps you're right, Goddess. It would be better to wash first."

But he didn't head back to the lake. He headed in the direction he figured the next prepared tree would be. And he counted his steps as he walked.

"That's the wisest thing to do. You'll have many opportunities in your life for self-love. There's no hurry to do it this moment."

Her voice faded behind him. He had to keep her talking. "Goddess, since I had my first Dream of Eros, I've been thinking of the girl in it."

"Do you think of her in erotic ways?"

"Yes." A partial lie. He was too busy thinking about the questions he had to have thought of Lethia more than a few times.

"Remember that you must not love any girl until you marry. It's a great sin to create a bastard child with no family."

"But what if I can't help myself? The feelings in my dream were strong."

"Which girl is it?"

The voice had come from ahead that time. He counted thirty-seven paces until he reached the tree. He smiled with satisfaction that Athena had fallen for his bait. He wanted her to give him the lecture on chastity before marriage to keep her talking.

He was about to answer her question when the realization hit him. She didn't know who the girl was! If she didn't know that, she couldn't see his dreams. She really was as blind to his mind as he was to hers.

Or was she humoring him again? The Gods were notorious for endless patience and asking questions they already knew the answer to. It made people think and come up with their own answers. It might be more time-consuming, but it was more beneficial to humans. It taught them how to think.

At least that's what Father taught him. But was this a question like that? He had to be sure. Carrying out his plans might confirm it.

"She's Lethia, the daughter of our neighbors."

"She is attractive," Athena agreed, "and becoming a woman. But that makes her dangerous. You must never be alone with her, especially when you two are naked. If you're truly interested in her, it would be wise to begin court-ing her."

Athena's voice was strong again, and Blinders could pick out the tree that it came from.

"But I'm not old enough to court yet."

"You're not old enough to *marry* yet, not for another year. But you could court her during that year."

Blinders ignored the tree and passed by it. As discreetly as he could, he veered his path deeper into the forest, wondering how soon Athena would no-tice. He began counting out paces.

"Where are you going, Blind Boy?"

The question shocked him, coming so soon. "I'm going to the lake to wash up." He could feel himself trembling as he lied.

"But you're going in the wrong direction. You might get lost."

Athena didn't seem to be aware what Blinders was thinking now either. Why would she warn him about getting lost if she knew he deliberately chose this direction?

Twenty paces.

"I am?" he said, trying to keep the excitement out of his voice.

"Blind Boy, you must turn back immediately. There is danger out there."

Thirty paces. All he could think about was getting away. He couldn't come up with another stalling remark, so he kept quiet.

"*Blind Boy, where are you going?*" Her voice was actually shrill. It wasn't the same formal tone she always used. It almost bordered on panic.

Forty paces. He broke into a sprint.

"*Blind Boy!*" The words reverberated like a chorus from multiple trees, all behind him. He ran and ran.

The ground started its upward slope to the foothills of the great Olympic mountain range. Although Mt. Olympus itself, the abode of the Gods, was several peaks to the south, he still felt the irony of climbing toward the mountains of the Gods while trying to get away from the Gods.

Athena's voice grew fainter and fainter until he couldn't hear her at all. Not one other tree spoke to him as he ran. He was certain of it now. There were no trees prepared to speak to him outside the boundaries of a circle encompassing his family's ranch.

Whether the Gods were truly blind to him would be proven beyond doubt on this flight. How soon would anyone find him? If the Gods could see him, they could direct a search party to him at once. If it took them a long time to find him, that meant the Gods could not direct the party to him. They could not see him.

The trees crowded in on him. He couldn't avoid multiple scratches as he pushed his way through the thickening brush. He should have worn more protective clothing before embarking on this adventure.

Ahead a small river splashed over some rocks and down the slope. The sweat from his running had moistened the filth on his body, causing it to reek. Getting scratched all over with horse droppings on his skin wasn't exactly a healthy thing to do. He headed for the river and removed his clothing, waded to a small pool where he sat and rubbed the filth off. It was probably the same river that fed the lake he was supposed to wash in.

That made him feel like less of a deceiver, since he really washed himself after all, and in water that would end up in the lake anyway. That was close enough for his conscience.

The water was icy mountain run-off. When he was clean, he leaped out quickly. The breeze that had been pleasantly cool in the heat of the day now chilled him. He needed to move again to warm up.

But heading further up the slope didn't appeal to him. It was more work to climb uphill, and the growth of the forest looked nearly impenetrable ahead. He rinsed his clothes in the river and put them on, then turned downslope, but in a different direction than he came.

Way below, Blinders heard voices shouting—male voices. A search party. The Gods wasted no time on that! But the fact they were shouting for him rather than coming straight to him had to be the verification he looked for. The Gods couldn't direct the search party to Blinders. They needed the humans to look for him.

The fact that the search party called out to him also confirmed the blindness of the Gods. You only call out to someone who wants to be found. If you call to someone trying hide, that'll make it easier for him to avoid you.

Which is exactly what Blinders did, thrilled that the Gods had no idea what he was thinking. Maybe being Godblind wasn't so bad.

He headed down the slope, but away from where the voices shouted, and away from the direction toward home. He decided, as he hurried along, to try one more test—a daring test. "Athena," he said out loud.

There was no answer.

"Athena," he repeated more loudly, "why do you let them shout? Don't you know I don't *want* to be found? Their shouting helps me hide from them. Why don't you tell them to stop?"

The shouting continued. Not only in the direction where he climbed up here, but also in the direction of home well behind him. The Gods may be blind to him, but they had the sense to send more than one search party—one where he'd last been seen, and one where he might be likely to go.

The chilly water slowly dried, and he felt warmer now. Ahead was a huge boulder perched on the slope—a big piece of mountain that had broken off and rolled down thousands of years ago. It could hide a dozen men.

He tucked himself behind it. Soon the second search party became louder. "Blind Boy!" some called, and others called, "Blinders!"

Someone came close enough that Blinders could hear trudging through the brush, then could see movement through the trees. The man's path would bring him just below the boulder.

If this man passes me, he thought, that proves beyond any doubt the Gods can't see me.

As the man neared, Blinders kept very still. His panting was gone so he could breathe quietly again. The man tromped past, calling "Blinders!" The voice was familiar.

Blinders hazarded a peak after the man passed. He recognized the clothing and the back of his head. It was Lethia's father—their neighbor. He'd recognize the shape of that bald patch anywhere. His name was Eusebius.

Carefully Blinders crept around the boulder into view. All Eusebius had to do was turn around to see him. By now Blinders didn't care. He'd learned all he intended to learn, and now he just wanted to play, taunting the Gods for *their* blindness, as so many had taunted him throughout his life for his.

He followed Eusebius, stepping carefully. The man was far enough now that he probably wouldn't hear, considering the racket he made plunging through the brush and calling out. Blinders took one last look at him to make sure he was still heading away, then bolted in the opposite direction.

"Blinders!" someone ahead of him shouted. The surprise made him stumble as he looked up to see who had shouted to him. He fell headlong and slid a couple meters, scraping skin here and there. A dead branch gashed a thin line of blood on his left arm.

It was Father who rushed toward him. "Are you alright?"

Blinders pushed himself up. His father grabbed his arm and helped him.

"You really should wear better clothes when you go gallivanting off into the forest," Father said as he inspected the gash.

Eusebius ran up from behind. "Is he okay?"

"Chewed up a bit, but he'll be fine." Father helped Blinders brush off the dirt and twigs and leaves that had stuck to him.

"Boys!" Eusebius said with a smirk. "You're lucky you didn't scrape your manhood off!"

Blinders wasn't happy about their conversation. Not today. Not after he'd been thinking of himself as a man for the first time, but acted like a boy in front of real men. That's how they thought of him still—a boy out doing boy's antics. He could see it in their eyes.

But it wasn't exactly amusement he saw. More like irritation. Maybe even a little anger? Were they *so* concerned about his safety? Was there something *that* frightening in the forest?

"Let's get you home, boy," Father said. His insistence on calling him boy didn't help. To Blinders, it meant both immaturity and his hated name.

Blinders noticed that all the shouting had stopped. The Gods knew at once that he was found and ended the search, now that men with Godsight stood by him. That seemed to confirm they really could hear the voices and see the visions of the Gods and weren't just teasing him. But it was small comfort.

Eusebius left for his own ranch. As they walked, Father said, "You never went to the lake, but you're—well, you're not *clean*—but you don't have the horses' filth on you. How did you clean up from the stables?"

How did Father know he never went to the lake? Did the Gods inform him of everything Blinders did? It gave him a sense of violation.

"I washed in the river back there."

"How did you know a river was there?" An alarmed look crossed his face. "Have you been this far into the forest before?"

"No, I just came across it." Blinders was irritated at how upset everyone was that he wandered a little deeper into the forest today. Why was it such a big deal?

"You shouldn't have done that. The Gods are not happy about it."

"But why? I went a little farther into the forest. So what? I'm becoming a man, you know. Am I to be trapped on the ranch forever?"

His father looked at him with disturbed eyes, but didn't answer.

Blinders studied him. Was it true? Was he really supposed to remain on the ranch forever?

They broke out of the forest onto the prairie. Ahead was the stables, the corral, and their house. Blinders stopped, forcing his father to stop as well. He had enough of being treated like a child.

"*Am* I supposed to be trapped on this ranch forever?"

His father peered at him. To Blinders' shock, his eyes teared up. "You'd better head to the lake and wash up before coming home to Mother."

Blinders refused to leave without an answer. Hands on his hips, he glared at his father.

"Just go to the lake and return home," Father said. "Don't go *anywhere* else."

He wasn't going to answer. Blinders realized that *was* an answer. Grimly he walked off toward the lake.

"Blinders," his father called. "By the time you get back, a God-eunuch will be waiting to speak to you."

A God-eunuch? Blinders didn't understand. A God-eunuch was serious business. What had he done that was so terrible?

Three young people swam at the lake, two boys and one girl. The boys were Thanos, his friend, and Bellerophon, someone Blinders tolerated. The girl, to his delight, was Lethia.

Blinders paused as he noticed her. She was naked as she swam. The sight of her brought back the image of her in his dream. The feelings came back too. He wasn't sure if he liked that. It made him feel self-conscious.

"There's the runaway!" Bellerophon said as Blinders appeared. "Thanks a lot for making us chase you down."

Great, Blinders thought. Even the boys were called out to search for him. How long before he'd live this down?

"Where'd you go?" Lethia asked.

"I just went for a walk in the forest," he said as he stripped down. "Why is everyone making a big deal out of it?"

"You mean the Gods?" Bellerophon smirked. "That kind of everyone?"

"Forget it," Thanos said. "Come in, Blinders. You need a rinse."

But he didn't feel like getting in just yet. He tried hard not to stare at Lethia, standing there looking at him with the water reaching only to her thighs. She stared at him as if she knew what he was thinking.

That thought excited as well as embarrassed him. He felt his penis twitching, so he sat down on a log and said, "In a minute."

Thanos shrugged and went back to cavorting in the water with the other two. Now that Lethia was preoccupied, he could gaze at her more openly. Whenever she glanced in his direction, he quickly looked away.

Until his Dream of Eros, he hadn't thought of her this way. He'd grown up with her and thought of her as another friend. She was attractive, even though she was still only halfway to womanhood. Her breasts were definite but small, and her hair below still only a tuft. But he couldn't help but see her as desirable now.

He must feel this way because of his dream. She was in the dream because she was the girl he knew best, he told himself, and now he associated the pleasurable feelings in the dream with her. Before that, he liked her, but hadn't thought of *loving* her.

"What by Hades are you doing?" Bellerophon roared.

Blinders jerked his head up. All three of them stood in the water staring at him.

He realized his hand was on his penis.

"He's pumping the staff!" Bellerophon shouted, pointing and smirking.

Thanos waded out of the water and leaned close to Blinders. "Why are you doing that here?" he said so only Blinders could hear.

Feeling chagrined, he didn't know what to say. "Doesn't everybody do it?" he muttered feebly.

"Sure, but not in front of people—*especially* girls."

"I'm getting out of here," Bellerophon said. "This is too weird for me." He climbed out and put on his clothes. "See you later, Thanos, Lethia. Have fun, Blind Bat."

"I need to go, too," Thanos said, and followed after him.

Lethia stood in the water, shivering a little, gazing at Blinders. He could feel his face burning red—he could *see* the red all over his body. "I-I'm sorry," he mumbled.

"It's okay," Lethia said. "A little strange, but it doesn't bother me. I think."

"I didn't mean to. I didn't really notice I was..." It sounded ridiculous to himself. What a thing to not notice he was doing!

"What were you thinking about?" she asked.

He could think of no way to get out of this. "I might as well just tell you. I don't think I can make a bigger fool of myself than I already have."

"I don't think you're a fool."

That emboldened him. "The truth is..." He took a deep breath. "I had my first Dream of Eros two nights ago. It was... I decided to try self-love for the first time yesterday. It felt...good..."

She smiled. "Yes, it does."

"I was thinking about...something...and I guess I just started playing with my penis. I didn't realize I was doing it."

"I can understand that. Sometimes I play with my hair without noticing."

He thought that comparison was a stretch, but he appreciated the effort.

She climbed out of the water and stood before him. "But what were you *thinking*? You must have been thinking about something if you didn't notice you were doing it."

The burning in his face deepened. Maybe he *could* feel more embarrassed. "I don't know if I want to tell you."

"Were you thinking about me? I noticed you kept looking at me."

His eyes dropped to his fidgeting hands, and he nodded.

"Were you thinking about loving me?"

His eyes shot up to look at her. "No! I mean...I was only thinking how beautiful you are. I wasn't thinking about...actually..."

She appeared relieved. "I'm flattered. But you know..." Her head cocked slightly to one side, as if listening to something. "It's not safe for us to think about such things. Boys and girls shouldn't be loving each other until marriage. It wouldn't be fair to any babies we create."

It was Athena's lecture all over again, as if Lethia were hearing it and repeating it. Blinders realized that's exactly what was happening. Athena, or one of the other Gods, told her what to say, and she repreated it to him.

That angered him. He didn't want to hear what the Gods thought. He wanted to hear what Lethia thought.

"I'm sorry," he murmured as he stood. "It won't happen again." He put his clothes back on.

"Blinders?"

He ignored her and marched away. He just wanted to get out of there.

He wondered what she would have said if the Gods hadn't interfered. *But you know, I couldn't love a Blind Boy anyway.*

Why *would* an attractive girl love him? He was defective. Why marry a Godblind man when you could have any number of whole ones?

The sun was low in the sky. He was halfway home before he remembered he never washed himself. He didn't want to go back to the lake, but he knew Mother would have a fit if he came home unwashed, and the dried blood all over his gashed arm would upset her. And—he suddenly remembered—there would be a God-eunuch there to meet him. He hated the idea of returning where Lethia was, but he had to be presentable.

Let Lethia be gone by the time I get there, he prayed to the Gods in his mind—bitterly, because now he knew they couldn't hear him. None of his silent prayers had ever been heard.

He returned to the lake. Fortunately Lethia had left. He bathed quickly, scrubbing at the dried blood to loosen it, then returned home naked, letting the breeze dry him as he walked. Before he reached home, he put his clothes on.

When he entered the house, Father sat with the God-eunuch, a pudgy, squinty-eyed "man" who would never have the pleasure of a Dream of Eros or self-love. After his embarrassment at the lake, Blinders wasn't so sure he didn't envy the eunuch.

"Blind Boy," the eunuch greeted, extending his hand while remaining seated.

Blinders touched the hand and bowed his head.

Mother came into the room and sat near Father. Blinders studied the eunuch. He couldn't tell if he'd seen him before. God-eunuchs were not a common sight—they only came around for important reasons—and as pudgy as they all were with the same bland white robe and shaven head, it was hard to tell them apart. Blinders couldn't ask his name either because God-eunuchs had no names. They were interchangeable servants of the Gods.

"Blind Boy," the eunuch said, "why did you run off today?"

Blinders had been raised with proper etiquette. He came from a respectable family. He knew that treating a God-eunuch with anything but deference would be a great affront. Yet it was all he could do to hold back the frustration he felt. This was getting very tedious, the way everyone made a big deal out of his little journey. What harm had come to anyone?

"I just wanted to go somewhere I hadn't gone before. I didn't mean anything by it."

"You ran away from Athena," the eunuch said. His composure never changed, as if nothing he said meant a thing to him. "Even when Athena commanded you to return, you did not."

"I—" A lie formed on his lips. Would the eunuch know? Why should a eunuch know any better than the Gods? "I didn't hear her. The wind was rustling the leaves, and my movement through the brush was noisy."

The eunuch impassively glanced at his parents, then looked back at him. "You ran away deliberately and hid from both Athena and the searchers she sent to find you. These are the acts of a rebellious heart."

This was more than Blinders could take. "What does it matter if I go farther into the forest? Why should Athena forbid me from doing it? What harm did I cause?"

The eunuch's brow wrinkled, apparently in confusion. "It's too dangerous deep in the forest."

"More dangerous for me than anyone else my age? Are other boys forbidden from going there?" As he asked it, he realized he didn't know. Maybe they *were* forbidden.

The eunuch extended his arm so the palm faced the floor. "By decree of the Gods, the forest is now forbidden to you, Blind Boy. You are not allowed to go in there at all."

Blinders was too shocked to react right away. Banned from the forest completely? Why?

The eunuch stood, his business finished.

"Thank you for coming, Sir," Father said. Mother nodded in agreement.

"May the rebelliousness of your son's heart calm, and happier days come to you," he said as he left.

Blinders leaped to his feet in anger. How dare he say such a thing!

Mother held him back as he took a step toward the eunuch. The man seemed not to notice as he disappeared out the door.

Blinders quivered with rage. "Why—" he choked out, then had to swallow before he could continue. "Why should I be banned from the forest?"

"Blinders!" Mother said. "What's happened to you?"

He whirled to face her. When he saw how horrified she looked, his feelings softened. As forcefully as he could without sounding harsh, he said, "I don't understand why it's such a terrible thing that I take a walk in the forest."

"You went farther than you were supposed to," Father said.

"*Why* shouldn't I go as far as I did? Why won't anyone give me a good reason?"

"It's too dangerous," Mother said.

"That's not a good reason. I didn't see any more danger there than any other part of the forest."

"If the Gods say it's dangerous, boy, who are you to challenge them?" Father said it with an edge to his voice.

"I'm not a boy anymore. I've become a man."

Father grabbed his arm tightly and stared him down. "If you think becoming a man means rebelling against the Gods, then you don't understand the first thing about being a man."

Blinders shrugged himself out of his father's grasp. "I do know what it means to be a man. It means taking on responsibility. Like I'm going to do right now. It's time for me to feed the horses." He headed for the door.

"You haven't eaten since breakfast," Mother said. "Why don't you have something to eat first?"

Blinders glared at her and kept moving. He was starving, but he wanted to show them he was a man. And he wanted to get away where he could be alone and think.

"Don't run off again, boy!" Father called after him.

Blinders whirled around and glared at him. "Don't call me that anymore!"

More calmly, Father said, "The Gods will track you if you run."

Blinders couldn't catch the laugh before it escaped his lips. "The Gods are as blind to me as I am to them."

Mother gasped and held her hands to her mouth.

"Where did you hear that?" Father asked.

Blinders turned away and headed for the stable.

"You shouldn't treat your parents that way, Blind Boy," Athena said as he neared the gate of the corral. Her tone expressed no disapproval.

He ignored her. He slammed the gate behind him, hoping the noise would hurt her ears through the gate post she spoke from, even though he was taught all his life the Gods felt no pain.

"Don't be angry with me," she said from the doorpost of the stable. "I was only protecting you."

He felt his anger melting. This was his second mother he'd grown up with, and her voice was eternally soothing, loving, forgiving, no matter what he did—except for that one panicky moment in the forest.

"I don't understand what you protect me from."

The horses neighed as he entered. They knew why he was here, since he maintained the routine so well over the years—because he *was* as responsible as any man. Blinders headed for the pile of hay in the far end of the stable and pulled the pitchfork from it.

"There are dangers in the forest you don't know about."

Her voice came from one of the posts holding up the roof of the stable. He shoved the pitchfork back into the hay and approached the post. "What dangers? Lions and tigers and bears, oh my?" It was a line he remembered from an ancient movie he watched years ago. He couldn't remember the name of it.

"Bears and mountain lions, at least."

"Am I the only thirteen-year-old boy who can be harmed by these dangers? Or are all the boys my age forbidden to enter the forest? Because none of them ever said anything about that."

"You are Godblind. We can't direct you away from danger like we can other boys."

Blinders touched the vibrating patch, about a dozen centimeters above his head. It felt soft to his touch, about four centimeters of softness within the hard wood of the post.

"You are blind to me too," he said. "I learned that today."

"I know," Athena said, hinting at no surprise.

He felt for the edges of the soft patch. Barely he could feel the abrupt seam of something on the apparently smooth surface.

"Can you see me now?" he asked.

"Yes, Blind Boy, I can."

"How?" He scraped at the faint seam, until he raised a small lip of it from the surface of the wood.

"I think you're about to find out."

He picked at the lip, slowly working it away from the wood. A thin layer of something peeled away. He kept pulling until a flat circle came off, revealing a circular hole in the post, four centimeters wide. The patch he pulled off had a wood-grain pattern to it, but was thin enough that he could see through it.

Packed inside the circular hole he found three strange instruments, all circular themselves, arranged in a triangle.

"This is the one I speak to you with," Athena said, and Blinders saw the one in the lower left corner of the triangle vibrate. "The one next to it is the one I hear you through."

The circle at the top of the triangle looked different than the others, glassy. He almost touched his nose to the post as he examined it.

"That's the one I see you with."

"Why can't I see you?" His breath steamed up the glassy eye.

"You are Godblind."

"No, I mean, you use these instruments to speak to me and to hear me and see me. Why can't there be one that lets me see you?"

"No human can see the Gods."

"Then why can't there be one to let me see the visions others see in their heads?"

"There can be. Now that you understand better how we communicate with you, we can show you visions through your linnix."

"Are these man-made instruments, or are they artifacts?"

"They are artifacts like the linnices, given by the Gods. We sent eunuchs to your ranch to install them as soon as we knew you were Godblind."

"Why couldn't you show me all this before?"

"We waited until you were ready enough to ask yourself."

He held the thin patch up. "Do you want me to put this back on, to protect the artifacts?"

"It won't stay on now that you've pulled it off. We'll have to send a eunuch to do it."

"You can send that eunuch who was here earlier. He must be the closest."

"He doesn't have the materials with him. It's not that important. But please don't expose any more of the artifacts, for their protection."

"I understand," he said. "How many of these are there?"

"Hundreds. Too many to find and destroy them all."

That made his heart jump. How did she know what he was thinking if she was blind to him? After all these years, she must know him pretty well.

A neighing horse reminded him why he was there. "I need to feed the horses." He hesitated, wondering what to do with the round cover in his hand. Even though his feelings towards the Gods were sour right now, he still couldn't bring himself to toss an artifact like this on the stable floor—something a God-eunuch had come and installed. Finally he decided to fold it and tuck it into the hole, off to the side where it wouldn't disturb the three instruments. When a eunuch came, he could deal with it.

He picked up the pitchfork and got to work. And meditated on what to do about all this new information.

"Tomorrow we go to the temple," Mother said, "so take a proper shower tonight."

A proper shower meant hot water and soap. Blinders didn't care for the perfumy soap smell that lingered after the shower, but he loved the hot water. Much more soothing than the chilly lake.

The sting from his scratches, and especially his gash, didn't make him feel any better about the soap. He rinsed it off as fast as he could, which meant even faster than usual. Heated showers were a luxury that no one who honored the Gods took lightly. It was the precious fire of the Gods, brought down through tubes from Mt. Olympus, that heated the water, so wastefulness was something everyone avoided. Most of his bathing was done in the lake.

The fire of the Gods heated the water, lit up the lamps at night, and most important of all, gave life to the linnices of the world. Through a linnix, people could search out any knowledge ever known to man, as well as call up any of the hundreds of movies that wizards had created in the ancient times for entertainment. Most of those movies told stories set in fantastic worlds, some of them virtually incomprehensible, but they were still fun to watch.

The shower felt refreshing, but Blinders wasn't too happy about the reason for it. The family had planned no trip to the temple tomorrow, so there could only be one reason for this sudden decision: to seek absolution for his acts today. How long would everyone rub it in?

In fact, the more he thought about it, the more it rankled him. There was no way he would go to the temple—not under these circumstances. But his parents would insist that he go.

Earlier today Blinders tried an escape just for a lark. He never intended to really, permanently escape. He just wanted to see what would happen.

Tomorrow's escape would be different.

He had to plan it carefully. He couldn't run off into the forest on foot like he did today. He'd have to be dressed properly and bring supplies and money. And this time he'd ride Phylo.

He lay in bed for a couple of hours until he felt sure his parents were in deep sleep. He gathered up everything he could think of that he needed, packed it, stole some money from his father's purse, and crept out to the stable. He didn't dare go inside the stable for fear he'd wake the horses, and they wake his parents. So he placed his pack next to the door. Since they were going to the temple first thing in the morning, he didn't have to worry about Father heading to the stable to do the early morning chores and discovering it there.

But Father was the least of his worries. All the while he prepared, his hair stood on end as he waited for the voice of Athena to cry out, "What are you doing, Blind Boy?" He tried to be as quiet as he could, hoping the night was dark enough with moonrise still a couple of hours away to keep the Gods from seeing him through those little round artifacts.

It was a dangerous gamble. He didn't know how sensitive the senses of the Gods were. They were Gods, after all. Perhaps he didn't have a chance.

Maybe their senses would be less divine filtered through the artifacts.

There was one other possibility he didn't know if he should dare hope for. Maybe the Gods slept. The ancient stories of the Gods from the original land called Greece indicated the Gods shared many of the weaknesses of men. Was the need for sleep one of them?

But he also knew those ancient stories mixed lots of fantasy with truth. He couldn't count on any of the details to be accurate.

So he knew he took one big gamble getting ready, even in the dead of night. But how else could he prepare?

All his hair-crawling was for naught. He was able to settle back into bed with everything ready, and not once did a God so much as sniff at him. Perhaps it was true after all that the Gods slept.

Or perhaps they were giving him lots of rope to hang himself with. He would find out in the morning.

If he had any sense, he'd ride off now. But picking his way through the forest in the dark sounded like real danger. And after everything that happened that day, he was exhausted. He needed some sleep before he left.

On the other hand, a horse galloping off would likely attract the attention of even a sleeping God. So it probably didn't matter when he left. The Gods would sound the alarm as soon as he fled.

He planned to wake up before everyone else so he could sneak away unnoticed and get as big a head start as possible.

Better to get the sleep he needed now and count on the speed of Phylo to win his freedom.

"Up, boy!"

It was Father. Blinders had slept well past sunrise, and everyone was awake!

He certainly got the sleep he needed, but at the expense of sneaking away. Now he'd have to make a run for it in full view.

He had to move fast, before anyone noticed the missing supplies—especially the money. He hurriedly dressed and came out.

"I'll saddle the horses," he cried as he dashed past his parents.

"We're having morning prayer," Mother called.

"I'll just take a minute," he called over his shoulder.

He knew the instant he grabbed the pack, the Gods would see his plan. They'd warn Father, and he'd come out to stop him. He needed to do this quickly.

He needed to saddle Phylo first, *then* grab his pack. He contemplated riding off bareback, but knew in the long run that would only slow him down.

The pack was still there. The Gods hadn't noticed it or hadn't figured out why it was there. That fact added to his cynicism about their powers. Just how divine were these Gods?

He tightened the saddle on good and made sure the bridle and bit and everything else was in order. He couldn't afford a slip-up once he began to ride.

When everything was perfect, he knew the moment of truth had come. The next thing the Gods would expect him to do was saddle Mother and Father's horse. When he went out to get the pack and climb on Phylo, the Gods would know.

He looked down and snapped his fingers as if he'd forgotten something, without quite being sure what it was he might have forgotten, then walked toward the stable door. Would this fool the Gods enough to buy him extra seconds?

He swung the door wide, then dove for the pack, dashed back to Phylo, hopped on as fast as he could, hooked the strap of the pack around the pommel, and dug his heals into Phylo's ribs. Phylo whinnied unhappily and took off in a gallop.

"Blind Boy, what are you doing?" a dozen voices of Athena cried to him from a dozen artifacts. It was a cry of alarm.

Father ran out of the house toward him, waving his arms wildly and shouting something Blinders couldn't hear with the wind whooshing past his ears and the hooves pounding. It didn't take much imagination for Blinders to guess what Father was shouting. "The Gods will punish you!"

But Father and the Gods were too late. Blinders pulled on the reins, urging Phylo to rise up triumphantly and whinny. As Phylo's forehooves hit the ground, Blinders kicked him once more in the ribs. The horse shot forward with a vengeance, running toward the forbidden forest.

"Blinders!" Father shrieked as the boy and his horse plunged into the trees.

The forest wasn't thick yet, so the horse could maintain his gallop. But Blinders knew from yesterday that this wouldn't remain true forever. He needed to find a path somewhere that Philo could move quickly along.

The river seemed his best bet. But he couldn't let Athena know where he was heading until he was past all the artifacts. He headed straight into the forest without veering toward the river until he reached the invisible perimeter where he knew he'd hear her voice.

"Please stop, Blind Boy." The voice was pleading this time and came from the two nearest trees. "If you turn back now, you will be spared. If you continue on, all is lost."

The word "lost" was nearly lost in the wind, because he didn't waver one bit as he rode past the talking trees. Phylo galloped all the way to the beginning of the slope, where Blinders reigned him in and quieted him down, then turned him to the right toward the river.

He kept his eyes peeled and his ears sharp for the inevitable search party that would come. The Gods were blind to him, but not fools. They'd send searchers to the likely places he'd go. The river had to be an obvious place, one he'd already been to before. Almost he decided to turn away since the river was the worst place he could go.

But where else? He really could get lost in the forest when he left familiar places. The Gods would raise all sorts of search parties this time after the fuss they made about going into the forest. Would any direction make a difference?

He should have thought this through more carefully. All he thought about was getting away into the forest. He hadn't thought one minute past that.

Which way should he go?

He realized with a shock that he didn't dare go where *any* people were. Meeting any other human on earth would be an instant alarm to the Gods.

He'd just exiled himself to the life of a hermit. He could never get near another human being again for as long as he lived.

Would that be so terrible? He loved his parents, but beyond that, what had any human ever done for him? All he was to them was the crippled Blind Boy, Godblind from birth. They all tried to be nice to him, perhaps at the insistence of the Gods, but no one ever truly made him feel welcome. Thalos had been his closest friend, and yet what had they ever done together? Mostly meet at the lake and swim or romp around the shore, or in the community center where activities were prearranged, or a glance and nod at each other in the temple. Lethia had been a friend as well, and most recently an object for his lust. But other than one Dream of Eros, she was no different than the others.

His parents had raised him, cared for him, loved him. But he was a man now who knew enough skills to take care of himself in the wild. He no longer needed them, although he'd miss them terribly. A man does not live with his parents forever—which was apparently what they had planned for Blinders for the rest of his life.

The Gods? To never hear the voice of Athena again? That held a troubling mixture of regret and relief. But what had Athena ever been to him? A second mother? Not really. Athena never held him, kissed him, sung to him. Athena hadn't even taught him as much about the Gods as his own parents had. She was more like a familiar aunt who spoke a few sentences to him each day, but offered little else. Not even a kiss or a penny to buy candy with.

In reality, Athena was a benevolent jail keeper, nothing more. He had no use for her. She couldn't even hear his prayers.

He'd get lonely, but he'd survive, and he'd get used to his isolation. Most importantly of all, he would be free—free of Athena's prison.

Free if no one caught him again. Standing in place, undecided, not far from where he entered the forest while search parties closed in on him, was about as foolish a thing as he could do. In fact, already he could hear the rustling of brush, the plodding of horse hooves. This time no one would shout for him. This time they'd quietly sneak up on him.

What a fool he was, waiting here for so long! He'd expected to hear voices. With the search party so near—with *any number* of search parties coming—he didn't dare move to the right or left. He plunged ahead, up the slope, away from the searchers, knowing that the path would become steeper very shortly, knowing that as Phylo struggled through the thick growth, he'd leave an obvious trail to follow.

Looking behind, he realized he was already leaving a trail. He changed his mind at once—he had no choice. He had to go for the river, because that was the only place Philo could pass without leaving a trail. Of course, the river itself would be an obvious trail, once Philo's path led the searchers to its bank. But at least the searchers wouldn't know if he had gone up- or downstream.

Blinders urged Philo into a gallop. The noise and the movement couldn't be very subtle, and sure enough, he heard a cry behind him and the thudding of multiple galloping horses. The only advantage he had now was a head start and the speed of Philo.

He wasn't sure how quickly the river would appear. He was on foot before and not paying much attention as he fled. But a horse can run much faster than a boy, so it shouldn't be long.

And indeed it wasn't. He saw the water as soon as he heard the babbling. He had no time to hesitate. He had to decide at once which way to go. He felt sure the Gods would send a search party along the river, so upstream was his only chance.

He hit the water and swung Philo hard to the left. Philo picked his way through the water and rocks as fast as he could. Would it be fast enough? There was a bend in the river ahead where the trees masked it. If he could get to it before the searchers came into view...

Then what? The searchers would see no horse tracks on the other side and immediately know Blinders took to the river. At least half of them would follow him upstream even without seeing which way he went.

He pushed Philo as hard as he could, risking a broken leg for his poor horse. Was it worth the risk? "All is lost," Athena had said. Her dire warning sounded like there was no turning back.

All what was lost? He still couldn't figure out why his actions were so terrible. Did she mean he'd assuredly be attacked by a bear or mountain lion and lose his life? That was a possibility, but an "all is lost" possibility? Especially perched atop a horse?

What was so awful about going into the forest? And what would be the awful punishment if he were caught? The Gods had always been so loving and benevolent that Blinders couldn't imagine them exacting a punishment at the level of "all is lost." But he didn't want to find out.

As he rounded the bend, a rumbling wafted out of the forest ahead of him, coming from another sharp bend in the river. Thank the Gods this river had so many bends, or his pursuers would see him in moments.

Philo rounded the bend. The rumbling turned into a thundering. A twenty-meter waterfall blocked his path. He was trapped!

He could ride Philo off into the forest again, but it looked pretty thick. Another trail left in their wake, easily followed. And how long could poor Philo keep this up? He'd tire eventually.

All *was* lost, whatever "all" was. Unless...

"Philo, my friend," he said, leaning forward and patting him on the side of his neck. "You know I love you. You were supposed to be my salvation, but now you're just a burden to me. Please forgive me."

He rode Philo to the shore, pulled loose the pack and climbed off, then whacked Philo as hard as he could on the flank. Philo whinnied and charged into the forest, leaving damage through the brush.

Blinders dove for the waterfall. It pounded his head and drenched his pack, but he was able to scramble through it. On the other side was just enough of a depression in the cliff that he could stand behind the water with only its mist soaking him.

The roar of the fall deafened Blinders from any other sounds. He had no idea how long he needed to stand here before he could safely emerge. Nor did he know how much time his ruse would buy him. How long would Philo run through the thick foliage? Probably not long. Probably the searchers would find him within a minute or two. They'd know what Blinders had done and start searching for him back at the river. They'd look for signs of a boy on foot—on wet feet—and find none. There would be no other place for him to hide than where he was. In moments hands would reach through the sheet of falling water and grip him.

What a fool he was!

He should run. They must have dashed into the forest by now, following Philo's path. In moments they would return and find him. He had a narrow span of time to bolt somewhere else in the forest. They'd return and find his wet trail and follow him again, but that was better than waiting here for hands to grab him.

He readied humself to rush through the waterfall when he heard someone shout, "Over here!" He froze.

Either they took longer to reach the falls than he expected and just noticed Philo's trail, or they already found Philo unmounted and returned to search for Blinders in the only place left to look.

Either way, he could only stay in place and wait.

Seconds passed. No hands grasped at him. They must have followed Phylo into the forest. Now was his only chance.

He dashed through the falls, coming out spluttering and wiping his eyes so he could see.

A lone man stood before him.

"Hello, Blind Boy." It was Eusebius, grinning carnivorously. He turned his head in the direction of Philo's path. "He's over here!"

As Eusebius shouted, Blinders dashed for the opposite shore. It was his last desperate chance.

"Oh, no you don't!" Eusebius cried as he lunged, barely grabbing Blinders' ankle. He fell face-first into the water. His left wrist twisted as it hit bottom. Blinders swallowed a mouthful of water and came up choking.

Eusebius put his mouth close to his ear. "Where do you think you're going, little Godblind boy? Little freak of nature?" He forced Blinders back to a sitting position in the river and clamped a strong rancher's grip onto his shoulder. "Your days of fleeing are over."

Two men appeared from Philo's trail, the second one leading Philo by the reins. Both of them were casual acquaintances of Blinders' family, other ranchers in the area, but he knew neither of them very well. He couldn't remember their names.

"Where was he?" the first one said.

Eusebius gestured with his free hand. "Behind the waterfall. Let's get him on the horse."

The first man grabbed Blinders on the other side, and the second man led Philo to them. "Heave ho," said Eusebius, and the two men launched Blinders into the air and onto his saddle. His pack flew out of his hands, and Eusebius retrieved it out of the water.

"I hope you packed everything waterproof," he said with a wicked grin as he slapped it into Blinders' gut.

He hadn't, but he hardly cared now.

Each of the three men took turns holding Philo's reigns while the others mounted their horses waiting nearby in the river. They didn't want Blinders fleeing again. But he had no intention of fleeing. Where would he go? He already tried and failed.

They stayed with the river until they exited the woods, then rode toward Blinders' home. Father met them coming out of the forest on his horse, taking Philo's reigns from Eusebius. His expression was ugly, and he neither spoke to nor looked at Blinders. "Thank you, gentlemen," he said. "I'm terribly sorry for this trouble, but I think this will be the end of it."

"I certainly hope so," Eusebius said, shooting one more glare at Blinders. The three of them rode off.

Blinders just wanted to get home and take a hot shower. He was soaked to the bone and shivering from icy mountain run-off. But when he held his hand out for the rein, Father said, "Where do you think you're going?"

"To the house."

"Not until I tell you to."

He couldn't remember a time when Father had been so coldly enraged. It was frightening to behold. Between the nasty remark of Eusebius in the river and Father's fuming wrath, Blinders began to think that maybe the "all" that was lost would be pretty bad.

By all rights, he should feel terror mixed with guilt. Yet for some reason he felt calm, but for the shivering and his chattering teeth. With the sopping fabric hanging from his body, he'd stay cold and wet for a long time.

That explained the shivering, but why did he feel so calm? Why wasn't he frightened of his punishment? Why wasn't he feeling lower than an earthworm because he defied the Gods?

It was because he didn't accept that he committed a sin.

Oh, he committed a couple of minor sins. He stole some money and supplies from his parents. He was deceptive.

But no one seemed to care about any of those sins, so he didn't care. All they cared about was the sin of running off into the forest. That's what seemed to infuriate everyone from the great Zeus himself all the way down to neighbors whom he barely knew.

And he had no idea why.

Father led Philo home and into the stable, then said to Blinders, "Get down." He complied, and Father clamped his own strong grip on his shoulder and led him to the house.

Stopping in front of the door, Father said, "You'd better take those dripping things off."

Gladly Blinders removed the sopping clothes. He didn't feel any warmer standing naked in the breeze, but at least he knew he'd dry faster and warm up sooner.

Mother appeared at the door with a big, fluffy towel. "Dry yourself off, son," she said. Her eyes were gleaming with half-formed tears.

He did so gladly, but her misty eyes troubled him. What in the world *would* happen to him? He almost felt like his parents were already separating themselves from him, as if he were on the way to his execution.

"The God-eunuch is here to see you," Mother said as she took the towel from him. "Be respectful, *please.*"

The news sent a chill through his spine. There could be nothing good about this. Yet what else could he have expected? A God-eunuch had appeared over his silly lark from yesterday. If that was bad enough to bring a eunuch around, today's antics must be atrocities.

Mother stepped away from the door, and Blinders entered with the towel wrapped around his shoulders. The God-eunuch sat in the same place with the same posture as yesterday. As far as he could tell, it was the same eunuch. It only made sense.

"Blind Boy, sit down," the eunuch said.

Blinders sat on the floor, his shivering calmer, but not quite gone.

"This boy is cold. Please give him something to warm up with."

Mother ran for a thick blanket, took the moist towel, and draped the blanket over his shoulders. Blinders pulled it around himself. The chill had gone to the bone and the blanket only helped a little more than the towel.

"Blind Boy, I have bad news for you." The eunuch stared at him, but showed no emotion on his face. "You were warned by the Gods to stay out of that forest, but you disobeyed. Twice in two days you disobeyed the warnings of the Goddess Athena. You must now pay the price for your rebelliousness."

Sharp in his mind was the fact that no one seemed to care about the real sins he committed: lying and stealing. Only entering that infernal forest.

"You will leave your home and family. You will never see them again. We gave them ample opportunity to show they could keep you under control, but the events of the last two days prove they no longer can. You clearly have the rebellious heart we thought you might have."

His brain went into shock. Leave home? Leave his family? Never to see them again? What is this nonsense? The punishment was so over-the-top in comparison to his misdeeds that the whole situation became surreal, a dream he could no longer believe in.

But a part of his mind said, isn't this what you wanted? To be away from everyone, to live on your own? Maybe they'll make you the hermit you wanted to be. Maybe they'll banish you from all civilization.

For some reason, when it was his own idea, it was a grand idea. But when it was forced on him, he hated it.

"You will live comfortably," the eunuch went on. "We'll take complete care of you and help you live as enjoyable a life as you can. But you can no longer live here."

"Where will I live?" He hadn't meant it as anything more than a question, but it came out sounding defiant.

The eunuch showed no reaction to his tone. "The location will be hidden from you. But you will be kept in a secure place, never to leave it."

"You mean thrown into prison?"

"It won't be a prison, but you'll be as unable to come and go as if it were."

"I'll be locked up somewhere, and will never be able to get out?"

"That's correct."

Darkly he said, "Sounds like a prison to me."

The eunuch ignored his comment. Tears streamed openly from his mother's eyes, but she stifled any sobs with her hands pressed against her mouth.

"This is the will of the Gods." The eunuch looked deeply into Blinders' eyes. "Do you accept your punishment?"

"By Hades, no!" Blinders spat.

That drew the first emotional reaction he'd ever seen from a eunuch. It was small, barely noticeable, but the eunuch's eyes flinched for an instant. The four of them sat in uncomfortable silence.

"So what does that mean?" Blinders finally said. "If I don't accept it, then I'm free to go?" It was a belligerent thing to say, but the punishment was outrageous, and if, as Athena had said, all was lost, what did he have left to lose?

"You are not. You must still obey the decree of the Gods."

"I will not," said Blinders.

The eunuch must be getting used to his rebelliousness, because this time he didn't flinch. He merely said, "You have no choice."

"Then why did you ask in the first place?"

That caused another wrinkle of confusion in the eunuch's brow. Twice he had confused a eunuch! He was proud.

And amazed at himself. Two days ago Blinders would never have dreamed he could be so arrogant with the Gods. How easy it had come to him! Maybe the Gods were right. Maybe he did have a rebellious heart.

"How can you not accept the decree of the Gods?" the eunuch said. "Their decree is merciful. It's the greatest mercy they can give you under the circumstances. By all rights, they should have you executed."

Blinders gulped. Executed? He'd made a joke to himself moments ago about being executed. He had no idea how close his joke had come to reality.

But his belligerence was not gone. If anything, it increased. Executed for going into the forest? Ridiculous! Insane! There were no words to describe the idiocy of this situation.

"I don't accept the decree of the Gods because it makes no sense. I haven't committed a crime worthy of one year in prison, let alone a lifetime, let alone execution. All my life my parents taught me the Gods are just and merciful. All my life I never saw any reason to disbelieve it. Now all of a sudden it's merciful to imprison me for life because execution is the only alternative? And for what? Because I took a casual walk into the forest?"

The sobs broke from Mother's mouth, filling the room. But Blinders trembled with so much rage that even that couldn't soften him. "If the Gods want me to accept their decree, then by Zeus, they'd better explain themselves!"

The eunuch opened his mouth to speak, but before he could, Blinders blurted, "And I don't want to hear anything about how dangerous it is out there. That just makes it poor judgment to go into the forest, not a sin."

"It's not dangerous to you," Athena's voice burst in, causing everyone but the eunuch to jump. "It's dangerous to everyone else."

The statement shocked Blinders. "*I'm* a danger to everyone?"

"Yes."

"Why?"

"Because you're a Blind Boy. You are Godblind."

"*A* blind boy?" Blinders said with a thrill going through his body. "Not *the* Blind Boy?"

Athena didn't answer.

"Are you saying there are other Godblind people in the world?"

"No. You're the only one."

His excitement crashed into disappointment. For an instant he thought he might not be alone.

"But there was another Blind Boy in the past," Athena added.

He needed a moment to digest this. "How long ago in the past?"

"Two hundred and fourteen years ago," Athena said.

"So he's been dead a long time."

"Yes, he was executed."

A sickening mixture of dread and anger filled Blinders. "What was he executed for? Going into a forest?"

"For sixty-nine murders."

This shocked him even more. He looked around the room. By his judgment, it should have come as a shock to every non-eunuch there. But his parents gazed steadily at him, as if they were gauging his reaction, not experiencing their own shock.

"You already knew this," he said to them.

Mother didn't move as she gazed at him. Her tears had stopped flowing, but they still glistened in her eyes. Slowly Father nodded in response.

"Why didn't you tell me?"

"The Gods forbade us," Mother said. Her eyes pleaded for understanding.

"Why?"

No one answered him.

Blinders turned to the eunuch, although he really intended to address Athena. "What was this other boy's name?"

"Gelasius," Athena answered.

"I see. *Not* Blind Boy."

Blinders continued to stare the eunuch down, since Athena wasn't there to glare at. "So I was forbidden to leave the ranch, and now I'm going to be imprisoned for life, because Gelasius from over two hundred years ago killed sixty-nine people."

"There were also beatings and rapes and thefts," the eunuch answered.

"When you were born," Mother said, "and we found out you were God-blind, the Gods wanted you killed immediately. But I pleaded with them to let you live. We swore we'd keep you under control so you wouldn't turn out like Gelasius."

"What kind of Gods have you taught me to worship?" he said icily.

She ignored him. "They agreed, but said if you ever became rebellious, they would take you from us."

"In these last two days," the eunuch said, "your rebelliousness has exposed itself for all to see. In two short days, you have committed astounding blasphemy and rebelliousness. The Gods were right to want you killed at birth." His face seemed tighter, and Blinders thought he detected emotion spilling into his voice. He got the sense the man was speaking his own feelings, not parroting the Gods.

"When you ran away this morning," Mother continued, "and this eunuch appeared at our door saying the time had come to take you, I thought he meant take you to be executed. When I learned they'd only keep you incarcerated, and that you'd live a happy life—"

"Happy?"

"A life of comfort, I wept with gratitude. It was a blessing from the Gods."

Blinders looked back and forth from his mother to his father. He couldn't believe what he heard. Father's face was grim and unreadable. "Does this make any sense to you, Father?"

His mouth pursed tighter than it already was. His eyes, dry until now, began to glisten like Mother's. "I'm sorry, my son, there's nothing we can do. These thirteen years we've had with you were a gift from the Gods. I cherish them. I wish there could be more. But your actions make that impossible."

"Father!"

"You were warned," he said with harshness, even as his tears slid down his cheeks.

"You were warned," Athena repeated. "All you had to do was obey."

"I was already in prison on this ranch," Blinders murmured. "I just couldn't see the bars." He turned to his mother. "Why didn't you explain all this to me? The reason I disobeyed was that it made no sense."

"She was forbidden to tell you," Athena said. "We had to know if your heart was rebellious. We had to know if you would obey the Gods because they commanded it, not because it made sense."

"And if I *had* obeyed?"

"If you had consistently obeyed over the years, even without understanding, the time may have come when we could let you roam the world freely."

"He's only thirteen!" Father cried, the tears now streaming. "All boys are rebellious at that age. It doesn't mean rebellion is in his heart."

"If you had told me," Blinders hissed. "If you had given me a real name instead of this insult. If you treated me with respect instead of suspicion, I never would have rebelled. I had no desire to rebel two days ago."

"The name was necessary," Athena said, "so everyone would know what you are. For the protection of people everywhere, your infirmity had to be named."

His rage reached its limit. He stood and threw the blanket aside. "Take me then. I spit on your mercy. I do *not* accept the decree of the Gods, but there's nothing I can do. I curse you, God-eunuch. I curse you, Athena. I curse all the Gods. You may as well execute me, because I will hate all of you forever."

Father hid his face in his hands. Mother burst out weeping again. Blinders wondered if the words he spoke now would horrify him later, but all he could feel was the rage.

"You will still be shown mercy, Blind Boy," Athena said. "We will not execute you. Eunuch, take him now. He will go naked with no possessions. All his needs will be provided, and the comfort of his dwelling will be such that he will never need the protection of clothes."

"You want me to remain naked so I'm easy to identify if I escape."

"You won't escape. Take him now."

The eunuch rose.

"Wait!" Mother said as she leaped to her feet and threw her arms around Blinders.

"He must leave now," Athena said softly.

"Wait! First let him... He needs one last hot shower."

"He'll have all the hot showers he wants where he's going," the eunuch assured.

"No, he's dirty and cold now. Let him have a shower before he goes."

"Very well," the eunuch said. "One shower, then he leaves with nothing, and you never see him again."

Mother put her arm around his shoulder and led him to the shower. Blinders didn't understand the point of this. She must be delaying the moment when she'd lose him, but it wasn't like Mother would spend the time in the shower with him. And when he finished, she'd still have to say goodbye.

But he *was* dirty and cold. A shower would feel good. Maybe that's all this was—her final gift for her son.

He turned to her and embraced her. "I love you, Mother. I'm sorry this happened."

"I love you too, my boy, my sweet boy. I'm sorry I can't help you."

They held the embrace until the eunuch drew near as a signal. Blinders left and stepped into the shower and drew the curtain. He turned the water on, steaming hot, and lathered up. He stayed in there, soaking in the heat, until the water started to lose its temperature. This time he wanted to waste as much of the fire of the Gods as he could.

———

The sun approached noon as the God-eunuch led Blinders naked to the stable and had him climb onto Phylo, still saddled.

"I'm hungry," Blinders said. He hadn't eaten all day.

"You can fast for your absolution," the eunuch said without passion.

"I don't want absolution. I want food." Blinders knew all his belligerence only validated everyone's belief that his heart was rebellious, but what did it matter now? It made him feel better.

The eunuch led Phylo by the reigns to where his own horse was tied. Blinders looked at the post, remembering the many times Athena had spoken to him from there. What would they do with all those hundreds of useless artifacts now? Remove them and bring them to the prison?

The eunuch let go of Phylo's reigns so he could mount his own horse. His abortive efforts to lift that large body into the saddle forced Blinders to suppress a laugh. He hated the Gods and the eunuch right now, but he still had no heart to make fun of the man for his weight. That had nothing to do with why he hated him.

The eunuch's horse was huge and powerful—it had to be to hold him up—but Blinders doubted it was fast. Phylo could probably outrun it. But that would only force the Gods to call out more search parties, and this time the searchers' mood might be ugly. The Gods were being merciful by not executing him, but he wasn't so sure his neighbors felt as merciful. If they had to search for him a third time, some of them might decide to carry out the punishment themselves.

Blinders studied the eunuch. If that pudgy creature were not alive to see for the Gods—if some accident happened to him on the way to whatever prison awaited Blinders—maybe he could get enough of a head start to succeed this time.

As they rode away, a loud sob came from behind. Blinders looked back. Father and Mother stood in the doorway, watching him go. They both wept, Mother noisily.

What had he done to them? What had he done to himself? Here he was, already contemplating his first murder like Gelasius, and he hadn't even left the ranch.

For the first time, shame for his acts filled his heart. Maybe the Gods were right. He *had* been rebellious. It came upon him quickly with only a little provocation. In two days he went from a good boy of Athens, a devout worshipper of Athena, to a man who cursed the Gods and dreamed of murdering their eunuch.

What had he done to his parents?

He wept silently himself.

But as his home fell out of sight and his mother's sobs died away, as the heat of the day formed a sleek layer of sweat on his skin and his stomach growled fiercely with hunger, his remorse died. He still felt a touch of guilt for contemplating murder, but he knew there was no way he'd have done it. He couldn't even laugh at the eunuch for being fat. How could he kill him?

But the anger at his unreasonable fate returned along with his determination to escape. It was terrible what all this did to his parents, but it was the Gods who did it, not him. The best thing he could do was escape, then try to get word to his parents that he was free. He still couldn't ever see them again, but his liberty should comfort them.

They approached the gate to Eusebius' ranch. Eusebius waited on horseback beside the road, watching grimly as Blinders rode by, a murderous glare in his eyes. No doubt ready to chase after him if he decided to flee.

His ranch house was set back fifty meters from the road, and Lethia and her mother came out to watch him ride by. On an impulse, he waved to her. Partly he thought it would irritate the Gods for him to act so casual about his punishment, and partly he hoped she'd like it. Would she miss him? Was she crying for him now like Mother had? She was too far away to tell.

She waved back hesitantly, then ran into the house. Blinders imagined she was on the verge of tears and didn't want him to see it. Why not assume that? They'd never be together again, so he could entertain any fantasy he wanted that would make him feel better.

Eusebius galloped up to Blinders and growled, "You'll never see her again, Blind Bat. Good riddance!"

The fierceness of his anger frightened Blinders. Had this man always hated him so much? He never showed it until this morning.

He felt certain if he fled and Eusebius caught him, he *would* carry out the execution.

"He's in the hands of the Gods, sir," the eunuch said, and Eusebius backed off. Had the eunuch feared for Blinders' safety, or was he just spouting some mindless nonsense?

Blinders wondered where they were going. He wasn't supposed to know where his prison was, yet here he was watching exactly where they went. Shouldn't they blindfold him or something? But he wasn't about to suggest it, and he was glad Athena couldn't hear his thoughts.

Other people at other farms and ranches stopped what they were doing to watch him ride by. He felt embarrassed that he rode passed them naked like a beggar. All the men seemed to be mounted on horses waiting for him to pass. None of them said a word to him, and he certainly didn't wave to them. He knew they were making sure he didn't flee.

Blinders hoped his friend Thalos would be somewhere, but he never saw him. That was the only other person he cared to wave goodbye to.

The road led to the center of town where the temple and the community house stood. He'd never been further than that in his life, alone or with his parents. Beyond that, he was told, was the city of Athens, but he had no idea how far it was or what sort of terrain or how many people there were along the way.

Blinders wouldn't kill the eunuch, but he still wanted to flee. This might be his last opportunity to escape for the rest of his life, and his best chance would be when no one but the eunuch was around. They hadn't been left alone one time since they began the journey. The Gods saw to that with the mounted men along the road.

He suspected there would be mounted men all the way to the prison. He felt it in his bones. Blinders began to tremble. He'd been clinging to the hope of escape, but the chilling realization sank in that he was going to prison for life, and there was nothing he could do about it.

Farmers selling their produce appeared along the road. They and their paltry number of customers stopped to watch Blinders pass. Did everyone on earth know what was happening, or was it the mere sight of a God-eunuch leading a naked boy through town?

The spires of the temple appeared ahead. It was small but beautifully wrought. Other structures appeared, including the largest in the city, the community house where social gatherings and courts and fairs took place, where local government representatives and the local police kept offices.

Blinders eyed the produce the farmers offered for sale. What he'd give right now for a fat carrot to gnaw on! "Let me get something to eat here," he said quietly. "Please."

The eunuch stopped his horse as he kept gazing straight ahead. "This boy is hungry. Will someone give an offering to the Gods?"

It was a formulaic phrase that meant to give alms to the poor. It made Blinders bristle to be labeled poor—his family had never been beggars. Yet what had he expected when he asked for food? He had no money, and he doubted a God-eunuch carried any.

A couple of farmers came forward, one with a tomato and apple in hand, and one with two carrots with wilted green tops. They both handed their offerings to the eunuch.

They must know who I am, Blinders thought, and they couldn't bring themselves to give the offering directly to a Blind Boy.

The eunuch handed the food to him, then eased his horse forward. It was all Blinders could do to juggle the four items in both hands. He gripped Phylo with his legs as Phylo lurched forth. He tried to figure out where to tuck the food away so he could eat one while still hanging onto the reins. Finally he wedged the carrots under his left arm, grabbed the reigns with his right hand, and held both the apple and tomato in his left hand. He bent his head down to bite into the tomato without losing his grip on the carrots. Juice squirted all over his chest and arm. He was glad he was naked now so the juice wouldn't stain any clothing.

The tomato gone, he worked on the apple. When all but a core was left, he hugged the carrots tight to his body, leaned forward as far as he could, and shoved the core into Phylo's mouth. His last gift to his beloved horse.

Now he could comfortably chew on the thin carrots. As he ate, the eunuch led him to the doors of the temple. "Get down and wash off," he commanded. Blinders dismounted and fed the remainder of the carrots to Phylo, then walked to the pool in the court of the temple and rinsed off the tomato juice.

The eunuch tied both horses to a post, then turned and faced him. They stared at each other for an instant.

"Is this where my prison is?" Blinders asked, hope rising in him. It didn't seem so bad to be incarcerated so close to home. Maybe his parents could visit him. Maybe Lethia would visit him.

But no, the eunuch had said he would never see his parents again. That enraged him once more. So close to home, and not see them? He knew now he had to escape—somehow. How secure could a prison be in this little community? Some day his chance would come.

"Your prison is not here," the eunuch said.

That disappointed him. He was back to not knowing. "Then where is it?"

"Please get back on your horse," the eunuch responded.

He sighed with frustration and remounted. Everyone in sight stopped what they were doing to watch.

A police officer approached him carrying two ropes. That didn't look good!

"Sit very still while I do this," the officer said. "If you fight me, you'll only make things worse."

The officer slung one rope over his shoulder. The other remained in his hands. He tied one end to Blinders' ankle.

"What are you doing?" he said in consternation.

The officer ignored him as he tossed the other end under Phylo's belly. It hit the ground on the other side.

He was tying Blinders up! There would be no escaping on this trip. As the officer moved to the other side of the horse, Blinders contemplated kicking him and running. But he knew it would do no good. There were too many people around watching, several on horseback. He wouldn't get anywhere.

"Is this necessary?" he pleaded.

The officer tied the rope to his other ankle, making sure it was snug enough to hold his feet against the horse's flanks.

"Now hold your hands together behind you," the officer said as he stood and faced him.

Dead silence permeated the community. Everyone watched as the officer used the other rope to tie Blinders' hands behind his back. He fought back tears as he felt humiliation creep through him. Naked and tied like a common criminal in front of everyone! He looked around to see if he could recognize a face.

Bellerophon sat mounted on his horse not too far off, watching grimly.

Anyone but him! Blinders wondered why he hadn't already come over to taunt him. But there was no gloating in his eyes. Bellerophon didn't appear to be in the mood to taunt. Blinders couldn't tell what mood he was in, but it didn't look compassionate.

He turned away and found a temple worker coming out of the temple with a white fabric in her hand. Was it a robe like the eunuch's? She handed it to the officer, who turned to face Blinders.

"Now, boy, tied the way you are to your horse, you need to ride carefully. If you slip, you'll find yourself hanging upside down with your head banging against the ground."

Blinders trembled at the thought.

"Men have died from that," the officer added. Blinders thought he heard hope in the man's voice.

The officer tossed the white fabric over Blinders' head. It fell down over his whole body, covering it. There was no opening for his head to pop through. All he could see was white.

He was blindfolded from head to foot! At least he could weep now without Bellerophon seeing him.

He heard the faint grunting of the eunuch as he tried to mount. Once up, he must have grabbed Philo's reigns, because Philo moved forward. He felt himself being led in circles a few times, then off in a direction he couldn't guess at. Even the sun didn't cooperate, being at noon. Had the Gods planned it that way?

There was no sound but the clomp of eight hooves. The Gods must have commanded everyone to remain silent as they left, so Blinders had no hint which way they traveled.

The horse steps quieted. Blinders heard the swishing of walking through tall grass. He wouldn't even be able to use the road to guess at a direction.

"I guess you really can call me Blind Boy now," he said with a disgusted smirk. The eunuch said nothing.

They rode endlessly. The shadow of trees passed by with increasing frequency, then faded away. The rope around his wrists and ankles chafed. His legs hurt from their unnatural position pressed against the flanks of Philo. His back ached with the strain of staying balanced on horseback without holding onto anything. His eyes stung from the silent tears that his pain forced from him. But he refused to beg for relief. Instead, he converted every miserable footfall of his horse into greater hatred for the Gods.

I *will* escape, he swore. I'll fight the Gods. If I can, I will kill them.

Now he understood Gelasius, his fellow Blind Boy. If they treated him like they treated Blinders, no wonder he became murderous.

At last the torment ended. Philo stopped. Blinders heard the eunuch dismount and felt the pull of the rope on his legs give way as somene untied first one, then the other ankle.

"We are here," the eunuch said.

"At my prison?"

"Please dismount now. I'll help you."

Blinders wasn't sure if he could. His legs were stiff and his ankles ached badly. He couldn't use his hands to dismount gracefully and basically had to slide to the side, hoping the eunuch would catch him. He did. In fact, it felt like two or three people caught him and eased him to the ground, then steadied him until his legs were ready to work again.

Gently but firmly they pulled him into motion. The light of the sun disappeared, and the natural sounds of outdoors gave way to an echoey stillness that had to be indoors. Blinders' bare feet padded against a cold, hard floor. The sandals of several people flopped against it. They led him back and forth through some maze of a path, then he heard a door open, and shortly after another, then another. Always the light changed with each new door, and always he heard each door close behind him.

Suddenly his escorts stopped him, and the fabric flew off his body. As he blinked, the eunuch said, "This is your home now."

He was in a large room, dazzlingly lit by lamps in the ceiling fueled with the fire of the Gods. The walls, floor, and ceiling were all white. Two large windows of glass covered one of the walls. Beyond them was a second room with more featureless walls and a long desk with three chairs facing him and three linnices on the desk facing the chairs. Some people stood in the room and stared at him through the glass. They all had white robes of temple workers on with differing insignia on each.

Was he imprisoned in a temple? Or had temple workers been assigned to observe him?

The eunuch untied his hands. Two other men, non-eunuchs, stood in front of him, their muscular arms folded. They seemed solemn, but their eyes held a hint of amusement.

Blinders ignored them and studied his new home. A comfortable bed stretched along the far wall. Next to it was a table and chair, cabinets hanging from the wall above the floor, a strange humming box with a couple doors, a small one above a large one, and another box that looked like a stove, but not like any stove he'd ever seen. In the middle of the room loomed a lengthy desk with three chairs and three linnices glowing away, mirroring the ones in the second room beyond the windows.

"What in the world am I supposed to do with three linnices?" he asked the two men standing in front of him. One of them shrugged a shoulder.

The final wall opposite the windows was completely blank. Facing it was a huge plush chair that looked more comfortable than anything Blinders had ever sat in. On a small tray attached to the arm of the chair was a linnix keyboard and mouse.

The eunuch had the rope off his wrists, and Blinders rubbed the circulation back into them.

"Farewell, Blind Boy," the eunuch said. "Have a happy life."

"Aren't you going to introduce me to my two friends here?"

The eunuch gestured to the one on the left. "This is X." Then to the one on the right. "This is Y."

For an instant he thought the eunuch was joking—an impossible thing to imagine. But he seemed deadly serious.

"Welcome, Blind Boy," X said with a smile, arms folded.

"My name is Blinders," he grumbled.

"Welcome, Blinders."

"They will be your assistants," said the eunuch. "When you need something, you can call them."

The eunuch headed for the door they'd come in through. It opened automatically. Blinders assumed it would *not* open automatically for him. The door closed, leaving a thin, dark seam in the wall to show its location. There was no handle on this side.

He noticed a similar seam on the other side of the room near the bed. There was no handle on it either. He nodded toward it. "I hope that's the privy."

"It is," said X.

"I hope it opens automatically for me."

"It does."

"Am I really supposed to call you X and Y?"

Y smiled at X, then said, "You can call us Chi and Psi if you want."

That sounded stupider than X and Y, so Blinders decided he wanted to call them that. "I take it X is Chi and Y is Psi."

"It's up to you," Psi said.

"They sound like names for cartoon characters."

The two men stared back without emotion.

"I'm making fun of you. Doesn't that bother you?"

Psi shrugged one shoulder.

"Don't you hate me? Don't you resent having to take care of a rebellious, Godblind heretic?"

"It's the calling the Gods gave us," Chi said, "and we're happy to have you tucked away where you can't hurt anyone."

"I could hurt you."

The two men looked at each other with a grin. "You can try," Psi said.

His response made Blinders feel creepy. Was the whole world gloating that he was in prison? Did everyone on earth hate him?

He headed for the plush chair and put his hand on the arm. "What's this for? Why is it facing a blank wall? Why is there a keyboard without a screen?"

"Try it," Chi said, grinning.

Blinders sat in the chair, sinking back deeply. It felt as comfortable as it looked. He reached for the keyboard and found that the tray it sat on was attached to an arm that let it swing in front of him.

"Clever," he smirked. He touched a key.

An enormous image blossomed before him, catching his breath. For a moment, he thought he was seeing a vision from the Gods. *Am I cured of my Godblindness?* he thought.

But he realized the image was the usual opening screen of all linnices, the black cartoon bird whose meaning no one could explain. And the image emanated from the blank wall.

"By Zeus, that's incredible!" he cried.

The two men laughed. "Have fun," Chi said. They headed for the door.

He jumped up. "Wait a minute! Where are you going?"

"We're leaving," Psi said.

"But aren't you supposed to be my assistants?"

Psi pointed at the bed. "That's where you sleep." He pointed to the table, the cabinets, the two big boxes. "That's where you eat. The cabinets hold food and utensils. That one is a fire-powered stove and oven, and the other is a fire-powered ice box. The top part freezes food to preserve it longer." He pointed at the far door. "That's where you shit and piss and bathe." Finally he swept his arm about the room. "And you have more linnices than one person needs in three lifetimes to keep your mind occupied. What more do you need?"

Chi said, "When you watch movies, be sure to watch them on the big wall. You won't believe it."

"But aren't you supposed to stay and assist me?"

"If you need anything you don't already have," Chi said, "just call for us, and we'll see what we can do. One or the other of us will be somewhere nearby at all times."

"But...aren't you going to *stay* with me?"

"What?" Psi said. "Locked up with you? We're not Godblind."

"What did you think, little Blind Boy?" Chi said. "That we're your *servants*? We serve the Gods, not you."

They turned and walked to the door. It opened for them. Blinders ran after them. Chi turned and grabbed him by the throat.

"*Never* try to escape, Blind Boy!" he hissed. "If you do, you'll die."

He released the grip, and Blinders coughed. "You're not my attendants. You're my prison guards."

"Smart boy," said Psi.

"I'm going to be in here all alone?"

"There'll be people looking in on you through those windows now and then," Chi said.

"But no one will ever be in here with me?"

"Didn't the eunuch tell you that?" said Psi.

Did he? Blinders couldn't remember. He was told he'd never see his parents again, but he didn't realize he would never be around *anyone* again.

The two men left, and the door sealed behind them. He noticed that only one person, an unfamiliar woman, remained on the other side of the windows. She gazed at Blinders for a moment, then disappeared out of the room.

Blinders was completely alone.

He stood there naked in the midst of that huge, white, sterile room, hearing the faint hum of the ice box. Its sterility made him feel like he should be cold and shivering, yet the temperature was comfortably warm. The enormous linnix screen suddenly flashed off from inactivity. There was nothing but a blank wall in its place—not even a seam like a door. As enormous as the room was, he began to feel the walls closing in on him. He didn't shiver from cold, but he began to tremble from dread.

This was his home. This was his prison. For the rest of his life. All thoughts of escape dissolved away. How could he escape from such a trap?

He ran to the bed, flung himself on it, and wept into the pillow. The bed was enormously soft, but he didn't care how comfortable it was. He didn't care how plush that chair was, or how warm the room was, or how abundant the supply of food was. He didn't care about how many movies he could watch on a gigantic screen. No matter how comfortable it was, it was still a prison.

All he wanted was to have Mother hold him again.

As his tears spent, he felt disgusted with himself. Bawling for his mother like a baby. Hadn't he become a man two days ago? A defiant man, cursing the Gods?

He hadn't heard a word from the Gods since he left home, but he knew they had to be watching. Artifacts had to be installed in this room before he ever came here. Was he going to give the Gods the satisfaction of seeing him cry over his punishment?

Angrily he wiped his tears away, sucked the mucous in his nasal passages down into his throat, hacked it up, and spat onto the floor. He stared at it glistening in the brilliant illumination, then shouted, "That's what I think of your punishment."

He half-expected to hear Athena's soothing voice comforting him, or maybe scolding him for soiling his living space. But there was no reaction. Now he felt foolish and vowed to never let the Gods see him act that way again.

He decided to examine the entrance door. As he expected, it didn't open for him. He pressed on it, but it was as unmovable as if it were the wall itself. The seams were too tight to get so much as a fingernail wedged in them. There was no chance of prying it open.

He walked to the other door. It opened as he approached. Good thing! His bladder complained fiercely. He stepped inside and found a basin, a toilet, and a shower, plus a cabinet and a small basket near it—probably meant as a wastebasket—and a taller container with a lid. But nothing like any of the basins, toilets, and showers he'd seen in his life.

The basin and toilet where white and made of a slick material, not quite glass, not quite rock. There was some kind of pipe hanging over the basin, and two knobs on either side of the pipe. The knob on the left had an H, and the knob on the right a C. There was a hole at the bottom of the basin.

He twisted the H knob. Water shot out of the pipe, splattering him. He turned it back until the water flowed more gently. The water only partially filled the basin with that hole in the bottom. In a moment he saw steam rising from it. He touched the water and yanked his hand back, stinging with pain.

That water was hot!

H for hot. He turned it off and turned the C knob. C for cold. The water was cold indeed, and felt soothing on his stinging fingers.

Turning the water off, he examined the toilet. All the other toilets he'd ever used were outhouses with wooden seats. He lifted the lid of this toilet seat and found another one underneath with the required gaping hole to shit through.

Inside, the toilet was a basin with a pool of water and a hole at the bottom. But the water didn't drain out through the hole like it did with the basin. How was that possible?

His bladder refused to let him wonder any longer. He had to relieve himself. The second seat lifted to allow him to piss into the toilet without splattering urine on the seat. Someone was being clever when they designed this.

He released his flow and enjoyed the feeling of relief. The loud noise his urine made as it hit the pool of water was entertaining. But when he finished, the pool just sat there all yellow and foamy.

This isn't good! Before long it would stink. Blinders thought maybe it would automatically drop through the hole when he was done, like the door automatically opened when he approached it. Was this part of the punishment the Gods had in store for him, to live in the stench of his own excrement?

Then he noticed the little shiny handle on the side. He grabbed it and tried to pull it. Nothing. But it seemed wobbly. He jiggled it up and down. Nothing happened. He jiggled it more. It seemed to go down more than up, so he shoved it down hard and cried out as a horrible explosive sound filled the room. He clamped his hands over his ears, waiting for the sound to go away. It did quickly. The yellow water swirled down into the hole, then clean water filled up to take its place.

This must be magic of the Gods! How could water stand in place with a hole beneath it, then fall into the hole at the push of a handle, then more water come and fill the basin up without falling through the hole again?

And how does a linnix screen suddenly pop out of a blank wall?

And how do doors open without being touched? Doors that can even tell who approaches and open only for those who are supposed to walk through.

This could only be a magical place.

He felt proud. The Gods may have imprisoned him, but they went to a lot of trouble to do it! Whatever else he may be to the world, he was important!

But then he fell into despair. If this place was teeming with the magic of the Gods, there truly was no way in Hades he'd ever escape. Athena was right. All was lost—he was not getting out!

The urge to weep came over him, but he pushed it away violently. The Gods would not see him weep ever again! They would see him enjoying his imprisonment! He would give himself that much satisfaction.

He opened the cabinet door and found towels, bars of soap, and rolls of thin paper. He noticed one of those rolls hanging from a stick attached to the wall next to the toilet. He pulled on the end of the paper, and a strip of it rolled off the stick.

He tore it off and studied it, then looked at the toilet. This must be for cleaning himself after shitting. But what flimsy paper! Wouldn't his fingers break through as he wiped?

Maybe the Gods had enchanted it not to tear while using it.

Next he examined the shower. It had a frosty glass door on it instead of a curtain. Opening it, he found two knobs sticking out of the wall like with the basin. A familiar nozzle hung over him from above, but there was no chain to pull like at home to get the water to flow. The knobs were also labeled H and C. It occurred to him that he could turn both on at the same time and control the temperature of the water. He couldn't do that at home!

Since he was already naked, he decided to try it on the spot. He turned the cold water on first because he didn't want to get scalded again, then added hot water. He was right about the control—by adjusting the knobs just a little, he could make the temperature perfect.

The spray of water drenched him. It was luxurious! Mother and Father would love this! How he wished he could share it with them.

The thought of his parents threatened to bring back the tears. He could feel them building up in his eyes. Blinders pushed his face into the stream of water to hide them.

At least Mother wasn't around to force him to use soap. That thought helped him regain control.

He stayed in the shower forever, trying to see how long the hot water would last. It never diminished. An endless supply of hot water—meaning an endless supply of fire of the Gods to heat it. If this was the punishment for rebellion, he wondered why more people didn't rebel.

Finally he turned the water off as his stomach growled at him. He stood while the worst of the water dripped from his body, then stepped through the door. There was steam in the air and a strange whining in the room. The whining came from above. He noticed a panel with holes in it attached to the ceiling that the whining came from. Steam sucked into it.

A magic breeze to remove the steam from the room! Blinders shook his head in amazement. What more would he find?

A puddle formed at his feet, so he grabbed a towel to dry off. Air-drying was best done outdoors where there was wind. An option he wouldn't have from now on, and he didn't want to track water all over his new home. So he used the towel.

After drying himself off, then wiping up the puddle on the floor, he wondered what to do with the towel. Maybe if he threw it in the air, it would disappear and reappear clean and dry in the cabinet. He didn't really believe it, but it sounded fun to try. He tossed it up. It fell to the floor.

He left it there. After everything else he'd seen, he couldn't imagine the Gods letting a soggy towel sit around forever. Let them deal with it.

Time to explore the food area. He noticed another, larger basket under the table—another wastebasket. The ice box teased his curiosity the most. He opened it. A light flashed on inside and cold air streamed out. Fire of the Gods seemed to power everything around here. What magic the Gods had to turn fire into cold air!

But the upper door held more wonders. Even colder air flowed out of it. The food inside was rock hard, like the surface of the lake in winter. His mind boggled that fire could cause a little chamber of winter.

The ice box was full of food he recognized and some he didn't. He grabbed butter and cheese and what looked like a container of milk and shut the door. The cabinets were full of dry food and produce and salted meat. He grabbed a loaf of bread and tossed it on the table. He rummaged around for utensils and found plates and pots and pans and cups. He grabbed a cup, found a sharp knife, and went to work on the table.

He cut four slices of bread, four thick slices of cheese, and troweled butter all over the bread. Each cheese slice went on a slice of bread.

Blinders bit into one. It tasted wonderful, but was dry and stuck in his mouth. Quickly he poured some milk into the cup and eyed it. Cold milk! What would that taste like? He'd heard of ice boxes before, but his family never had one.

He took a sip, mixing the milk with the food in his mouth. It tasted exquisite! Greedily he stuffed bread and cheese in his mouth and slurped at the milk.

Maybe it was because he was so hungry, and maybe it was because of the cold milk. Or maybe it was because the Gods provided this food. But he swore it was the best food he ever tasted.

Once finished, he sat back and enjoyed the sensation of fullness, then decided the milk and butter and cheese should go back in the ice box. The table was full of crumbs, the knife and cup dirty with butter and milk.

Let the Gods deal with it.

Gazing around the room, he knew in an instant what he wanted to try next. Blinders plopped into the plush chair and swung the keyboard tray in front of him. He grabbed the mouse and moved it. Instantly the wall came to life. He clicked and brought up a menu, selected "Movies," and found thousands of possibilities listed before him. More movies than he ever dreamed existed! His linnix at home only had a few hundred choices.

How was he supposed to decide which one to watch? Most of the titles were meaningless to him. He decided to select one he'd seen before, one that seemed to be about some demigods who trained for battle in strange flying chariots, and who had passionate love affairs to rival the Gods. He figured they must be demigods because one of them crashed and died, so they couldn't be Gods. But they couldn't be humans either, because humans would never have magical flying chariots to battle with.

He found *Top Gun* under the T's and clicked on it. The screen lit up with the mountain, then the words he never cared about. When the enormous carriage appeared and shot into the sky, his head and stomach swam.

The music crashed around him. The chariots launched into the sky. Their roar blasted throughout the room. Sound came from everywhere! It was as if he were in the chariot himself with the demigod Maverick!

His stomach tickled with delight. It was almost more than he could bear. Never in his life had he experienced anything like this. He could turn on the linnix at any time and become whoever he wanted to be, placing himself right there as if he were experiencing it in person.

If this was punishment, let him have more!

"Athena," Blinders said out loud, "I beg your forgiveness. I never knew how powerful your magic could be. And I never knew how compassionate you could be, to give a rebellious soul such a wonderful life, even as a prisoner."

Athena made no response. Maybe she couldn't hear him over the roar of the chariots.

Mother lay in her bed all day, not eating, not speaking. Just weeping and dozing. She knew Father was afraid for her, but she couldn't bring herself to arise. What she dreaded for thirteen years had finally happened, and the pain was so great she couldn't imagine ever being consoled.

As the daylight waned, she refused to turn on any of the lamps. She wanted to lay in darkness, echoing the darkness in her soul. Her son, her sweet boy, was gone, never to return. Athena promised he'd live a comfortable, happy life, but she didn't know what that meant. Only that it meant a life away from her. She could never see him again.

Oh, Athena, why? she cried out in her mind. *Why was he cursed with God-blindness? Why couldn't you heal him?*

She didn't expect a response, and she didn't get one.

The vile needs of reality pressed on her. She needed to empty her bladder. She was in such a state that she considered emptying it right onto the bed, but in the end, her decency prevailed, and she struggled to her feet. Where Father was, she had no idea, but he wasn't around the house. She drove him away hours ago with her shrill wails each time he tried to comfort her.

She trudged to the outhouse in the gloomy twilight and took care of business. The sheer effort of movement brought, not relief from her mourning, but a lessening of its intensity. Returning to her home, she sat in a chair instead of falling back into bed and stared at the place where the God-eunuch had been, announcing the end of her world.

"Athena," she prayed in a whisper,"at least let me know he's alright. At least let me know that he's as happy as you promised he would be."

"Blind Boy is well," the familiar voice came into her mind. "He arrived at his new home and is exploring it."

Mother's heart ached to hear Athena's voice again through the air, the way she used to speak to Blinders. But she didn't dare ask for it. No matter. It would probably tear her heart out to hear Athena's voice in a way meant for Blinders.

"Please, Athena, let me see that he's happy."

An image formed in her mind. Blinders in a bright white room with wondrous surfaces that she couldn't identify. Nothing like the rugged wooden furnishings of the home he left. She saw him piss into a toilet that washed the urine away with the touch of a handle, and soak forever in a steaming shower, obviously enjoying every minute of it.

She laughed through her tears as she slowly shook her head. "Of course he's not using soap."

Blinders grabbed some bread and cheese and devoured it hungrily, washing it down with his first taste of cold milk. Everywhere he went, he left a wake of debris—a wet towel, crumbs, dirty utensils.

"Oh-h-h-h," she moaned tenderly, "he's such a slob."

"He'll learn," Athena soothed.

Then he sat in a chair that Mother couldn't believe. It engulfed him and embraced him the way she wished she could embrace him again. He swung a linnix keyboard in front of him and moved the mouse. The wall in front of him blazed with an impossibly huge image. She watched him, mouth wide open, as he selected a movie he'd watched and loved at home. The wall filled with dazzling images of flying chariots, and the room boomed with the noise of it all. Blinders' eyes were agog in wonder.

"Is this a true vision?" Mother said. She knew it was blasphemous to ask such a question, but she had to know. Surely Athena would understand.

"It's a true vision. He's happy."

"Yes," Mother said with tears streaming down. "He's happy." She fell to the floor on her knees and wept uncontrollably. "Thank you, thank you, Athena, for being merciful to him."

"You must never ask for such a vision again. Blind Boy is dead to you now, and you need to grieve for him and move on."

"Yes, Athena," she said, wiping at her tears. "I understand. Thank you for showing me."

The towels and plates and crumbs and wrappers from the food piled up. The Gods did not deal with them. Finally Blinders washed the dishes, using some liquid soap and one of several cloths he found in the cabinet. He tossed the garbage in the wastebasket. He had no idea what to do with the towels, until he realized the taller container in the privy must be for them.

That took care of tidiness for the moment, but the wastebasket and the towel container were nearly full. What was he supposed to do with them?

He dragged them both to the entrance and called for his assistants to find out. He had no idea how to call them, so he just called—he stood in the middle of the room and shouted, "Chi! Psi! I need you!"

Chi showed up. "What do you need?" he said calmly, but without warmth.

"What do I do with these? They're almost full. And what happens when I run out of food? Or towels. Or that paper in the privy?"

"Just call. We'll take care of it."

"Oh."

Chi grabbed each container with a hand and dragged them as he backed out of the room. Blinders toyed with the idea of making a run for it while the door was opened, but remembered the powerful grip of Chi's hand around his throat. The door closed for several moments, then Chi returned with both containers empty.

It was like having a maid! Blinders decided to test his limits. "Next time I want you to come in here and clean up all the towels and stuff for me."

Chi belted out a laugh and left without a word.

Okay, maybe not a maid.

―――――

Sleep. Showers. Food. Movies. Games on the giant linnix. Blinders' life.

The games were dazzling on the big wall. Their explosions and crashes and music filled the room. He could immerse himself in them for hours and forget his home was a prison.

Periodically the bright lights dimmed to twilight. He assumed that co-incided with nighttime outside. As he lay on his bed before falling asleep, a feeling of despair would settle on him. It was alone in the darkness where he most felt imprisoned. The movies were thrilling, the games exciting, but how he longed to visit the lake one more time and splash with his friends, especially Lethia.

Occasionally he awoke with a need to clean himself up from a Dream of Eros. Wearing no clothes and needing no blankets thanks to the perfect tem-perature of the room, cleaning up was like at home his first time. He'd hop into the shower, dry off, and simply wipe any residue from his bed that remained with the wet towel.

At first he felt self-conscious about those dreams, knowing the Gods must be watching him. But after a while, he became accustomed to the idea and stopped caring. Let the Gods watch him all they want, if they had nothing bet-ter to do. What did he care what they thought of him? He was already a rebel-lious, fallen sinner they had to imprison. What more could they do?

In fact, he enjoyed a new-found freedom he never had on the ranch and taking walks to the lake and into the forest. Here he could do what he wanted without fear of what the Gods might think. They'd already done their worst, except execution, and they seemed unwilling to resort to that.

He put it to the test. He never said his morning or evening prayers. He cursed the Gods enthusiastically whenever something happened he didn't like. The rare times Chi or Psi appeared, he taunted them unmercifully. Once he shat on the floor in the middle of the room and left it there until he couldn't stand the stench anymore.

Occasionally that one woman who remained the longest in the room on the other side of the glass returned and sat watching him, studying him. Al-ways she wore the white clothing of a temple worker. She never spoke, even when he spoke to her, even when he goaded her to get her to speak. Maybe she couldn't hear him through the glass. Sometimes her face changed with emo-tions, but usually she just looked somber, almost pitying, and that irritated him to the point where he began to loathe her.

One time he stood before the windows as she peered at him and pumped his staff until it exploded onto the glass, all the while gazing suggestively at her. She reacted with nothing more than a furrowed brow and a tighter face, but otherwise did nothing, and left the room after he finished.

No matter what he did, nothing happened. No scolding from Athena, no appearance of Chi and Psi to punish him, and certainly no execution. He discovered a curious sort of freedom with the curse of "all is lost." Losing every-thing meant nothing left to lose, so he could do anything he wanted without consequence.

Anything he wanted *alone*. Of course there needed to be no consequences. His actions couldn't impact anyone but himself. No one else smelled the shit on the floor but him. His childish displays of rebellion only affected himself and probably made everyone else all the more certain he was the monster they thought he was.

That aggravated him, so he stopped. But then he had no outlet for his ag-gravation, so he found himself having childish outbursts from time to time without warning. A cup of milk flung across the room. Food pelted onto the floor and stomped on. Used towels flung at the glass when the woman was there. She seemed to be there more often, and seemed to gaze at him with a deeper concern on her face.

The movies became boring. The games became tedious. He began to fan-tasize attacking Chi or Psi as they entered the room and bolting through the open door. Never mind he wouldn't get far. Just to get out of this damnable room for a moment. At least it would be something different.

He discovered the nude women on the linnix. At first it shocked him. These were never available on his linnix at home. And they weren't just women go-ing about their lives nude as he sometimes did back home. They tried to be sexy with their poses and expressions. Blinders never experienced a girl com-ing on to him with sexual intent, but he realized this must be what it looked like when they did.

He viewed them more and more, first on the desk linnices in some mis-guided notion that he could be more discreet about it there, but eventually on the wall where they towered over him with their enticing bodies. It wasn't long before he pumped his staff on a regular basis with female flesh filling his eyes, then felt a terrible emptiness inside when he finished.

And every time, even though he had many beautiful women to choose from on the screen, he ended up fantasizing about Lethia. She was the girl he'd been in the presence of physically, had touched the skin of incidentally as they frolicked in the lake.

His self-love became more angry as time went on. It turned into self-loath-ing, but he couldn't stop doing it because it was a few moments of distraction from his tedious life. He'd feel disgusted and worthless afterward, feel that his life had no purpose whatsoever, but those dark feelings only made him crave the moments of distraction all the more.

One time he broke down into uncontrolled weeping afterwards, bent over on his knees from the despair in his soul. When his emotions were spent, he stood back up and saw the woman in the other room, standing near the glass and gazing at him with a look of anxiousness.

She placed her palm on the glass. He stood stupefied, gaping at her, then approached. He studied her flattened palm for a moment, then placed his own palm on the glass over hers. She gave him a forlorn smile.

A couple of men charged into her room, causing her to drop her hand and back away. She turned to face them as they approached her. They spoke forcefully at her. Blinders couldn't hear a sound.

The woman spoke back to them, showing no submission. They seemed to argue for a while, then the men strode out of the room frowning deeply. The woman turned back to Blinders, gazing at him with intensity, then went to the edge of the glass and pressed something on the wall.

"Hello, Blinders," her voice came through.

That shocked him. If she could speak to him through the wall, she probably heard everything he ever said. He went over to where she stood and said, "Can you hear me?"

"Yes, I can."

"Who are you?"

"My name is Selene."

A thrill ran through him. "The *Goddess* Selene?"

She smiled. "No, I was just named after her."

He felt foolish, but the joy of talking to another human being—a *woman* especially—overcame that feeling. "Why do you watch me?"

"To see how you're doing. To make sure you're alright."

He shook his head. "But I'm Godblind. You're supposed to hate me."

A sadness touched her face. "I'm sorry how they've treated you. They do it out of fear, not hatred."

"They *should* fear me. They taught me to hate them. If I could—"

She put her hand up to the glass close to his mouth and whispered, "Not a wise thing to say."

He gazed at her, not sure what to do next.

"May I ask you a personal question?" she said.

He nodded.

"What do you think about when you self-love with those women on the screen?"

That was a question he didn't expect. He felt embarrassed to answer. But she peered at him with such a concerned expression, and she was the only person who'd ever shown him compassion since he was torn from Mother, he felt compelled to be honest.

"Lethia," he said softly.

She cocked her head. "The girl who was your friend back home?"

How much did she know about him? He nodded, feeling his face flush.

She nodded back. "You were attracted to her."

"She was my friend ever since I can remember."

"You didn't have many friends, did you?"

He lowered his eyes.

"I'm sorry for what they've done to you," she said again, as if she hadn't already said it. "Gelasius murdered people, but you've done nothing except be a boy testing his independence."

"But I... I mean, I think I could murder now."

She peered at him sorrowfully. "Could you have before they did all this to you?"

He pursed his lips and shook his head.

"I warned them. I told them treating you this way could drive you to become like Gelasius."

"But I'm harmless here, so what do they care?"

She nodded. "But I care."

That sent tingles through his body. It was beyond his ability to imagine someone could still care about him. "*Why* do you care?"

"It's my job."

"What *is* your job?"

"Caring for people. Helping them. The old Greek word is psychologist."

"So you care because it's your job?" he said with a hint of disappointment.

"It's my job because I care about people."

He wasn't sure he believed her, but he wasn't sure that mattered to him. And he wasn't sure he had a choice. She was the only one who showed concern, regardless of her reason.

"Why are you different from the others?" he said. "You seem...wiser."

"There's a handful of us. We preserve much of the ancient knowledge the rest of the world has forgotten."

"You rule society?" he said with hope.

She chuckled, but there was no humor in it. "We're servants of the Gods like everyone else." She looked around the room. "I'm watched as much as you are."

"Why have you never spoken to me before?"

"I was forbidden to."

A thrill shot through him, and he smiled. "You rebelled too?"

She chuckled, and this time there *was* humor. "I suppose, a little. But it was clear you were sinking into darkness. I had to do something."

"Those men... They didn't look too happy."

"I don't answer to them. I was assigned to observe you, make sure you're... as happy as you can be here."

"Who assigned you?"

"Well...Athena, actually."

Blinders didn't know how he felt about that. A part of him wanted to resent Athena. A part of him was glad she hadn't really abandoned him completely, even though she never spoke to him anymore.

"I should go," Selene said with a touch of sadness. "But I'll do what I can to help you have a more normal life. Living in isolation for the rest of your life will drive you insane."

"Thank you, Selene," he said with all his heart.

"Just don't be talking anymore about...dark things you might want to do."

"I...somehow I think...I don't think I could really murder anyone, now that you've talked with me."

She smiled broadly and warmly. "I'm glad." She put her fingers to her lips and kissed them, then pressed them on the window. "I'll come back."

She pushed the spot on the wall where she'd pressed before, then mouthed a *goodbye* he couldn't hear and left the room.

Blinders sat at the middle of the three linnices staring off into space. He was sick of the games. He was sick of the movies. He was even sick of the towering nude women that always behaved as if they felt passion for him, but he could never touch or talk with.

He was sick of living. He wondered if the mercy of the Gods putting him in this prison was crueler than execution.

It had been days since he saw Selene. He became more and more convinced she abandoned him. Or maybe the Gods had forbidden her from seeing him again because she spoke with him.

He thought of the knives in the cabinet he carved the bread and cheese and other food with. He imagined carving his own flesh and watching the blood flow across the floor. That was a mess the Gods *would* have to deal with, because he wouldn't be around to clean it.

The magic door opened. Blinders turned his eyes listlessly toward it. He felt no curiosity at who might be there. It was always either Chi or Psi.

This time it was both, and he perked up at that. They never came together, probably because they worked in shifts.

"You have a visitor," Psi said.

Blinders was shocked. That had never happened before. He stood, uncertain who it could be. Mother, he hoped.

They stood aside. Slowly with trepidation, Lethia crept into the room. Blinders gaped as his head spun. She looked at him with strong emotions playing across her face that he couldn't identify.

"Lethia," he murmured.

"Hello, Blinders," she said. She peered about the room. "This is where they took you?"

This is my prison, he wanted to say, but he was so taken aback at her presence, he couldn't get any words out.

Her eyes returned to him. A long silence pulsed.

"How have you been?" she said.

He couldn't think what to say. To anyone else, even Mother, he'd have launched into a lurid description of the horror of living isolated in this prison, but he couldn't bring himself to spew his frustration at Lethia.

She took a few steps toward him. "It must be terrible living alone."

Those words forced tears from his eyes. He hated that he couldn't hold them back. They broke into sobs that he couldn't control. He buckled over and sank down to his knees.

Lethia ran to him and knelt down before him. She reached out tentatively with her hand, hesitated, then pulled him into an embrace. She patted him on the back, but said nothing.

He wept for a few moments, then regained his composure. He straightened up on his knees, wiping his eyes. "I'm sorry."

"No, no," she said, gazing at him with pathos. She helped him up and sat him back on the chair. She sat in the next one. They peered at each other. The emotions in Blinders churned so much, he could find no words to say.

She looked back at Chi and Psi. They stared somberly at them with arms folded. "I'll be okay," she said.

"You're not going to harm her, are you, Blind Boy?" Chi said.

"She's my friend," Blinders said with indignation. "I would never do anything to her."

Psi and Chi looked at each other, then left the room. The door swung shut and sealed.

"Why are you here?" he said. "*How* are you here?"

"I came to see how you were doing." Her eyes darted about uncertainly as she spoke.

He gazed at her. She had a simple but elegant tunic on, and her hair was done up in a way he'd never seen her do before. She seemed more a woman than a girl, and he wasn't sure, but he thought her breasts were larger.

"They said I'd never see anyone I know again."

She fidgeted with her hands as she looked down at them. "It was Athena. She...asked me to come."

He immediately thought of Selene. Had she been able to convince the Goddess to send her?

Lethia looked at the large chair facing the blank wall, at the bed, at the ice box and table and cabinets. "That's where you have your meals?"

"Yes. I have an ice box powered by the fire of the Gods."

Her eyebrows rose. "You do?"

"The upper part even freezes things into blocks of ice. It preserves them longer that way."

She looked at him in amazement. "They've blessed you with that?"

It bothered him that she called it a blessing. He'd trade all that for his home with no ice box.

"What's that large chair for?" she asked.

He grinned. "Let me show you." He brought her over to it. "Have a seat."

She looked at him, then sat down. He swung the keyboard and mouse in front of her and pushed a key. The wall flared up with the opening screen.

She gasped. "It's a gigantic linnix!"

"Call up a movie."

She looked at him again uncertainly, then worked the mouse. She picked a movie called *The Notebook*. It began to play, and she gaped at it in astonishment for some time. "I feel like I'm there."

Suddenly she stopped the movie and pushed the tray away. "But I didn't come here to watch movies."

She stood and looked at the bed. "Is that comfortable for you?" She walked over to it and sat, pressing her hand down on it. Her face broke into a smile. "Very comfortable!"

"I suppose it is." He hadn't thought about that for a long time. It was just his prison bed.

"Come sit with me," she said, patting the bed beside her.

He wanted very much to sit close to her, but felt guilty about it. To sit with a girl on a bed, especially a girl he was attracted to, especially when he was naked, was a sin likely to result in producing a bastard. He pushed those thoughts away, reminding himself he no longer cared what sin he committed. What more could the Gods do to him?

But they could do a great deal to Lethia. She'd be committing a sin too. If a bastard resulted, she'd be the one that was shunned. He couldn't do that to her. He couldn't do that to the baby.

She studied him as he hesitated. "Please. It'll be alright, I promise."

She was the one with Godsight. If she was fine with this and the Gods didn't scold her for it, why should he hesitate? He walked over and sat down.

She gazed about again. "I'm glad they put you in such a nice place."

He wished she'd stop saying things like that. This was a prison, no matter how comfortable. He didn't want to feel any irritation while she was here.

"What's behind that door?" She pointed at the privy door.

"That's...uh...where I go to...uh..."

"Oh." She smiled a sweet smile at him. "Do you—" She stopped abruptly. The smile disappeared. She looked down. "Do you remember the last time we were at the lake together?"

He became immediately uncomfortable.

"You...uh..." She pointed at his penis and whirled her finger.

He nodded, feeling his face turn red.

"And you said you dreamed a Dream of..." She trailed off.

Suddenly he wished she wasn't there. His excitement at her presence dissolved into humiliation.

"Did...were you...did you want to...with me?"

"I'm sorry! I should never have—"

She pressed her fingers against his lips to silence him, then gazed deeply into his eyes. He couldn't tell what emotions they reflected.

She grabbed him in an embrace and kissed him hard. He was so shocked he couldn't respond, until desire welled up in him. He pulled her into an embraced and kissed passionately.

What happened next drowned in a confusing flood of emotions. Without understanding how, she was naked in his arms, then she lay on him, then the amazing sensations of pumping his staff overwhelmed him with an intensity he hadn't experience before. Something soft and moist squeezed his penis, and his body involuntarily thrust back and forth. The explosion that came made him cry out. Lethia gave out a squeal that lasted for several seconds.

She lay on top of him as they panted with exhaustion, sweat glistening on their bodies. His penis was still inside her. The weight of her lying on him was gentle compared to the powerful sensations, but it had a comforting pleasure all the same.

But as the thrill faded, guilt swept in, and he cried out with anguish. "What have I done to you?"

She rolled off of him, breaking the joining of their bodies. "Blinders, it's alright. We've done nothing wrong."

"But we loved without marrying. We might have created a—"

She pressed her fingers to his mouth again. "We haven't. I promise you, nothing's wrong." She sat up and gazed down at him. "Athena commanded me to come here and love you."

His head swam with confusion. None of this made sense. "But you could have a bastard with no family. A bastard from a Blind Boy! How could Athena possibly—"

"Blinders!" she shouted. It silenced him. "Listen to me. Athena commanded it. I said those same things, but she promised me we wouldn't create a child. Before I came here, a God-eunuch brought me little things to swallow each day. He called them pills, and taking one each day would keep a baby from forming. Athena said it was unnecessary for us to marry if it was impossible for us to create a baby."

He gaped at her, trying to understand her words. "Athena commanded this? You can't have a baby?"

She nodded.

"Ever? Not even if you marry?"

"As long as I swallow the little pills."

"Why?"

"Athena said you were sad and lonely. You behaved as if you'd gone insane. She said you needed companionship."

It must be true! Selene did talk to Athena and convince her that Blinders needed this. Another thought occurred to him. If Athena *commanded* her to love him...

He sat up. "Lethia, tell me truly. Did you want to do this, or are you only obeying the command of the Gods?"

"I...missed you. I was sad to hear you were not well. I wanted to help you."

"But did you do this out of love, or...or pity."

"I have...affection for you."

She carefully avoided the word *love*. "Are you to be with me always now?"

"I'm to come here once a month and be with you for one day."

It was clear to him. She didn't come out of love for him. It was her duty. She said she had affection for him. But she didn't love him.

"I enjoyed it," she said reassuringly. "It was more than I expected it to be."

He gazed at her, trying to sort his feelings out. She was beautiful—even more than he remembered. Did loving her make him feel that way? Her naked body was even more enticing to him, now that he'd loved her.

But he remembered how his prison also seemed grand at first. New and dazzling, but the excitement wore off. The passion they shared was also new and dazzling, but if there was no love behind it, would it also grow wearisome?

He wanted her to stay the day, but he wanted her to leave. He wanted to hold her in his arms again, fondling her as they writhed in passion. But he also felt the indignity of receiving love from her that she didn't feel.

"Do you want me to leave?" she said as she studied him.

The thought of being alone again was unbearable. "No." He looked around, wondering what to do next. "Do you want to watch a movie?"

Scrunched naked together in the large chair, they watched two movies, then had a meal. As time went on, they felt more comfortable with each other. There was no more talk of love or commands of Athena. It was as if none of this had happened and they were friends again. In some ways that was more delightful than the loving. Maybe she didn't love him, but it was clear her friendship was genuine.

Lethia remained naked with him. She didn't want to make him uncomfortable being dressed when he had no clothes. They slept together and loved each other again. This time was calmer, gentler. He decided he liked it more that way. It seemed more genuine. The first passionate time was driven with a hope for love. This gentler kind of love seemed appropriate for friends, and he could enjoy it without feeling humiliated.

Two more meals and one more time of love, then she showered in preparation to leave. She took a long time, and when she came out, she declared his shower a blessing from the Gods.

As she dressed, he decided with all his heart he wanted her to come back next month. Her affection, her friendship—even if it wasn't love, it was wonderful. And he couldn't bear facing the isolation again.

Psi and Chi appeared to escort her away. They kissed fondly. As she walked out the door, she turned and gave him one more look full of genuine affection.

The door sealed shut, and he was alone again. He began counting the days until next month.

Two days later Selene visited him in the other room. He stood before the glass, hoping she'd talk to him again, but instead she sat at one of the linnices and gestured for him to sit at one of his. He chose the middle one.

Words appeared on the screen. *I'm forbidden to speak to you anymore, but I'm allowed to communicate this way.*

Did you arrange to bring Lethia here? he typed.

I asked Athena. She refused at first, but I convinced her it was necessary to keep you from going insane. I told her execution would be more compassionate than the isolation.

That sent a shiver up his spine. *What if she chose execution?*

She peered at him through the glass, then typed, *If she refused to let Lethia come, wouldn't that have been the better choice?*

He remembered how he considered doing it to himself, and nodded.

It was worth the risk, and I trusted in her mercy, Selene typed.

How is Lethia?

Her face became somber. *I'm not allowed to tell you about her while she's away.*

That disappointed him and seemed unnecessarily harsh. But it didn't surprise him. The Gods still wanted him in isolation. He should be grateful Athena was willing to do as much as she did.

Selene appeared from time to time and typed conversations with him about how he was doing. He asked her lots of questions, but she evaded any that had to do with the outside world. She wouldn't say a word about Lethia.

The time approached for Lethia to come again. His anticipation grew to where he could barely contain it. Curiously, Selene stopped visiting him for a week before the date arrived.

The night before Lethia was due, Blinders couldn't sleep. He showered early the next morning, wanting to be fresh for her. He watched movies to distract him from his excitement, but it didn't work. He couldn't concentrate on them.

The day passed slowly. He stared at the sealed door, waiting for it to open. The hours crawled unmercifully. When the lights dimmed to twilight, he was horrified.

She hadn't come.

That night he lay on his bed in turmoil. Was he never to see her again? Was his isolation back? Did he count the days wrong? How long should he wait before he gave up in despair and ended this nightmare with blood flowing across the floor?

He pumped his staff, but it was a hollow experience and comforted him not at all. It only reminded him how it felt to have those sensations with Lethia in his arms. When he finished, he flopped down on the bed and wept into his pillow.

Another day passed with no visitor, neither Lethia nor Selene. Not even Psi or Chi, since he had no need to call them, and they never appeared without a reason. As he lay in bed staring at the dimly lit ceiling, all the feelings of hopelessness came flooding back. He couldn't endure this anymore. If Lethia didn't come, if Selene didn't appear and explain what was happening, he refused to endure this vicious curse of the Gods any longer. He would have his escape at last in the only way available to him.

That night he lay awake considering ways to execute himself.

A knife seemed the simplest way. He could bury it in his belly. He could slide it across his throat. He could slice his wrists open. He thought of all the ways he'd seen knives used in movies to kill.

He fell asleep. In the light of the morning, he grabbed a knife and pressed the blade against his throat. He stood there for some time before he realized he could never slide it across.

He sat in the large chair and wept.

The door swung open. He leaped to his feet with excitement.

Selene rushed in with a wild look in her eyes. She ran to him and put her mouth to his ear. "Get on your linnix. Search and study. Learn all you can. Find a way to save yourself." She pressed something into his hand and closed his fingers over it.

Psi and Chi barged through the door. She stepped away from him and gazed into his eyes. "I'm sorry."

They grabbed her by her arms and dragged her away.

"Leave her alone!" Blinders shrieked and dashed for them.

The door swung closed. Blinders tried to catch it, but it forced itself out of his grasp and closed tight.

He stood gaping in shock. The feel of the thing she pressed into his hand intruded into his mind. He almost held it up to look at it, but realized he didn't want the Gods to see that Selene had given him something. He looked around, wondering what to do. He headed into the privy and sat on the toilet. It was all he could think to do. He hoped the Gods didn't watch him in here.

In his hand was a crumpled scrap of paper. He spread it flat. There were words hastily scrawled.

Type this into your linnix. Search and study
everything you can. Learn the truth. Find a
way to escape.

sudo cd /marshill/unknowngod
Password: 01032019.17.23
exec rabbithole -a hyperuser

He gaped at the words she wanted him to type. It was gibberish! Even the words he recognized had no meaning to him.

It must be some form of communication of the Gods. No matter what it meant, Selene had gone to great trouble to get it to him, by the way Psi and Chi dragged her out. He feared for her safety.

He crept out of the privy, feeling the eyes of the Gods bearing down on him. He clutched the paper tightly in his hand so it couldn't be seen. He wasn't sure how to type the words in without the Gods seeing, but he had to know what this scrap of paper meant. He dreaded what judgment Selene might be going through right now just to get it to him. For her sake, he had to follow her instructions.

He took a deep breath, then strode to the linnices as if nothing was different. He sat at the middle one, his hands hidden beneath the table. He stared at the blank screen, wondering where the artifacts might be installed they used to spy on him.

His eyes were drawn to a spot on the linnix just above the screen. A small hole stared right at him. That must be one right there! He looked at the other two linnices on either side and saw similar holes. There were probably more placed throughout the room, but one thing he thought unlikely. There were probably none aimed at his lap and his penis while he sat at the table. Why would the Gods want to stare at that?

He fumbled around without looking down, laying out the paper on his lap so he could read the gibberish, then activated the linnix with the mouse and studied the screen. *Type this into your linnix*, the note said. He wasn't sure exactly where to do that. There were only little icons on the screen—no boxes to type anything into.

He studied the icons one at a time, reading their titles, trying to find one that might be where to type it. Most of them were familiar. But he noticed one that never appeared on his linnix back home. Its was labeled with the word *Terminal*. He'd never clicked on it before because he had no idea what it meant and didn't want to do something that could damage the linnix.

He stared at it feeling trepidation, then impulsively clicked on it.

A little box popped up that was nothing but black except for a strip on top with the title *Terminal — bash — 96x30*. More gibberish he didn't understand.

There were two lines of white words in the black part of the window that also made no sense:

Last login: Fri Feb 20 3294 10:49:25 on console
Olympus:~ zeus$

They were followed by a small horizontal line that blinked on and off.

Trying not to shake, he glanced down at the paper and typed out the words *sudo cd /marshill/unknowngod*, then pressed the return key. *Password:* appeared automatically followed by the blinking line. He typed *01032019.17.23*.

A line saying *Olympus/marshill:~ unknowngod$* appeared. Barely able to breathe, he typed *exec rabbithole -a hyperuser*.

The screen exploded with icons, more than he'd ever seen on any linnix. They were colorful and intriguing, and most of them displayed unfamiliar labels. He didn't know where to start.

He began clicking. He searched everywhere and studied everything, as Selene instructed. Hours passed without him thinking of the world around him once until his bladder demanded attention.

Forced back to reality, he felt his stomach gnawing with hunger, so he ate, then went right back to the linnix. The lights in the room dimmed before he pulled himself away to get some sleep.

The entire next day, his only obsession was clicking and searching and studying screen after screen of information. It was tough going at first because everything was so foreign to him, but slowly he began to piece things together. For the first several days, his hair prickled as he waited for Athena's voice to cry out, "What are you doing, Blind Boy?" But she never did. He finally stopped wondering why.

When he clicked on one icon, he froze in shock. It pulled up a set of icons with labels that sent chills down his spine.

Aphrodite
Athena
Hera
Hermes
Poseidon
Zeus

The names of the Gods!

He remembered the final word that always appeared on the black screen of *Terminal* when he typed Selena's instructions in: ~ *unknowngod$*.

Unknown God?

What was all this?

He clicked and studied these parts furiously. Days turned into weeks, weeks turned into months, months extended into the next year. His whole life was eating, sleeping, using the privy, the occasional movie for a break—and studying the information on the linnix.

During that year, his world expanded beyond anything he could imagine.

Blinders lay in his bed when the lights dimmed, but he couldn't sleep. He stared at the ceiling and contemplated all he'd learned.

Athens was not really Athens. Mount Olympus was not really Mount Olympus. All those things were on the other side of the world.

There was a war, a terrible war, using powers beyond anything that existed today. Cities exploded to dust. People disappeared by the hundreds of thousands. Poison filled the land. At one time he'd have considered such power the fire of the Gods, but it wasn't that at all. Humans created it and humans tossed it about, devastating the planet.

Pockets of civilization remained. The one that Blinders lived in and called itself Athens had a gigantic machine that could think like a man. It was almost as if it were a lifeform all its own, but created by humans, not Gods. To recover from the war, those who had built it and operated it used it to control many aspects of their society. Whimsically they used the names of Greek Gods for different parts of it: Zeus, Hera, Aphrodite, Hermes, Poseidon—and Athena.

The humans also studied their own minds. They tinkered with them at a tiny level, something they called *genetics*. They bred people to bring out desired characteristics, like breeding horses.

One of those characteristics was the undeveloped ability of human minds to sense things they normally couldn't see. For hundreds of generations humans thought of it only as premonitions, hunches, but the learned people who called themselves scientists came to recognize it as an ability they could breed into greater strength. They called it psychic abilities.

They also learned how to make their great machine be able to communicate with humans through this newly developed ability. It could send a signal out through empty air that people's minds could detect and pick up the signals their minds sent out. After many generations, everyone in Athens had this ability, born with it from all the genetics tinkering and breeding.

Except for one boy who was born with something called a *mutation* that made him blind to the signals. A boy named Gelasius. Because of his blindness, he was an outcast and became an enemy to society.

The records Blinders searched only made reference to a single Blind Boy. They considered the mutation extremely rare.

But not rare enough, he realized. More than two hundred years later, the mutation struck again in the mind of a newborn ranch boy named Blinders.

He couldn't decide if it made him feel better about himself knowing why he was Godblind. It made no practical difference. He was still feared and still imprisoned, without even the promised monthly visits from Lethia.

What impacted him more was what he learned about the Gods.

There was a large wall in the mountains of the Gods called a dam. It blocked the water of a great river and let it flow only through passages on either side of the wall that caused gadgets to spin. Those gadgets generated the fire of the Gods that powered all the things Blinders had considered the miracles of the Gods.

But that power was created by men, not Gods, and they called it *electricity*.

Because the power was limited, most people of Athens had limited access to it. They lived simple lives, mostly farmers or ranchers or merchants or tradesmen. In the city of Athens was where most of the power was used to keep all their wondrous machines running, to power the machine that was the great thinker for Athens.

The very same machine that controlled all the linnices of Athens and controlled every marvel within Blinders' prison. He learned both he and the machine were in the great city of Athens itself, inside the very temple of the Gods.

Those who ruled Athens after the war were among the learned people. As they aged, and as they discovered the secrets of the human mind itself and how it could connect with the machine, they devised a devious plan. They moved all the information in their brains—their entire minds—into the machine. They adopted the whimsical names they'd given the parts of the machine: Zeus, Hera, Aphrodite, Hermes, Poseidon—and Athena.

Some stayed behind. They refused to become part of the machine. These must have been the origin of the people Selene belonged to.

Blinders learned the Gods were not Gods at all. He learned there were no Gods. The Gods were only humans who turned their minds into parts of the great machine that ruled all citizens of Athens.

All but Blinders.

He couldn't sleep that night. The rage he felt over his discoveries consumed him. He'd been treated as an outcast all his life, had been feared and hated and imprisoned, all because of dead humans who stored their minds in a machine and called themselves Gods.

All because of a lie.

Blinders spent another day searching the knowledge in the machine. He learned that the part of the machine he had access to through Selene's instructions was the part that ruled over the entire machine. The Gods were each in a lesser part of the machine, separated as individuals. They had no access to the part Selene led Blinders to, and that explained why Athena never cried out,

"Blind Boy, what are you doing?" She was as blind to his poking around in the machine as she was to his brain. The only thing the Gods knew about the ruling part was to call it the Unknown God.

And Blinders was in it.

The realization hit him like a horse kicking him in the gut. He had access to the Unknown God. He could control the Unknown God.

Blinders *was* the Unknown God now. And the Unknown God had power over the other Gods.

A thrill shot through him. Now he understood why Selene had led him here, why she talked about escape. He could arrange his own escape and return home to Mother, to Father, and to Lethia. He could marry Lethia.

With that thought, he was consumed with an urge to find out what happened to Selene and Lethia. But no matter how much he searched, the Unknown God portion of the machine had no information about them. In fact, the Unknown God seemed to have no information whatsoever after a certain date—that very same date that appeared when Blinders first clicked on *Terminal*.

Last login: Fri Feb 20 3294 10:49:25 on console.

It appeared the Unknown God had been neglected ever since.

He had no idea how long ago *Fri Feb 20 3294* had been. That was a dating system used in the machine, but not in the communities of Athens. It had to be less than two hundred and fourteen years ago, since he found information on Gelasius within the Unknown God.

He avoided poking around in the parts that were the Gods themselves. He didn't want to risk being detected by any of them. But he continued to search all the places within the Unknown God with obscure names that meant nothing to him, hoping to find more useful information.

One of them was something called *System Log*. He scanned it, finding many labels he didn't understand that had some kind of notes in them that were mostly gibberish to him.

He was about to give up there, until one label caught his eye.

User ~Selene.

He pulled that up and found notes that must have been typed by Selene. There was a lot of things she wrote that Blinders didn't understand, notes about other people he didn't know. But he reached a point where the notes started including the name Blind Boy.

He read about himself and what she thought of him. He couldn't understand all the words she used, but it was clear she had great concern for him.

He reached the point where she wrote about her conversations with Athena about Lethia. Athena finally agreed to send Lethia to him. She was supposed to come once a month.

But three weeks after Lethia's first visit, Selene wrote a note that horrified Blinders.

> Learned today that Lethia became pregnant.
> The pills they gave her were too old and lost
> their potency. She was sent to a home for
> wayward girls.
>
> I fear for Blinders. This will probably push
> him over the edge. He needs to get out of that
> prison. I have to try to find the administrative
> commands to access Unknown God. These
> Gods must be stopped.

He stared with horror at the note. Lethia pregnant and shunned! No wonder she didn't return. He could only imagine what Eusebius thought of her getting pregnant without marriage from a Blind Boy.

Even more disturbing was how Selene wrote openly about defying the Gods. He hoped because the note was in *System Log* in the Unknown God that the other Gods hadn't seen it. But he didn't know enough about the machine to be sure.

In the next note, Selene reported that she found the login to the Unknown God and would study how to use it to stop the Gods. He dreaded what would come next, considering what she ended up doing with the login.

The next note was short and seemed rush.

> They found me out. Must get login to Blinders. Last hope for him.

Only one note followed, and it wasn't written by her.

> Subsystem ~Zeus admin exec
> Firewall breach user ~Selene
> Execution ordered citizen Selene
> User account ~Selene purged

He gaped at the note, too shocked to think, too shocked to feel. His eyes couldn't look away from that word *execution*. A terrible sickness arose in his gut. He had to jump up and run into the privy. He buckled over the toilet and spewed his last meal into it.

He fell back onto the floor leaning against the wall and wept loudly. The Gods killed her! She gave her life to help him! It was more than he could bear.

He fell forward, resting his forearms on the floor. He couldn't get his wailing to stop. The pain flooded over him, overwhelmed him, consumed him, for Lethia, for Selene.

When his energy drained away, he rolled onto his back and stared at the ceiling. The pain gave way to numbness. Within the numbness a deep wrath formed and seethed up to consume his entire soul.

Realization hit him.

You are a God, as much as any of the other Gods. You just don't live inside the machine.

He could take control of the Unknown God, thanks to Selene. She did not die in vain. He could end this tyranny of the Gods. He could rule Athens in their place and be the benevolent God he thought all his life the Gods had been. He could share the knowledge in the machine with the citizens of Athens, share the fire of the Gods hoarded for the luxuries of the elite in Athens with everyone, especially his parents. Mother could enjoy endless hot showers as he did in his prison.

He could save Lethia from the humiliation her pregnancy brought her. He could get his revenge on the Gods.

Kill the Gods, as he once vowed to do.

He pulled himself to his feet and rinsed his mouth out, then headed back to the linnix and stared at the screen. The evil words were still there. He shut down *System Log* and contemplated his next move.

He realized with consternation, he could only do all that by remaining in prison. He was still Godblind—his only access to the power of the Unknown God was through the linnices here. None of the linnices among the people had such access.

He lay on his bed throughout the night and thought. As the Unknown God, he could command the other Gods, and they'd never know it was him. He could open the prison door that wouldn't open for him and wander the halls of the machine's great building, wander the streets of Athens. He could arrange a dwelling place where he and Lethia could live as husband and wife to remove her humiliation.

But he could never truly leave this prison room. His power depended on the access he had here. He'd have to stay near it for the rest of his life. And if the Gods ever found out it was him, they'd cut him off from this room and surely execute him.

And what about Lethia? Would she want to live such a life with him? Would she want to marry him at all? She made love with him, but she avoided saying she loved him. Visiting him once a month was one thing. Marrying him another. Would it be too loathsome for her to marry a Blind Boy? Worse yet, would she marry him only to escape her humiliation, but resent him for life?

His anger darkened even further as he thought about what happened to her. She suffered right now because of his brief moments of love with her, all because they trusted a machine. Why didn't Athena know the pills might not work? Did the machine even care? *Could* the machine care? What kind of a mind was stored away when a human placed theirs in a machine? How smart would it be? How compassionate could it be truly? Was it even a mind at all?

Blinders thought back to all the interactions he had with Athena. Ever calm, ever patient, ever understanding—like a machine. Always only one emotion, compassion. Nothing ever upset her except when he tried to flee, an act of rebellion the Gods never experienced except with two mutated boys.

He had to leave this prison. He had to save Lethia from her prison. He had to end the rule of the Gods. But how, without being bound to this place?

He needed his own access, some kind of linnix he could take with him anywhere. If the machine could send and receive signals to human minds throughout Athens, surely it could do so with a portable linnix. It would just have to be a linnix with access to the Unknown God.

It could act as his Godsight.

He leaped out of bed and searched on the linnix. He learned there was such a thing as a portable linnix at one time. But as far as he could tell, they'd not been maintained, not been distributed, and ultimately were destroyed. Perhaps the Gods didn't want such a thing getting into the hands of the people.

But if such a thing once existed, it could exist again, even if he had to build it himself. He wondered how long it would take for him to learn, if he could even get the pieces to build it. But there must be something he could use, some remnants of such a machine. The Gods had used something to move their minds into the machine.

That was it! He searched for such a thing. It didn't take long. Some kind of metallic cap that covered the entire scalp with protrusions all over it, probably where the signal was sent out to the machine. If the Gods could send their entire minds through that thing, certainly Blinders could send commands through it to the Unknown God.

It was called a transference cap, and he'd have to wear it at all times to maintain his control.

He gazed at the image of the contraption, wondering what excuse he could give for wearing it. Telling everyone he controlled the Gods through it would be a very bad idea. He pictured it sitting on his head. What might it reasonably look like to other people? It could look like a...like a...

Crown.

After more investigation, Blinders figured out how to establish a connection between the Unknown God and the rest of the Gods. His first goal: to get out of this room. He opened up the connection and typed.

Athena, this is the Unknown God. Blind Boy has been chastised long enough. He understands the error of his rebelliousness. You may release him now without danger.

Words appeared on his screen. *We think it wise to contain him.*

He typed, *It is my command. Release Blind Boy. Let him go home.*

He waited for some time. No new words came. Was she ignoring him?

The door swung open. A scowling Psi stood there. "What did you do, Blind Boy?"

A chill ran through him. Was he found out?

"How did you convince Athena to let you go?"

He shook his head. "I don't know what you mean."

Psi glared a moment longer. "You can leave any time." He whirled around and left. The door closed.

Blinders rushed over to the door. It opened for him. He grinned with satisfaction and let it close. He returned to the linnix.

Athena, we will help Blind Boy no longer be blind. You will instruct your God-eunuchs to prepare the transference cap. He will wear it throughout his life and will have Godsight at last.

I don't know what a transference cap is, Athena answered.

He panicked. He assumed she'd know about it. He thought hard, then looked up the information he'd found about it and typed.

This is the transference cap. With that he sent the information to her. He held his breath, hoping it would work. A moment passed.

Why have we not done this for him before? appeared Athena's response.

His eyes misted. Even knowing she was only a machine, only a lie, a machine that had participated in destroying Lethia and Selene's lives, it still affected him that her first thought was his well-being.

He had to answer somehow. He smiled when he thought of something that should please her. *We needed to make sure he overcame his rebellious heart before we could release him.*

Another moment pulsed, then Athena responded, *It is done.*

Blinders watched the door as he waited, not sure what to expect. Nothing happened. He had no idea how long it would take for something to happen. He headed for the kitchen area and prepared a meal. He finished it and dozed off sitting at the table before the door opened.

Two God-eunuchs entered, one carrying the cap, the other a black cable with attachments on either end. It reminded him of the cables that connected every linnix to the fire of the Gods.

"Please sit over there," the God-eunuch with the cap said, indicating the middle chair at the linnix table.

He hurried over, realizing he left his conversation with Athena on the screen. He closed out everything until the linnix bird appeared. The eunuchs came to him. The one with the cable pushed one end of it into a hole in the cap, then leaned down and reached under the table with the other end. "This will fill the cap with the fire of the Gods. You'll have to do this every few days."

Blinders looked underneath and saw the cable plugged into the holes where the cables for the linnices also plugged in.

"Sit perfectly still," the other eunuch said.

Blinders sat stiffly as the man lowered the cap onto his head, then pressed down. There was a soft click as it gripped his head.

"To remove it, press here," the eunuch said. He pressed with fingers on either side of the cap. The click released the pressure, and the cap came up. The eunuch pressed it back into place with a click. The two eunuchs stood back and waited.

"Can you hear me, Blind Boy?" Athena's voice filled his head.

He jerked with shock. "Yes, I can."

"Don't speak. Think it to me."

Yes, I can, he thought.

"Can you see me, Blind Boy?"

An image formed in his head of a beautiful, lordly woman in a flowing robe with a sash tied around her waist. Her hair flowed in the wind.

Yes, I can! he thought forcefully. It was dazzling! This is what every other person experienced?

"That's good. I can see and hear the things you think to me."

That shocked him. He hadn't thought of that. Would she see everything he had planned?

"Why are you troubled, Blind Boy?"

He felt some relief. She apparently could only hear thoughts he directed at her. He responded, *I'm not used to this. It's so personal.*

He'd have to be guarded about what he envisioned in his mind.

"You'll become used to it over time."

Thank you, he thought to her and meant it. He almost felt grateful that he had Godsight at last, but then he remembered the *System Log* notes.

"The Gods can communicate to the minds of everyone," the eunuch who had the cable said, "but your cap will only work within a mile of Athens." He produced a small gadget from some pocket in his robe. "If you connect this to any linnix near you, the cap can send signals back and forth through the linnix." He handed it to Blinders.

"Never take the cap off except to swim or bathe or sleep," the other eunuch said. "You may live a normal life now. But if you show a rebellious heart again, you will be executed."

That sent a chill through him. He had nothing but rebellious acts in mind once he stepped out that door. "May I return to my home?"

"Your parents are excited to see you again. Be sure to plug that into the nearest linnix wherever you go. To be out of contact with the Gods for an unreasonable time will be considered rebellion."

The eunuchs turned and left without another word. Blinders sat at the desk in a bit of a daze. At last he had his portable linnix on his head. He had access to the Unknown God. He had control over all the Gods. But he was still restricted. He could travel up to a mile away from Athens. Beyond that he'd have to communicate with the machine through this gadget attached to other linnices.

But other linnices had no access to the Unknown God. He'd still have to accomplish his plans right here in Athens. At least he didn't have to remain in this prison.

He was ready to begin his plans. But first he wanted to find Lethia.

Athena, he thought, *I'm going home now.*

"Your family is eager to see you."

I prefer not to go home naked.

No response, but presently Psi entered the room and dropped some clothes on the bed. "Goodbye. I'm as free from my prison as you are from yours. No longer do I have to serve an accursed Blind Boy."

"I'm not a Blind Boy anymore."

Psi sneered. "A crutch for your broken brain."

"A crown of freedom," he said smugly.

Psi smirked and walked out the door.

Blinders faced the linnix and gazed at it, feeling apprehension. It was time to put his plans to the test. Could he control the Unknown God through his cap, or was he doomed to stay here sitting at these linnices until he changed all of society? He closed his eyes and thought the gibberish commands Selene gave him that he'd burned into his mind for the last year.

The Unknown God screen filled his head. He connected with Athena.

Blind Boy needs a horse to travel home.

It will be ready for him at the exit.

He smiled with satisfaction. It worked.

He removed the cap and left it on the table where it could continue to be filled with the fire of the gods. He used the toilet and took one more long, luxurious shower. He put the clothes on Psi brought him. They were a size too large, but he didn't care. He wasn't at all happy with how it felt to have fabric smother his skin after all this time and considered going home naked, but he refused to travel naked like a prisoner again.

He sat in the comfortable chair one last time to access the linnix. A part of him wanted to watch one more movie on the giant screen, but he was eager to get out before something went wrong. He didn't connect with the Unknown God this time. He looked up the location of the home for wayward girls and memorized the directions.

He swung the tray aside, put his cap on, took the cable and the connector, and felt a thrill as the door opened for him. He stepped out, wandered the halls until he found the exit, and walked into the sunlight. He let it splash on his face with closed eyes and breathed in the fresh air with its wonderful aromas. He took the reins to his horse from the eunuch that waited for him, mounted, and galloped away in the direction he'd memorized from the linnix.

The home had once been large and majestic, but now was old and in disrepair. Children played in the yard full of weeds as mothers with hollow eyes, many almost children themselves, watched them and scolded them. They all wore filthy, tattered clothing.

Blinders paused his horse and peered at the sight, his heart breaking. He felt sorrow for every one of them, but especially for Lethia that had to live in these conditions. This was something he'd have to change as the Unknown God. But for today, it was Lethia he focused on.

And their child. He didn't even know if he had a son or daughter.

The mothers and the children stared at him as he approached, whether because they never had visitors or because of his strange cap, he didn't know. One mother rushed into the house.

By the time he arrived and dismounted, an older woman came out, eyeing him suspiciously. "What is that thing on your head?"

"It's..." His plan to call it a crown sounded stupid now. "It's something from prison."

She scowled. "Leave and return after dark. These girls need time with their children."

It took him an instant to realize what she meant. "I haven't come here to whore with them!"

Her glare darkened. "What *did* you come for?"

"I came for my wife...and my child."

"There are no wives here," she growled.

"I'll make her my wife."

She laughed. "You should have done that before you loved her and abandoned her."

"I never abandoned her. I—"

"You went to prison."

He took a deep breath. "Are you telling me the Gods allow you to turn these unfortunate girls into whores?"

Her face became sorrowful. "We are the Godforsaken. We no longer hear from them, and they don't pay attention to us."

"So *you* make them become whores?" he said angrily.

She glared at him. "How else do you think we survive?"

"And make more bastard children to be shunned by society?"

"Absolutely not!" she said with a sharp gaze, then her expression softened. "They...have no wombs."

He gaped at her dumbfounded. "You cut the womb from my wife and forced her to be a whore?"

"I don't force any of them. They choose to. Those that do live better lives."

He sneered at her as he waved his hand. "You call this a better life?"

"Better than the ones who refuse!" She scowled at him, then said more calmly, "Who's the girl you're here for?"

"Lethia."

She nodded. "The one with the baby girl. You'll be happy to know she's one who refused."

He sighed with relief.

"But she and the baby are in poor shape. We've helped her as much as we can, but I can't ask the girls who work to share equally with those who won't."

They stared at each other.

"Wait here," she said and disappeared into the home.

Blinders peered at the mothers and their children, who tried to avoid looking at him. The sight killed any last vestige of positive feelings he had for Athena and the Gods. Their compassion was nothing but a machine's farce. These girls broke their rules and, with machine-like efficiency, were forsaken.

As Blinders had been the moment he became rebellious. If they hadn't feared him, would he have been banished to a place like this?

A girl crept out from the door holding a baby, a few months old. They were both thin and sickly. It took a moment for Blinders to see Lethia in her face. His heart broke. "Lethia," he said and headed for her.

She backed away a step. He stopped, unable to read her emotions.

"They let you go?" she said.

It was the obvious question to ask. He didn't know how to respond. How could he explain to her all he'd learned? But he didn't want to lie to her either.

She looked at the cap on his head. He realized that was the answer. "The Gods created this...this artifact." He touched the cap. "It gives me Godsight." He forced a smile. "I can hear the Gods in my head!"

Her eyes widened, and he thought he saw a trace of hope in them. He stepped forward with an inviting hand out. "Lethia, I can go home. *We* can go home. You, me, and our child."

In her eyes was shock, maybe disbelief. "I...we're...our daughter's a bastard. We can't go home."

"Athena commanded you to love me. She promised you wouldn't give birth. *This is not your fault!*"

"But we're not married."

"We'll get married. Our daughter won't be a bastard anymore."

Her face was troubled as she stood silently. She gazed at him, at their daughter, then looked back at the other mothers and the older woman watching them silently. She turned back to him. "Have the Gods instructed this?"

Her words were chilling, and his heart sank. Even now, after what Athena had done to her, she was afraid to act without the approval of the Gods. What if she couldn't accept what he knew? Would he have to let her believe a lie all her life? Would he have to play along with that lie to not upset her?

No! He came to free her. Not only from this physical squalor, but also from the iron grip the Gods had on her mind.

But not here. Not now.

He smiled. "It's not for the Gods to decide. It's our choice to marry." He stepped forward again so he stood right before her. This time she didn't step back. "I love you, Lethia. I want to be your husband. And..." He stroked the flimsy hair of their daughter. "I want to be her father."

She watched him stroke her hair, then looked up at him with genuine hope shining in her eyes. She looked back at the older woman.

"Go, child," the woman said. "Fewer mouths for us to feed." Her expression was somber. Several of the mothers had tears in their eyes.

Lethia peered at him with her eyes gleaming. She whispered, "Take me away from here."

They ran to the horse. Blinders held the infant while Lethia climbed up. He handed the child to her, then mounted behind them and kicked the horse into a gallop. His spirit soared as the wind rushed by, fluttering Lethia's hair against his face. They were both free at last!

"Blinders," Lethia cried over the wind. "What will our families think? What will the townspeople think?"

He remembered the hatred her father Eusebius displayed as the eunuch led Blinders to prison. *Good riddance! You'll never see her again.* No, he probably wouldn't accept them with the hatred he felt toward the Blind Boy.

"Lethia, will you come with me to Athens and marry me in the temple there? Then we can return home with honor. Married with a legitimate daughter and a Blind Boy who's no longer blind."

"Yes!" she said intensely.

They reached the main road. Blinders slowed the horse down. This was the beginning of their freedom, of their life together as a family. He didn't need to rush in fear anymore.

"What's her name?" he said.

"Callista."

He could hear the affection in her voice. "It's as beautiful as she is."

They traveled until the spires of the temple in Athens showed above the trees, so much more magnificent than the small temple back home.

Blind Boy, where have you been? Athena's voice in his head startled him. They must be within a mile of Athens.

"I went to get Lethia and our daughter," he said without apology.

You were to connect with us through a linnix.

"There are no linnices at the home for wayward girls." He wasn't positive that was true, but if they were the Godforsaken, he thought it likely.

"Who are you talking to?" Lethia asked.

He realized he'd spoken out loud. "Athena. I'm used to speaking to her with my voice."

Why have you returned to Athens?

It bothered him that the Goddess challenged him so much. He feared that wasn't a good sign. Immediately he recited the commands in his mind to connect with the Unknown God.

Athena, you will allow Blind Boy and Lethia to marry in Athens, then return to their homes as an accepted family of society. You will instruct Eusebius, Lethia's father, to welcome them.

A moment passed, then Athena said, *Blind Boy, come to the temple.*

"Athena told me we should go to the temple," Lethia said.

"She told me too."

They rode into the city and followed the spires to the center. Blinders felt apprehension at entering the building that had been his prison for over a year. But it was also where he and Lethia could legitimize their family.

They dismounted and handed the reins to a God-eunuch. Another eunuch said, "This way," and led them inside. Blinders put his arm around Lethia, and she smiled at him. He gazed down at Callista, feeling amazed that this was his daughter. The love he and Lethia shared would soon be sacred after all.

He realized the eunuch led them to the room where he'd been imprisoned and stopped. "This is not where marriages are done."

The eunuch turned to him and with no emotion said, "The marriage will be conducted here out of sight. The people are not ready to accept you as one of them. You must give them time." He walked to the door, which opened for him, then headed to the middle of the room and waited.

"Athena says we're to be married here," Lethia said.

A foreboding fell upon him. He never intended to come here again, and now Athena was leading him back into the prison. But how could this be a trap? He had access to the Unknown God that ruled over the Gods, and the Gods didn't even realize it. It must be nothing more than what the eunuch said. The Gods were concerned the people weren't ready for this, after being taught all their lives to fear the Blind Boy. They were only exercising their usual machine compassion for the people.

He stepped in, leading Lethia with his arm. They stopped before the eunuch, who gazed at them with an expressionless face. Blinders waited for him to begin the ceremony. But he did nothing.

"We're ready to be married," Blinders said.

The eunuch continued to gaze at them without moving.

Something was very wrong. *Athena, instruct the God-eunuch to begin—"*

A deafening buzz pulsated throughout the room over and over. Red lights flashed. The door slammed shut. An unknown voice filled Blinders' mind, machine-like, neither male nor female.

Firewall breach. Location main console room. Lockdown in effect.

The eunuch grabbed Blinders by his clothing and threw him to the ground. For the first time in his life, Blinders saw a powerful emotion in the face of a eunuch—a snarling wrath.

Lethia backed away in alarm and pressed her back against the wall. The large screen behind her came to life, flashing the same words Blinders heard in his head. Lethia screamed and ran to the foot of the bed, cowering on the floor, protectively clutching Callista to her breast.

All the linnices flashed the same message.

Firewall breach. Location main console room. Lockdown in effect.

The eunuch fell upon Blinders and grasped at his cap.

They knew! The Gods discovered what Blinders was doing. He grabbed the eunuch's wrists and fought back.

Firewall breach. Location main console room. Lockdown in effect.

The door flew open, and Psi and Chi charged in. Blinders shoved the eunuch off and scrambled to the privy door.

It wouldn't open.

He turned to see Psi and Chi running at him. Desperately he called up the help command in the Unknown God and scanned the available commands for the one he remembered seeing in *System Logs*.

Firewall breach. Location main console room. Lockdown in effect.

"Get that cap off his head!" the eunuch cried, pointing.

Blinders slid to the floor with his back against the privy door. He kicked at Psi as he arrived, shoving him back onto the floor.

There was the command! The one he saw in Selene's notes. *Purge*. Quickly he read the instructions for it.

Firewall breach. Location main console room. Lockdown in effect.

"Purge subsystem Zeus!" Blinders cried.

Chi dropped onto him and reached for the cap. Blinders pushed against the door and launched the cap into his chin. He cried out with blood trickling from wounds from the protrusions.

Firewall breach. Location main console room. Lockdown in effect.

"Purge subsystem Hera!"

Psi grabbed his feet. Blinders kicked hard, trying to release them.

Firewall breach. Location main console room. Lockdown in effect.

"Purge subsystem Aphrodite!"

Chi leaned on him, pressing him to the floor. "I got it!" He fumbled with the cap.

Firewall breach. Location main console room. Lockdown in effect.

"Purge subsystem Hermes!"

Blinders punched Chi on the side of his head. Chi cried out, but kept struggling to grasp the cap. Blinders grappled with his hands, keeping them from getting a good grip.

Firewall breach. Location main console room. Lockdown in effect.

"Purge subsystem Poseidon!"

Psi kicked him in the groin. Blinders howled in pain. His grip on Chi's hands loosened.

Firewall breach. Location main console room. Lockdown in effect.

"Purge subsystem—"

Blinders! Athena called in his head. Her voice was filled with pleading. *Please don't kill me. I've always loved you. I've always cared only for your well-being.*

He hesitated. Her pleas brought back the feelings he had for her all his life.

"I've got it!" Chi shouted. Blinders heard the click that loosened the cap.

"—Athena!" he shouted.

The cap flew off. Blinders foot connected with Chi's face. The man sprawled back with blood running from his nose. The cap sailed out of his hands, then landed and rolled across the floor.

The pulsating buzz stopped. The flashing lights disappeared. The words on the linnix screens dissolved into the bird icon. The entry door swung open. The privy door gave out a grinding sound as it pushed against Blinders trying to open. He scrambled away and stood up.

The room was deathly still. Psi and Chi and the God-eunuch looked about in shock. Lethia peered at him with her face contorted and tears streaming down her cheeks.

Blinders looked around himself. What had happened? Had he completed the command in time?

Psi glared at Blinders, motionless as if waiting. Suddenly his face wrinkled with concern. "Athena?" he said. "Athena! What do we do with Blind Boy?"

Nothing happened.

Chi stood up, looking as confused as Psi. "Zeus?" He became more alarmed. "Hera? Aphrodite? Hermes?"

Psi cried out, "Poseidon?"

The eunuch gazed around with fear in his face.

"What's happening?" Lethia whimpered. "Why don't the Gods answer?"

Blinders scrambled to the cap and jammed it back on. Furiously he thought the login and the commands to enter the Unknown God. The others watched in apprehension, frozen in place.

Zeus, Blinders called out. *Hera. Aphrodite. Hermes. Poseidon.*

There was no response.

Athena!

"Is that you?" Lethia said as she gazed at him with a confused expression.

Blinders gaped at her. "You could hear me?" He looked at Psi, at Chi, at the eunuch. They peered at him with horrified expressions. Had they all heard him through their Godsight? Had all of Athens heard everything that happened? Did the firewall breach, whatever *that* was, open all communication?

Did he have the ear of every person in Athens right now? A thrill shot through him. He stood tall and sent out his thoughts.

I am the Unknown God, the ruler of all the Gods.

Lethia stared at him with her lip trembling.

Don't be afraid of what you heard. Everything is under my control now.

Psi and Chi backed off, keeping their eyes fixed on him.

The Gods rebelled against me. They have kept you in darkness and robbed you of prosperity.

The eunuch's face filled with dread.

I have sent them away. I will be your only God now.

Blinders peered at the terrified people in the room, thinking what to do next. Did they realize he was the Unknown God? That was not a good thing. He was only human, and eventually everyone would realize that. He needed some other explanation.

He thought of his cap, the artifact—the manmade instrument, he corrected himself—that allowed him to connect with the Unknown God. He remembered what he thought it looked like when he first saw it, and smiled.

The God-eunuchs will no longer have authority over you.

A panicked look spread across the eunuch's face.

From this time forth, my chosen king will be the only authority over you. I have placed my crown on his head. He's the one you've known as Blind Boy. I have cured his Godblindness.

The shock on everyone's face, including Lethia's, almost made Blinders laugh, but he suppressed it. He had a dignified role to play now. He turned to Psi and Chi. "Leave us. Return to your homes. Your service here is done."

They gaped at him for a moment longer, then reluctantly slunk away.

To the God-eunuch he said, "You and your brothers will be taken care of. The Unknown God will teach you how to live your own lives. Go tell them."

The eunuch nodded and hurried out the door.

Blinders gazed at Lethia. Her face was full of emotion.

"It's you, isn't it?" she whispered.

He came over to her. She stiffened up.

He knelt down before her and took her hand. "Please don't be afraid of me. Remember, it was the Gods who taught everyone to fear me. It was their treatment of me that pushed me to rebelliousness. It was the Gods who forced you to that terrible home to live in poverty."

Her head shook. "How...did you...?"

He smiled and stood up, then extended his hand. She stared at it, then took it and let him lead her to the plush chair. "Have a seat." She sat, adjusting Callista in her arms. Blinders swung the arm where he could reach it and typed the *sudo* command that had started it all, that Selene had given him.

The wall filled with the icons of the Unknown God. "This linnix has knowledge in it that our linnices back home can't show us. I've spent a year learning everything I could. What I've learned you might find impossible to believe, but I swear it's true."

The look she gave him expressed apprehension, but it grew into anticipation. "Will you teach me?"

"I will. But it's too much to give you now. I'll teach you over time, as we live as husband and wife." He smiled at her.

She smiled as she blushed. "But we're still not married."

"I promise we will be. You'll be my wife *and* my queen."

The smile on her face grew. He offered his hand and helped her to her feet.

"Let's go talk to the people of Athens and introduce ourselves. They're probably terrified about what happened."

They left the room. This time Blinders didn't vow to never return. It didn't matter anymore. There were no Gods left to entrap him. He could come and go as he pleased.

Outside the temple people stood about in a buzz of heated conversation. When they saw him, they all fell silent. Someone knelt down, then another, and another, until everyone in sight was on their knees.

Blinders lifted his arms as he imagined a king would when addressing his people. As he spoke the words, he sent the same thoughts out for the Unknown God to share with everyone.

"People of Athens, I am the king of the Unknown God. The reign of the Gods is over. Only the One God will rule now. That's what you'll call him, the One God. He's no longer unknown to you."

He glanced at Lethia, who watched him with wonder.

"Your lives will become better now. The temples of the Gods have used most of the fire of the Gods, leaving little for you. That will change. The fire will be spread out to all of you."

The people peered at one another. An excited buzz passed through them.

"The homes of those girls who have been shunned for giving birth without marriage will be shut down. They are no longer to be shunned. They and their children will be welcomed by their families with open arms."

He reached out to Lethia, who joined him as he put his arm around her. "This is Lethia, and this is my daughter Callista. They lived in such a home, in poverty with little to eat. That will never happen again. She and I will wed before you today, and she will become your queen."

The buzz became more excited. Lethia beamed at him.

"You'll be taught the learning of the Gods that they've withheld from you. You'll learn how to do wonderful things you never dreamed of. You will enjoy prosperity that you've never seen."

A cheer went up among the people.

He took Lethia in his arms and kissed her deeply. They peered into each other's eyes. The crowd cheered again.

It's true? her voice came into his mind. He was thrilled he could hear her thoughts as the Gods had all her life. *You're the king, but also the One God?*

Yes.

Her expression became somber. *Will you become like the other Gods?*

"No!" he said out loud. "I'm *saving* the people from the rule of such Gods."

"And putting them under the rule of the One God. You."

He looked out at the people. "The Gods used them, kept them in the dark. I'm saving them from that."

"By keeping them in the dark about you?"

"Lethia, they don't know how to live life without the Gods. They'd be lost. I have to teach them, wean them away from a life full of Gods." He stroked Callista's hair. "Like a mother slowly weans her child from the breast."

She gave him a smile, but it was forlorn. "I know you mean well. But I don't want you to become like those Gods that imprisoned you and sent me to that home."

"I won't!"

"Promise me you'll stop playing God."

"I promise!" he said with conviction. "But not yet." He gazed out at the people on their knees peering at him with the same expression of adoration he'd seen on the faces of his parents at the temple, an expression now directed at him and the One God he played. It exhilarated him that these people who once loathed him now venerated him.

"Not yet," he whispered.

The Dreamcatcher

Cassandra finished putting on her shoes, feeling nervous about tonight. Her client was young, a mere thirteen-year-old boy. It shouldn't make any difference, but she always felt nervous poking around in such an underdeveloped brain.

The dreamcatcher hung on the wall in her bedroom by a single nail. She put her jacket on as she stood before it. The hoop was made of willow. The network of fibers stretched within it represented the web of Spider Grandmother of Native American folklore. From the lower half of the hoop dangled a thick clump of feathers and strings of beads.

She tried to remember when she purchased it. About four years ago? That would have been when she was thirteen herself. She purchased it from a Navajo family with a booth alongside a dusty road in the Four Corners area of Utah, Colorado, New Mexico, and Arizona. It symbolized the abilities she was born with. From that time forth, she called herself the Dreamcatcher.

Gently she lifted it from the nail and turned to get her mother. It was time to go to work.

The Campbell family sat around their living room. Margaret sat next to her husband Tom on the sofa, fidgeting as she waited. She resented that the others weren't as nervous as she was.

Their older son Ethan, almost an adult, sat in a chair reading a book. Kevin sat on another chair, typically motionless, studying his hands in his lap. Their youngest, preteen daughter Robyn, huddled in the corner on the floor, quietly playing with her dolls.

When they heard the sound of a car pulling up, Margaret, Tom, and Ethan looked at each other. "Is it her?" Ethan said.

The three of them rushed to the large window, lifted one of the blind slats, and peered out. A teenage girl stepped out of the passenger side, paused on the sidewalk to examine the house, then turned and wave to the silhouette of a woman in the driver's seat. The car pulled away.

"I thought she'd be a withered old gypsy woman," Ethan said.

"Tom," Margaret said, feeling apprehension grow inside her, "I'm not so sure about this."

"We've tried everything else."

"She's just a child."

"Scott recommended her."

"He's only your best friend from high school. That doesn't mean he knows what he's talking about."

Tom sighed. "I trust him."

"I don't."

"I have a hunch about this."

It irritated her when he used that as an argument. "You and your hunches! I'm the one who's supposed to have intuition."

Tom chuckled. "You do."

"And my intuition says this won't turn out well."

Tom glanced at her, shaking his head just enough so she could notice it, then turned and said, "Kevin, you'd better get ready for bed now. She didn't want you here while she talks to us."

Kevin looked up from his hands, then stood and plodded up the stairs.

Cassandra gazed at the house, assessing it. A two-story building with an attached two-car garage in a neighborhood of carbon-copy homes, some of them mirror images of the Campbell's house, all crammed together on post-age-stamp lots. Upper middle class.

She waved to her mother so she'd drive away, then walked up the sidewalk to the door. In the window on the right, a blind slat was pulled open, and eyes stared at her. She stopped and stared them down, feeling like a freak in a circus side show.

The slat snapped shut.

With a weary sigh, she continued to the door and rang the bell. When the door opened, three people crowded around it, gawking at her. A father and mother, obviously, and a young man who was probably their son. She scolded herself for letting a flutter of emotion react to how attractive he was.

"You must be Cassandra?" the father said.

She nodded and walked in without waiting to be invited. The three moved aside to give her space. The door closed behind her.

She examined the living room. Nice furnishings, an impressive entertainment center, a book case with important-looking books that were probably never read, tacky landscape artwork on the walls, family photos that included two other children not gawking at her right now. One of them was the girl sitting in the corner preoccupied with dolls. The other must be the thirteen-year-old boy.

"We're the Campbells," the father said clumsily to break the ice. "My name is Tom. This is my wife Margaret."

Cassandra nodded curtly. Margaret reluctantly held her hand out. She gave it a brief shake.

"And this is our son Ethan," Tom said.

Ethan extended his hand with a broad smile. "Hi, Cassandra."

Again she had to squelch her emotions. She needed to remain professional with clients. She shook his hand with nothing more than politeness.

"What's your last name?" Ethan said.

"Tonight I'm just Cassandra."

One of his eyebrows raised. It was obnoxiously adorable, and in spite of herself she let a tiny bit of emotion in. She gave him a slight smile. "But you can call me Cassie."

"Okay, Cassie," he replied with an even bigger smile.

"May I take your jacket?" Tom said.

"Thank you." She removed it and handed it to him, shifting the dreamcatcher back and forth between her hands to slide her arms out.

He hung it on a nearby coat tree. "Would you like to sit down?"

She walked over to a chair and sat, resting the dreamcatcher on her lap. Tom and Margaret took the sofa, and Ethan sat in a chair that faced her. All four of them stared at each other for an uncomfortable moment. The daughter played in the corner as if nothing were happening.

Ethan gestured at the dreamcatcher. "What's that you have there?"

"It's a dreamcatcher."

"I thought *you* were the Dreamcatcher," Margaret said.

This was a typical conversation she endured multiple times until she was sick of it, but she held her irritation back. "I am. This is for Kevin."

Margaret studied it. "It's pretty small."

"Size doesn't matter," Cassie said.

Ethan smirked. "That's what she *didn't* say."

"Ethan!" Margaret spat.

A corner of Cassie's mouth twitched before she was able to suppress her smile. Ethan gazed at his mother with chagrin that was tainted with a hint of satisfaction. "Sorry, it just slipped out."

"Tell me about Kevin," Cassie said.

Both parents immediately became guarded. "Well," Tom said, "he's had nightmares for a long time, but he seemed to be okay otherwise. Then one day he suddenly stopped talking and—"

"What happened that day?"

"Nothing we're aware of. He's never talked since."

"How long ago was that?"

"About a year." Tom glanced at Margaret, who studied her lap with a scowl. "We've taken him to a couple of therapists, but they don't seem to get anywhere."

People could be so clueless! Especially parents. "Don't you think something happened to him that day?"

"Of course we do!" Margaret snapped as she shot an annoyed look at Cassie. "But we have no idea what. Kevin won't tell anybody."

"The therapists couldn't figure it out?"

"He wouldn't talk to them," Tom said. "They wanted us to...commit Kevin to some facility. But we're not—"

"No way is that happening!" Margaret said.

"My friend Scott recommended you," Tom said. "We figured it was worth a try before we did anything...drastic."

"Tom thought that," Margaret said. "I have to be frank. I'm not comfortable with this."

"My mom is suspicious about everything," Ethan said.

Cassie glanced at Ethan, then studied Margaret. She was the one who would be resistant. There was usually a resistant one. "As long as I'm here, why not let me try? Even if I fail, no harm will come to Kevin."

"I just have this..." Margaret looked at Tom. "Well, I...I suppose...I mean... What will you do?"

"I'll watch him while he sleeps, and I'll listen."

"That's all?"

"Pretty much."

"What good will that do?"

"What harm will it do?"

Margaret's brow knotted as she frowned. "What will you listen to?"

"His dreams. I'm a Dreamcatcher."

Margaret shook her head. The woman couldn't accept any of this.

There was usually one.

"Like she says," Tom said, "what harm will it do?"

"It'll create false hopes."

"Like taking Kevin to therapists?"

Margaret gave him a sharp look.

Cassie gazed at the girl in the corner as their drama played out. The girl continued to ignore all of them and focus on her dolls. "Who's this?"

"Oh, that's our daughter Robyn," Tom said. "She's pretty quiet and shy."

That caught Cassie's attention. "Like Kevin?"

"Oh, no, not like Kevin. She talks. She's always been shy. Kevin changed suddenly."

Cassie nodded, thinking, *Parents!* She stood and walked to Robyn, crouching down before her. Robyn watched her approach.

"Hi, Robyn. I'm Cassie."

"Hi."

"I like your dolls. They're pretty." She picked one up. "What's her name?"

"Angie."

"That's a pretty name."

"What's that?" Robyn said, gazing at the dreamcatcher.

"That's my dreamcatcher."

"It catches dreams?"

"That's what they say. It was made by Native Americans."

"Can it catch my dreams?"

That was the sort of thing Cassie looked for. It could be a question of mere curiosity. Or it could be a plea for...something. "Maybe so."

Cassie smiled warmly at her and stroked her cheek with the back of her hand, then returned to Tom and Margaret. "I think it's time I see Kevin."

Margaret scowled as the three of them stood. "How do I know any of this is real—"

Cassie held up her hand. "I don't deal with skepticism. Either you want my services or you don't. Do you want my services?"

"Yes, we do," Tom jumped in quickly.

"Then bring me to Kevin."

"Don't you want to hear more?" Tom asked.

"Is there more to tell?"

"Well, we think he might—"

Her hand stopped him. "I'm here to learn what you don't know, not be biased by what you think you know."

"Um...okay." He held his hand to the stairs. "This way." Tom and Margaret moved to lead the way.

"If you don't mind, I'd prefer you two don't come with."

Margaret glared at her. "This is getting—"

"But I could use an assistant." Cassie turned to Ethan. "Do you think you could help me?"

A huge grin popped out on his face. "I'd be happy to."

"We're his parents!" Margaret growled.

Cassie's irritation got the better of her. "What is it you think I'm going to do to Kevin?"

"It's alright, Mom," Ethan said. "I'll protect him from her wily ways."

Cassie looked down to hide her smile.

Tom and Margaret stood helpless as Ethan led Cassie up the stairs.

The stairs connected to a hallway at the top heading right and left. To the left it ended in a single door. To the right were two other doors. An open bathroom door faced the stairs.

Ethan turned right and led Cassie to the nearer door. "What kind of help do you want me to give you?"

"You've already given it. I don't want your parents there, but your mother would've never let me be alone with him."

"What have you got against my parents?"

"Nothing. I just don't like parents hovering over me. They're too intrusive...too protective."

He paused at the door. "Are you really going to just listen?"

"More or less."

"What does that mean?"

"Is this it?" she said, looking at the door. He nodded. She opened it and walked in, followed by Ethan.

A boy, barely a teenager, sat upright on his bed in a fetal hug with nothing but boxer shorts and a T-shirt on. His back pressed against the backboard.

The bedroom contained a desk and chair and lots of baseball paraphernalia, a glove and ball on the desk, and a bat leaning against the wall. Baseball trophies sat on a shelf above the desk. Photos of Kevin with a man dressed like a coach and other photos of another man dressed like a scoutmaster hung on the wall.

Cassie stood at the foot of the bed and smiled at the boy. He looked right through her, never moving his eyes. Ethan stood next to her.

"Hi, Kevin. My name is Cassie."

He didn't twitch a muscle.

She moved to sit on the side of the bed. "I know something happened to you a year ago."

She waited to see if he'd react. Nothing.

"It must have been a terrible thing. So bad you can't talk about it." Delicately she reached out to stroke his bare foot with the back of her hand. "I'm here to help you let it out. All you have to do is go to sleep, and I'll catch your dreams...with this."

She held up the dreamcatcher. His eyes drifted up to look.

"It's a dreamcatcher, made by Native Americans. It'll catch your dreams, and I'll listen to them."

Kevin looked at her. She smiled, pleased at the reaction, then went to the wall opposite his bed, pulled down a photo that she set on the desk, and hung the dreamcatcher in its place. She returned to sit on the bed. "Now Kevin, you just need to relax and go to sleep. I'll sit over there with your brother and wait."

Kevin looked at her, then at Ethan. His expression never changed.

She said to Ethan, "Is there another chair you can get?"

"Be right back." He headed out the door.

She turned to Kevin. "Lie down now and I'll tuck you in."

His brow twitched.

"Don't worry. I won't read you a bedtime story," she teased. She smiled as she gently pulled his arms down from his legs and stretched his legs out onto the bed. Ethan returned with a chair and paused at the door to watch.

Kevin still remained motionless.

"Now Kevin, if you don't lie down yourself, I'll have to gather you up like a baby and lay you down."

He peered at her, then settled down flat and stared at the ceiling. Cassie stood and pulled the covers over him. "You're as stiff as a board!" She sat next to him and prodded him. "Turn over."

She finally got him to lie on his stomach. She massaged his shoulders. "Relax, now, Kevin. Fall asleep. Everything will be okay."

Ethan watched as she rubbed his back. Kevin's eyelids drooped until they closed. Before long soft snores came from his lips.

Carefully to avoid waking him, she slid off the bed and sat in the chair. Ethan set his chair next to her and sat. He leaned over and whispered, "You've got a great bedside manner."

She blushed. "It's no big deal."

"No, I mean it. I can tell you have lots of empathy for people."

"It's just what happens when I can get to know them so well."

"Through their dreams?"

She smiled.

He looked up at the dreamcatcher on the wall. "Are you serious about catching dreams with that thing?"

"It's just a prop. Something to distract Kevin from me."

"If we're not really going to catch dreams, what *are* we doing?"

"We *are* going to catch dreams. *I'm* the Dreamcatcher."

He cocked his head with a skeptical look. "Are you seriously saying you can hear my brother's dreams?"

"Hear them, see them, feel them." She realized she was bragging, so she forced a more neutral tone. "Whatever he hears and sees and feels."

"No offense, Cassie, but that's a little hard to swallow."

She sighed in disappointment and felt foolish for expecting something different from him. "So don't swallow it. I'll catch his dreams whether you believe it or not."

"But...aren't you gonna try to convince me?"

She stood up and moved over to the desk to examine the trophies. "Why should I care if you believe me?"

He came over to her. "I didn't mean—"

"Kevin's really into baseball."

"Home run king for his team. At least...back when he was talking."

"That's his coach?" She pointed to a photo.

"Mm-hmm."

"And this is his scoutmaster?"

Ethan cocked his head to the side. "You thinking something?"

"No...not yet."

Kevin moaned slightly and stirred in his sleep. He flopped over on his back. Ethan was about to say more, but Cassie put her hand up to quiet him. He whispered, "Did you catch a dream?"

"I just don't want to wake him."

She crept over and crouched before the bed, gazing at Kevin's face. Ethan crept to the other side of the bed, watching. Kevin's eyes began to move back and forth behind his lids.

"It's starting," Cassie whispered.

She settled into a comfortable kneel and focused on Kevin. The view of his face unfocused and dissolved into a grey fog that materialized into a sunny day in a park. The fog never went away entirely.

The Campbell family sat at a picnic table appearing to enjoy themselves. Kevin looked at the food on the table. A bowl of rotting fruit. Sandwiches spotted with green mold. Potato salad with flies crawling all over it.

Ethan grabbed a sandwich and bit into it, ignoring the mold. Frowning, Kevin turned away.

Robyn took him by the hand. They walked along a path in the park that plunged into a grove of trees. The day was suddenly dark as if an ominous storm had swept in. The wind picked up into a gale. The trees swayed creepily above them.

Shadowy movement roamed among the trees. Kevin jerked his head back and forth, never quite catching a glimpse of what they were.

Ahead a mist flowed into the trees. Robyn led Kevin directly into it. The trees were shadowy silhouettes in the gloom.

A ghostly figure leaped out at them, a black-hooded robe with glowing red eyes where the face should be. Kevin cried out and fell back. In the bedroom, Cassie jerked and gasped.

Kevin ran from the ghostly figure. Robyn was nowhere to be seen. The ghostly figure jumped into Kevin's path from the right, grasping with skeletal fingers.

Kevin cried out and veered away, but the figure jumped in from the left, grasping. Kevin darted away in another direction, but the gloomy grove of trees never seemed to end.

The figure emerged from the mist ahead. Kevin couldn't stop in time before running into its open arms. They clamped around him.

Kevin cried out.

Cassie and Ethan jerked back as Kevin bolted up to a sitting position with a gasp. He stared straight ahead for an instant with a wild look in his eyes, then turned his gaze to Cassie.

She stroked his cheek with the back of her hand. "It's okay. It was just a dream."

He stared at her, then looked up at the dreamcatcher on the wall.

"Yes, I caught your dream. The black robe, the glowing eyes."

His head jerked toward her in surprise.

"Is that what you saw?" Ethan said.

"You asking me or Kevin?"

He pondered an instant. "Both, I guess."

"Is that what you saw, Kevin?"

Kevin stared at her without moving.

"Guess we'll never know," Ethan said.

She stroked Kevin's cheek again. "Go back to sleep. I'll be here with you. Whatever you dream, I'll dream with you."

Kevin lay back down and closed his eyes. Cassie kept stroking his cheek until his breathing became even. She and Ethan returned to their chairs.

"What did you see?" Ethan said.

She took a deep breath. "His dream was shadowy...like a fog. Usually they look clearer."

"Does that mean something?"

"I don't know what."

"No guesses?"

"No, I...I have to think about it."

"What was the dream?"

"It's private."

"Oh."

They sat quietly, Cassie watching Kevin, Ethan watching Cassie. She could feel his eyes on her. Normally when boys did that, it bothered her. They were probably staring at her because she was a freak. But she didn't feel that coming from Ethan. It gave her pleasant tingles, but she didn't want to get distracted by that while working.

"I was kind of hoping you *would* try to convince me," he said.

"What for?"

"I don't know. I guess...it's kind of disappointing that you don't care what I think."

"It's not that I don't care. I'm just sick of trying to convince people. Everyone's a skeptic."

"I didn't say I was skeptical. Just...that it's...hard to swallow."

She gave him a stern glance. "What's the difference?"

He leaned in closer. "Maybe I *want* you to convince me."

She could feel her face burning, so she turned away. "I wouldn't know how to convince you. It's something I just...do."

"Maybe if you explain to me how it works."

"I don't know how it works. I listen. I hear the dream."

"Maybe...could it be...you're just imagining it? How do you know you're hearing real dreams?"

"Because when they tell me their dreams, it's the same thing I saw. Kevin's the only one who doesn't talk."

"The same all the time?"

"Some don't remember their dreams. But when they do, I get it right."

"Sounds like you're psychic."

She hated that word. People used it dismissively. "If that's what you want to call it. Mediums. Crystal balls. Tarot cards. Palm readings. It's all the same."

"Crystal balls?" he smirked. "Tarot cards?"

"They're just props. It's really the...*psychic*...doing it."

"I always assumed they were frauds."

"Many of them are. But that doesn't mean they all are."

"I take it you claim to be one of the real ones."

She gave him a dirty look and tried to mean it. It irked her that she couldn't feel that way toward him. He seemed to be teasing her, but it was more affectionate than malicious. She felt like she was in uncharted waters. This was the first time she'd ever bantered with a boy, and she liked it. She wasn't sure what she thought about that.

"Can you read my mind?" he asked.

"No."

He reacted to the blunt answer. "Why not?"

"You've got a barrier set up around your thoughts. Everybody does."

"I'm not *trying* to put up a barrier."

"It's a reflex. If I try to hear someone's thoughts while they're conscious, they sense it. You know, like that eyes on the back of your head feeling? And the barrier goes right up."

"Whoa! That almost makes sense."

"Thanks a lot," she grumbled.

"Can't I try to drop the barrier?"

"You can *try*. That's what all the props are for. To distract people from their barrier."

"So that dreamcatcher thing helps people drop their barrier, and you read their minds?"

"Our family does things a little differently. We wait for dreams when the barrier automatically drops."

"Your whole family does this?" he said incredulously.

"Well, no. I'm the only one in my immediate family. But I do have an aunt and a cousin who are like me. And a great grandmother who was the strongest of all. It's tradition in our family to catch dreams. That's how we practice our..." She waved her hand. "...ability."

"So when Kevin dreams, *then* you can read his mind."

"I wouldn't call it *reading* exactly. You know how dreams are. Weird and distorted. I have to figure them out."

"Sounds like plain mind reading would be simpler. Maybe you should just get some tarot cards."

She laughed. "Like people's thoughts are any less chaotic! At least dreams have a story, bizarre as it is, not a jumble of random thinking."

Gently the bedroom door opened. Tom and Margaret appeared. Cassie took a deep breath to hide her irritation.

"How are things going?" Tom whispered.

"Fine," whispered Ethan.

Looking at Kevin, Margaret said, "Is everything okay?"

"Everything's fine, Mom."

"Has anything happened yet?" said Margaret.

"Cassie caught a dream. It was pretty vague."

Margaret scowled.

"Mom, everything's fine. All she did was kneel beside him and listen."

"What did he dream?" Tom asked.

"I'm not ready to talk about it," Cassie said. "I need to study more dreams." She added more pointedly, "We'll talk in the morning."

Margaret looked around the room once more, focused on Kevin, then returned her gaze to Cassie and Ethan. "Can I get you anything?"

Ethan said, "If we need something, I'll take care of it. Go get some sleep."

"Let's go, Margaret," Tom said.

Reluctantly she pulled the door closed.

"That's why I wanted you here," Cassie said.

———

"You knew she was going to listen," Tom said as Margaret closed the door.

Irritated she said, "Yeah, but—"

"So why get your shorts in a knot when she does?"

"Don't mock me, Tom!"

She peered down the hall at Robyn's bedroom door on the end and, on an impulse, headed over and quietly opened it. Robyn was sound asleep. She closed the door.

Tom, still standing by Kevin's door, said with a smirk, "Is everything alright? Did the boogeyman get her?"

She scowled at him as she approached him. "I just have a bad feeling about tonight."

"I'm sorry."

They went into their bedroom at the other end and closed the door.

Cassandra stood at the window, gazing out at the full moon, now high in the sky. "Beautiful night, isn't it?" Ethan said, coming up to her.

She nodded .

"Does the full moon help you catch dreams?"

"Don't be silly."

"I love your hair. It's so full and luxurious."

He lifted his hand as if to touch it, but pulled away. She took a step back, but also felt a touch of excitement that he wanted to. "Thank you. Do you always stand so close to girls?"

He blushed. "I...don't...actually." He walked away from her. "I've never been any good at talking to girls. Especially..." He paused, then faced her. "I don't really know how to flirt. It would probably come out stupid if I tried."

She found it hard to imagine he had any trouble with girls.

He looked down at the floor. "So I'm just gonna come right out and say it. Cassie..." He took a deep breath. "I'm attracted to you."

A thrill shot through her. "Because of my hair?"

"Your hair, your face, those gorgeous eyes, your cute butt—" His eyes popped wide with embarrassment. "See? It came out stupid!"

She tried to hide a smile and failed. "That was...sweet...I guess." She felt her face flushing, so she returned to her chair. He sat beside her. She fought back an urge to put her hand on his. "Since you were honest with me, I'm attracted to you too."

"You are?" he said with surprise.

"Your face, your eyes, and..." She smiled self-consciously. "You have a cute butt too."

He laughed. "I've never said those things to anyone before."

"I've never had anyone say them to me before."

"You've got to be kidding. No one every complimented you on your hair, your eyes?"

"Oh, aunts and grandmas, I suppose. Not boys."

"That's impossible to believe."

"I'm just too weird."

"That's what I like about you."

"That I'm weird?"

"That you're different from the other girls."

"Different equals weird."

"You're exotic."

"Weird."

"Sophisticated."

"Weird."

"Okay, you're weird."

She frowned like she was wounded.

"It's a good thing," he said. "Normal is boring."

"Then I'm definitely not boring."

He reached his hand out and paused. She tingled with anticipation. When she didn't balk, he brushed some hair from her face. "I like how smart you are. How you came in and took charge. Nothing seems to ruffle your feathers."

"You sure you're thinking of me?"

"You've been that way since you got here. I've never seen anyone handle my mom like you did."

"I'm just a shy girl that was born with a *weird* talent."

"Shy you're not."

"On my job. Here I'm a professional. You should see me at school. I don't get straight A's. I don't get much attention, except to get *you're weird* looks."

"They're morons."

"I won't argue with that."

"See how good a match we are?" He rested his hand on hers. "I think you're beautiful on the outside and on the inside."

She blushed deeply. "I don't know what to say."

He grinned. "Say thank you, Ethan."

"Thank you, Ethan."

"Say I love you, Ethan."

"I like you, Ethan."

"Say I worship the ground you walk on, Ethan."

"Screw you, Ethan."

He laughed out loud, then quickly put his hand over his mouth. Kevin moaned and shifted position. "Sorry," he whispered, cringing.

Kevin moaned again. Cassie perked up, studying him.

"Another dream?" Ethan said.

"I think you may have triggered one." She headed to the bed and leaned over Kevin. His eyes darted back and forth. She knelt beside him and focused. Ethan stood behind her.

Her consciousness melted into Kevin's. He stood before a playground in the park. Everything seemed foggy again. Robyn played on a climbing playset with Ethan watching her. Tom and Margaret sat on a park bench not far away, talking and paying no attention to the kids.

Robyn climbed up to a tube slide. Ethan came behind her. She jumped into the tube, and he followed. A moment later they shot out the bottom laughing. They gestured to Kevin to come play.

Reluctantly Kevin joined them on the slide. First Robyn, then Ethan disappeared into the tube. Kevin climbed in and launched himself.

Halfway down a clown grinned up at him, grotesque and leering with sharp teeth.

In the bedroom, Cassie jerked in shock at the image.

"What did you see?" Ethan whispered.

The clown laughed wickedly and reached out with clawed fingers. Kevin scrambled back up the tube. He crawled out of the top and climbed down the ladder. The clown followed close behind him. Kevin broke into a run to the outskirts of the park.

Tom and Margaret continued to talk, oblivious to what was happening. Ethan and Robyn continued to play.

Kevin ran up a trail that was surrounded by sparse scrub oak as it climbed a foothill to a mountain range. The wind picked up, thrashing the trees. Clouds rolled in and cast a dark pall across the landscape. The clown followed behind him, leering his impossibly wide grin with bloodstained fangs in his mouth.

The trail switched back and forth several times. The clown kept close behind. The trail plunged into a thick knot of trees. When Kevin came out of it, the clown leaped out at him from the side. Kevin balked and dashed away.

The trail clung to the side of a steep hill. The clown remained on his heels. The trail rose up to a level place where a small lake churned with the wind kicking up waves. Kevin passed some boulders. The clown stood on one of them grinning down at him.

Kevin reached a steep slope where one fork of the trail plunged down sharply and the other fork headed sideways into more woods. On the steep fork below, the clown grinned up at him with claws raised. Kevin fled into the trees.

He came to a flat bridge over a rushing creek and ran halfway across it, but stopped as the clown leered before him at the other end of the bridge, blocking his path. Kevin turned around to flee, but the clown blocked the way there, halfway between him and the end. He whirled around again, but the clown was there, halfway to him. He turned again, and the clown was a handful of feet away. Another turn, and the clown loomed over him with arms above him.

The clown pounced. Kevin screamed.

Kevin jerked awake with a cry. Cassie panted as she straightened up on her knees. Ethan gazed at them both with concern.

"Oh, Kevin!" she said as she gave him a hug. "I'm so sorry you're having these dreams."

She pulled back and looked at him. His gaze was wild and peered past her.

"Please tell me what happened to you a year ago."

His lips trembled as if to speak. He looked at Ethan, then at Cassie. His lips parted. She held her breath and waited for words to come out.

His lips closed, and he lowered his eyes.

She shook her head and took his hands. "It's okay. You're not ready yet."

He lay back down, his gaze lingering on her for a moment, then he stared up at the ceiling.

"Would you like some warm milk to help you sleep?"

She looked up at Ethan, who mouthed *Warm milk?* at her with an amused look. Sternly she said, "Think we could get some warm milk?"

His expression changed to chagrin. "Uh, sure."

"Be right back, Kevin."

As they headed down the stairs, Ethan said, "What did you see?"

"Ethan, it's pri—"

"Cassie, he's my brother!"

She stopped midway down the stairs and peered at him, considering. Maybe it *would* help if he knew. Maybe he'd have some insight. "In both dreams he's chased by something frightening. He gets boxed in."

His eyebrows rose. They began walking again.

"It's something he thinks will harm him, or overwhelm him, or...destroy him." They reached the bottom of the stairs.

"But you don't know what?"

She followed him into the kitchen. "The dreams are too symbolic. Fantasy monsters chasing him." She considered whether to mention his entire family in the dream ignoring him when he was in danger, but decided against it. That could make Ethan defensive.

He opened the refrigerator door and removed a jug of milk. He filled a cup from the cupboard.

"I hope he dreams about the thing he's really afraid of tonight," she said.

He placed the cup in the microwave and closed it. "How long?"

"One minute."

He punched the buttons. The microwave beeped and droned into operation. They stood next to each other, leaning against the counter.

"My mom and dad are paying you, right?" he said.

"Yes."

"How much?"

"That's confidential."

He rolled his eyes. "You act like I'm a stranger off the street, not part of the family."

"Let's just say it's enough."

"Enough for what? Your music downloads?"

"My Mustang." His face showed he was impressed. She dragged her next words out for effect. "My metallic burgundy drop-top Mustang."

"Why didn't you drive it here?"

"I didn't want to park it all night in a strange neighborhood."

He bristled. "It's a safe neighborhood."

"I'm protective of my baby."

He pulled a spoon out of the drawer. "You can keep up payments on a Mustang with dreamcatching? Teach *me* how to dreamcatch!"

She smiled smugly at him.

He paused with the spoon raised and peered at her. "What?"

"I'm not making payments."

"What...how are—"

"I paid cash."

"*What?*"

The microwave dinged. He placed the cup on the counter and stirred it. "People pay you enough to buy a Mustang with cash?"

"Eventually. I started saving before I had my license."

"That sounds like one sweet ride."

"It is. I love going for a drive in the country with the top down."

He gazed at her mesmerized as he continued to stir.

"I start out slow so I can smell the wildflowers and hear the birds sing. Then I speed up. The wind catches my hair and blows it straight back."

"That must be a beautiful sight, your hair flowing in the wind."

"It feels like I'm flying. I think you've stirred that enough."

He looked down at the cup and smiled self-consciously, then put the spoon in the sink. As they climbed back up the stairs, he said, "I'd love to see that, your hair flying in the wind. Think I could ride with you sometime?"

"Possibly."

"Think I could drive it sometime?"

"Not a chance!"

He pouted at her at the top of the stairs.

Kevin lay motionless in the bed, still staring at the ceiling. Cassie took the cup from Ethan and held it out. "Here you go."

He sat up and took the cup, downing it in several gulps as she sat next to him on the bed. Ethan stood by watching. Kevin gave the cup back to Cassie.

"Good," she said and handed the cup to Ethan. He took it and looked around perplexed, then walked over and set it on the desk.

"Now go back to sleep," she said.

Kevin lay back down. She pulled the covers up to his neck, smiled down at him, and stroked his cheek with the back of her hand. "Don't worry. We'll figure all this out for you."

Kevin gazed at her for an instant, then closed his eyes. She and Ethan went to their chairs. They sat quietly for a moment, then Ethan leaned in toward Cassandra. "Are you sure I can't drive it, just once?"

"Nobody, Ethan."

"Not even your husband?"

"I'm not married."

"But when you are?"

She thought about it. "*Maybe* my husband."

He paused dramatically, grabbed her hand, and fell to his knees. "Cassandra, will you marry me?"

She rolled her eyes and threw his hand off, but she couldn't keep the smile off her face the whole time. "Your love is so sincere."

Outside a car drove up, and the engine shut off. A car door opened and closed.

"Sounds like Coach is coming home," he said.

"Who?"

He pointed at a photo of Kevin with his baseball coach.

"He lives next door?"

"Yeah."

She jumped up and headed for the window. He followed and stood next to her. They peered out. A middle-aged man walked away from the car. It was the man in the photo. He glanced up, noticed them looking at him, and waved with a friendly smile.

She took an impulsive step back. Ethan waved.

Coach headed for the side door to his home and went inside.

"How well do you know him?" Cassie said.

"He was my coach too."

"You played baseball?"

"For a while. I never got into it like Kevin."

She stared at the door in the next yard, even though Coach was gone, mulling over the possibilities. It was usually someone they know. "Why didn't you tell me he lives next door?"

He shrugged. "I didn't know it mattered."

She sighed. "You never know what matters."

"You think Coach has something to do with this?"

"I have to consider everything."

"He's a good guy. The kids love him."

She perked up. "They do, huh?"

"Cassie! You don't really judge people that quickly, do you?"

She shook her head. "You're right. I'm sorry."

"It's okay."

She headed back to the chair with Ethan accompanying her. "Tell me about Coach."

"Well...he's Australian. We all love his accent. Reminds us of Crocodile Dundee."

"You're old enough to have seen that movie?"

"He showed it to us once."

"Where?"

"At his home."

"He had the team over to his house?"

"You're being suspicious again."

"Just curious."

"I really can't see him doing what you're thinking."

"Well, how about the scoutmaster?" She indicated one of the photos with him in it.

"He lives across town."

"Was he your scoutmaster too?"

"No, he came along later. I don't know him. You gonna ask about our Catholic priest next?"

"You're Catholic?" she said with surprise.

"No, but you're covering all the stereotypes."

She laughed with embarrassment and felt her face flush. "Got any friendly uncles?"

He chuckled.

"Ethan, something happened to Kevin, and most of the time it's someone they know."

"You haven't even figured out what happened yet, and you're already accusing people you don't know."

"I'm not accusing anybody. I'm exploring possibilities."

"Sounds like accusing."

She placed her hand on his knee. "I'm not the cops. I'm here to help."

He looked at her hand, then took it and pulled it to his lips. He planted a kiss on it. She blushed and smiled. "Are we still being straight with each other?" he said.

"Sure."

Slowly he leaned forward, drawing her closer with her hand. She was breathless with anticipation. Their lips crept together. A fraction of an inch away he paused, gazing at her closer than any human ever had before. Her heart pounded.

He closed the space between them and let his lips brush hers. He pulled away, a mere inch, then brushed his nose against hers. Her whole body tingled with sensations she'd never felt so strongly.

He pulled away several inches, then swooped in and kissed her. It was the most exciting thing she'd ever experienced.

They broke apart, and suddenly she noticed Kevin sitting up watching them intently. "Kevin!" She stood. "I'm sorry. I...we were just waiting for you to fall asleep."

Kevin scrutinized them with squinting eyes. She ran to the side of the bed and knelt before him. "I wasn't ignoring you. I was just waiting for you to sleep. I'm sorry."

His mouth moved, and for an instant she thought he might say something. But he licked his lips, then lay back down and turned his back to her.

She crept back to her chair and sat, trying to calm herself. That was careless of her! Ethan watched her silently. Finally she turned to him and whispered, "We shouldn't have done that."

"You didn't want to kiss me?"

"It's not that. It's... This is my job. It was like kissing at work."

"Then what time do you get off?"

He gazed at her with a silly smile. At first it irritated her that he was treating this so lightly, but she could still feel the pressure of his lips on hers and the thrill she felt. She couldn't help letting a smile escape. She glanced at Kevin. His eyes were closed, and it looked like his breathing was even. "Actually, I could use a break."

Ethan's face brightened up.

"A *bathroom* break."

"Oh." The smile disappeared. "I'll show you."

He led her into the hallway to the next door over. But he stood blocking her way and smiled invitingly. "Since you're taking a break from your job..."

She smiled coyly and lowered her eyes as he leaned in. They kissed, but in seconds she felt the pressure inside her and broke away. "I really do need to go."

She went in the bathroom, swung the door mostly closed, but peeked through it and smiled, then shut and locked it.

She stood before the mirror, gazing at herself. Slowly she lifted her hand to her mouth and brushed her lips with her fingers. A smile broke out.

It was her first kiss.

Ethan gazed at the closed door with a content smile, then returned to the bedroom. He crept quietly inside and paused at the foot of the bed. Kevin's chest moved slowly and evenly.

Ethan went to the side of the bed so he could peer down. He cocked his head as he studied his brother.

What could be going on inside that head of his? What secrets might Cassie discover? He still wasn't sure he believed she could catch dreams, but a disquieting feeling crept up on him that somehow this might be a real thing. That was something that didn't fit his worldview.

He bent over when he noticed movement under Kevin's eyelids. He rushed out the door.

Cassandra jerked up with a wad of toilet paper in her hand when a knock came to the door. "Cassie!" came a harsh whisper.

She whispered back in a loud hiss. "I'm busy!"

"He's dreaming again."

Hurriedly she wiped and flushed and did a quick token dip of her hands under the faucet. She flung the door open and locked eyes with Ethan for an instant, then rushed to the bedroom.

She knelt before the bed. Sure enough, Kevin's eyes were moving. Ethan stood behind her.

"Come on, Kevin," she whispered. "Show me what really happened this time." She let her consciousness slip into his.

Again the dream was foggy. Kevin sat at a table in a dark room. A birthday cake rested on the table before him. He stared at it with a confused look. Its frosting was completely black and decorated with a skull and crossbones in white frosting. Thirteen candles made a wide circle around it.

On the opposite end of the table stood Tom, Margaret, Ethan, and Robyn, smiling at him.

Kevin stared at the cake anxiously. Margaret came over and lit the candles. They glimmered in Kevin's eyes and cast orange flickers on the wall behind him. In the flickers were the shadows of two grotesque figures in profile, one on each side of him. They had horns on their heads and long noses and chins protruding out. Hands with wicked claws reached for Kevin's shadow.

His family continued to gaze at him with warm smiles.

The claws reached for Kevin's throat. His family called to him in distant, echoing voices, repeating over and over, "Make a wish, Kevin! Come on, make a wish!"

Just as the clawed hands were about to grasp the throat of Kevin's shadow, he leaned forward and puckered his mouth to blow out the candles. The grotesque shadows froze in place.

A clawed hand thrust out of the middle of the cake right through the skull and crossbones. Smeared with crumbs and frosting, it grabbed Kevin's throat. He tried to scream, but nothing came out.

In the bedroom, Cassie's eyes were wide and her mouth quivered as she stared.

Kevin reached for the hand and yanked it away. The shadows on the wall pulled back and disappeared into the flickering. Kevin leaped out of the chair and ran.

Margaret looked at him in confusion. "Kevin, make a wish!"

Kevin ran past erect headstones in a graveyard. The night was pitch black. He stumbled and fell forward, landing on his stomach with a headstone directly in front of his face.

A clawed hand burst through the grass, covered with fresh dirt. Kevin, wide-eyed, scrambled to his feet and turned to flee. The hand suddenly held handcuffs. It slapped them on his ankle with a locking clack. Kevin fell forward, landing hard.

Another hand burst from the ground with handcuffs that it locked to his other ankle. Two more hands burst out and locked handcuffs on his wrists. He lay spread-eagle on his belly, struggling to free himself.

Two legs walked up to him, dark silhouettes. They stopped near his face and stood silently.

Cassandra said, "Kevin, look up! Look at who it is."

Kevin continued to struggle. He didn't seem to hear her.

"Kevin!"

He didn't respond.

She gave out an exasperated cry. "I'm going in."

"What?" cried Ethan.

Cassandra knelt beside Kevin in the graveyard and looked up at the figure. It was an unrecognizable silhouette of a man. "Kevin," she cried as she leaned forward, "you have to look up!"

He ignored her and continued to struggle. She placed her hands on the ground and leaned down to his ear. "Kevin, look at me!"

His head jerked up in shock and gaped at her.

"Look at the man's face!"

He stared at her with horror and shook his head.

"Look, please!"

Slowly he turned his head and lifted his eyes. Cassandra watched the man, but he remained a silhouette. Kevin craned his head up as far as it could go. A gloomy light slowly crept up the man's body, illuminating it. The shadows receded, and when Kevin stretched his neck as far as it would go, the light shone on the man's face.

It was Coach.

Cassandra jerked back up, startling Ethan. Kevin moaned and thrashed about weakly.

"Oh my God," Cassie murmured. "It *is* Coach."

"What are you talking about?" Ethan said ominously.

She grabbed Kevin by both arms and jostled him. "Wake up!"

He woke up, stared at Cassie with wild eyes, then sat up and grabbed her in an embrace.

"It's okay, Kevin, it's okay," she said as she hugged him and rubbed his back. She looked into his eyes. "Tell me what happened. Tell me what Coach did to you."

He looked at her with a troubled expression, trembling.

"Talk to me, Kevin. It's okay. Coach can't hurt you now."

A tear trickled down his cheek as his lower lip quivered. Cassie waited with anticipation. He glanced at Ethan, then closed his eyes and bowed his head.

She pulled him into another hug. "Oh, Kevin, what did he do to you?"

"Coach did something to Kevin?" Ethan said. His eyes burned with a smoldering flame. "*Coach...hurt...Kevin?*" He marched to the window and peered out at Coach's house. His face grew dark. He whirled and grabbed Kevin's baseball bat.

"Ethan?" she said.

He marched for the door.

She stood. "What are you doing?"

"If Coach hurt Kevin..."

She ran to stop him, but he brushed her off and left.

"Ethan, wait!"

She ran after him. When she reached the top of the stairs, Ethan was already at the bottom. She ran down as fast as she could. He threw the front door open and marched out. She rushed up behind him. On the porch, she grabbed him and pulled him around. "What do you think you're doing?"

He glared at her with flaming eyes. "He's gonna tell me what he did."

"It was just a dream."

He pulled away from her grip. "If I have to beat it out of him, he's going to tell me." He stormed down the porch steps.

"Ethan, I don't know if Coach hurt him." He whirled in his tracks as she ran up to him. "It was just a dream image. I don't know what it means."

"You said it! *Oh, Kevin! What did he do to you?*"

She lowered her head. "I know, and I'm sorry. I jumped to conclusions. But it's not enough evidence to bash someone's head in."

"If he didn't do it, then what the hell's going on?"

"I don't know. I need to learn more." She looked up to the second story. "I have to go back into his dream."

"What's this crap about going into his dream?"

She took a deep breath. "You remember I said I listen—more or less?"

Suspiciously he said, "Yeah..."

"Well, that's the more."

"You go *into* his dream?"

"I go in and become a part of it."

"You can go in and affect it?"

"I can't change anything. But I can talk to him, influence *him* to change it."

"How come you didn't mention that before?"

"You saw how your mom reacted to just listening."

He visibly calmed down. "You could have told *me*."

"I was hoping I wouldn't need to go in at all."

He squinted his eyes. "Is it dangerous?"

"It's uncomfortable...confusing to the dreamer. Often they resist. That barrier I told you about?"

He though about it a moment. "It'll help Kevin?"

"That's what this whole night is about." She turned to head back, but he remained in place. She faced him. He had a plaintive look on his face.

"Cassie? Can you really do all this?"

"Yes, I can."

They found Kevin staring out the window at the moon when they returned. He turned and looked at them.

"Kevin, can you tell me what happened with Coach?" Cassie said.

He gazed at them, glanced at the photos of Coach and himself, then walked to his bed and climbed under the covers.

"I understand," she said. She sat in her chair.

Ethan put the bat down and joined her. "Still won't talk."

Kevin peered at her with the covers pulled up to his neck. She nodded to him. He closed his eyes and rolled to his side. Quietly to Ethan she said, "But he wants me to find out."

"And if Coach did do something?"

"We call the police."

"And tell them what? Dreams are not evidence."

"We need to get Kevin to talk. He's afraid of something. If we can find out what, we can help him feel safe from it."

"*Will* you be able to get him to talk?"

Slowly she shook her head. "We'll just have to see. Next dream I'm going in right away. See if I can influence him from the beginning."

He put his hand on hers. "I really appreciate you helping Kevin. It means a lot to me."

She smiled warmly at him. "My pleasure."

"So..." He became self-conscious, although he still kept his hand on hers. "After you're done tonight, what are you going to do?"

"Sleep!"

He chuckled. "After you sleep...then what?"

She gave him a coy look. "Are you asking me out?"

"I'd like to get to know you better."

She got all perky. "What do you want to know?"

"Where to start? Um... Okay, when did you first know you had this...gift?"

"I don't know. I guess I always had it. My family watches for signs, and they nurture it when they find it."

"It's genetic?"

"Seems to be."

"Wow. So how did you become a Dreamcatcher? Is there some kind of school?"

"Like Hogwarts?" She giggled. "No. I guess you could say I apprenticed under my aunt. I played her assistant, but really I was practicing. Then we'd compare notes. I'd tell her what I saw, and she told me what she saw, then she'd explain how she interpreted everything."

"When was the first time you did it on your own?"

She grinned mischievously. "Officially or unofficially?"

He laughed. "Both."

"Officially about two years after I started training. My aunt had the appointment, but she got sick. She sent me to do it alone. She said I was ready."

"Were you?"

She smirked. "No! Turned out to be multiple personalities. Talk about a mess inside! My aunt had to come the next night and start over."

"Wow!"

"An experience like that is rare. Just my luck to get it the first time."

"What about unofficially?"

She chuckled. "I practiced on my brother and sisters and cousins."

"I bet they loved that!"

"They hated me for it! Especially when my brother had his first wet dream."

"Oh my hell!"

"*That* was educational," she said with a laugh. "He dreamed about a girl at school. I'm pretty sure she didn't look half as good naked in real life as she did in his dream."

"Uh...I'm not sleeping anywhere near you!"

"Guess you're not driving my Mustang then."

"Huh?"

"I'm not marrying anyone who won't sleep near me."

"Hmmmm...guess it's a risk I'll have to take."

She leaned in close. "Does that mean you're not skeptical anymore?"

He thought about it. "Open minded. *Something's* going on. I'm not sure what yet."

She shrugged. "I guess that's a start."

"I'm ready to accept it as soon as I see real evidence."

"Does that mean I'm not nuts anymore?"

"I never said you were."

"You never *said* it."

"Okay, I thought it. But not anymore."

She gazed at him with a smile forming."I think that deserves a kiss."

She checked to make sure Kevin wasn't watching. They kissed for a long time. She couldn't believe what was happening. Never had a boyfriend in her life, and suddenly she's kissing this boy over and over in just a few hours. And feeling so comfortable about it. *He* made her feel comfortable.

Something stirred in her mind. She broke free of the kiss and looked at Kevin. He was dreaming again. She ran to him and knelt down. Ethan came up behind her.

"I'm coming in, Kevin," she whispered.

They were in a dark room, empty. A single shaft of light with no apparent source shone down on Kevin. Still the dream was foggy. Cassie wondered what that was all about. She'd never experienced dreams that weren't clear.

Kevin sat on the floor rolling a baseball back and forth between his hands. A baseball glove lay in front of him. A bat leaned against the wall in the corner behind him.

Cassie stood off to the side facing him. He didn't notice her. With all the baseball trappings, she couldn't help think of Coach.

"Kevin," she called. "Kevin?"

He ignored her and kept rolling the ball.

"Kevin, please show me what happened."

He didn't react. She crouched down before him.

"Kevin, look at me."

Footsteps, slow and definite, came from outside the room. Kevin looked with fear toward a door that was suddenly in the wall. Mist seeped in through the gap on the bottom.

The door slowly opened with an unnerving creak. Mist poured in and flowed along the floor. A male figure stepped out of the mist into the room. Kevin looked up with great apprehension. Cassie stared at the figure. Its face was covered with a ghoulish mask with horns and a jutting nose and chin.

The figure stepped further into the room. Kevin stood slowly with the ball in his hand. The figure stopped in the middle of the room. The two faced each other, unmoving.

Cassie went to Kevin. "Focus on his face. Let me see his face."

Kevin stared at the man without moving. The man stepped toward Kevin. The ball in Kevin's hand dropped to the floor with a thud and rolled away noisily.

"Kevin, grab the bat," Cassie said.

He didn't move, except to follow the man with his eyes.

Loudly she said, "Kevin! Run and grab the bat!"

The man stopped a couple feet away from Kevin, who looked down at the floor. A silent moment pulsed, then Kevin pulled his T-shirt off over his head.

She gasped in horror. "Kevin, no! Stop! You don't have to do that."

He dropped his shirt to the floor. The man crouched down and gripped Kevin's arms.

Tears formed in Cassie's eyes. "No, Kevin, run! You can stop this!"

Suddenly Kevin broke free from the man's grip and walked like a zombie right at her. She had to back away to avoid a collision. "Kevin?"

Kevin sat straight up in bed and threw the covers off. As if in a trance, he swung his legs over the side. Cassie and Ethan jumped back out of the way. He stood up and walked like a zombie to the door.

"Why didn't you tell me he's a sleepwalker?" she said.

"I didn't know."

Cassie and Ethan followed Kevin out the door and down the hall toward the door at the end.

"What happened in the dream?" Ethan asked.

"I think Kevin was molested."

Ethan's eyes squinted darkly. "Was it Coach?"

"I couldn't see. The molester had a mask on."

Kevin opened the door and went inside.

"What room is that?" she said.

"Robyn's bedroom."

As Cassie and Ethan were about to enter the room, the door at the other end of the hall opened. Tom and Margaret appeared. "What's going on?" Margaret said.

"Kevin's sleepwalking," said Ethan.

"Why didn't you tell me about this?" Cassie said to her.

"He doesn't sleepwalk," she said with a scowl.

Cassie went into the room. Kevin stood beside Robyn's bed, gazing at her as she slept. The others began to enter, but Cassie stopped them with a hand up. "All of you, stay there."

She went to the foot of the bed. Ethan paused, then crept into the room a few feet behind her. Tom and Margaret peered in from the door.

Kevin reached out and brushed Robyn's cheek with his fingers. Robyn whimpered and stirred.

"I need to go inside again," Cassie said.

"*What is going on?*" Margaret said in a harsh whisper.

"Shut up, Mom!" Ethan whispered.

Kevin continued to brush Robyn's cheek. Cassie knelt beside them and entered his consciousness.

Kevin stood in the middle of the same room, but this time it was brightly lit. The dream still remained foggy. A full-length mirror hung on the wall. Kevin stared into it. Cassie watched with anticipation.

Kevin crept closer to the mirror. Cassie came and stood behind him and looked.

The reflection in the mirror was Robyn.

The fog disappeared and the dream became clear. Robyn stood before her, gazing at her own reflection. Cassie gasped. Kevin was nowhere in sight.

Slow, deliberate footsteps sounded outside the room. Robyn turned with horror in her eyes. Suddenly a door existed in the wall. Mist oozed out from its crack.

The door creaked open. Mist poured into the room. The figure with the mask stepped in. Robyn stared at him with dread.

The man slowly crossed the room to her. Robyn watched him without moving. Cassie pressed her fists to her chin. "Robyn, run away!"

The man stopped before Robyn. They looked into each other's eyes. Her hands dropped to the hem of her blouse. She began to pull it up.

"*No!*" Cassie cried.

Cassandra leaped to her feet and shook Robyn, then Kevin. "Robyn, wake up! Kevin, wake up!" Kevin and Robyn roused to a groggy wakefulness, looking stunned.

Cassie turned to Ethan. "It wasn't Kevin. It was Robyn!"

"What?"

"Robyn's the one that was molested."

Ethan gaped at her. Cassie turned to Tom and Margaret. "Someone molested Robyn."

"Are you out of your mind?" Margaret said.

Tom's face had a tight expression.

"Don't you see?" Cassie said, frustrated. "It was never Kevin. It was Robyn all along."

Ethan said, "But you saw Kevin—"

"I saw Kevin's dreams. But they weren't his dreams. They were Robyn's dreams. That's why they were so murky."

"What are you talking about?" Tom said.

She glanced at each of them with a pleading look. "Don't you get it? Kevin's a Dreamcatcher too. He caught Robyn's dreams and dreamed them himself."

"That's as much as I'm going to take of this, young lady!" Margaret grabbed her arm and pulled her to the door.

"Wait! You need to know—"

"It's bad enough I let you into my house. You're not going to accuse my family of all this hocus-pocus!"

Cassie fought and broke free before Margaret could pull her out of the door. "You can't throw me out now! I'm almost there!"

"Oh, yes I can! Tom..."

He looked at Margaret, then at Cassandra. "Please, Cassie. I think it's best you leave."

Tears formed in her eyes. "Please! Someone molested Robyn. Probably still is. I need to find out who."

"You said it was Coach," Ethan said with a stern look.

"Coach!" Tom cried.

"I did not! I don't know for sure."

"Now you're accusing our neighbors?" Margaret growled.

"No! I don't know who it is. I have to find out."

"Tom, get her out of here."

She ran and sat next to Robyn, who gazed at her in confusion. "Tell them. Tell them what happened."

Tom wrapped his hand around Cassie's arm, squeezing hard.

"Ouch!"

Robyn sat up in the bed as Tom pulled Cassie out of the room.

"Tell them, Robyn!" she cried.

Margaret and Ethan followed. Kevin and Robyn gazed at them with troubled expressions.

Tom dragged Cassie to the stairs and kept pushing her down. She fought him. "You're making a terrible mistake! I have to help them."

She broke away and ran down the stairs, stopped at the bottom and turned to face them.

"Why won't you listen to me? Don't you care about your son and daughter?" She focused on Ethan. "Ethan, tell them."

He gazed at her, then shrugged his shoulders. "It's their house."

She gaped at him in disbelief.

"Enough of this!" Margaret marched down the stairs and pushed Cassandra to the door. "Get out, or I'm calling the police."

Margaret opened the door and shoved Cassie. She stumbled out. It slammed behind her. She threw her body against the door with a cry of rage.

"My jacket! My dreamcatcher!"

For a moment she stood facing the door, breathing heavily with anger. The door opened, and her jacket flew out at her. She caught it.

The dreamcatcher sailed past her and landed on the sidewalk past the porch steps. The door slammed closed.

She threw her jacket against the door in a rage, then turned and pressed her back against the wall. She stood there for a moment fighting back her tears and frustration, wiping at her eyes with a finger. After she calmed her breathing, she picked up her jacket and put it on. She sat on the porch steps, still fighting the tears.

She pulled her phone out of her jacket and almost dialed her mother, but stopped. She couldn't bring herself to abandon Kevin and Robyn. But what could she do? They threw her out. If she tried to get back in, they could accuse her of trespassing.

She looked about the yard, up at the stars, then at the dreamcatcher lying on the sidewalk. She went and picked it up, then turned and studied the house.

No, there was no way she could abandon those kids. She had to reach out to them—somehow.

She marched around the corner of the house and slunk into the backyard. She looked up at the second story and tried to map out in her mind which window would be Robyn's. The one she thought it was had a light on inside.

She paced slowly back and forth, her eyes on the window, muttering under her breath. "Come on, Robyn. Go back to bed."

The light remained on. "Hurry up, Robyn. It's almost morning."

She stopped and sighed with relief when the light turned off. She walked to the house immediately under Robyn's window and leaned her back against the wall. She slid down until she sat.

With the dreamcatcher in her hand, she lifted her arms to the side, pressing them against the wall, and closed her eyes. Softly she said, "Now sleep, Robyn. Sleep."

She breathed evenly to relax herself. "That's it, Robyn. Sleep. Sleep."

Slowly she lifted her arms until they rose above her head. She grasped the dreamcatcher with both hands and pressed them against the wall.

"Now dream."

She felt when the dream started. Her consciousness rose up to the window and entered Robyn's mind.

Cassandra found herself in the same room. The view was crystal clear, no fog. One pale light streamed down from nowhere, shining on Robyn standing in the middle. She looked about fearfully. Cassie approached her with a smile. "Hi, Robyn."

It startled her. She peered at Cassie. "Hi," she said uncertainly.

"It's me, Cassie."

Robyn smiled and said warmly, "Hi, Cassie."

"Do you want to play?"

She nodded eagerly.

A bright light flashed on in the corner where her dolls lay on the floor. Robyn walked over to them and sat, picking one of them up.

Cassie sat across from her and picked up a doll. "Does this one have a name?"

Robyn nodded. "Angie." She held her doll up. "And this one is Lizzie."

"Are Angie and Lizzie friends?"

"Very good friends."

"That's nice. Do you want to be friends with me?"

Robyn smiled coyly and nodded her head.

"Good!" Cassie said. "I like you." She looked around at the darkness. "It's so dark in here. Can we turn on more lights?"

She stiffened up. "He'll see me."

"Who?"

"Him," she said fearfully.

"What's his name?"

Robyn's brow wrinkled anxiously. She dropped her head and stared at the floor. Almost inaudibly she said, "Him."

"I want to see him."

Her head jerked up in alarm. "No-o-o!"

"I won't let him hurt you. I promise."

"No," she whimpered.

"I need to see him so I can stop him from hurting you."

Robyn shook her head back and forth slowly. She perked up as the sound of footsteps came from outside the room. Cassie turned her head around and peered into the dark.

The door was there. Mist flowed from underneath. The door creaked open. The mist billowed in.

Robyn's face contorted with terror. Cassie scooted next to her, put her arm around her, and whispered, "I'll protect you."

Robyn looked at her. Cassie nodded assurance.

The man entered the room. The mask seemed even more grotesque now.

"Show me his face," Cassie whispered.

Robyn buried her face in Cassandra's bosom.

"Please, Robyn, show me his face."

Robyn whimpered, keeping her face hidden. The figure stopped in the middle of the room.

"Show me his face!" Cassie said forcefully.

Robyn looked up at her, then at him, then slowly rose to her feet.

"No, Robyn!" Cassie tried to pull her down, but in the dream her hands were powerless.

Robyn crept toward him, gazing at him intently, trembling all over. Cassie pressed her fists against her mouth.

Robyn stood a few feet away, peering up at him. Cassie's mind raced, wondering what she could do, what she could say, to stop this.

Robyn pulled the hem of her blouse up.

"*No!*" Cassie shrieked.

Robyn stopped. Slowly she lifted a hand up and grasped the chin of the mask. In a quick move, she whipped it off his face.

It was Ethan.

Cassandra gasped.

Cassie's eyes popped open. A face loomed above her. "Ethan!"

He glared at her with a fierce expression, reached down with both hands and grasped her throat. He pulled on her. She slid to her feet to keep from choking. The dreamcatcher dropped to the ground.

Ethan pushed his face up to hers. "You really do catch dreams," he snarled. "How is that possible?"

He pulled her away from the wall and threw her to the ground, then jumped on her and pressed his hand over her mouth. She fought back, but his weight was too much for her.

"Why couldn't you stay focused on Kevin? Why couldn't you give them Coach for your suspect?" A tear formed at the corner of his eye. "I really liked you, Cassie."

He leaned down, pulled his hand away, and planted his lips on hers. She jerked her head away from him. He pressed his hand on her mouth again and kissed her cheek.

"What am I supposed to do with you now?" He stroked her hair with his free hand. "You'll tell them everything." He shook his head with a dismal look. "I'm sorry, Cassie. I really liked you, but..."

He grabbed her throat again with both hands and squeezed as tears streamed from his eyes. She gasped for air, but none came. The pain in her throat became intense.

A cry of rage filled the air, and Ethan looked up in alarm. Kevin charged him with his baseball bat held high. Ethan fell back with eyes wide as Kevin swung hard, catching him on the head. Ethan collapsed onto his back.

"You're not hurting her!" Kevin shrieked.

Cassie struggled to her feet, coughing and gasping for air. Kevin swung the bat, bashing Ethan on the chest. Ethan lay motionless.

"I'll kill you, you son of a bitch!"

Kevin swung once more before Cassie could grab him from behind and pull him away.

"No, Kevin!" she cried. She pulled him farther away as he struggled to break free.

Tom and Margaret rushed out the back door. "What in God's name is going on out here?" Margaret cried. She focused on Cassie clinging to Kevin. "You little monster! What are you still doing here?" She noticed Ethan lying on the ground. "What did you do to my son?" She ran to him.

"Mom!" Kevin dropped the bat and shoved Cassie's arms away. She let him go. He ran to Margaret and buried himself in an embrace. "Mom, it's Ethan. He's been doing things to Robyn. He made her do things to him."

Margaret gaped in horror. Tom stood beside her in shock.

"I had to stop him. He's been doing things—doing things! I don't know how long."

"No, no. That's impossible."

"I saw him, Mom! I saw him, and he saw me. He choked me. He said if I ever said a word, he'd kill me."

Kevin broke out in weeping. Margaret and Tom stared in total shock, unable to move. Cassie watched, hardly able to breathe.

"I should have stopped him. I should have stopped him a long time ago."

Cassie rushed over to him and crouched before him. "No, Kevin. It's not your fault."

He peered at her with streaming eyes. "I should have! I should have! I was scared."

"*It's not your fault*," she emphasized.

Robyn crept out of the house, stopping some distance away. She clung hard to one of her dolls. Cassie ran to her, knelt beside her, and embraced her. "Robyn, are you okay?"

She looked past Cassie at Kevin, then at Ethan. Cassie noticed where she looked. "It's all over."

Robyn peered into her eyes, then brushed Cassie's cheek with her fingers. Part chuckle and part sob broke from Cassie.

Robyn noticed the dreamcatcher lying on the ground. She pulled away and went to pick it up, then brought it back. She held it up. "Did you catch my dreams?"

"Yes, I did. He'll never hurt you again."

Robyn offered the dreamcatcher to Cassie, but she pushed it back. "No, you keep it. My gift to you."

"But you need it."

"I can get another one."

Robyn smiled and gazed at the dreamcatcher. She looked over at Ethan. "Is he dead?"

Cassie peered over at him. "No, he's...I can still feel his...

His head moved. He moaned.

"I..." She sensed his mind becoming active, hurried over and knelt down beside him.

"What is it?" Tom said.

"Everyone be quiet!" She entered Ethan's consciousness.

A young boy that looked very much like Ethan was with Coach. In a chaotic series of images, they interacted with each other, first with the team on the baseball field, then alone together as they practiced throwing and hitting. Gradually images intermixed that had nothing to do with baseball. Ice cream. Watching a movie. Talking alone together. More and more touching occurred. The touching became intimate. Cassie watched in horror.

"Is everything okay?"

Cassie jolted back to reality, disoriented.

"Is Ethan hurt?" The voice had an Australian accent.

She looked up to see Coach standing above her. She leaped to her feet and stood defensively before Ethan. She looked around, trying to get her bearings. Ethan moaned and muttered incoherently. The rest of the family stood frozen, uncertain.

Cassie composed herself. "No, he's fine. He slipped and hit his head, but he'll be okay."

Coach looked at Ethan again, who came to consciousness enough to look around in confusion. His head seem to clear. He sat up, looked at Cassie, then at Coach. His eyes became troubled.

"Maybe we should call an ambulance," Coach said.

"No, he'll be fine. Just a little bump."

Coach gaze at her challengingly. "I don't know you."

"Oh, I'm..." She looked at the family, down at Ethan, then back at Coach. "I'm his girlfriend."

Ethan did a double-take.

"I've never seen you around before," Coach said.

She forced a broad smile. "Well, we're new together."

Coached peered at Ethan, who looked back at him, then struggled to his feet as Cassie helped him.

"I'm okay, Coach," Ethan said. He broke out in a smile. "Thanks for coming by to check."

Coach studied Cassie and Ethan once more. "Well, okay. I'm glad you're alright, mate."

His gaze turned to Kevin. "How's Kevin doing?"

Margaret glanced at Cassie and Ethan, then pulled Kevin closer. "Oh, he's doing much better now."

"The team sure misses you, Kevin. We all hope you come back to play."

Kevin nodded.

"Thanks for saying that," Tom said.

"Well, you all have sweet dreams. G'night."

Coach gazed at everyone once more, then headed back to his house. Cassie waited until he disappeared, then whirled around to face the family.

"Quick! Call the police!"

Afterword: My Confession

It's confession time (even though I'm not Catholic). Forgive me, Readers, for I have sinned.

My dirty little secret is, every story in this book was originally conceived for a purpose other than inclusion in this anthology. Most of them weren't even intended to be published in written form. They're—I tremble to confess the word—adaptations!

Two of them were intended for publication. The rest began as screenplays. And it shows. You could probably pick out the ones that began as screenplays by the fact that they're heavy with dialog, more than I usually write. But movies are a different animal, and the adaptations reflect that.

Still doesn't mean the stories aren't fun to read. In fact, they might be funner to read because they read so effortlessly, like a good screenplay should.

Here are the origins of each of the stories include in *Twisted Soul*. I love to read such revelations by my favorite authors, so I figure my fans (one day numbering in the millions, which I verified with a time machine) will enjoy reading about the origins of my stories too.

Alexandra

I don't remember where the original idea for this story came from. Such moments are fleeting and fragile and unexpected, and immediately my creativity goes to work chugging out a story from it. The original inspiration for the idea is lost in the chaos.

What I do know is, this idea came to me when I was in the screenplay-writing phase of my life. So "Alexandra" was destined to become a feature-length movie, which means I should write *Alexandra* in italics, not in quotes.

I wrote most of the screenplay, but struggled with how to end it. I never did finish it until it occurred to me to adapt the story to a novella and include it in this anthology.

I still struggled with the ending. I came up with multiple ideas that never seemed quite satisfying enough, until at last I stumbled on the current one.

Even then, I tinkered with it more after receiving feedback from a first reader or two. It's still the same ending, but I presented it in a different way. In the first incarnation, Alex and Noah conceive the plan and prepare it together. There's no suspense for the reader except for one question—will it work?

Someone pointed out it would be more powerful if the reader only knew there was a plan without knowing what the plan was, and didn't learn what the plan was until it unfolded before their eyes. Doing it that way—suspense! I kicked myself for not thinking of that obvious strategy that zillions of stories have used. That's why I always use first readers to find such defects that I miss.

But there was one problem. If I have my two characters strategize together and prepare together and watch the plan unfold together, all the while knowing what the plan is, I couldn't keep the plan from the reader. One of them needed to be the point of view character, and it's cheating to keep hidden from the reader something the point of view character knows.

Seriously, it *is* cheating!—even though I know a few authors who don't think so and do that very thing. But they do cheat their readers doing that, and I refused to do it.

I changed the ending so Noah had no clue what the plan was and Alexandra conceived and prepared it alone. Then I stayed in Noah's head the whole time. Now the reader didn't know and I wasn't cheating. In the process, I also beefed the final scene up to a dramatic level the story deserved. It was over too fast in the first version.

In the denouement I had Alex describe to Noah how she prepared. That shortened the story over the original ending, and that was a good thing. The preparation scene wasn't that important to the drama.

To a person, every first reader has loved the story, but had a couple issues. One was the age of the children. Eleven- and twelve-year-olds don't talk like that, they said. They need to talk like kids their age or I need to make them older.

Well, I already knew that! It wasn't a mistake. It was a choice with a justifiable reason behind it. I thought I made that reason clear in the story, but apparently not well enough. So I beefed up that aspect to make it clearer, and still a reader or two said the same thing. WTF? The reason is, these kids with the power they have dip into adult minds constantly and have learned many things beyond their age, including more sophisticated speaking. Alexandra explicitly states that right there in the story, for heavens sake! So I never changed the way they speak.

The other is the nudity of the children. That was also a deliberate choice. I've watched endless movies where people have out-of-body experiences of some kind, whether astral projection, dying and becoming a ghost, or whatever. In every case, the character has on the *exact same clothes* their body had on. Or alternatively when they die, they appear with some kind of robe on.

An obvious example is the movie *Ghost* with Patrick Swayze, Demi Moore, and Whoopi Goldberg. Great film, but when Swayze dies, he runs around as a ghost in the exact same clothes he died in. And the stickler in me cries out, "Where'd the damn clothes come from? Is there a spiritual wardrobe somewhere that magically appears on them at the moment they die?"

That's just nuts, so I refused to do that because I don't cheat in my stories. I also don't have the neurotic paranoia over human bodies like most of America seems to have, so if the story warrants it, the nudity goes in, period.

I'm not alone in this. The legendary science fiction author Theodore Sturgeon in his novel *More Than Human* imagined an ad hoc family of mutants with various psychic powers. Two of them are young black women who are twins and are mentally deficient in their ability to speak, but can teleport themselves anywhere with a thought. When they teleport, they show up completely nude, because they can only teleport themselves and nothing else, including clothing.

Do I even need to point out that the *Terminator* movies do the same?

That's why my preteens are nude when they astral project, because as Alex points out, you think there's an astral wardrobe somewhere? She also points out that it's not quite the same as real nudity because there's no physical body involved, just a spirit or soul. Plus she's invisible to everyone when she does project, so it doesn't really feel like nudity to her. I did all I could to avoid any suggestion that the nudity was sexual.

And that's why I made the characters eleven and twelve years old. I didn't want the complications of post-pubescent sexuality to contaminate the nudity if I made them fifteen or sixteen or more. I wanted it to remain innocent. There's absolutely nothing sexual about their out-of-body nudity, and I wanted to keep it that way.

I'd like to think the story's extreme anti-sexual-predator theme makes clear there's no devious motive for including the nudity, in case any of my readers want to go there. America's attitude toward the human body and sexuality is downright neurotic, if you compare it to other places in the world like Europe and Japan, and I refuse to play along. My small contribution in trying to normalize America's attitude toward human bodies is to include nudity whenever the story warrants it.

So the nudity in "Alexandra" stays.

The First Mormons in the Moon

To die-hard H.G. Wells fans, the origin of this title should be obvious. It's a play on his novel *The First Men in the Moon*. But apparently that's not one of his more well-known works, although I was familiar with it in my youth, because none of my first readers picked up on it.

The title isn't the only thing I borrowed from H.G. The entire story is based on his book. The idea came to me when I encountered a call for submissions for an original anthology. The theme was steampunk science fiction with a Mormon twist, obviously intended for the Mormon niche market, which is not trivial, if you're familiar with the unusual number of prominent science fiction and fantasy writers with a Mormon heritage. I'd never written steampunk before, so I was intrigued and wanted to try my hand at it.

But what would the story be? I don't write steampunk and I don't read steampunk. When I think of it, I primarily think of Will Smith and Kevin Kline's abortive movie *Wild Wild West* that I never could bring myself to watch all the way through. Blecch!

I thought and I thought and was coming up empty, until I had one of those marvelous *Eureka!* moments when the idea came in a flash. I laughed out loud at how genius it was. I'd steal H.G. Wells' story and plop Mormon prophet Brigham Young into the middle of it. The rest fell into place. I added that classic trope of one of the characters living the story first before going on to write it later in life to justify my thievery of H.G.'s story.

If you sense a hint of the movie *Time After Time* starring Malcolm Mc-Dowell, Mary Steenburgen, and David Warner, you're absolutely right! That also influenced my choice. In that one, H.G. Wells really invents a time machine and goes forward in time, only to return and end up writing *The Time Machine*.

I dug in and researched H.G. Wells and found fascinating elements of his youthful life to include. I also looked up how and when Brigham Young died—since he dies in my story—and included that information. At the same time Brigham died, Herbert George Wells—or Bertie as he was really nicknamed in his youth—was ten years old. His father and mother really were Joseph and Sarah. They really owned a sports and glassware shop across the street from their basement dwelling on High Street in Bromley, Kent. Bertie really attended Morley's Academy that really taught "girl's handwriting and tradesman arithmetic," and Bertie really hated it. Joseph Wells really played cricket professionally enough to earn a wage from it, and he really was the first player to achieve a "double hat trick." Bertie really did break his leg and ended up reading profusely while he convalesced from science-themed library books his parents brought him.

Their experiences on the moon were adapted straight out of *The First Men in the Moon* with various tweaking at my whim. In the story, when Bertie goes home with the determination to write the book, he's writing his own experiences, except with fictional characters and lots of embellishment.

But I did cheat with authentic history in a couple ways. First of all, the stable behind the house and the wellsite spheres inside, I made up (in case you hadn't figured that out yet). And during the period of time this story is supposed to have happened, Brigham Young was old and ill and bedridden. But a bedridden old man makes for a poor adventure hero, so I spryed him up into the feisty Brigham Young we all think of when we think of Brigham Young. Thank God for dramatic license!

The rest fell into place—except for one problem. The anthology I wanted to submit it to had an upper limit of 8000 words. Before long it became very obvious that my word count was going way beyond that. Astronomically beyond that, one might say. It clocked in at over 10,000 words *more* than the anthology's limit. I never submitted it.

But I did finish it, because it also became obvious that I could include it in *Twisted Soul* where there wasn't an upper limit for the word count.

A Face in the Window

When studying film production in college, I made three short films for my first production class. For the next semester, I was tired of doing short films. I wanted to try my hand at a feature film. That film became *Geeks & Goblins, Elves & Elliot*. Made on a budget of exactly zero, it didn't turn out half bad, although I can point out a zillion cringeworthy things I could have done better.

After that, no way was I going back to short films again. For my next project, I conceived of another feature film called *A Face in the Window*. It was intended as a horror film. One night as my wife and I watched one of the endless lame sequels to *Friday the 13th*, I told her even I could write a better horror movie than that, in spite of the fact that I'd never written a horror story ever.

This film is what I ended up writing. Not a slasher (ugh!), not full of scare jumps (blecch!), but a psychological thriller worthy of my creative genius.

I have no doubt I was influenced by Octavia Butler's novel *Wild Seed* with a villain that couldn't help but hop from one body to the next, and by the Denzel Washington movie *Fallen* that made the body-hopping villain a demon called Azazel. I took the body-hopping spirit in my own direction and came up with *A Face in the Window*. "My own direction" included a novel way of defeating the unstoppable villain, where those other two influential stories never defeated the villain in the end.

Or was my villain defeated? Yes, I went for the ambiguous ending, because sometimes an author has to satisfy his evil-twin alter ego. Bwa-ha-ha-ha!

I began production on the film for a school project, only to have it utterly torpedoed by the female lead actor who had only acted in theater and never in a film. Turned out, she hated the filming process as tedious and made up some bullshit excuse to quit. By then I couldn't start over because of my school deadline, so instead I made another (gag! vomit!) short film—well, sort of short, clocking in at eighteen minutes. As I contemplated the stories to include in *Twisted Soul*, I decided to adapt *A Face in the Window* into a novella.

Godblind

This was always supposed to be a standalone novel. The concept intrigued me of a society where everyone could telepathically receive visions from the Gods, except for one child who was born "blind" to the visions. I think the concept came to me when somehow the term "Godblind" popped into my head: someone who couldn't commune with God. The title might have been free-associated from, once again, Theodore Sturgeon, whose novel *Godbody* was published posthumously.

I placed the thirteen-year-old boy Blinders into a future society that at first appears to be an ancient Greece-based society, but slowly the revelation comes that there's modern technology mixed in here and there, so clearly it's not ancient Greece.

The theme of "Godblind" is the "other" and how society fears them and treats them poorly. It acts as a metaphor for any marginalized population, whether race or religion or sexual orientation or whatever. Society comes up with its own justifications for ostracizing the "other," but those justifications still result in cruelty.

Nevertheless a soapbox was not my intent. I just thought up a cool story idea and wrote the story honestly. The theme emerged of its own accord.

Like "Alexandra," I struggled with the ending. I wrote myself into a corner when Blinders was thrown into his gilded cage, and I kept coming up with cliche ideas for how he escaped. The story collected dust on the shelf for many years, leaving Blinders in prison limbo indefinitely because I couldn't figure out a satisfying ending at all, let alone how he escaped his incarceration.

When I decided to include it in *Twisted Soul*, I had to bite the bullet and struggle to find an ending. But it helped when I realized my stories for the anthology were all turning out to be novellas. That meant I didn't want *Godblind* to be a novel anymore, but a mere novella so it could fit the pattern, and that helped me think in more economical terms for the ending. (It still ended up being the longest of the stories.) Gradually an ending formed in my mind that was more satisfying than any other I'd considered before, and I could implement it in a shorter number of words, avoiding the status of novel.

It also turned out to be a darker ending than I'd anticipated and a bit ambiguous itself. More satisfaction for my evil twin.

The Dreamcatcher

Remember my abortive attempt to film *A Face in the Window*? I made a third attempt in school to produce a feature film, *The Dreamcatcher*. We got well into filming, perhaps a third of the way through, when my *male* lead actor bailed on us this time.

What made matters worse was, he was the same actor cast in the male lead for the first failed movie. He and I badmouthed the girl who quit on us in that movie, then he turned around and did the same thing in this one. The asshole!

What made matters worser was, it was his family's house we filmed at, so we lost our location. I warned the family what it would be like for us to film there, how inconvenient and intrusive it would be, but they assured me they were excited about doing it. Then they got sick of how inconvenient and intrusive it was.

Film making seems so glamorous to the lay person, until they experience it first hand.

That torpedoed that project, and these two failed attempts is why I've only produced one feature film.

But all was not lost. As with *A Face in the Window*, I adapted this screenplay into a novella to include in this collection. It's a slow burn of a suspense story, a bit of a mystery story. And lots of talking heads because Cassandra and Ethan sit around a lot waiting for the next dream to happen. Don't think it wasn't a challenge to make talking heads interesting! I *think* I succeeded. At least I find it engaging.

But after I completed it, the damn thing ended up being shorter than the others and only qualified as a novelette.

Well, that screwed everything up. With *Twisted Mind*, the first book in my series of original anthologies, I subtitled it *6 Science Fiction Stories by D. Michael Martindale*. I also included a bonus story that was the first version of one of the stories in it, to show my progress from first draft to completed product. The two were *very* different stories, different enough to consider them separate stories.

For this book, *Twisted Soul*, I planned on following the same pattern and subtitling it *5 Slipstream Novellas by D. Michael Martindale*. Except one of them wasn't a novella, but a much smaller novelette.

So I *really* followed the same pattern and decided to label "The Dreamcatcher" as a bonus novelette and made the subtitle *4 Slipstream Novellas by D. Michael Martindale*. Now I've developed a pattern of having bonus stories in each volume of the series, so I guess I'll always have to have one.

"The Dreamcatcher" was inspired by—you guessed it—Native American dreamcatchers. They made me think what kind of story could I tell if that thing really could catch dreams. In the end I made the dreamcatcher a mere prop because I wanted the story to be about a person, not a magical item. So Cassandra became the Dreamcatcher. I made dreamcatching her profession to justify why she came to this family to help.

I asked myself, what case could she be on for this story? A boy who suddenly stopped talking for a year seemed like an intriguing one. The rest fell into place as I contemplated why he stopped talking, with a red herring (Coach), a twist ending (Ethan), then an extra twist making the red herring the real cause of all this (also Coach).

It's pure coincidence that the first and last stories in this book involve a girl with psychic powers of some kind. My readers will probably notice a little overlap with certain characteristics of their powers between the two stories, but that's also unintentional. I devised the two stories years apart from each other, and any similarities in the powers came strictly from the fact that when working out the rules for either of them, certain rules worked well for both stories.

Plus a dash of my bias in thinking how such powers really would work. Why mess with a good thing?

About the Author

D. Michael Martindale is a storyteller. It doesn't matter which medium the story is told in—whether it be film or television or books or music—what's important is telling stories that people enjoy.

He was born in Minnesota and has been telling stories since before he could write. He started out by drawing comic strips and having his mother fill in the dialog balloons for him. He developed a taste for science fiction and fantasy, and although he's written screenplays in all sorts of genres, he continues to gravitate back to speculative fiction.

Martindale earned an Associate Degree in Film Production at Salt Lake Community College and a Bachelor Degree in Screenwriting and Cinematography at Utah Valley University.

For a period of time, he focused on telling stories about his religious community, Mormons. He considered the quality of Mormon literature subpar and preachy and wanted to tell stories about his people that he'd want to read, quality stories that were honest and edgy and not the least bit preachy. He's glad to see that the quality of Mormon art has been improving over the years.

He served three years on the board of the Association for Mormon Letters, a nonprofit organization that promotes Mormon literature and other arts, and acted as their Writers Conference chairperson for four years. He wrote a number of articles and book and film reviews for their literary journal *Irreantum*.

He worked for a time as a staff writer for *The Sugar Beet*, an Internet publication of Mormon satire patterned after the infamous website *The Onion*. Many of these online articles of alleged Mormon "news" were eventually collected into the popular book *The Mormon Tabernacle Enquirer*.

The editor of *The Mormon Tabernacle Enquirer* decided to start his own publishing company, Zarahemla Books, and chose as its flagship publication Martindale's second novel *Brother Brigham*, which he categorizes as "Mormon speculative fiction." *Brother Brigham* went on to receive substantial critical acclaim and was even used as reading material in a college comparative religion class one semester. He also had a science fiction short story "Bokev Momen" published in the anthology *Monsters and Mormons*, which has been included in this collection.

Inspired by *Jesus Christ Superstar*, he composed the musical *General Prophet Joseph Smith*, based on the events leading up to the assassination of the Mormon prophet Joseph Smith. He produced a concept album recording of it on CDs, and is currently developing a film adaptation of it. He calls it "Les Mis for Mormons."

Martindale has written two other novels. His first, *The Power of the Seeker*, is the beginning installment of a science fiction series called *The Reincarnate*. It remains unpublished, and he describes it as "crap." He may rewrite it someday. His third novel is a fantasy called *Celeste & the White Dragon* which he's in the process of bringing to publication. It's the first volume of a fantasy series.

For nine years Martindale focused on screenwriting and film making as a director and editor. Film is his favorite medium in which to tell stories. He wrote, produced, directed, and edited eight short films and a feature-length fantasy film called *Geeks and Goblins, Elves and Elliot*. He has multiple other screenplays ready to be developed into feature-length films, including an adaptation of his short story "Solar Butterfly" that appears in this collection. Additionally, he's been on the development team for three television/web series.

He resides in Salt Lake City, Utah, and is the father of three grown children and the grandfather of the best granddaughter in the world. Do not debate him on this.

Twisted Mind:
6 Science Fiction Stories
by D. Michael Martindale

From the twisted mind of D. Michael comes six science fiction stories that disrupt the status quo of our world in the spirit of The Twilight Zone and Black Mirror. Whether the new world that arises is better or worse is a question each individual will have to decide for themselves.

A Growth in the Backyard
Eternal Rectangle
Solar Butterfly
Bokev Momen
Mary Mother of Nanites
Eyes of the Beholder
Bonus story: **Time Forks**

twistedstories.worldsmithstories.com

Brother Brigham
by D. Michael Martindale

Like many young boys, C.H. Young grew up with an imaginary friend. In his case, it was his ancestor Brigham Young—or rather, "Brother Brigham" as C.H. knew him. During his formative years, Brother Brigham filled the boy's head with grand expectations of an important mission in life.

Now grown up with a wife and two young sons, C.H. has sacrificed his dreams to earn a living for his family. Brother Brigham is just a distant memory—until one day he returns in a most unexpected way. As Brother Brigham's appearances and instructions grow increasingly bold, C.H. struggles to hold together his faith, his marriage, and his sanity.

brotherbrigham.worldsmithstories.com

Celeste & the White Dragon
by D. Michael Martindale

Queen Tamara, thrown into a dungeon by the rogue sorceress Gwendolyn, is about to give birth. There's something about her baby that makes Gwendolyn want to possess it, and when Tamara delivers, Gwendolyn will kill her and take the baby.

But Tamara's chambermaid Zenia will not let that happen. At great risk to her life, she rescues Tamara and helps her flee out of the kingdom of Gallea. But in the midst of Fenweald Forest, Tamara dies while giving birth to the baby, and Zenia discovers the terrible secret that makes Gwendolyn want to possess it. She puts her life in peril seeking a way to hide the infant.

A great search for the child begins, with kings and sorceresses and wizards and accursed monsters and village witches all struggling to find and possess the young princess, whom Zenia names Celeste. The fate of three continents depends on who succeeds.

celeste.worldsmithstories.com